Love Song (Liebeslied)

I0638506

Book One
of the Captive Heart Trilogy

Stephanie Baumgartner

To Adam, the first one to understand my heart and love the real me;

And to Sara, who has given me the joy and privilege of being her big Sissy.

"There are three things that are too amazing for me,
four that I do not understand;
the way of an eagle in the sky,
the way of a snake on a rock,
the way of a ship on the high seas,
and the way of a man with a maiden."

—Proverbs 30:18-19

I have been here for five months, one week and four days.

Time stretches out before me like a desolate desert road. I don't move. I don't blink, torpefied by the repetitiveness of my surroundings. I fade in and out of awareness, my few moments of clarity giving the illusion that larger amounts of time have passed.

I tear my gaze away, chin burrowed in the heel of my hand. Outside the window, olive, wispy tendrils of a willow tree sway in the idle spring breeze. It reminded me of two girls I'd seen in grass skirts doing the hula in one of Cecilia's copies of Seventeen magazine. Bright pink flowers pinned back one side of their raven black hair. Their white teeth were blinding against their copper skin as they danced in the sand, the peacock blue sea endless in the background. They embodied what I used to imagine it must have felt like to be free.

I used to think running away was the only way I'd gain any license over my own life. I imagined my mother setting places at the table for breakfast. She'd sit down to eat, feeding my baby sister, annoyed that I wasn't up yet. After putting away their dishes, she'd come up to my room, staggered to find my bed empty. What she wouldn't know was that I'd left some time in the night. By train or by bus, I wouldn't stop until my bare toes were sinking into the west coast sand, out of their reach forever.

That was always fun to envision, but I knew I'd never do it. In my naiveté, I thought I had to leave to escape the oppression I'd endured for so long. I know now what a foolish misperception that was. Independence isn't found in running from one's fears; it is found in facing them. All this time, I thought I wanted to run from my mother, from my father, from that small town—but that wasn't true. The truth was I'd been running from myself...

Until he came along.

I breathed in the memories like air, every corner of my mind filled with thoughts of him. He had the alluring, smooth face of a boy, contoured by the afternoon shadows of a man. Eyes the color of the morning sky, I missed the way they crinkled as we talked, out of a sincere enjoyment of my company. No one had ever looked at me that way before.

A screeching, cringe-worthy scrape on the chalkboard brought me back to the classroom. I was relieved that Mrs. Evans had her back to us, using a ruler to guide the chalk as she drew a line, connecting points A and B on the board. The other girls were attentive at their desks, writing or staring ahead. I turned back to the window.

In hindsight, I understand why my actions scandalized the people in my hometown. I was shy and quiet; a well-mannered, obedient child who did what she was told and sat in the same pew every Sunday with her mother and siblings. That was perhaps the most erroneous impression of me— thinking I was a child. I was seventeen when it happened, more of a woman than a child by that point.

But the way my parents controlled me had distorted the way I perceived myself, bleeding over into the way everyone else saw me, too.

Everyone, except him.

It's kind of humorous that my parents thought sending me away was a punishment. It was supposed to weaken my feelings for him; break my spirit. The irony was that home had been doing that to me for years. Placing me in a boarding school—taking me out from under their direct authority—has had the opposite effect.

Because the truth is, I've grown a little stronger each day. I've never felt more aware of myself—the real me—than I do now. That first day at the camp, neither of us could have known how our lives were about to change. I didn't realize when God found a way to heal his heart, He'd also found a way to heal mine.

Chin still bearing down on my palm, I grinned, rolling my pencil between my fingers.

I hope you're thinking of me, Friedrich...wherever you are.

"Miss Wyndham!"

My blood iced over. The other girls became rigid in their seats, none of them daring to turn their heads in my direction. It could have been just myself and Mrs. Evans in a class full of mannequins for how still the room had become.

On the other side of her horn-rimmed glasses, Mrs. Evans peered down her pointy nose like a gun sight at me. I swallowed, glued to my seat.

Mrs. Evans clasped her hands behind her back. "I'm sorry that you find arithmetic so uninspiring that you'd rather prolong your ignorance with daydreams. Or perhaps you find it beneath you to pay attention with the rest of the class?"

Oh, how I yearned to answer honestly. "No, ma'am."

My pencil bent, almost snapping in half from how tightly I held it. I knew what was coming. I could see her mulling over the inevitable.

Her heels clacked on the floor as she walked out from behind her desk. "Front of the class, Miss Wyndham."

I stared at her—but not for too long, lest it worsen my impending discipline—heaving a heavy sigh as I pushed out from my desk.

Mrs. Evans lifted her chin. "We'll add yet another slap for that sign of exasperation, Miss Wyndham."

My penny loafers were soundless as I traipsed up the aisle, never breaking eye contact. I refused to give her the satisfaction of knowing I was nervous.

Up close, her eyes were the size of golf balls through her lenses. I raised my left hand—my non-writing hand—palm-side down. Using the ruler, she struck my knuckles, surprising me more than it hurt. The second slap stung enough that I scrunched my face; the third actually made me wince.

Mrs. Evans grimaced. "Now, Miss Wyndham, is there anything you'd like to say to the class?"

Yes. It didn't hurt as bad as four slaps.

I faced the sea of white collared shirts, brick-red jackets and gray skirts. "I sincerely apologize. I hope I've not offended any of you with my disruptive behavior. I assure you it won't happen again."

My eyes fell on Kate, one of my roommates. Her playful brown eyes were twinkling and she pursed her lips. I simpered in return before my throbbing hand reminded me that I was still standing next to Mrs. Evans.

I prayed a silent prayer of thanks that I'd worn my hair down that day, my curled, dark brown tresses blocking my face from Mrs. Evans' line of vision. I chanced a peek at her to make sure she hadn't noticed before heading back to my seat.

I passed Anna, my second roommate, on the way. Her arctic blue eyes surveyed me in concern until I was too far for her to see without turning her head. I knew she'd ask me later how terribly it had hurt.

I took care to keep my desk from creaking as I sat down. I crossed my ankles, folding my hands over the desktop, trying to appear like a good girl once more. Mrs. Evans resumed talking about the Pythagorean theorem and the Euclidean distance. The second hand on the clock continued to tick like an eternal metronome and my eyes glazed over.

Mrs. Evans is just like my mother. A slap on the hand, separation from all I've ever known—it's all peanuts. These trivialities hold no sway over me, because the worst has already happened.

At the board, Mrs. Evans filled in a circle on her chalk line; that's where I am now, somewhere between where I used to be and where I'm supposed to be.

All the rest is just what I must endure while I wait.

Two

On a white, blizzard-like evening in January 1926, my brother Amos was born. He was all my parents had dreamed their first child would be: perfect and beautiful, with a black head of hair and an even-tempered demeanor, and a son. The hopes of my father and grandfather were fulfilled, knowing the family business would be preserved through another generation of Wyndhams.

As a young man, my grandfather, Robert Wyndham, made his living as a coal-miner, until the phenomenon of the Wright Brothers at Kitty Hawk inspired him to change the course of his destiny.

Fueled by the belief that flight could someday replace train travel, my grandfather founded Wyndham Aero Industries in 1911. He began with a handful of employees, including one invaluable aeronautical engineer. His hard work and patience paid off at the onset of the Great War, when he was approached by a Navy captain in search of a manufacturer. By 1917, Wyndham Aero Industries had produced sixty seaplanes for the United States Navy.

As much as the company had flourished during the war, it began to struggle when it was over. Determined not to fail, he kept the company from going under in those meager years by constructing furniture and sea-sled boats from his remaining lumber stocks.

And because of Grandpa Robert's perseverance, my father was able to attend Cornell University. He graduated with a degree in business, the first in the family to attend a higher institution of learning.

It was my father who suggested they start employing their planes as mail carriers. With Grandpa Robert's approval, a new branch of the company—Wyndham Aero Transport—was created. As head of the division, my father made the maiden voyage with a few fellow passengers, carrying mail from Virginia to Texas. With over three hundred and fifty tons of mail and a hundred tons of express packages—and the government paying subsidies on every pound—my grandfather's company flourished in a time when many others floundered.

So the birth of my brother was a grand event. Spencer and Miriam Wyndham's first child, a son, would one day take over the business my grandfather and father had worked so hard to build and sustain.

At nineteen, my mother spent the first few months after Amos' birth learning how to be a wife and mother on her own. My father worked countless hours during the week, often not even making it to dinner. Unable to count on her own mother for help, my mother was alone in trying to solve every fever, cough or illness Amos had; in keeping him entertained; in keeping the house up and having breakfast and dinner on the table whether my dad showed up or not.

After five months of all her attempts at a routine being thrown into turmoil, she broke down on my father, begging him to cut his hours at work or else hire a maid for her. He told her it was impossible and that a maid was an expensive luxury; she just had to improve on managing her priorities. So my mother, not wanting to disappoint my father, dried her tears and told him he was right.

It was a month later when she found out she was pregnant with me.

My father was overjoyed with the news, but my mother cried for two days after she found out—a detail she never fails to mention when the subject arises.

The announcement of my birth generated a less enthusiastic reaction compared to my brother's. My grandparents were happy to have a second grandchild, but I didn't hold the value my brother did. To my father, I was a spare; to my mother, a millstone around her neck. Even once I was old enough to understand, my family loved musing over what great things Amos might accomplish once he inherited Wyndham Aero Industries. Afterwards, to show they also held great hopes for me, they speculated on which affluent family I might marry into someday.

Some of my mother's friends said that it was not fair to Amos that she got pregnant again so soon. He would not be allowed the time and attention a new baby deserves, since all my mother's focus would be on me. My mother assured them all that would not happen, and I'll be the first to admit that she kept her word.

There's never been a moment when I didn't feel hidden in the dark of my brother's shadow. Growing up, his pictures were the ones that made it onto the refrigerator, because he had talent beyond what someone his age was supposed to have. He drew detailed crayon cowboys on palominos and appaloosas, chasing Indians with multi-colored feathers on their heads. Mine were ordinary, maybe of a horse in a field or a little dog being walked by a stick figure. I drew one once of the family, our little stick hands interlocked in front of a likeness of our house, but Amos' drawing of Dad's car made it up instead of mine.

When he was six, my parents let Amos join a local little league baseball team. Every week, I would sit on the wooden bleachers, watching with my mom and sometimes even my dad. One day, while we were driving down Main Street on the way home, I saw a girl my age on the sidewalk. Her blonde hair in elegant curls, I coveted her satin leotard and the sleek pink skirt around her waist.

For weeks, I begged my mother to let me dance, too. She told me no, saying it would be too much trouble. But I was persistent.

She sighed. "I don't know, Cassandra. I'll think about it."

After talking it over with my father on the phone, she took me to the dance studio in town. I was beside myself with excitement. My mother bought me my very own blue leotard and pale pink ballet slippers. I loved wearing them, prancing around the house in them even when it wasn't a dance practice day.

I'd been dancing for six months when Amos' baseball practice time changed to five-thirty in the afternoon and he signed up for football, too. My dance classes conflicted with his schedule; my mother couldn't make it to both.

My second recital was two weeks away when she pulled me out of ballet. I cried and told her it wasn't fair.

"Amos was playing baseball before you were in dance, Cassandra. Stop being selfish. We'll find you something else."

My dad suggested getting me a kitten, but my mother rejected that idea, saying she'd be the one taking care of it. He then proposed buying me a piano and having a tutor come to the house.

I could hear him on the other end of the receiver. "That way you don't have to go anywhere and Cassandra can learn the piano. Everybody's happy."

Amos was lying on the floor, tossing a baseball up and catching it.

"Will Daddy come watch me play?" I asked her. He hadn't come to my only dance recital.

My mother's grip on the phone tightened. "Your father's busy, Cassandra. You know that."

Not even the thought of having my own piano thrilled me as much as my ballet shoes did. I wanted to dance; I reminded my mother of that, just in case saying it one more time would change their minds.

"You can't dance anymore, Cassandra. It's the piano or nothing," she said in annoyance before talking to my father. "Are you listening to this? This is what I have to deal with every single day. You have spoiled your daughter, Spencer."

I didn't say no to the piano lessons, but with tears in my eyes, I kept telling her that ballet was what I really wanted to do. She sent me to my room, saying I would do neither. I was okay with that; I'd rather do nothing than commit to an activity I found no interest in. I continued practicing what I had learned at home until my leotard could no longer be pulled over my shoulders. After that, I threw it with my slippers under my bed and never wore them again.

My brother never flaunted the fact that he was the favorite in front of me, even though we both knew it. He used it to my advantage on many occasions.

My mother's criticisms of me were limitless. She found fault with the way I dressed, how much I ate, the way I spoke, even the way I sat at the table. It only escalated as I got older. Amos would run interference during our disagreements. He'd give our mother his famous winsome smile, his green eyes glimmering as he made cracks until she laughed. I was never sure if it was intentional—or if her love for him simply surpassed her displeasure with me—but she always seemed to forget what she was upbraiding me for.

But even Amos knew when he was risking his position as the favored child. In those instances where his charm was insufficient, he would abandon me, leaving me to suffer my mother alone, even when he knew she was wrong.

I loved my brother, but I couldn't deny my envy of him. I always wished that I could be more like him—*genuine*. He didn't hide who he was; he wasn't afraid of what people thought of him. He was good-looking, with his jet black hair and emerald green eyes, his brilliant smile and perpetual confidence. He had high marks in all his classes and was the star player on both the baseball and football teams. Everyone in town knew his name. Everyone in school wanted to be his best friend or his girl. It was obvious to us all that my brother was meant to be someone great.

And it only made them love him more when, the night before his eighteenth birthday, the principal announced before the football game that it would be Amos' last; he would be joining up the very next morning. It had been a little over two years since the Japanese attacked Pearl Harbor, and I was certain it was the impassioned speeches from my father and the vows to enlist from his friends that had impacted him to do the same. The girls in the crowd all cried or swooned; my father's chest swelled with pride, while my mother dabbed at her cheeks, kissing my baby sister's forehead. Amos would be one of the first to leave his class, since most of the other boys wouldn't turn eighteen until summer.

My brother scored the winning touchdown that night, a fairytale ending. I sat with my friend Holly, watching as my brother's teammates carried him away on their shoulders. My parents were stopped every couple of steps by well-wishers, while Holly and I slunk off to the parking lot. I avoided being harassed because no one knew who I was.

I woke up the Sunday morning after to the sound of my mother's laughter carrying up the staircase, a sure sign that Amos was up, too. Through my bay window, it looked like any other day. I could see Mr. Stewart's big red barn in the distance, swirls of smoke rising from his chimney while the grass in the surrounding fields rippled in the winter wind. With a cavernous yawn, I slid into my slippers, heading down the hall for the bathroom. After brushing my teeth, I put on the dress I'd picked out last night; a navy blue one with a white collar. I loved it because it reminded me of Ginger Rogers' dress in *Swing Time*. Whenever I spun, the skirt would flare out, and I felt like I was her—which was hard to do since I had no Fred Astaire, and my mother thought I was too young to wear pumps. I wore my black and white saddle shoes instead.

"Much more appropriate," my mother had once said.

She'd called me ungrateful when she caught me kneading them on the grass and in the driveway soon after buying them. It was only because Holly said they looked too new, when we were supposed to be making do and mending. I tried to explain to my mother that it was my patriotic duty, but she just yanked them away from me, making me scrub them with soap and water at the bathroom sink.

I sat at my vanity, the very one I would sit in front of when I was a little girl, patting on pretend make-up and making faces in the mirror. It used to be my mother's, but my father had bought her a new one a couple years ago. It was old—with cracks in the wood and the gold handles either loose or missing—but it was mine and I liked it.

I untied the rags in my hair, running my fingers through the curls before pinning the sides. I looked over my shoulder, making sure my bedroom door was closed.

Two containers of foundation and rouge sat in the darkened corners of my vanity drawer. I'd found I could wear a little make-up without my mother noticing. She didn't approve, always saying, *"You're only sixteen!"* I didn't think it was fair. Holly and all my other classmates already knew what made them look best and what their favorite brands were; some of them even made their own make-up. It was Holly who'd given me the foundation powder. Her mother had bought it for her, but it was the wrong shade. It felt like Christmas when she gave it to me, along with the rouge.

I looked myself over in the mirror, accepting that this was as good as it was going to get.

My mother was chuckling, scrubbing a pan in the kitchen sink when I got downstairs, while Amos, my father and Lucy ate at the table.

I kissed my father's cheek. "Morning, Daddy."

His mouth was full. "Morning, Sweetheart."

"Sleeping Beauty arises. It's about time," Amos said, his voice muffled by food. "I thought you were going to let me leave without saying goodbye."

Plate in hand, I divvied up my breakfast from the stovetop. "Don't be silly. Someone should have woken me. I would have come down sooner if—"

"Cassandra, take your sister into the living room. Your father and I want some time alone with Amos."

My mother hadn't even looked at me as she spoke. Over my shoulder, my father was already regaling my brother with what he considered to be a great accomplishment at Wyndham Aero Industries. (In a twenty-four hour period, the company had assembled sixteen planes. My father's biggest competitor here on the east coast hadn't even managed to do that.)

I wanted to tell my mother she wasn't the only one who wanted to spend time with Amos; I wanted Amos or my father to protest. Instead, I swallowed my anger, taking Lucy by the hand and heading to the living room.

My parents and Amos continued their conversation without me as Lucy knelt on the floor, rifling through her toy box. Fuming, I wasn't sure how long she'd been trying to get my attention.

She held up blocks with two chubby hands. "See, bocks." *Sissy, blocks.*

"I see your blocks."

Her dress flipped over her head, revealing her diapered bottom as she pushed herself up. "See, pay me."

"I can't play right now, baby. I'm eating."

She put the blocks in my lap. "Pay me."

"Maybe in a little bit." I set them on the couch. "Let Sissy finish eating first, okay?"

Her eyes were a lighter shade of green than Amos' and my mother's. She blinked, toddling back to her toy box.

Lucy was an anomaly in our family. She should have had black hair, like my mother and Amos, or dark brown like my father and me, but she was blonde. Like me, she had been a surprise, but like Amos, she had been wanted.

She was also the only person that I felt could see the real me. That sounded ridiculous, considering she wasn't even two yet, but I wondered if it was because she was so new to the world that she could see people for who they truly were, not for who they pretended to be.

Lucy gave me at least one way to be useful to my parents. I never refused an opportunity to care for her whenever my mom was too busy, or too tired, or simply didn't want to. There had been many instances where it had been inconvenient for me, but I didn't resent Lucy for that. I adored my baby sister.

Lucy was grunting, her diaper peeking out beneath her dress as she tried to climb up beside me. I helped push her up, rolling my eyes upon hearing my mother's laugh in the next room.

Lucy dropped her favorite book, *The Princess and the Prince*, onto my plate. "Ree me."

"Lucy," I groaned. Despite some of my eggs sticking to the back of it, I laughed, spreading the book out between us.

It was a generic fairy tale, not like Cinderella or Snow White. The main characters' names were in fact 'the Prince' and 'the Princess.' The princess had been kidnapped and placed in a tower ever since she was a little girl. No one had ever come for her, and she had never been able to escape because of the vicious dragon that guarded the tower. Until one day, a prince from a faraway kingdom fell in love with her after hearing her singing from a window. He charged the castle the next day, slaying the dragon and taking the princess away on his white horse to his kingdom.

And they lived happily ever after.

I closed the book. "The end."

"Ree me."

I chuckled as I chewed, but I read it to her again.

Lucy sat the book on her lap afterward, staring at the long hair of the blonde princess on the cover. She loved that book—and that was exactly why everyone had stopped reading it to her. The second my mother closed it, Lucy would make her read it again. Amos had tried to convince her that other books were just as good, but Lucy didn't care. She only wanted to hear about the princess. Now she knew I was the only one who would read it to her.

I put my empty plate on the coffee table, slumping so I could be on her level. "Did you know you're a princess?"

Her eyes sparkled as she beamed at me. "Uh huh."

She stood on the couch, and I held her as she wrapped her arms around my neck, not even worrying about my hair. Lucy kissed me, her hands on either side of my face. "See prins."

"You think I'm a princess, too?"

She only smiled, asking me to read to her again. I did.

For a long time, I was just like Lucy. This house was my tower, and I used to imagine being rescued by a prince. He would take me to his kingdom, far away from my oppression; a place where I could be free. While no one else even looked up when I entered a room, he would see only me. He would think I was beautiful; he would understand my heart in a way no one else ever had.

But no prince had ever come to save me. I was in my junior year of secondary school now, so any prince who crossed me at this point would be too little too late. My grandfather had set up a trust fund for both Amos and me before he died. If the worst were to happen and the business were ever to go under, he wanted to make sure Amos got the same education my father had. He said mine could be used for school too, but more importantly, he wanted to ensure I could make a good marriage. I'd heard my whole life that I would never finish college. College was a place for girls to meet husbands, and then it would be my responsibility to make a home for my family. My trust fund would then go to the man I married...

Because having just me would not be enough.

Eyes burning, I took a sip of milk, watching Lucy admire the cover of her book.

Of course, deep down I still wished there was someone who would come along, hear my cries for help and fight for me.

Fight for me.

The only thing my brother ever fought for was his status. The only thing my father ever fought for was his work. The only thing my mother ever fought for was herself. People didn't fight for other people. Whatever I wanted out of my life, I was going to have to do it myself. The moment I turned eighteen and could access the money in my trust fund, I was going to leave this place and never look back.

My mother's heels were sharp on the hardwood. "Spencer, will you come get your suitcase?" she called out, lifting Lucy over the back of the couch. "Come on, my Sweetheart. Mommy needs to change your diaper."

I passed my father on my way into the kitchen. Amos was no longer at the table, to my dismay, but I could hear him in the adjacent bedroom. When my father bought the house, that room had been a servant's quarters. My parents used it as a guest room until Amos turned sixteen and asked to move from his bedroom upstairs. My mother wasn't comfortable with the idea, but my father said he was becoming a man and deserved his own space.

I was the only one who knew that he wanted the room so he could sneak out and sneak people in at his leisure. Amos was aware of this, but he knew I wouldn't tell.

His rucksack was packed, resting at the foot of his bed. I lowered onto the edge, reading his name tag as he rummaged around in the connecting bathroom.

He noticed me, carrying his shaving kit as he reentered the room. "Almost forgot some essentials."

I suppressed a smile. There had only been a light shadow on his upper lip the last time he tried to grow out his facial hair. He placed them in the bag, glancing at me. "Sorry about earlier."

I shrugged. "It's fine."

"You know Mom. She would've asked Dad to leave, too, if she thought he wouldn't get mad," he said with a conciliating grin.

I only nodded. He was always trying to justify her actions to me. *What about the fact that I'm going to miss you, too? Why didn't you tell her it wasn't fair to me?* I wanted to ask him. Perhaps I would have, if I were brave. "I'm glad Dad's here to see you off. I can't remember the last time he spent a whole weekend with us."

Amos snorted. "I know. I guess that means it'll be another three months before you see him again. Even longer for me."

My father had become president of Wyndham Aero Industries in 1933, after Grandpa Robert's unexpected death from heart disease. They had retired the biplanes by that point, building an innovative monoplane instead. With a smaller production factory in Montana now, my father inherited more than Grandpa Robert ever dreamed of. It wasn't until the war began, however, that my father felt the full weight of his responsibilities. Unlike most might have, though, he didn't buckle beneath it; he thrived on it. Where my grandfather had produced sixty seaplanes in 1917, Wyndham Aero Industries was now producing three hundred and sixty bombers a month under my father. We all understood that what he was doing was crucial to the war effort, and he promised to never go more than three months without coming home.

Still, even when he was home, he would lock himself away in his study until it was time to return to Maryland. Mom always said it was because he was busy, but Amos told me once that he didn't think Dad was happy here. The older I got, the more I began to think he was right: we were no longer enough to make him want to stay.

Amos was shaking his bag around, trying to make room. His hands trembled as he tried to zip it closed. He was always unruffled, on the edge of a smile, but not this time. I worried for my fearless older brother.

"Are you scared, Amos?"

He saw I had been watching him and his mellowness returned. "Are you kidding? I can't wait. Jimmy's almost through with basic. At this rate, he's going to get to see some action before I do."

I could tell from his face that it was a lie, but I wasn't sure if it was for my benefit or his. My chin didn't even reach his shoulder as I hugged him, my voice cracking. "I'm really going to miss you."

He didn't speak, his arms tightening around me. Mom's heels clunked down the stairs and I wiped at my cheeks.

Amos chuckled, but his eyes had misted over, too. "Cry baby."

I left him to finish packing. My mother was standing at the sink with Lucy on her hip when I returned to the kitchen. I'd left my plate in the basin while I talked to Amos.

"I hope you're going to wash that."

"I am, I was just—"

"You're not going to wear that, are you?" my mother asked, her emerald eyes looking me over. "For goodness' sakes, Cassandra, it looks like you're going to a funeral. Wash your plate, then go upstairs and change."

That dormant ball of fury inside me spun. She handed Lucy off to my father in the living room and I cleaned my dishes before starting upstairs with a heavy gait, the only way I could think of to express my disgruntlement.

In spite of her contempt of me, my mother was a beautiful woman—when she smiled. She had straight black hair that went just past her shoulders when it was wet, and well-defined, arched eyebrows that every woman she met coveted. She had a long, straight nose, perfect lips and a perfect figure, even after having three children.

And even though she and I had our issues, I knew that she was the reason I had a relationship with God. He tried to remind me of that every time I thought I hated her.

I held up a couple dresses in front of my vanity mirror before settling on a pastel yellow eyelet dress she had given me with a peplum waist and short, puffed sleeves. I couldn't fill it out the way she had, but at least it would keep her from complaining about my taste again.

My mother yelled from the bottom of the stairs. "Cassandra, let's go!"

"Yeah," Amos called out behind her. "Mom's in a hurry for me to shoot some Huns."

Smiling, I smoothed my hair, listening as she scolded him.

The drive to the station wasn't as sad and heavy as I had anticipated. My brother kept us laughing as he talked about how he might react to those drill instructors yelling in his face, touching their noses with his. I watched the way my mother looked at him, eyes crinkling every time he spoke, and

I couldn't help wishing she looked at me that way, too. Sometimes I wondered if it was because of my dad. I looked more like my father, though the hazel shade of my eyes was specific to me. I wondered if that was why it hurt her to look at me; I made her think of him.

Parking the car at the train station, my father got his suitcase and Amos' bag out of the trunk. I held Lucy, trailing behind my father while my mother looped her arm around Amos'. Dad bought their tickets and we sat inside the station talking until their train arrived. Lucy and I said goodbye to my father while my mother embraced Amos, her voice splintering. Then, we switched.

Amos reached for Lucy. "Come here, little pumpkin-head."

He had an endless supply of nicknames for her, my favorite being 'Lucy-fer.' Whenever she wailed, Amos would yell, "Mom, Lucy-fer's calling you!" To which my mother would grit her teeth and ruffle his hair.

Lucy laughed as Amos kissed all over her cheeks. "Bee, dop!" *Bubby, stop!*

Squeezing his face, she kissed him on the lips before hugging his neck. She didn't understand what was happening; that our brother was leaving for war. She just knew that she loved him.

We watched her totter over to our parents. Amos adjusted his bag on his shoulder. "I'm gonna miss you, Cass."

"I'm going to miss you, too. I don't know what I'm going to do without you."

I glanced at my mother. She lifted my baby sister, still talking to my father. My anxiety must have been evident to my brother.

"You'll be fine. Just stay out of her way."

"I *do* stay out of her way. All I have to do is breathe and she complains about it."

He shrugged. "So hold your breath in front of her."

I shook my head at him. He grinned.

We said our final goodbyes, my mother, Lucy and I watching them board the train. My father was going to ride with Amos all the way to Richmond, where they would part ways. Dad would head to Baltimore to work while Amos would take a separate train to Fort Bragg in North Carolina.

My mother sniffled as they boarded. "Come on. I don't want to see them leave."

Mom and I didn't speak the entire way to church. A few times, Lucy prompted one of us but other than that, I was silent. Mom had held a conversation with Amos the whole way to the station, but with me, she had nothing to say. I guessed it wasn't fair to blame that on her; I had nothing to say to her, either.

I hadn't noticed how many people had put up service banners until now—the rectangle ones with blue or gold stars that hung in almost every window. I assumed that would be the first thing Mom did when we got home.

In fact, I hadn't thought about how many men had actually left to fight until now. With so many men gone, a lot of women had taken up the jobs left behind to provide support for the war and to keep the economy running; over half of my father's employees were women now. They were all noble people working for a noble cause. Even my mother volunteered as a nurse's aide at the local hospital some evenings, and she always took an active role in scrap drives and helping to collect medical supplies. I was sixteen, and while my brother would soon be off to fight the Germans or the Japanese; while my father was supplying Superfortresses and Flying Fortresses; while my mother was providing relief for nurses and companionship to invalids, I was at home with my baby sister. My family was making sacrifices and I was doing nothing to fight for my own freedom.

Forehead to the glass, I closed my eyes. Why did I have to wait until marriage—until I was a mother—to be able to say I'd contributed to society in a meaningful way? I couldn't fight on the front lines like my brother; I couldn't work overnight like my mother since I was in school; I knew nothing about the construction of airplanes. I felt the sudden urge to ask my mother what she thought I could do before hearing her voice in my head say, *"Make my life easier. That's what you could do."*

At church, we sat in our regular pew on the left side of the sanctuary. I distracted myself with Lucy as people came up to tell my mom they'd keep Amos in their prayers. It was comforting to hear, though I wished they hadn't mentioned him at all. Part of me was still hoping we'd go home and he'd be there. Maybe he was sick and just couldn't make it to church today. I decided to let myself believe that for now.

As the sanctuary filled, someone plopped down beside me. It was Holly, her voice as bland as her expression. "How'd it go with your brother?"

"Fine. As you would expect, I guess."

"So he's gone?"

I nodded. Holly's amber eyes were on Lucy. I watched her for a moment, wondering if she was going to say more. Instead, she leaned back against the pew, flipping through the hymnal.

Holly was the best friend I had. I'd always been kind of a loner and the transition into secondary school exploited that. My freshman year, I would often eat lunch by myself, except for the few times my brother had come over to pity-sit with me. Sometimes, even Jimmy had tagged along.

A few months ago, Holly—who always seemed like a voluntary loner rather than a helpless one like me—asked if she could sit with me. I said yes, and we'd stuck together ever since. Holly was different from me, though. She smoked. She had the potential to be popular, but chose to be an outsider. I, however, wasn't brave or strong enough to break out of the glass shell I was in. I wished I could say that Holly and I were kindred spirits, but the truth was, we weren't. We didn't really see each other outside of school or church. On occasion, we might walk downtown after school to the soda shop or to Crewe's Department Store. I didn't know why she chose to be my friend. Maybe it was like being on a train and sitting next to a stranger; we were both on separate journeys, but it was nice having someone to talk to during the ride.

I stood with Holly and my mother as the choir began to sing. Mr. Jenkins, the music minister, led us in prayer afterwards.

Lucy tugged on my dress. "See."

Smiling, she closed her eyes, clasping her little hands. I chuckled into my hand, meriting an admonishing glance from my mother.

We sang a couple hymns before Pastor Gilbert walked up to the pulpit. He was in his early sixties, his hair a faded gray. He had a knobby nose and pockmarked face, though he still looked younger than his age.

Pastor Gilbert set his Bible on the pulpit. "For it to be the middle of winter, it certainly is a beautiful day. Days like this, I know God just wants us all to remember that there are still reasons to be happy; to not give up the fight, because there's still good here worth fighting for. Like the rainbow after the flood, He's showing us that He's still present and that all the strife in the world hasn't gone unnoticed by Him."

That warranted some "amens." My mother unraveled a tissue, sniffling.

He continued. "These are dark times we're bearing witness to, but I can think of no better circumstance where God can be glorified more than in a time like this. Our boys are fighting for a good cause and they're not alone in this battle. This is bigger than a war of nations. This is a war between good and evil, and God does not abandon those whose trust is in Him. Let's go to the Lord in prayer. Father, we come to you today..."

Pastor Gilbert was right; this was an unprecedented evil, and measures had to be taken to keep it from breaching our shores. I may have been a girl—I may have been just me —but I wanted to take up my part in this. But what could that possibly be? I was a nobody; just a plain and powerless American girl who could only hope to become another man's burden someday.

I had to be meant for more than that. My spirit felt on fire for some obscure purpose, my heart ready and willing to take part in a sacrifice that meant something, even if only to God—even if only to me.

What do you see in me God? What do I have to offer to this war, to this world? To You? Show me. Show me what I have to give. Show me that I am someone of value. Please Lord. Am I worth anything at all to You? Please tell me, because right now I feel so empty, so incompetent. Please show me…

"Amen."

Pastor Gilbert's prayer had ended, signaling the pianist to come play another hymn. We all stood to sing.

Pastor Gilbert preached, but I seemed unable to focus. Sitting amongst all those people, I felt like the lowest kind of life form; a tick drawing off others what it needed to sustain itself. It felt like Pastor Gilbert was preaching only to me whenever I caught pieces of "letting God use your skills" and "this is a fight for the freedom of all people."

Holly and my mother rose with the rest of the congregation and I hopped to my feet a second behind them. The choir was singing "Just As I Am" and I made the wreath on the altar my focal point. It felt like holding a searing hot iron to my skin. How could I be of any worth to God when I was of so little worth to everyone else? He wanted me to come to Him just as I was, but how was that enough?

I didn't want anyone to see that I was affected by that song; that the events of the day had stirred an awareness of inadequacy within me. I hadn't made any sacrifices. I was just a schoolgirl living my life the same way I had before there was even a war.

Crouching down, I pretended Lucy needed entertaining to keep my mother from noticing my tears. They would only irritate her and she would ask what I possibly had to cry over; "*Self-serving tears,*" she would call them. Pulling my Bible and purse closer, I was ready to leave.

"This week, I was asked to remind the congregation that the Red Cross is always in need of volunteers, whether it's for rolling bandages or providing auxiliary care at the hospital," Pastor Gilbert announced. "Donating blood is also of the utmost importance at this time. There are two Red

Cross chapters in town, for those interested in getting involved."

I pondered on this; I *had* just asked God to show me how I could help.

"Remember, often it takes more than words to make a difference in life; it takes action. If you have faith that God will help bring this war to an end, then you have a responsibility to do your part. Give what you can for Him to use. Ladies, the military is in dire need of stockings in order to make powder bags for naval guns. Even bacon grease donations are essential to the war effort. In Joel, the Lord says, 'And I will restore to you the years that the locust hath eaten...' Everything that is given up for the Lord will be given back in due time."

My mother was restless beside me, pulling Lucy into her lap and buttoning her coat. Pastor Gilbert folded his glasses, setting them on the pulpit, and a peculiar silence rippled through the church. He hadn't dismissed us, but it was as if he forgot we were still in the sanctuary. I looked at Holly to see if she found it odd, but she was yawning, staring ahead.

Pastor Gilbert's voice dropped. "One last thing...before we go. I was approached this week by an administrator from the local POW camp. As most of you know, Rockmont was one of the towns chosen to host some of the men captured overseas—mostly Germans. This war isn't going to last forever. There is some concern about one day returning these men, just as they are, back to their country when it's over. These men don't believe Adolf Hitler is a man of God—they believe he *is* God."

My heart was hammering in my chest. The gold letters on the hymnal in front of me held my gaze.

"They have a fierce devotion and loyalty to Hitler, particularly the young ones, because Nazism is the only way of life they've ever known. Our government wants to find ways to rehabilitate them. There have been many secret programs developed over the last couple years to introduce democracy into the prisoners' lives in the hopes that it'll replace Nazism once they return. We've been invited to take part in a smaller program still in its trial stages—to re-familiarize the prisoners with the roots of Christianity."

Why was I shaking? Lucy whined, pushing away from my mother and crawling into my lap.

"Our church has been assigned twenty prisoners who are fluent in English." He took a deep breath. "If there are any among you who feel called to do this, there's a sign-up sheet in the lobby. The first meeting at the camp will be Saturday, February 5th. I will be handing out discussion guides and answering any questions after service the Sunday before."

Murmurs of dissent filled the sanctuary. Pastor Gilbert's eyes roamed over us all.

"I understand how difficult this must be to grasp. Many of you have sacrificed your husbands, sons or brothers to fight these men. But before we are Americans, we must remember what God has commissioned us to do as Christians; to love one another. Even our enemies—*especially* our enemies. We would do well to remember that these men —though misguided—are still sons of God. I humbly ask that if you do decide to do this, please, do a thoughtful, prayerful self-evaluation first and make sure your heart is in it for the right reasons."

Miss Doris began to play the piano. Mom hoisted Lucy from my lap before walking out into the aisle to chat with Mrs. Webb. I felt frozen.

Holly thawed me. "Come on."

Grabbing my belongings, I followed her in the opposite direction from my mother.

The lobby was crowded. Holly and I stood against the wall, waiting to slink past the queue of people and head out the door. The cork board in the entrance hall was covered with multi-colored flyers and announcements. There were a few people huddled around the table in front of it, and I pushed against the current to make my way over. They'd all walked away by the time I got to it, a clipboard with the sign-up sheet for camp volunteers.

A green wooden pencil lay next to it. There were only three signatures so far.

"You're not going to do it, are you?"

I hadn't realized Holly had followed me over. I turned back to the clipboard. "I don't know. I was thinking...maybe."

There was a battle raging inside me. I could do this. I loved God; I believed He could change lives...

But the Germans were hardened and aggressive, in opposition to everything I believed in.

Why was I still standing there? Why hadn't I gone out to the car already? It was impetuous; I hadn't even prayed on it. Somehow, I knew if I went home without putting my name on that sheet of paper right now, I never would. I was just a girl; these were violent men. My presence wouldn't change anything. I lacked the savoir faire to even make friends at school; how did I stand a chance at converting a Nazi?

The deepest pit of my being was on fire. Words appeared on the wall of my soul, written in flame, declaring that I did have something to offer, even if I didn't know what it was.

I gripped the pencil, my name on the list before I even realized I'd written it myself. I waited for lightning to strike me, preparing myself for spontaneous combustion.

Holly plucked the pencil out of my hand, writing her name beneath mine.

"You're signing up, too?"

"Why not?" she asked, monotone before walking away.

My mother called my name from across the lobby, motioning toward the door with her head. With a final glance at my name, I followed after her.

Holly was getting into her mother's car. "See you tomorrow."

I gave her a nod. Getting into the front seat of my mother's navy blue Ford Deluxe, she handed Lucy to me, starting the car. For once, I was grateful that she wasn't talkative. It kept me from telling her I'd enrolled in a program that would have me face-to-face with Nazis without asking her first.

Three

What had I done? *What had I done?*

In the weeks that followed the signing of my name to that cursed list, I stumbled through a maelstrom of anxiety. In the same manner in which she had written her name, Holly didn't seem to give it a second thought. Every time I brought it up, she reacted the way she always did—bored.

The only person who offered an opinion was Donald —a friend of Holly's and mine—except it wasn't an uplifting one. "That can't be safe. It sounds dangerous to me."

I looked at Holly for support, but she continued scribbling on the paper on her desk. "Uh—well, I...I don't think they'd put us in a life-threatening situation."

His cheeks were becoming red. "Still. Are there at least going to be bars between you?"

I looked at Holly again. I didn't know how to answer. The truth was, we didn't know very much about what the program was going to be like yet. "I don't...I don't really know."

Donald smirked, revealing his overly-large front teeth, his eyes becoming half-moons. "Really, Cassie. You probably should've done a little more research before signing up."

I could tell he thought he was joking, but I felt like he was mocking me.

Holly sighed. "Really, Donald, maybe you should mind your own business."

He reached forward, flicking her ear. I saw the spasm of a grin as she kept her head down, still writing.

Holly had hinted to me a few times that Donald was keen on me, but he'd never acted on it. From my point of view, it seemed like Holly was the one who liked Donald. We were in some kind of bizarre triangle on the fringes of the school hierarchy, but to be honest, I wasn't interested in Donald; I wasn't interested in anyone, not when I knew I was months away from leaving Rockmont.

I still hadn't worked up the courage to tell my mother about the camp. There was a chance I could still back out before having to tell her. I wanted to, every time I imagined myself talking to a blond-haired man with red eyes. He jerked on the cold, steel rods between us like a chimpanzee, trying to reach for me. Every time I gave him a Bible, he would tear out the pages and scream something about hating Jews and fighting for Hitler.

I wasn't sure I was qualified to work with someone like that.

As much as the vision disturbed me, I tried not to let it be what deterred me. I truly didn't think Pastor Gilbert would put us in such a pointless and frightening situation. There had to be some hope for these men or else this program was a farce.

Though my imagined German terrified me, the idea of telling my mother did so even more. I knew she was going to be furious that I hadn't asked for permission. With the meeting at the camp only a week away, I couldn't keep it a secret any longer. It was a miracle Pastor Gilbert hadn't mentioned it to her long before now anyway.

After dinner, I got ready for bed and trudged down the stairs as if I were being led to burn at the stake. Lucy was at the table, playing with her dolls.

I gulped, gripping the back to one of the dining chairs. "Uh—Mom, I wanted to...talk to you about something."

She was washing a glass. "What's that?"

"Well..." My palms were sweaty. "I wanted you to know that I signed up for that program at church; the one where we'll be going to that POW camp to talk to prisoners."

The glass in her hand clinked against the metal sink as she dropped it, eyebrows raised in disbelief. "You what?"

I tried to gauge her reaction before nodding in response. She stared at me a moment before shaking her head, turning back to the foamy suds. "And how are you going to get there? I'm not driving you."

"I've already worked it out with Holly. I'm going to ride my bike to the schoolyard and then we'll ride together to the camp."

She continued scrubbing. "*Why* are you waiting until now to tell me?"

I wanted to give her the obvious answer, but I knew it was apparent only to me. "I don't know."

She scoffed. "So typical. All you ever think of is yourself—"

"How...how is this me only thinking of myself?"

"I work every Friday night, Cassandra; you *know* that. I count on you to watch the baby on Saturdays so I can sleep, and now what am I going to do?"

"I know, Mom. I'm sorry. I didn't think it would be imposing on your sleep time—"

"Of course not. You never *think* about anything. You just go headlong into whatever you want to do without giving a single thought to anyone else."

Perhaps she was right; I hadn't thought about the fact that she had to sleep. "I know. I'm sorry. It shouldn't be more than a couple hours. I can watch Lucy before I go and when I get back."

Lucy was untwisting the strands of red yarn that was her doll's hair, untroubled by my mother's bone-chilling silence. I didn't want to ask her if she was going to let me go; I decided to put on as if it couldn't be changed.

"Pastor Gilbert wants to meet with all of us after church tomorrow, to go over everything. Is that all right?"

31

"Well, I guess it has to be," she snapped, rinsing off dishes. She turned, pointing her finger at me. "Don't expect me to drive you to that camp. If you can't make it there yourself, you're not going. I'm not wasting gas rations on a drive into town for that."

I breathed in my fragile victory, picking up my baby sister. "Thanks, Mom. I'm sorry about your sleep, but I promise you, the whole rest of the day, I'll watch Lucy."

I hurried upstairs before she could say anything else, getting Lucy ready for bed and tucking her in. I hated the way I had to steel myself every time I spoke to my mother. I'd predicted having to beg her to let me go—or worse, having to back out because she didn't approve and not because I wanted to.

Every night leading up to Saturday, my prayers seemed to lengthen, my misgivings increasing. Whenever the camp crossed my mind during the day, I prayed about it then, too:

Give me wisdom, God, to know what to say...

Give me strength not to falter with this...

Please, speak through me, Lord. Use me the way that You need to...

Please don't let him try to hurt me...

Give me guidance to lead my prisoner in the right direction, Lord...

Please take my fear away...

What do You want me to say? Give me Your words, Your courage, Your strength...

I anticipated clear, undeniable answers from Him each time. I knew God didn't work like that, but part of me wished He would make an exception. I would feel better knowing ahead of time what exactly He wanted me to do when I walked into the camp. I was supposed to trust that He would reveal it to me in His own time, but how would I know I was truly doing what He wanted to begin with?

Lucy and I fell asleep Friday night in my parents' bed, as we always did when my mother worked. I'd had trouble staying asleep, easily roused when my mother came home in the early morning hours. I stole down to my own bedroom, trying to sleep another couple of hours before the light in my room became too bright. Stretching, I walked over to sit in my bay window. I loved that Mr. Stewart's farm was the first thing I saw in the mornings. The fields surrounding his house had once been covered in large stalks of corn, but now they were carpeted in a sea of green. It had been that way for the last two years. Both of Mr. Stewart's sons had joined the Marines after Pearl Harbor and all the farm hands had enlisted as well. It was too much work for just one person. Mr. Stewart never replanted his corn, now only tending to a small Victory Garden behind the barn.

I frowned upon seeing myself in the mirror. My father's old pale blue pajamas looked ridiculous on me, but they were comfortable. Mom had tried to bunch up the fabric in the back to make the bottoms tighter, but I still had trouble keeping them on my hips. The assessment of my reflection became more disparaging the more I looked and I left my room, certain my nervousness would only worsen as the day wore on.

Lucy was lying awake next to Mom, entertaining herself by examining the corners of her baby blanket. I chuckled at her patience; I wondered how long she'd been waiting for me.

"Hi, sweet girl," I whispered. "Want to come downstairs for breakfast?"

She raised her arms, reaching for me as I picked her up. Closing the bedroom door behind me, I tickled her neck as we started down the stairs. "Your hair looks like a little mouse tried to make it into a home last night."

She giggled, hiding it under her hands. "No!"

Down in the kitchen, I made breakfast, saving some of the scrambled eggs and toast for Mom for later. After cleaning up, Lucy and I played in the family room before I needed to start getting ready. I bathed Lucy first, combing her hair and putting her in a tartan frock with a Peter Pan collar.

I sat her on a quilt on my bedroom floor. "Will you play with your blocks while Sissy gets dressed?"

She didn't respond, too busy trying to stack the cubes on top of one another.

I didn't know what to wear. I didn't want to look like I was trying to impress anyone; I also didn't want to look like I didn't care. Searching through my closet, I chose the sky blue dress my mother had made out of old linen, only because it had a Peter Pan collar, too.

I pointed to it. "Look, Lucy. You and Sissy are wearing the same kind of dress."

Her little jade eyes scrunched at me and she turned back to her blocks.

Taking the rags out of my hair, I groaned upon realizing one of the curls toward the front was still damp. It fell straight as it unfurled, an eyesore amongst the rest of my ringlets.

Why did it have to be in the front? I tried to pin it back to keep it from being noticeable, but still, it hung frizzy and straight from behind my ear.

Sighing, I angled myself out of Lucy's view from the mirror and put on my foundation and rouge. I doubted she had the awareness or the vocabulary to tell my mother, but I didn't want to take any chances. With one last remorseful look at my unremarkable appearance, I grabbed my sweater, purse and Bible, taking Lucy down the hall.

I set Lucy on Dad's side of the bed with her blocks and princess book. "Sorry, Mom, but I have to go. Play with your toys on the bed until Mommy wakes up, okay, Luce?"

"Otay." She drew the word out as if exasperated. I laughed, kissing her head.

My mother had already rolled over facing Lucy, eyes closed as she hugged her pillow. I'd kind of hoped she'd have shown some interest or even wished me luck, but I tried not to dwell on it.

Downstairs, I put on my green and brown plaid coat and ivory beret. My bike was in the yard, against the front porch where I always left it. Placing my belongings in the wire basket, I rode it down the driveway and onto the road.

The trip to the school felt quick, probably because I was making my way toward the camp with escalating dread. As the brick school building came into view, I saw Holly's bike propped on its kickstand. She was leaning against the outer wall with a cigarette, watching with indifference as I drew near. Flicking the smoldering stick into the grass, she mounted her bike.

I hoped she wouldn't notice my hair. "How long have you been waiting?"

"Dunno." She biked past me. "A few minutes."

I caught up with her, wondering how she was able to act as if it were any other day while I was trying not to vomit. We were about to be in the company of Germans—*Nazis.* Wasn't she the least bit edgy? Maybe it was the cigarettes.

We cycled around Main Street so we could stay on the sidewalks. The handle bars were becoming slippery in my grasp. It felt difficult to breathe, either from the peddling or from nervousness; I wasn't sure. On the outskirts of town, Holly and I got off our bikes, pushing them down a winding road into the woods—the way Pastor Gilbert had told us to go.

The camp came into view. Tall fences enclosed most of the area designated to the camp, ominous with barbed-wire across the top. We continued up the road, riding again, passing the officers' and nurses' quarters. At the intersection just ahead, lofty watch towers sat on each corner outside the fence. There were large, brick buildings on the inside that the towers looked over, one of which appeared to be a hospital. This area was sectioned off from the rest of the camp.

Across the street were the guards' quarters. The entire area was much larger than I had imagined. Everything was spread out and sentinels were posted at checkpoints and vantage points throughout the camp.

Just ahead, the road was blocked by a pair of colossal wooden gates. A small group of women were gathered in front of them and I recognized their faces from church. Pastor Gilbert was even there already, talking to two of the guards. On the other side of the gates were countless rows of buildings, also split up into different sections.

It wasn't difficult to deduce that those were the prisoners' compounds.

Pastor Gilbert was smiling. "Cassie, Holly. Everyone's almost here."

One of the guards—a man with a sallow complexion —pointed behind us. "Ladies, you can leave your bikes at the stockade office there."

We left our bikes with the others parked against one of the buildings we'd passed on the way in; a couple cars were parked there, too. I was glad to see the same curiosity and trepidation I was feeling on some of the other women's faces. I hoped that meant Holly was the odd one and not me.

It surprised me to see Ruth Howard there. She was nineteen and a newlywed, having only gotten married three months ago before her husband was shipped off to the Pacific. Miss Jean and Miss Fannie were also there, the only two talking as if they had simply met somewhere out in town. They were both widows and very sweet old ladies, though they had earned the reputation of being gossips. Nancy Claremont was chattering with Sharon Nichols, who was standing next to her. They had both graduated from secondary school last year and Sharon was already engaged to Teddy, a boy she had gone steady with since eighth grade. Teddy had been sent to England almost a year ago for the war.

The other women were around my mother's age. I knew them because of her, but I'd never really talked to any of them.

"Ah, and here comes the cow's tail," Pastor Gilbert said, causing the rest of us to turn and look.

Pastor Gilbert's niece, Shirley, held onto her hat as she came to a screeching halt on her bike. "I know, I know. I'm late. But I'm here now."

One of the guards laughed.

"Better late than never, I suppose," Pastor Gilbert said.

The pale guard addressed us while the other put Shirley's bike away. "Let's get started. My name's Rich; that's Dennis. We'll be escorting you today. Before meeting the prisoners, we'll be taking you to the Visitor's Reception Building. There, we'll go over some information about the camp, what the prisoners are like, what we expect from this program...things like that. So stick together and follow me."

In spite of how detached Holly often was with me, she kept unusually close as the gates opened. In fact, it was almost as if all of us were no longer individuals; our group had packed so tightly together that we moved as if we were all one body.

Past the gates, yet another fence separated us from the prisoners. I couldn't keep from looking, now that we were closer to the barracks. Most of the men in sight were in collared blue, gray, or black shirts tucked into pants. Some were pacing the grounds or smoking outside the barracks, the letters 'PW' stenciled in white on the backs of their shirts or jackets. A couple of them noticed us, watching until we were out of sight behind the Visitor's Reception Building.

We followed Rich down a long hallway once inside, passing a few other men in American uniform along the way. Rich stood by an open door, directing us inside. "Two to a table, please."

As Holly and I got closer, I was able to see another man standing inside, smiling and shaking hands with everyone. The pins on his uniform made him look more important than the other guards we'd seen. He was also older, with thick white hair and wrinkles that made his face less stern. He shook my hand. "Hello. General Turner."

"Cassie," I returned. He greeted Holly the same way. She followed me as I headed straight for one of the vacant tables in the back.

General Turner seemed to have already been familiar with Pastor Gilbert. Bible stowed away under his arm, Pastor Gilbert sat next to one of my mother's friends near the front.

General Turner looked over the room. "Good afternoon, ladies. In case you've already forgotten, I am

General Turner, the commandant here at Camp Rockmont. I trust that all of you know why you're here, and if you don't, it appears you've taken a wrong turn somewhere."

Miss Jean and Miss Fannie laughed.

"I wanted to be the one to inform you about our camp today. Usually, this is left to one of my guards, but since this is a new and exclusive program, I felt that merited my personal attention."

Rich had already pulled down a projector screen on the wall behind the general. Dennis, a younger guard with strawberry blond hair, was at the back of the room with us, the projector whirring and clicking as he turned it on. Rich turned off the lights and a map appeared on the screen.

"Camp Rockmont hosts close to five thousand prisoners-of-war, most of whom are German. This little rectangle here," General Turner said, using a pointer, "is where we are right now, the Visitor's Reception Building. All these little boxes are the prisoners' barracks. As you might have noticed when you came in—and as you can see here— the prisoners' area is divided into three compounds. Each compound contains, on average, sixteen hundred prisoners, along with four mess halls, four lavatories, at least one work building and a post exchange. You will also see near the front of each compound, here, that there is an infirmary and administration building. There are two fences, each one eight to nine feet in height, that surround all three compounds. That includes the hospital, dental office, work buildings and storehouses down in this corner. A fence also runs between each compound to separate it from the others. The prisoners you will be working with are from compound two."

I hadn't realized my fists were clamped together under the table. I couldn't believe I was here, that in just a few moments, I was going to be talking to a German. If we weren't already in the heart of the camp, I wondered if I would have walked out.

General Turner paced. "We have one guard for every three prisoners. Now, before anyone gets antsy about that, I can assure you, we maintain a very strict and controlled environment here at Camp Rockmont. Our prisoners maintain obedient dispositions and are very respectful to our American guards. We expect no less of their behavior towards you."

My eyebrows knitted closer together. He had to be lying just to make us comfortable. The Germans were cruel, ferocious men; that's what I'd always heard.

"For our prisoners, reveille takes place at five-thirty each morning. They make their bunks, get dressed and are at the mess hall for breakfast by six. They are allotted thirty minutes to eat, before being marched back to their barracks to shower and shave. By seven-thirty, they begin their work projects, which range from local physical labor to cleaning the barracks. They are given a break for lunch before getting back to their work assignments. Dinner is from six to seven and the time before lights out is theirs to use as they wish."

General Turner gave Rich a nod and he turned on the lights.

"Sundays are typically their only day off," General Turner continued. "They are permitted to wear their uniforms then, as well as for special occasions. We do have a chapel on site for the men to attend morning services, if they wish. Afterwards, they often spend the rest of the day playing sports—usually soccer—out in the recreational field behind the barracks. Probably the next popular way they utilize their time is by putting on plays or skits. Sergeant Bell—Dennis—and I have sat in on many. I'm not ashamed to admit that they can be quite entertaining."

He had to be kidding. I peeked at Dennis to see if he showed any sign of being part of an inside joke, but he was nodding in agreement.

"Our prisoners have also formed a Music Committee, from which they've gone about recruiting men who can sing for the choral groups. They've also selected men who are talented instrument players for the camp orchestra. We have a large library with books written in both English and German for the prisoners to choose from. Recreational rooms have been set up for the men who prefer more discreet entertainment, such as chess and card games. The prisoners have the opportunity to attend classes, one of which is an English class. That's how most of the ones in the group you'll be working with today became fluent."

He looked over the classroom. "Are there any questions?"

I was stunned. These men played sports, performed in plays, performed in orchestras; they sang, they acted...they laughed. This conflicted outstandingly with the animalistic, murderous man I had envisioned.

Nancy Claremont's hand was raised. "Yes, um...where will we be talking to the prisoners? In their cells or...?"

General Turner chuckled, glancing at Rich. "Excellent question. These men are not here because of anything they've done besides fighting on the wrong side of the war. Only the ones who have committed a crime during their time here are put in cells. The rest of the prisoners are free to roam about the grounds as they wish, as long as they stay a good distance away from the fences. You'll be working with the selected prisoners from compound two in one of the mess halls. Yes?"

"I hope I'm not the only one wondering this," Mrs. Hall—one of the women my mother knew—said as she glanced around the room for moral support, "but are we in any real danger by doing this?"

General Turner gave what I thought was another patronizing chuckle. "I'd conjecture that there's an element of danger anywhere you go these days, but in regards to our prisoners, we have taken every precaution to ensure your safety. There will be guards posted throughout the room, so if anyone is made uncomfortable, all you have to do is raise your hand and someone will come over. However, these prisoners are not only extremely well-mannered, but I'm certain they will be on their best behavior considering you are the first women they have seen in a very long time."

Mrs. Hall harrumphed. "That's why I had to ask."

Everyone laughed except Holly and me; me because I was skeptical, Holly because she was Holly.

"I assure you all that you will be safe, or else I have failed as this camp's commandant. Any other questions?"

When no one spoke, he glanced at Pastor Gilbert. "Pastor, is there anything you'd like to add?"

Pastor Gilbert stood. "Thank you, General. Did everyone remember to bring both discussion sheets I handed out last Sunday?"

Pastor Gilbert had given us two packets; one for ourselves and one to give the prisoner we were assigned to. There were verses to read and study, followed up with questions to be asked and discussed with our prisoner. I'd read over mine at least once every day since.

He was handing out spares to Shirley and Ruth. "Remember, you are not here to hate these men. If it is not your intention to share God's word and Christ's love, you need to leave that attitude in here. You do not have to like them, but you are in a position to bring God back into their lives. Please don't counteract it by condemning your prisoner for his current beliefs. I implore each of you to remember why you are here; to do the work each of you have been called to do in Christ. Stay focused."

"Pastor Gilbert, what do we do if the prisoner starts talking about Nazism?" Ruth Howard asked.

Holly rolled her eyes, shaking her head. I covered my mouth to hide a smile.

Pastor Gilbert answered. "You have to remember, Nazism has been both their lifestyle and religion for years. Most of the younger men were in school just for that. Chances are, they *are* going to talk about it, but that is a good thing. Talk to him about it. Show him what the Bible says. These specific men have been chosen for this program because they appear the most likely to be swayed from Nazism."

"There is also one more thing I feel the need to address," General Turner said, stepping forward. "I'm sure you will agree with me on this, Pastor. We are not blind, nor are we totally oblivious, to the fact that we are about to send a bunch of women into a room full of lonely soldiers."

A couple of the women adjusted in their seats.

"I have to remind my guards all the time: these men are charming, dignified—they are slick. They'll say and do whatever they must to get you to drop your guard. One of the most important things to remember is that you can never trust a German."

Pastor Gilbert's eyes flinched. He opened his mouth to speak, but he must have decided otherwise.

"If you remember that, you'll be fine. Most of the time, whatever they say is a lie. That, is the only thing you can be sure of. As I said before, there will be guards posted all along the room. If you get frightened for any reason, all you have to do is raise your hand and one of them will come to you."

He glanced at Pastor Gilbert before stepping back.

Pastor Gilbert hesitated. "All right. Before we go, let's go to the Lord in prayer."

I tried to steady my breathing, saying my own prayer alongside Pastor Gilbert's.

Rich opened the door. "Take only your Bible and the worksheets when we leave. Any other belongings must remain in here and may be picked up on your way out. I'll now be taking you down the hall for an inspection with Nurse Watson—which we'll do every time—and from there, we'll head over to the mess."

"Inspection?" Holly whispered in my ear, once we were out in the hall. "What do they think we're going to be doing with these Germans?"

I blushed. Standing in a line with the rest of the women, I prepared to run if the nurse so much as asked me to get on a table. Instead, she merely pat us all down, making Holly take her comb out of her sock to check that it wasn't a weapon.

We followed Dennis out of the Visitor's Reception Building and back outside. The sun warmed my face, despite how cold the air was. As we walked through a second set of gates, into compound two, there were still many POWs standing outside their barracks, watching us in interest as

Dennis led us forward. Word must have spread that there were women in the camp because some of the men rushed to their doorways to see us. I fought the urge to wrap my arm around Holly's at the risk of showing fear or weakness; at least the prisoners were keeping their distance.

The mess hall was empty when we entered, except for some guards with rifles overhead, peering down at the long rows of tables. Each table sat eight on each side and it was impossible for me to count how many tables there were. We crowded near the door as Dennis walked down one of the aisles.

"One person to a table," he said. "Find yourselves a seat, evenly spaced from your neighbor and don't be afraid—there's plenty of room."

Everyone began to fill the tables closest to the door. As much as I longed to do the same, I felt the need to step out of my comfort zone. If I was going to make a difference, I had to be brave; this was my first test. Swallowing, I lifted my chin, headed for the aisle Dennis had walked down. Setting my sights on one of the farther tables in the middle row, I became aware that I would be the only one on that side of the room. I tried to appear casual—regardless of how I was squirming on the inside—as I set my Bible down on the table and slid into the chair. Noticing movement to my left, Holly sat at the table next to mine. I beamed at her.

Good ole Holly!

Taking off my coat and beret, I positioned my Bible and the worksheets on the table. While Pastor Gilbert was still passing out pencils, the first of the POWs began to trickle in through a door on the opposite side of the room. I was surprised to see that they were not all blond, as they were so often portrayed. Most of them were, but some had different shades of brown hair. Their curious murmurs echoed throughout the room. One of the men, a dark-haired German whose hair was almost black, wore a broad smile as if he were enjoying the fact that so many women were in such close quarters. His eyes met mine and I looked down at the table, stiffening in my seat. Most of the rest of the men stood in silence close to Dennis with curious, solemn expressions, while others were smiling or laughing amongst one another. I was surprised at how human they all looked. Their faces were smooth and shaven, their hair combed and their clothes clean.

Dennis' voice boomed throughout the mess hall. "All right, ladies. When I call your name, please raise your hand so the prisoner you're assigned to can find you."

The smiling prisoner blurted out something in German, and the others erupted with laughter. Nervous, I glanced at Holly, surprised to see that she looked amused.

"Enough!" one of the guards barked. Dennis eyed the prisoners until their laughter died down.

He began calling out names and I watched as prisoner after prisoner sat down—some being sent off with chuckles. It was then that I began to pray; I didn't care which prisoner I got, all I knew was that I did not want that smiling German. There was something about him that I didn't like. He was still one of the last ones standing, and I had yet to be called.

Dennis continued reading off the list. "Holly Morgan."

I held my breath for her, watching her arm raise in my peripheral vision.

"Egon Wulf."

It was hard to be grateful knowing I would not be placed with the smiling German when he had been assigned to Holly. His smile widened as he strutted down the aisle, his thick lips proportionate with his high, prominent cheek bones. He winked at me and kissed the air as he pulled the chair out across from Holly.

"Cassie Wyndham."

My blood felt hot underneath my skin. Taking a deep breath, I raised my hand. Dennis looked at the blond German standing closest to him.

"Friedrich Naumann."

Friedrich perked up, unfolding his arms. He searched the room before his gaze locked with mine. One of the Germans still waiting to be placed grabbed Friedrich's arm, whispering in his ear. Friedrich looked at me, responding with a mischievous grin.

I distracted myself, flipping through my Bible. He must have noticed my hair or the fact that I wasn't wearing as much make-up as the others. Maybe he was joking about Friedrich being placed with one of the uglier girls in the room.

He was walking up the aisle now. I realized right away what General Turner had meant about their charm. His perfect white teeth, attractive face and confident stride only added to his charisma.

He smiled down at me, extending his hand. "It is nice meeting you."

"Hi," I mumbled, shaking it.

His brand new Bible thumped on the table as he gave it a careless toss, pulling out the chair across from me. He spoke with an accent. "I hope you forgive me. My English is not so good."

I still wasn't able to meet his eyes. "It sounds fine to me."

"Thank you."

I pulled out the folded worksheets from my Bible, handing him a copy. "So, apparently we're supposed to make this something of a getting-to-know you session."

"Wonderful."

His unblinking sky blue eyes hadn't left my face. And still, he smiled.

I gulped, picking up one of the pencils. "Uh—anyway. What...what's your name again?"

"Friedrich Naumann."

I wrote the 'Fr' in his name then paused. "Sorry. H-how do you spell that?"

He spelled it out for me. I wrote it down before going to the next question. "Okay, and where are you from?"

"Whoa, whoa, wait one minute." He picked up the other pencil. "I believe it is my turn asking a question."

"Uh—okay."

"What is *your* name?"

I recoiled at the thought of giving him any information about me. Yet, that was why I was here; if I didn't open up, it would be hypocritical of me to expect him to.

"Cassandra Wyndham."

His eyes widened as he snorted. "I think you have to spell it for me."

I hadn't meant to grin, but I did. "Well, actually, everyone just calls me Cassie."

I spelled it, watching him scribble away beneath the question on his sheet. He studied it when he finished. "You have a very pretty name."

"Thank you."

"It matches you."

My cheeks grew warm as I looked down at my worksheet. What was he doing? I was certain he'd go back to tell that other German later that he told the ugly girl she was pretty. I'm sure they'd get a good laugh over that.

I read the next question aloud. "Where are you from?"

"Köln."

Unfamiliar to my ears, I looked at him on impulse. He smiled, and I began to wonder if he'd done that on purpose. "My apologies. I forget. Americans say—I believe it is—Cologne."

I wrote it down. "Right."

"And you?"

"Here. I'm from Rockmont...Virginia."

His forehead rumpled in concentration as he wrote. I waited until he was done before moving to the next question.

"The next part says to tell a little about yourself."

His lips pulled up on one side as he shrugged. "I am born and grow up in Köln. I have an older brother, Hans, who is in Germany. My mother is a homemaker, my father is a farmer; he is dying when I am a boy. I am in the Hitler Youth since a few years, and after, I join the *Wehrmacht*—the military—and am a part of it ever since."

"How old are you?" I asked without thinking.

"Twenty-one."

I nodded, writing all this down. "I was going to say, you don't look like you could be much older than me."

"How old are you?"

"Sixteen."

He laughed. "You are still a baby."

My face hardened at the insult. "I am not."

"Yes, you are," he said with a chuckle.

"Well, you...you're not that much older than me."

"Ah, but I have more experience."

I gaped at him. Even though I knew he was probably right, I resented the fact that he already believed so. "You don't know that."

"Have you been out of the country?"

I fiddled with my pencil. "No."

"Have you ever leaving this state?"

I smiled in triumph. "Yes."

"Oh really?"

"Yes. I had grandparents in both New York and Maryla—"

"That counts not."

I scoffed. "How does that not count?"

"Have you not ever leaving home without your parents? You know, going somewhere for no reason, without an idea what you will meet or what you make there?"

I tapped the eraser from my pencil on the table. "Well...no."

He was smug. "This is what I think. You are still a baby."

"No, I'm not."

He began writing under the 'Tell a Little About Yourself' section.

"What are you writing?"

"Stubborn."

He simpered, as if daring me to contradict him. But that would only prove him right.

My toes curled in my shoes out of frustration. "I think we're getting a little off topic."

"I frustrate you, am I not?" he asked in amusement. "There is no harm in it. I try to understand you."

His expression was innocuous, as if all of this truly was just a game, but I hadn't forgotten what the general had said; I didn't *want* this person to figure me out.

Friedrich sighed, scrawling something in German before looking back up at me. "Okay. Your turn. Tell me a little about you."

I cocked an eyebrow. I could tell he was enjoying himself.

"I quit, I promise. Please. Continue."

Watching him for a moment, I sighed. "I'm about to start my last year of secondary school. I plan on going to college this autumn for—"

"Have you a boyfriend?"

I blinked up at him. "I'm not looking for one, if that's what you're asking."

He burst with laughter. "No. I ask because distance is bad for a relationship. I know."

"Right, because of all your experience," I said with a sarcasm that reminded me of my brother.

He found this funny, too. "Exactly!"

I couldn't hide that I was humored myself. "Is someone waiting for you at home? In Germany?"

Friedrich's eyes relaxed. "No. Not anymore. She marries someone else."

"Oh. I'm sorry."

"No need for being sorry. She finds someone better."

He was no longer smiling, looking down at the worksheet. I had the feeling it was he who was trying to avoid my eyes now. The tone in his voice had been too heavy for me to believe he was indifferent, as he put on to be.

I went to the next question. "Okay, so—"

"Tell me about your family."

That wasn't anywhere on the sheet. "What do you want to know?"

Friedrich shrugged. "Tell me anything."

"Well, I...I have an older brother, Amos, who just left to fight, and a little sister, Lucy. I was born in New York and —"

"I think you say you are from here?"

"I said I'm from here because I don't remember living in New York. My parents moved soon after I was born."

"What is making them move?"

A fleeting fever came over me. "Oh...it was actually to get away from my mother's parents." I rolled my eyes. "You know how parents can be."

"Ah. Yes, I understand."

"Let's go to the next question." This had been the one I had been most eager to hear his answer for. "What are your spiritual beliefs up to this point in your life?"

Friedrich glanced at the same question. "What means this?"

"In reference to God, what are your beliefs?"

He straightened in his seat. "Oh. I believe He is an all-powerful being, looking down on us."

I nodded. "What about Jesus?"

"The Son of God."

He smiled at me as if he had said all he needed to say.

"What else about Him?" I asked.

For the first time since meeting him, Friedrich seemed irresolute. "He is the Son of a carpenter."

I waited for him to continue before realizing he wasn't going to. I prayed a quick prayer in my head for guidance, understanding that this was going to be a little harder than I thought. "What would you say your testimony is?"

"Testimony?" Friedrich shook his head. "What mean you, 'testimony'?"

"I'm sorry. I mean, what has God done for you in your life? How has He changed you and allowed you to grow in Christ?"

Friedrich stared at me. He looked as if I were asking him to paint the Mona Lisa on a toothpick. "I am not knowing what means this."

I reached for my Bible. "Okay."

"Is this bad?"

I gave him a reassuring grin. "No. It's okay. This is what I'm here for. Even though you aren't sure now, it doesn't mean God hasn't been with you. Hopefully, after this, you'll be able to acknowledge His presence in your life and experience it as it's occurring."

He nodded. While he soaked this in, I searched for the first verse to study.

"Do you need help finding the Book of John?" I asked.

"No. New Testament, right?"

"Right!" The brightness of my tone gave away my excitement. He smirked, thumbing through his shiny, crisp leather Bible.

"Chapter three," I repeated. "Go ahead and read John 3:16 out loud."

Crossing his arms over the table, he leaned forward. "For God so loved the world, that he gave his only begotten Son, that whosoever believeth in him should not perish, but have everlasting life."

"Are there any words that jump out to you in that?"

He raised his shoulders. "Uh—"

"Okay," I said, rescuing him. "I think the most significant words—at least to me—are 'loved,' 'gave' and 'whosoever.' This verse tells us what God was willing to give up in order to save us and why—because He loves us. And He gave up his Son to die for everyone, which is saying there is no one who can't be saved. Do you understand that?"

"Yes."

"Do you have any questions or anything you want to say about this?"

Friedrich seemed to think for a moment. "I think not."

I was a little disappointed, but became mindful of the fact that if he already had all the answers, I would have no purpose being there.

We read more verses together. There was one in Jeremiah he thought was interesting, talking about how God knew us even in the womb. He also liked one in Ephesians saying that every gift was to be used for the glory of the Father. Some he simply could not grasp; I knew he wasn't unintelligent. I could only assume it was because of the language barrier, or that what we read didn't fall in line with what he already believed. He seemed to be an inert listener but I was still disheartened that he wasn't more responsive.

Pastor Gilbert called out that there were only five minutes left, and I put my pencil in my dress pocket. "I guess our time's up."

"Too bad," Friedrich said, closing his Bible. "I enjoy it."

"Well, you can still read on your own. You don't have to wait until the next time we meet."

"But it is the company I enjoy." He gave me his charming smile, to which I looked away out of bashfulness. "Bye, Cassie."

I picked up my things. "Bye, Friedrich."

Holding my breath, I bit at my lip as I headed over to Pastor Gilbert and one of the guards by the door.

What kind of impression had I made on him? Had I begun to make a difference yet? Or had he not really listened, viewing this as time to flirt with a female and not an opportunity to strengthen his faith? There was no way for me to be sure.

Holly came up to me, and I chanced a peek over my shoulder. Friedrich was laughing with one of the other prisoners as they headed toward the door they had come in from. It already looked as if everything we had discussed was far from his mind.

Whether he had paid attention or not didn't change the fact that I had done it. I had been scared—terrified even —of being so close to a German; the enemy, the very same men who were responsible for this war. Yet, I had recognized my fear and for the sake of my faith, I had acted in spite of it:

I had faced a German.

Four

Despite the former potency of my angst over the POW camp, it all seemed to vanish from my thoughts the following week. My mother never asked how my first meeting went. I assumed she must have forgotten since she was always so preoccupied worrying over Amos, thinking about Dad and taking care of things at home. She was volunteering at the hospital every other night during the week now. I often only saw her when I came home as she was walking out the door and by that time, she was in too big of a hurry to ask how my day went, or anything else for that matter.

We received a letter from Amos on the second of February. He thanked Mom for our letters, telling us about all the training he'd done so far and that he had indeed touched noses many times with one of his drill sergeants. He said that he wasn't sure where he was going to be sent from there, but probably couldn't tell us even if he knew. He asked how we were doing near the end, and thirty minutes after reading it, Mom had already written a response.

Walking down the halls of my school that week, I couldn't help noticing that my steps seemed a little more self-assured. I stopped watching my feet as I walked, allowing myself to look up as I made my way to each of my classes. I smiled at a few other students whenever their eyes met mine, which I didn't usually do. I wondered if it was just me or if anyone else noticed a difference in me. Donald and Holly, the closest people I had to friends, never mentioned any changes, so I assumed it must have been my imagination.

"Have you looked over the study sheet for Saturday that Pastor Gilbert gave us?" I asked Holly as we walked with Donald to our lockers.

Uninterested, she focused straight ahead. "No. I'll look over it before I leave Saturday morning."

"Well, you're both still alive and planning on going back so I'm assuming that means it went well?" Donald asked.

I smiled, adjusting my books in my arms. "Yeah. Actually, it did."

Donald's cheeks turned red as his eyes fell to my books. "Would you like me to carry those?"

"Oh, no, thank you. I'm all right. Our lockers are just down the hall anyway." I turned to Holly. "I never got to ask you how it went with your prisoner."

I was curious to know if Egon had been as insufferable as he seemed.

Holly shrugged. "It was good."

I watched her a moment, hoping she would elaborate. "Well, did he seem receptive to you?"

"He was okay."

I sighed as the three of us turned down the hall. I was still hoping to talk to someone about my experience and since my mother had no interest in what I was doing there, I'd kind of hoped Holly would ask me how it went with my prisoner. Instead, there was nothing but silence on the other side of my locker door.

Donald leaned against the lockers as I organized my books. "What do you have next?"

I pulled out my history and English books. "English."

"Oh. Right. Hey," Donald said, a lift in his voice. "I wanted to ask you: I'm having a little get together at my house Friday night. It's just going to be a few friends. I was hoping you could make it. Holly's going to be there."

I shut my door in time to see Holly dabbing tinted Vaseline on her lips, pretending to look in her mirror when seconds ago, she had been looking at us. I hadn't really ever seen Donald outside of school. The thought of even making some new acquaintances didn't seem unpleasant. I smiled, unfamiliar with this new confidence inside me. "You know, that sounds nice."

Donald beamed. "Really? That's...that's great. Do you need to ask permission first or anything?"

"Yeah, I should. My mom works at the hospital on week nights so..." I gasped, slapping my forehead in embarrassment. "Actually, Donald, I can't. I have to stay home and watch Lucy."

His face fell. "Oh."

"I'm really sorry. I would if I could. But hey, I'm sure you'll both have fun without me."

Donald gave me a weak smile. "Yeah. I have to go to class. See you both later."

Holly seemed fixated on rearranging the items on the top shelf of her locker. As usual, she didn't even speak as she shut her door, walking with me to English.

I woke up that Saturday without an anvil of panic weighing me down. I met Holly at the school just like before and we rode together to the front gates of the camp.

Sitting in the same seat as I had the previous week, I felt a twinge of anticipation as the POWs dispensed into the room. Friedrich searched for only a second before spotting me. Something in my chest warmed as I comprehended that the breadth of his smile had been meant for me.

He pulled out his chair. "Miss Wyndham. How is your week?"

I wavered for a moment, realizing I couldn't remember the last time someone asked me that. "Good. Normal. How was yours?"

"The same. Normal," he mimicked, giving me that enchanting grin of his again.

I laughed in politeness before handing him the extra worksheet. "Ready for round two?"

"Certainly."

We read the four given passages together before starting on the questions. A few of them were easy, the answers found in the verses. The reflective ones were harder, particularly since the verses were written in Old English. I circled the troublesome ones on his study sheet, hoping he might look them up in a German Bible later.

"Is there anything you would like to ask God to give you a wise and discerning heart over?" I read aloud.

"Why is this Solomon referring him as a little child?" Friedrich asked, ignoring my question as he flipped through the pages. "What kind of people want a man like this on the throne?"

At least it was a response. "Solomon was a great king. The reason he was a great king was because he humbled himself before God. His people trusted him because of this."

He raised a cynical eyebrow. I chuckled.

"He sought beyond his own abilities to be a great ruler. He asked for wisdom with a pure heart and God granted that to him."

"But why he asks not be a warrior? A kingdom cannot trust a soft, childlike man what uses religion as a seat cushion. It needs someone what can defend it. And look, God rewards him for his cowardice, saying, 'I will give you what you have not asked for—both riches and honor.'"

"God's not rewarding him for being passive; He's rewarding him for not being too proud to acknowledge that a kingdom can't flourish without God's help. And riches and honor weren't the only things He gave Solomon. He gave him a wise and discerning heart because it's what he *did* ask for."

Friedrich sighed. "I think I cannot respect a man like this."

I stared at him, wondering if there was any chance I could redeem Solomon's actions or if I had already lost my battle with this passage.

"Is there anything you would like to ask God to give you a wise and discerning heart over?" I repeated.

Friedrich's lips puckered as he shook his head. "I think not."

I watched him before looking down at the question. It couldn't be left unanswered, whether he was the one who had a response or not. Remembering that the only way I could reach out to him was if I opened up, I had to take down the barriers that surrounded my heart, if only for an instant. "Then...maybe I'll answer this one."

Friedrich set his pencil aside, giving me his rapt attention. "Okay."

I looked around at the other pairs, collecting my thoughts. "I think the thing that I need a wise and discerning heart over the most is how to...matter."

His eyes lost their crinkle. "What mean you?"

I was hesitant, unsure whether I was about to reveal too much about myself. I was certain he was going to think me strange, as if I divulged my true feelings to everyone, but it was quite the opposite. I hid my true self from others because they didn't care about how I felt or how I perceived things; I wanted to tell him the truth in case he did.

"I don't mean that in a self-important sort of way, like in regards to money or status. I'm talking about on a raw, personal level—much like Solomon meant here. It's something I've struggled with my whole life. My father's not around much and I've always felt that if I were a better person, or a more interesting person, or a more significant person...he might stay."

I flipped the pages of my Bible out of discomfort. "My brother's the favorite in the family. I never have and never will do anything as great as him. I'll never be as talented —never be as *perfect*. So, I guess...I guess what I'm trying to say is, since I have no value in my family, maybe I have value to God."

I distracted myself with the ribbon hanging from the spine of my Bible. "I guess that's why—"

Friedrich burst with laughter. My cheeks burned.

He leaned on the table. "You are joking. Right? Is someone telling you to say this? Because you cannot be serious."

I wanted to melt onto the floor. I kept my eyes on the words in my Bible out of embarrassment. This was what I got for making myself vulnerable.

It was a moment before he spoke again. "You...you are serious?"

I closed my Bible.

He glanced around. "You are really feeling this way?"

I gave a feeble shrug, too ashamed to say more.

"I...I am sorry," he said. "It is just...you seem to have you together. Why else are you here, talking to a prisoner-of-war about Christianity?"

I ran the ribbon between my fingers. "I'm here because of what I just said."

I picked up my pencil, looking at the set of questions for the last passage. "Let's go to the next one: Why is it important not to conform to the ways of the world, but to allow your mind to be transformed and renewed?"

I looked at him. "Will you answer this one?"

He scrutinized me. Leaning back in his chair, he crossed his arms. "I think I am wanting you to answer again."

I dithered, wondering if I should just go to the next question or tell him he had to answer. I wasn't there for myself, I was there for him. Still, giving my own reply was better than leaving it blank.

I peeked at Holly to see if she was listening, but she was oblivious, talking to her own prisoner. "Okay. I believe the power of this verse depends on your perspective."

"Why?"

"This verse will mean nothing to you if you hold no value for God's will...or His mercy, or His love for that matter. I, however, do. This verse is asking us not to conform if we wish to be a catalyst through which God can be glorified. So...back to what I answered with before: I could choose to talk to my mother the way she talks to me; I could choose to be absent physically and emotionally from my father. But I choose not to because God's presence is more important to me than hurting them—even though I may want to."

"But this is going back what I am saying before," Friedrich rasped. "Why not fight them? Why *not* hurt them when they care for you so little?"

"I'm sure it appears that way—that I'm being passive—but just because I'm not reacting to my parents doesn't mean I'm not reacting at all; I'm reacting to God. I'm hoping He'll be the one who changes them for me, because that's the only way this is ever going to change."

He studied me from across the table. I flipped over the worksheet, my skin growing clammy. Here I was, pouring out my heart to some Nazi when I was supposed to be ministering to him. "Please, let's...let's go to the next one."

He leaned over, his nose mere inches from his worksheet. "Is there an area of your life where you may not be thinking of yourself with sober judgment?" He looked at me. "Answer."

My lips parted. "Why?"

"Because I am wanting to hear it."

He wasn't wearing his typical grin. I felt guilty. This was becoming about me and not where he stood in his faith—what I had been brought here to discuss.

"No. Friedrich. Please, can't you answer this one?"

"I want you to answer."

I hid my face in my hand. He was doing this to avoid answering them himself—to avoid deliberating over how they applied to his own life. I only answered the first one because I thought it was a step toward helping him figure this out on his own.

I clenched my eyes before lifting my face. "I...I don't know. I try to humble myself. I try to be what I think is a good person. But I'm not perfect. And then sometimes, I don't believe I'm good at all. Sometimes I think being a valuable person is so far out of reach because I don't have what it takes to be that. I'm ordinary. If I wanted to be someone extraordinary, I should've been born my brother."

Friedrich snickered under his breath at that. He began to write under the question. Hoping it was his own response, I tried to read it, disappointed to see he was writing in German.

"What are you writing?"

He didn't answer and I gave a heavy sigh as Pastor Gilbert called out that we had only five minutes left. We hadn't even discussed the questions for the last two passages. I placed my worksheet in my Bible as Friedrich finished writing.

"You and I have much in common," he said, folding his worksheet in half, "and yet we are still very different."

"What do you mean?"

"I am not unfamiliar with how you are feeling with your family. I see many similarities, but we handle it different."

He stood with his Bible under his arm, tilting his head much like a man who was lifting his top hat would. "It is a pleasure. Until next Saturday."

I could only nod in response. That dashing smile returned and I stared at his back as he walked away. Grabbing my belongings, I headed in the opposite direction.

Befuddled by our conversation, I wondered the whole way home if I'd said too much. It was difficult for me to understand why he had been so insistent on hearing my thoughts. Was it because he thought I was foolish and wanted a laugh over the sheltered American girl's limited perspective? Or had it been genuine curiosity? Part of me felt abashed for revealing so much of myself, yet another part of me—a much more embarrassed part—felt a guilty pleasure at the possibility that he had been interested in what I had to say.

The weeks leading up to April went by rather quickly. Thanks to my mother's night job, I didn't see her often, which prevented her from having too much time to find something to be annoyed with me about. Most days, we saw one another only in passing. Only on a few of those occasions did she use that brief interchange to correct my posture or remind me of something I did wrong with Lucy the night before. She never asked how my meetings at the camp went, but I kept telling myself that it wasn't because she didn't care; she was just busy.

Each week, I counted down the days for that one hour of conversation with Friedrich on Saturdays. In spite of how sealed up he kept his spiritual and personal details, he seemed to rather enjoy hearing about mine. I kept praying that I wasn't wasting God's time, and that there was a reason Friedrich kept asking for my opinions.

I reveled in how attentive he was whenever I spoke. No one but Lucy had ever smiled at me the way he did, so honest and sincere. Looking into his eyes was like catching a glimpse of the sky from a dark, hopeless place. Whether he was earnest in allowing what he learned in our meetings to change him, I couldn't be sure, but he was always respectful. From our first study together, I knew that he believed in God, but I speculated that that was as far as it went for him. I wasn't sure if he had a deeper faith than he wanted me privy to, or if he was self-conscious on some level because he didn't have one at all.

We got another letter from Amos in the middle of April wishing me a happy birthday and saying he was being sent to Georgia for more training. There was a different tone in his writing than there had been before; he didn't talk so much about himself, or in what ways he was being prepared for battle. He mentioned some of the men who had become his friends (it seemed strange calling them men; I imagined most of them couldn't have been much older than Amos) and how he wished they would just send them to fight already. His enthusiasm disturbed my mother, but I admired Amos more than ever. He sounded strong and determined. He seemed more like a man, as if the high opinions that had been bestowed upon him all these years had now been rightfully earned. I'd always wrestled with the concept that maybe I loved my brother just because everyone else did. The reason my parents esteemed him so meant nothing to me. Why should I admire him as they do? Now I had my own reason.

The last week of school dragged on, making it feel as if the weekend would never come. As much as I looked forward to the break from school, summer meant extended time alone with my mother. She wouldn't let me get a job as long as she was working; someone needed to be home to watch the baby. I hoped that since her schedule would be changing to day shift, I could be in bed before she got home.

On my last day as a junior, I got on my bike with a sigh of forbearance, knowing there was just one more year of secondary school to get through. Pedaling off, I slowed down upon hearing someone jogging behind me.

I stopped in surprise. "Donald."

He was breathing hard, his eyes in their typical crescent shape. "Hey Cassie. On your way home?"

"Yeah. We're officially seniors now," I added.

"I know. Any plans for the summer?"

"Not really. Just babysitting, church and going to the camp."

He nodded in thought. It felt awkward, and I twisted my handlebars as he looked at the ground.

"Since it's the end of the year and everything," he said, "I had a question...for you."

I swallowed, wishing Holly was there. "Yeah?"

"Would you, um...I was wondering if you might want to go to the movies with me tonight."

"Oh. Well, I...I would, but I have to watch Lucy."

"I thought your mom was going to start working day shift?"

"Next week."

"Then how about Saturday night?"

I stared at my shoes. The truth was, I didn't think I wanted to; I didn't like Donald like that. At least, I didn't think I did. I hadn't really had those kinds of feelings toward anyone except my brother's friend Jimmy once and even then I hadn't been sure. Whether I liked Donald or not, I had no desire to have connections to this place after I left; I knew he had other plans in mind.

"I can't, Donald."

His cheeks were the color of raspberries. "Why not?"

I could have told him my mother wouldn't let me—which wasn't a lie—but I didn't have it in me to tell him the truth. I couldn't hurt him. He was one of my only friends.

"My mom already told me she might have to work Saturday night this week. I'm sorry."

He avoided my eyes. At the risk of appearing rude, I looked at my watch. It felt like a bucket of cold water had been dumped over me; I was going to be in so much trouble. "Oh my...I really have to go."

He yelled my name as I pedaled away. "Can I come visit you this summer?"

"Sure. Bye Donald," I called out over my shoulder.

I cringed over yielding that much to him, but what else could I have said? He'd want an explanation if I said no and I didn't have time for that right now. I could only hope that he would forget or else wouldn't be able to work up the courage to stop by.

I biked home as fast as I could. My mother would be furious if I caused her to leave even a few minutes late. I was supposed to come straight home after school. The times I'd pedaled too slow or dawdled by getting caught up in conversation with Holly or Donald, I wound up getting grounded, having what few privileges I had taken away. I refused to ruin my summer before it even started.

My bike rattled as I let it fall in the grass, my steps pounding the porch like a drum. Mom opened the screen door in her blue chambray pinafore and white button up just as I reached it. I could tell by the absence of fury on her face that I had made it on time, though she noticed my hair sticking to my forehead.

She sighed as the door slammed behind her. "You left late, didn't you?"

I tried to answer before leaning over to catch my breath, hands gripping my knees.

"I told you before, Cassandra, if you ever make me late again—"

"But I didn't. Sorry, Mom. It's the last day of school. I'm not going to be seeing Donald again until next year."

She scowled, brushing past me. "You'd better be thankful you got here on time. I'm picking up James and Mrs. Williams to drop them off at the bus stop before work, so I'll already be running late."

I stood up straight, arm wrapped around the porch column. "Mom, what...what would you do if someone asked me to go to the movies?"

She paused, looking at me from behind her open car door, one of her perfect black eyebrows arched. "Someone asked *you* to go to the movies?"

I took umbrage at the skepticism in her tone, though I nodded. She clenched her jaw. "You know how I feel about that, Cassandra. You're not ready."

"But, Mom, you always let Amos go when he was seventeen. You even let him take the car—"

"You're not Amos; Amos is more mature than most people his age." She checked her watch. "I don't have time for this. You're not going to the movies. That's the end of it."

She slammed the car door shut. I waited on the porch as she backed out, driving down the road. Sighing, I went to pick up my bike. Hearing her say no like that made me want to go with Donald out of spite. I knew she'd react that way, but I wished she'd have asked me whether I liked the boy or if I really wanted to go. Instead, she looked like she couldn't believe someone had even noticed me. Dust stirred up from her tires floated in the air and I went inside to eat dinner with Lucy.

I was glad this week's Bible Study was a little more lighthearted than the others had been. This one focused on using one's spiritual gifts.

"What is something you're good at that could be used for the glory of God?" I asked, reading the question. Friedrich shook his head.

I snickered at his expression. "What? What are you thinking of?"

He scratched at his forehead. "I have a talent, but I think it is not something good."

"No, you can't do that. God can use anything. What are you good at?"

His eyes twinkled. "You are going to think I am an animal."

"I already think you're an animal."

He laughed.

"I'm teasing," I said. "What is it? Tell me."

"Fighting. I am good at fighting."

My grin wavered with uncertainty. "What do you mean?"

With a sly smile, he beckoned me forward with his hand. A hot flash swelled over me from being so close to him.

"I may not always be the victor, but you ask any of the men in this room what they are not wanting to fight and they say me."

"Why?"

"Because I am..." He paused, pondering the right word. "Strong. Even if I know I am losing, I stop not. I am not giving the other man a chance to take a breath. So, now that you know," he said, rising upright in his seat, "tell me you still believe this is something good—that it is something God can use for His glory."

"I do."

He turned somber. "What?"

Thinking, I began to nod. "Yeah. That's definitely something He could use, under the right circumstances."

"Why?" he asked. "How?"

I shrugged. "Sometimes, I think you view God as you see Solomon. As sappy and childish—but He isn't. People put too much focus solely on His emotional side—the fact that He's loving, that He's forgiving, that He's beautiful. They miss the full scope of Him because they don't pay attention to His other side; that He's a fighter, a protector. He rescues those who can't rescue themselves and defends the ones who love Him. Just because He's a good warrior doesn't mean He isn't good. The same can be said for you."

He stared at me.

"Who do you think God counts on when He tells that soft, childlike king who uses religion like a seat cushion that it's time to send his people to war?"

Friedrich's eyebrows tightened. "This is interesting."

"That's why Solomon had to be childlike. If he was strong and independent on his own, he wouldn't have asked for God's wisdom and help. That's also why God puts a desire in a person's heart to be a fighter—like you said— because He needs to be able to use you in the right way. If the king's heart isn't in the right place and the fighter's heart isn't either, the kingdom will fall."

He looked at me before gazing toward the table in deliberation. I stayed quiet, afraid of overwhelming him with an excess of my thoughts.

"I never think of it this way," he finally said. "I hope you are right, though. I never can follow the other thing."

This piqued my curiosity. "What other thing?"

An uncomfortable grin positioned itself on his face and I realized I'd never seen him look embarrassed before. "Ah, never mind. Tell me what you are good at."

I snorted. It was always just a matter of time before the questions came back around to me. "I don't know. I'm good with my baby sister, I suppose—though I don't know how that could be used. I like to write."

"What are you writing?"

"Mostly I journal, though I've written a couple poems, too. I really only do it when I'm sad or angry. I've come to discover that my mother's my biggest inspiration."

That humored him. "I am sure."

Internally, I felt like a fraud. I hadn't known my whole life what God wanted to use me for. I did enjoy writing my thoughts, but I had yet to experience that clarifying moment where I discovered what my purpose in life was.

After finishing the rest of the worksheet, I glanced at the clock on the wall. "Hmm. We finished early."

He closed his Bible. "Are you noticing a difference since turning seventeen?"

I pushed my Bible aside, recalling my birthday a few days prior. "No, not really. I'm still a baby."

He shook his head. "You are not a baby."

"I wasn't the one who said it."

"And I am not right to say it. I am sorry."

He seemed to search my face for a response I felt too dumbfounded to give. He was afraid he'd hurt my feelings. He was apologizing—for hurting my feelings. Why did I feel so surprised?

"It...It's okay."

He rolled his pencil between his fingers. "You are not telling me what you get."

"Oh. I got a new sweater from my mom. She knitted it herself. And Lucy..." I chuckled, thinking of it. "Lucy gave me a little sock puppet she made. Its eyes are crooked and it doesn't have a nose, but I think it's adorable."

Friedrich smiled.

"And then, my dad sent me a record of 'O mio babbino caro.' It's from—"

"Gianni Schicchi. The opera by Giacomo Puccini."

I gaped at him. "You know it?"

"I know it."

I laughed. "Wow. Of all the people I've told that to, you're the only one who's had any idea what it was. It's my favorite song."

"Why this one?"

I played with the ribbon bookmark dangling from my Bible. "It's stupid, really."

"I am never hearing you say anything stupid."

I wanted to hide my face from how much it was burning.

"Okay," I began. "When I was little, my dad got free tickets to see Gianni Schicchi from one of his colleagues whose daughter was making her debut. My brother groaned and complained the whole way there, calling it a sissy girl's show. I remember my mother looked so beautiful that night. She was so pretty and I prayed I might be as lovely as she was someday. It was also the first time—and only time—I'd ever seen my father in a tuxedo. My mother was so excited to have the entire family together—for my dad to be there—that she dressed Amos and me without a single cross word. She smiled the whole night."

Friedrich continued listening.

"Then," I shifted in discomfort, "as funny as the opera was, watching Rinuccio and Lauretta was the first time I'd ever wondered what it would feel like to love and be loved like that. Just when Lauretta believes she's going to be separated from Rinuccio forever, she breaks into 'O mio babbino caro.' I didn't understand what the words meant, of course, but the melody was so mournfully beautiful, so heartbreaking. I fell in love with that song because of what it meant to Rinuccio and Lauretta...and because it made me feel like it could happen to me someday."

Friedrich didn't speak, and the way my mouth had gotten away from me made me want to implode on myself. I glanced at him to see if he was laughing at me. "I'm sorry. I know it sounds sentimental and childish—"

"No. It is not."

The way he was looking at me made me feel more exposed than ever, my skin prickling. I felt the most disappointment I had yet as Pastor Gilbert instructed us all to wrap up our sessions.

I gathered my things, standing up. "I've really enjoyed today, Friedrich—as always. To be honest, I really hate to leave."

His voice was low. "I hate watching you go."

Tittering, I found I was only able to look at him indirectly from beneath my lashes. "Until next time, then?"

He gave me the same smile that kept turning up in my head. "Until next time."

The women from church had begun to accumulate in the doorway. Looking over my shoulder, Holly was talking to

Nancy Claremont as they walked together in my direction. My eyes wandered over to the POWs leaving on the opposite side of the room. Friedrich was trailing behind the other prisoners, and I didn't expect him to cast a casual glance over his own shoulder. We smiled as our eyes met, and I quickly looked away before anyone else noticed.

Five

I struggled to keep my thoughts on track Sunday morning. The church could have gone up in flames from Pastor Gilbert's passionate sermon, and I wouldn't have known. I'd gathered quite a collection of mental notes on how attractive Friedrich was, reviewing them often. His face was faultless: the gold hair that graced his head, in gentle waves over his forehead; the definition of his cheekbones; the perfect angle of his nose; his soft, square jaw; all could have been painstakingly carved by hand. The pine-like scent I'd been lucky enough to catch a whiff of when he'd leaned in close to me had stuck with me, even in my dreams. The intensity of his gaze, the light blue of his eyes made my heart beat a little harder in my chest. He had exquisite eyes...

Maybe if my mother had been more engaged with my life, she would've demanded to know the source of my inexplicable smiles, of my dreamy sighs. If he were a boy at school, I would have told her that he made me feel like my thoughts and ideas were important; that he made me feel like I was special.

But my mother wasn't observant. I wasn't supposed to be capable of feeling the things I was feeling, and Friedrich wasn't a boy at school; he was a German prisoner-of-war.

Someone shouted "Amen" and I snapped out of it. I was lucky no one could hear my thoughts. If anyone knew...

I shuddered. This had to be some kind of slip on my part. Perhaps my weakness was that I liked his attention; I'd constructed something that it wasn't in my head. Attachments were bound to arise, considering how familiar we had become with each other. Whatever was between us was nothing beyond a friendship, if it could even be called that.

I was grateful when Pastor Gilbert dismissed the congregation, distracting me from my inner turmoil.

My week dragged by at a snail's pace. My daily routine was even more monotonous than it had been while I was in school. Mom left the house every morning at seven. Lucy was usually up by eight o'clock. We'd play in the family room or outside, eat lunch at twelve, then I'd lay her down for a nap. I'd use the next two hours to read or tidy the house. Once Lucy awoke, we'd play for another few hours until dinner time. I'd always try to leave a little extra food for Mom, so she'd know I was thinking of her. I knew it was difficult working twelve-hour shifts every day.

I'd have Lucy in bed by seven-thirty and would then hide in my room until I heard Mom come home. Sometimes, she'd open the door to say goodnight to me. Other times, I'd listen to her peek in Lucy's room before heading back down the hall to her own.

Every night, I laid awake, staring at the stars glittering through my bay window, and I thought of Friedrich. I justified it with the knowledge that no one besides myself would ever know I was intrigued by this enemy of my country. Friedrich had dedicated his heart and soul to a man —an evil, terrible man—who was, at this moment, attempting to take over the world. He'd been bred and raised to fight and die for this man; to hate and strike down everything that stood against this man. Perhaps it was my privileged, foolish adolescence that allowed me to disregard that I was part of the latter; that my brother was part of the latter. How could I possibly feel anything other than resentment towards someone like Friedrich?

Because—and I had come to sincerely believe this—I knew there was a part of him that was good. Just because this was the person his world had created—the person he had been brought up to believe he was—I knew in my heart that he was not truly himself; not yet.

Saturday morning, I got Lucy fed and dressed, taking her into Mom's room. Though Mom was working the day shift now, she still looked forward to Saturday being her sleep-in day. I felt bad for disturbing her, but I did have a responsibility to tend to. I hoped she understood that; maybe even respected my diligence, though she hadn't voiced it. I had yet to skip a day at the camp and never complained about doing it, even though she never asked.

I couldn't wait to see Friedrich again. We peeled another layer of ourselves back every time we met. Even though he still hadn't completely opened up, I could tell he'd gotten comfortable around me.

At what had become our usual table, I waited for the prisoners to enter. Seeing Friedrich, I fought to keep my smile from completely spreading off my face.

"How are you today, Miss Wyndham?" he asked as he approached the table. It was what he called me when he was being politely playful.

"I'm well. Dreading the ride back from here, though," I said as we opened our Bibles and worksheets. "Looks like it's going to rain."

"And you still come."

I reflected his smile. "Of course."

"How many times you hear 'O mio babbino caro' since I last see you?"

"Plenty. Lucy's starting to learn the words, if that tells you anything. How's your week been?"

"Same as always," he said. "Same boring routine. I look forward to Saturdays."

I laughed under my breath, too timid to ask him to clarify if it was time with me he looked forward to or if he meant something else.

We began to read the verses out loud together. I started, reading Psalm sixty-two, while he followed with a couple verses in Isaiah. I read again in Ephesians. The last segment had two short verses from two different books that Pastor Gilbert had placed to be read together. I didn't hear what Friedrich read as Holly's laughter rang in my ears. She'd thrown her head back and I was appalled to see Egon eyeing her chest. I was still grateful I hadn't ended up with him.

"...For there is no difference between the Jew and the Greek," Friedrich read from Romans, "for the same Lord over all is rich unto all that call upon him. For whosoever shall call upon the name of the Lord shall be saved."

I tore my eyes away from Holly and Egon. "Okay, so——"

"This I am not agreeing with," Friedrich said.

I looked at him. "What don't you agree with?"

"Christ comes to wage war against the Jew. It is unbelievable that His blood is also meant for them."

I gaped at him. Never once, in all our time together had he even hinted at being anti-Semitic. I'd heard that not all Germans were; many were submissive to the idea so as not to be seen as disloyal to the Nazi Party. Up until now, that was what I thought Friedrich had been.

"I...I'm sorry?"

"It is a fact that the Jew is inferior," Friedrich continued. "They are also the ones responsible for killing Christ. Their blood is dirty, not worthy of redemption. This is why they must be destroyed."

I couldn't extricate my gaze from his, the hairs on the back of my neck standing. I wasn't prepared for this. In no way had I ever expected to confront this topic at this level of conviction with him. I was trembling, though his eyes revealed his opposing placidness.

I was breathless. "What? No. Friedrich, w-what makes you say that?"

He shrugged. "It is what I believe."

"But the Bible says that's not so."

"Cassie, I agree with what a lot of the Bible says. Just because I am not agreeing with this part means not that I am not believing the Bible in general."

"It doesn't work that way, Friedrich. You either agree with all of it or you don't believe it at all."

"It says in the Bible that it is the Jews who rally around and crucify Christ. I read it."

"Then you've also read that it's because of the world's sin—past, present and future—that Christ had to die," I said, glad to hear that he'd been reading but disappointed it had come up now, like this. "The culpability of His death falls on all of us."

"But it is the Jew who carries it out," he countered.

I tried to hide my horror, not wanting to show my frustration. His calm demeanor enlightened me to the fact that this was indeed what he believed; he was not just saying it to pick a fight.

"And this is not the only thing they are guilty of, Cassie," he asserted. "You must believe it in some ways, too."

I studied him as I scanned over my beliefs and ideas in my head; it only took a second for me to know he was wrong. But I also realized I had reserves that might make him reconsider.

"What's your definition of a Jew, Friedrich?"

He narrowed his eyes in contemplation. "The Jew is the rotting of the foundation of society. Their blood is dirty, guilty, and we must prevent their blood from contaminating the pure bloodlines."

I gazed toward the ceiling. "So...someone who's half-Jewish—they have contaminated blood?"

"Yes. The only time a person has Jewish blood and is not a threat is if it is an eighth or less."

I nodded in response. "And you believe that full Jews, half-Jews and quarter Jews should be...wiped from the earth?"

"Yes." He hadn't flinched, hadn't even hesitated.

I watched him, tapping the eraser from my pencil against the table. "Do you think I deserve to die, Friedrich?"

Smiling, he gave a slight chuckle. "No, why are you...?"

He paused, the humored expression melting from his face. I didn't look away.

He withdrew one of his hands from the table, his back stiffening. "You—you are Jewish?"

The summer blue eyes that had always looked at me with such fondness turned frigid as a winter lake. His sudden change in demeanor startled me.

I swallowed. "My mother converted to Christianity before she met my father. My grandparents disapproved of her new way of life, as well as her marriage to a Protestant. That's why we left New York. My father wanted to get my mother away from the stress and pressure. They didn't want my brother and me to grow up with the fighting."

He spoke through his teeth. "Why are you not telling me this?"

He'd never spoken to me that way before. Where I shook in alarm, he was shaking with anger. I tried not to let it daunt me; God could still redeem this.

"It doesn't change anything," I said quietly. "I'm still who I am."

He continued to glare at me, his jaw jutting forward as his breathing accelerated.

I leaned far enough on the table to where only he could hear. "So I'm asking you, Friedrich: I may not practice the faith, but Judaism is still a part of my ancestry. Do you think I deserve to die for that?"

My eyes were soft as I watched him. I didn't want to appear as if I were trying to break him; I only wanted him to think.

I could see a battle raging behind his eyes. Everything he had once known and everything he had discovered in the past few months with me was coming to a crossroads in this moment. The knuckles of his clenched fist on the table had turned white. His eyes slackened and I knew he had chosen a side.

He spoke in a gruff whisper. "Yes."

My lips parted. He knew me. He knew more of my heart than I think he even realized; more than I'd ever shown to anyone. This wasn't supposed to happen. I'd believed it would make a difference, that he would see he was wrong. I thought God was going to use it. How stupid, how injudicious could I possibly be?

Tears filled my eyes. His fist had loosened, along with his tight expression, but it wasn't in remorse. Instead, he almost looked confused.

I bowed my head over my Bible, tears splashing on the black letters. I cut them off; I could not, would not let him see me cry.

His face hardened, eyes blazing, as my hand shot into the air. I didn't break my gaze from his until a guard was standing next to me.

"Everything okay here, Miss?"

"Uh..." I glanced at Friedrich, his frosty eyes unblinking. I didn't want him to hear my voice crack, but it splintered anyway as I stood. "I'm not...I'm not feeling very well. I don't think I can stay any longer."

The guard turned a suspicious gaze toward Friedrich.

I was backing away. "Can you, um—can you make sure he gets his full lesson today?"

I fought to hold in my tears. I looked at no one as I walked up the aisle, headed for the door.

The concern on Pastor Gilbert's face caused me to spill over with a couple drops anyway. "Cassie, is everything okay?"

I held at my stomach to make it believable. "Yeah, I'm just—I'm not feeling very well. I shouldn't have come today." I motioned behind me though I didn't turn to look. "I asked the guard to make sure he still gets his full lesson today."

"Certainly, certainly, don't you worry about that; you're doing a great job. Go on home and get some rest. Make sure your mother lets me know how you're doing. Fred here will walk you out."

Fred—a guard I hadn't talked to before—walked me to the front of the camp. The instant the gates closed behind me, I burst into tears, speeding away on my bike. Sprinkles dampened my hair and shoulders. Thunder and lightning beleaguered the sky by the time I was out of the woods, rain pummeling at my back, and I pedaled faster.

Main Street was deserted. I rode to the last corner, stopping in the doorway to the dance studio. With the rain coming down at such force, coupled with the lightning and the fact that all resolve had been drained from my body, I sat under the awning over the doorstep. Wringing out the skirt of my lightweight cotton dress, I didn't even care that my underclothes were visible through the wet fabric.

Drops of water fell from my hair, streaming down my face. I gripped at my saturated hair, leaning onto my knees as I sobbed. Despite how desperately I tried to block it out, I kept seeing his utter revulsion as he gave the answer that changed everything between us. I heard him say it, over and over, slicing at my heart like a surgeon's scalpel each time.

The thunder roared as the rain battered the pavement all around me. I was glad; it kept my cries from being heard.

As much as I hurt from my mother, as much as I agonized over my father's near nonexistence in my life, Friedrich's betrayal hurt worst of all. At least when it came to my feeling of lesser value with my parents, I could retreat to an inner oasis of solace knowing they didn't know the real me; that one day, when I was strong enough, I would be enough for them.

But I had exposed the wounds of my heart to Friedrich because I trusted him—because I thought he was safe. My worst fear had life breathed into it today; he had been the one to show me that the real me wasn't enough, either.

I screamed, punching the door with my fist. "Why? *Why?*" Knuckles throbbing, I clutched at my hair. "I'm not enough. I'm not enough."

My mind overflowed with voices from my past; barbs of poison that had never been expelled, lingering in my system to accomplish the only thing toxins were good for:

"Daddy!" I said in the black receiver of the telephone, twisting at the waist to see how pretty my feet looked in my ballerina slippers. "Will you come see me in my recital? It's three weeks away!"

"No," he said. "Daddy has more important things he has to do, Cassandra."

My mother and Amos after dinner one night:

"Can I have a cookie?" Amos asked. I lifted my head from the couch to listen.

"Shh," Mom whispered. "Don't tell Cassandra I let you have one. She's gotten so pudgy."

While meeting one of my mother's friends when I was fourteen:

"Hmm," Mrs. Kelley said. "You'd be prettier if you looked more like your mother."

I stared at her as my mother chuckled. "She's still in that awkward stage."

And finally, the arrow shot by the one person I'd foolishly chosen to open my heart to:

"I may not practice the faith, but Judaism is still a part of my ancestry. Do you think I deserve to die for that?"

"Yes."

He said yes.

I might as well have asked him if I was worthless. I could have asked him if my creation had been a waste of time, if my life was without purpose, and he would've had the same answer:

Yes.

It couldn't be a coincidence that so many people— people I was close to—saw me in near the same exact way as the next. They had full view of an endless truth I couldn't outrun. It was I who turned out to be wrong.

My entire life, I'd fought to be someone who deserved being loved, to be someone whose company could be enjoyed, to be someone who was valuable.

Why? It had never changed anything. It didn't make my father come home, it didn't make my mother like me, it didn't inspire Amos to defend me, and it didn't make a Nazi give his heart to God.

I closed my eyes, breathing in the scent of sodden pavement as I hugged myself. Facing another onslaught of tears, thunder continued to roll in the distance.

"Hold me," I whispered. "Please just hold me."

Six

The storm didn't let up. I no longer worried about any punishment. My mother's fury wouldn't worsen by the minute; it was already as bad as it was going to get now. I sat there, leaning against the damp doorframe for hours. The burden of my thoughts had drained any willpower I might have had before, but I rifled about my being to find an ounce of it somewhere; I would be biking in not only rain, but total darkness within the hour.

I tried to cover my Bible with my purse and sweater the best I could before stepping back out into the rain. It pounded my back as I climbed onto my bike, my teeth chattering. I pedaled fast at first, but I knew it wouldn't change the fact that I was already drenched and riding into the eye of my hurricane mother. I slowed with reluctance to a steady pace as night began to fall.

The sky was black by the time I reached my driveway. Bringing my bike onto the porch, I wasn't sure my already wounded heart could withstand another beating.

And yet, nothing she could say or do could be worse than the blow I'd already sustained today. As morbid as it was, this soothed me.

Squeezing out what I could from my dress to keep her from yelling at me for soaking the floor, I opened the screen door and stepped inside. I let it slam shut, just so she would know I was home; I wanted to get it over with.

She came stomping out of the kitchen into the living room. Her entire body was tense as she zeroed in on me. "Where the *hell* have you been? I have been waiting for you for *hours*! I called Holly's house, I called Pastor Gilbert and both of them told me you had left the camp early because you weren't feeling well. Where did you go?"

"I'm sorry." It was all I could say.

She scoffed, her hands on her hips. "You're sorry? You're *sorry*? That's all you have to say for yourself?"

I shut the front door behind me, quavering from the cold of my dress clinging to my skin.

"Answer me!" she shouted.

I couldn't lift my gaze from the floor. "I got sick. On the way home it began to rain. I tried to wait for it to stop but it never did."

"Don't lie to me, Cassandra. You were with a boy, weren't you?"

I stared at her. "What?"

"I'm not stupid!" she yelled. "I *told* you that you weren't ready and I meant it. How dare you——?"

"I wasn't with a boy."

"Well, it's awful funny to me that just last week, you asked if you could go to the movies and now you think since Mom told you 'no,' you'd do it anyway."

I gave an unintentional chuckle at this. Her eyes widened in a frightening way. "You think this is funny, young lady? I'll show you funny. You're grounded. For two weeks."

This didn't scare me. What could she possibly ground me from? I didn't see Donald or Holly outside of school. I spent my days with Lucy while my mom worked, so she wouldn't keep me from doing that. The only thing she could ground me from was going to the camp. Little did she know, I wouldn't be going back there anyway.

She crossed her arms, shaking her head. "I cannot believe you. Your brother *never* would have done something like this."

Every jab on my heart pulsated as one more puncture wound was added to my soul.

Her barrage continued. "I don't even know what to do with you. You are so irresponsible. You act like you're the only one in this family that matters. Is it not enough that I have to worry about Amos every minute of the day? Why do you *do* this to me, Cassandra?"

My lower lip began to tremble and I closed my eyes as tears rolled down my cheeks. I told myself that if she knew what had happened to me, she wouldn't have acted that way; if she could see how badly I was hurting, she would have held me instead.

As much as I wanted to believe that, if it were true, she would have consoled me a long time ago.

I opened my eyes at the creak of a door, hoping her bombardment was over. Instead, my father stepped out of his study and into the living room, coffee mug in hand.

"Dad," I said in astonishment.

I hadn't realized how much I missed him until I saw his face. He had become far too serious the last few years, but tonight he looked relaxed. I loved that face when I was little; it was the one most likely to distort into a funny expression just to get a laugh out of Amos and me. It was when he looked like that that he was most likely to play a game or spare a few minutes to sit and talk with us.

His mustache and goatee a new addition, he took a couple steps closer, his free hand in his pocket. "Cassandra, Sweetheart."

"I didn't see your car," I said.

His bronze eyes rumpled in concern. "I parked around back to surprise your mother. Why are you all wet?"

My shrew of a mother was still vicious. "Tell your father why you're just now getting home."

Dad didn't look that concerned. He was softer than she was, usually because reacting to us meant taking time away from his work to discipline us. "I've been volunteering at the POW camp to talk to the prisoners about God. I was feeling sick so I left early and got caught in the rain downtown. I would hug you, but—"

"That's okay, Sweetheart."

I knew he wouldn't want to get wet, but I had mentioned it in the hopes he would disregard his comfort and insist on a hug. I couldn't express how desperately I needed someone's arms around me right now.

My eyes were burning again and I inched toward the stairs. "I'm really sorry, Mom. I know what I've done, and...and I know why you're angry, but...if it's okay with you, I really want to get out of these clothes and just go to bed. I promise I'll talk with you about this tomorrow."

"You don't tell me when you'll talk to me and when you won't, young lady. You don't get to—"

"Miriam." My father was using his authoritative work voice. "Look at her. Let her go. You can talk to her tomorrow."

She glowered at me and I almost ran to my dad and hugged him anyway.

"Fine," she growled. "But after church tomorrow, you and I are going to have a little talk. And you are still grounded."

I didn't dispute this. Neither of them spoke, but I could feel their eyes on me as I plodded up the stairs. Changing out of my clothes and into my pajamas, I hurried to the bathroom to brush my teeth.

When Amos and I were younger, whenever we misbehaved, my mother would scold us before directing us toward my father's dreaded study. Sometimes we'd be sent together, sometimes alone, but it never made the experience less intimidating. We'd watch my father smoke a pipe or cigar, continuing paperwork in his big red chair behind his desk as we sat in the cold, wooden ones across from him. We'd sit in silence until he spoke, discussing what we did, why we shouldn't have done it and what our punishment would be. I hoped Dad had prevented her from reprimanding me tonight because he felt sorry for me, not because he knew it would become his problem.

I turned off the water, pressing a hand towel to my wet, puffy face. All I wanted was to feel the warmth of someone's love, to have someone's arms around me; to be in the company of someone I didn't have to be afraid of.

Hanging up the towel, I froze, a remedy popping into my head.

Lucy couldn't have been in bed but maybe half an hour, if that. Tossing the towel on the counter, I tiptoed down the hall, grateful that both my parents were still downstairs.

Pushing my baby sister's door open, I could see her pixie-like silhouette in the moonlight.

"Lucy?" I whispered.

A small ointment of joy touched my heart as she turned her head, pushing herself up. "See."

I chuckled through my tears. Sitting on the edge of her tiny bed, she reciprocated as I cuddled her. I held her for a moment, drawing as much love from her as I could.

"You're such a special little girl, did you know that? Sissy loves you so much."

"Wuv you."

It made me feel even better to know she wouldn't let go until I did. Kissing her temple, I leaned her back onto her pillow.

Out in the hall, I could hear the low murmur of my parents' voices downstairs. I was certain they were talking about me, but I was too cold, too tired and too distressed to eavesdrop.

I huddled beneath my sheet, bringing the quilt up to my chin as I quivered. Catching sight of the stars from my bay window, I began to tear up, crying into my pillow.

Is there any way at all—with the vastness of the universe, with the number of people who are suffering at the hands of war right now—that You are still aware of the pain that has been dealt on my heart today? Is there any chance that You're crying with me? That You're already trying to whisper that this is only for now; that it isn't going to be like this forever?

Once more, I wished that He would give me some kind of sign, something obvious to tell me that He saw me, that He heard me——but there was nothing but silence. The crickets sang their chorus out in the fields as the night breeze tickled the oaks and firs just outside our house. The stars glimmered in the night sky and Lucy was nearing sleep in her bed across the hall.

I was all alone.

Whether by good fortune or by curse, my mother never sat me down to discuss my punishment the next day.

I woke up that morning with a fever, the chills keeping me from leaving the womb of sheets and quilts I was in. The congestion made me feel like my head was going to bust open.

I could tell by the severity of my mother's heels in the hallway that she was coming with the intent to berate me for not getting up for church. My door swung open and I used what energy I had to turn my head to look at her.

Her eyes softened, though her expression remained stern. "Are you sick?"

"Yes," I answered, the blockage in my sinuses audibly apparent.

She watched me before tightening her jaw and stepping back out into the hallway, but not before I heard her grumble, "This is *just* what I need."

I didn't have the strength to call after her; I didn't have the strength to cry.

In the short time it took her to return, I'd already dozed off. Seeing the thermometer and glass of water in her hand, I struggled to sit up, shivering without the coverage of my blankets.

"Here." She lowered the thermometer to my mouth, poking it underneath my tongue. She sighed when she saw how high the mercury was rising.

I got back under the covers. "What is it?"

"One hundred and two. Here, take some aspirin." She dropped the oblong white pills into my hand, raising an eyebrow at me. "You must have caught a cold. That's what you get for being out in the rain all day yesterday. You'll be lucky if you don't catch pneumonia."

I ignored her, swallowing the medicine. Setting the glass of water on my nightstand, I retreated back into my blanket-cave.

"Your sister and I are going to church, but your father will be here; I'll have him check on you and bring up breakfast, if you're up to it."

My eyes were burning with heat and I curled into a ball. "Thanks, Mom."

I tried to sleep after she left, but I was too congested and too achy to get comfortable. My limbs felt slow and clumsy as I placed wadded tissues among the growing heap on my nightstand. Gripping my blanket and pulling it up to my nose, Mr. Stewart's big red barn looked like a picturesque painting on the other side of my window.

I had no defense as my mind dredged up memories of the camp yesterday. Either out of sickness or repression, it almost felt as if it hadn't happened; like it had been a bad dream. The good-natured, smiling, bantering Friedrich I knew wouldn't have been so cruel; it was as if he had become another person.

I cowered, recalling my stupidity. Not many knew the truth about my family. It had been a well-kept secret; my mother hadn't even mentioned it to some of her closest friends.

I wasn't uneducated on the consequences of her decision to become a Christian. She had been born into a Jewish family, without any inquisitiveness of other religions. A couple of girl friends she made in secondary school who were Christians had begun to talk to her about their beliefs, even inviting her to church with them. She was reluctant at first, certain her parents wouldn't approve.

So she didn't tell them. Church each Sunday with her friends became a ritual, until one day, my mother decided to make a permanent change. After giving her life to Jesus, she knew she had to tell her parents.

They were outraged; in disbelief, mostly because they hadn't even realized she was going to a church of a different religion. They told her that her actions were disgraceful, sinful; they threatened to disown her if she did not come back to her former faith.

And, if there was anything I admired my mother for, it was this:

She didn't back down.

The last straw was when she decided to marry my father, yet another revelation that my grandparents claimed came out of nowhere. She hadn't even told them she was seeing anyone, especially not a Protestant.

The day of their wedding, the only people to show up were my father's family and friends and what few friends my mom still had left after secondary school. It was a foreshadowing of how my grandparents would come to treat every milestone in her life from that point on. They visited her for only a day after Amos was born, waited a month before coming to see me for the first time, and for Lucy—for my precious baby sister, they sent my mother a card.

Somewhere—between her marriage to my father and my birth—was when her new foundation began to crack. I've tried many times to convince myself that it wasn't my arrival into this world that was her breaking point, but I'm more than certain it was. It was in that stage of her deterioration that she began to believe she was being punished, not rewarded for the choice she made.

I assumed that was why she was always so adamant about attending church and reading her Bible, as well as making sure her children did the same. That was why she still went today, even though I was sick and my father was too busy. She was still clinging to the hope that she hadn't made a mistake; that one day, she might be vindicated...

That one day, she could forgive herself.

A couple of birds were dots in the distance, swooping toward Mr. Stewart's barn and perching with grace on top. My eyes began to droop, coaxing me to lie back down beneath the covers.

I was close to sleep when I heard my father ascending the staircase, becoming alert as his footsteps passed my parents' bedroom. With a couple light knocks, he slowly opened my door. I sat up in bed, leaning against the metal headboard as he entered.

His dark hair was disheveled and I noted the new wrinkles around his eyes. He wore a vest and tie, the sleeves to his white collared shirt rolled up to his elbows. "Hey Sweetheart. How are you feeling? Your mother said you're running a pretty high fever."

"Better," I said, though I fended off shivers. "I can't breathe, but..."

He reached forward, his rough hand scraping across my forehead. "You're still pretty warm. Are you hungry?"

"A little."

He nodded, picking up my empty glass. "I'll get you some more water, too. You should probably drink more. I'll be back."

I rested my eyes until he returned. He set a full glass of water on my nightstand, handing me a saucer with a biscuit.

"Your mother said you shouldn't eat much...but you tell me if you want more."

I smiled, noticing he'd already spread the jam on for me. "Thanks, Daddy."

It surprised me when he pulled my desk chair over to my bedside. "How'd you like your birthday present?"

My portable gramophone was on my desk, "O mio babbino caro" never having left the turntable since I'd received it. He must have seen it.

"I love it. I haven't stopped listening to it."

"I assumed that would be the case." He leaned back in the chair, studying me. "Your mother's concerned you're sneaking around with some boy. Is that true?"

It sounded as ridiculous now as it had yesterday. "No."

He nodded. "What's this about someone asking you to the movies?"

"It was just Donald."

"Oh." He seemed to think about it. "Hmm. I didn't know you liked Donald."

"I don't. Not like that. I was just...curious to see if she'd let me. I *am* seventeen now."

The wrinkles around his eyes became more pronounced, and he watched as I ate. "What's it been like without having your brother here?"

I took a sip of water, holding the glass in my lap. "It was different at first. I guess we've all adjusted now."

We sat there in mutual silence. I liked that he was there, talking to me, but I didn't feel as connected to him as I wished we were. Every time he came home, we might spend a few minutes catching up before he would lose interest, returning to the lair of his study. I knew this time wouldn't be any different.

And yet, despite the lack of depth in most of our conversations, I still loved my father's presence.

I closed my eyes just to feel the coolness of my eyelids. "Isn't Lucy bigger since the last time you saw her?"

I heard my father laugh under his breath, taking the glass out of my hand. "Yes, she is. My little girl's growing up so fast."

I felt the cool of his lips on my forehead, and I was asleep before he even shut my bedroom door.

My father left to go back to Baltimore sometime that afternoon. He came up to say goodbye and hugged me before leaving. My mother brought up soup for me for dinner later and I could see the frustration on her face and hear it in her voice. She didn't have to say what was vexing her. My father hadn't stayed but for a day after having been away for four months. I was sick, and she was probably fretting over what to do with Lucy until I got better. In the past, my father had suggested the obvious: *"Just take off work. It's not like it's a paid position."* This always riled her and they could usually be overheard arguing later in their room. She hadn't taken off then, and I knew she wouldn't now—not with Amos in the Army. She wasn't just doing her part for the war anymore; she felt she was doing her part as the mother of a soldier.

Monday morning—though I felt the same, if not worse than the day before—my mother did what she could to make things a little easier on me. She'd already given Lucy breakfast and left a little for me on the stove when I came down. An old wool blanket and a pillow were on the living room sofa when I took Lucy in there to play, along with a box of tissues on the coffee table. Her thoughtfulness was appreciated and not at all expected. At least she was trying to make sure I was comfortable. Just as my mother trudged on through less than ideal circumstances, I did, too.

As horrible as I felt, I was somewhat grateful. My mother had told Pastor Gilbert Sunday morning about how sick I was, which made my urgent departure from the camp seem legitimate. Holly had even called once to ask how I was doing.

Her voice crackled through the receiver. "You sound terrible. Are you going to the camp this weekend?"

I twirled the black cord around my finger. "Probably not. Listen, I'm not feeling well. I think I'm going to go lay down."

"All right. I'll call you again next week sometime."

I hung up, not feeling guilty over the fact that my symptoms were instead diminishing. I preferred everyone to assume later that I just fell out of the habit of going rather than catching on to what had happened between Friedrich and me.

As the week neared its end and I started regaining my strength, I became aware of how the thought of Friedrich didn't make me sad anymore. Instead, I began to wrestle with a new emotion:

Anger.

I couldn't pretend I wasn't hurt, but at the same time, it was infuriating that someone could be so ignorant, so deceptive, so...*stubborn*. He didn't care about me. General Turner had been right. Friedrich had done everything he had warned us that the Germans did. He was polite, he was handsome (or at least, I used to think he was), he was suave, and he had yanked the rug out from under my feet with his stupid charm. Perhaps I shouldn't have been angry that it worked out this way. At least I knew now how fickle he was.

On my weaker days, I thought maybe he hadn't really meant what he said. There'd been moments where I thought I could see him reflecting on what we were discussing; moments where he had been engrossed in my explanations of meanings behind verses, or the things I believed in. His intrigue seemed authentic; I never got the impression he was putting on an act. After all, if he had only been feigning interest for sinister purposes, would he have revealed his anti-Semitism to me? He would have known better.

I'd been so certain of his potential goodness before, but now I wasn't certain of anything. I sighed. It no longer mattered what I thought; I was never going back. Whatever role God had wanted me to play in Friedrich's life had been written out.

Saturday morning, I sat in my bay window to read, checking my watch:

Eleven-thirty, the time I would start gathering my Bible and the worksheets, fixing my hair and make-up.

Twelve-fifty, the time I would come downstairs to say goodbye to Mom and Lucy.

One o'clock, the time I would get on my bike.

One-thirty, the time I would meet Holly at the school. (I wondered if it felt strange to her, riding without me for the first time.)

Two o'clock, the time I'd sit at the table I had come to view as Friedrich's and mine. (I wondered if he was looking for me; if he was happy to see I hadn't shown up, or if he felt even a twinge of disappointment.)

And finally, three o'clock, the time I would look over my shoulder to see him walking out with the other prisoners.

I wondered afterwards if anyone else even noticed I wasn't there. Holly would notice, but it wouldn't matter to her; I was just the person she happened to choose as a friend for...well, even I didn't know the answer to that. Pastor Gilbert was probably too distracted with the other volunteers and their prisoners to remember I was absent. The guards certainly wouldn't notice which girl hadn't shown up today.

The only person who would notice I was missing was the only person who knew why.

I felt much better the next day, but I lied to Mom, telling her I was still too weak to get up for church. Pastor Gilbert would expect to see me at the camp the following Saturday; I'd rather lie to my mother than lie to a pastor. I was going to have to go back to church someday, though. I hated that it would appear as if my heart had never been in the program, but I—and *he*—would know that the reason I wouldn't return was because it had been.

On Tuesday, my nose was raw and I had a slight cough, but that was the worst of my symptoms. Holly called again that afternoon to check on me.

"Have you talked to Donald at all?" she asked.

"No. Not since we got out of school. Have you?"

There was silence on the other end. "Yes. He was at the soda shop last week. I went shopping with my mom and ran into him. We sat and talked for a little bit."

"Oh."

"Yeah. He said he hopes you feel better soon. Are you going to the camp this weekend?"

Running my fingers in thought over the dial, I tried to come up with an excuse in my mind. "Uh—I don't know. It's been really hard on my mom. She doesn't get to sleep in when I go. She works all week, you know?"

"Yeah. Well, I've got to go. If I don't see you Saturday, I'll see you at church."

I didn't feel guilty for lying to her. I kept telling myself that if anyone knew the truth, they wouldn't blame me. Whether that was true or not, I supposed I'd never know.

I waited that night in my room like I always did before Mom came home. I pulled out my journal from my desk drawer, sitting cross-legged on the bed. It was the first time I'd felt like writing since getting sick. I skimmed through some of the poems and entries I'd written in the past. It was strange that most of what I'd written had been composed because of my mom; this would be one of the only entries that was about someone else.

I heard the front door, signaling that my mother was home, but I stayed at my desk writing. It wasn't until she was standing in my doorway in her nurse's aide uniform that I looked up.

Her hand gripped the door knob. "You look like you're feeling better."

"I am, I think."

"Did you have any trouble with Lucy tonight?"

I grinned, remembering the way she'd splashed me with water from the tub earlier. "No. She was perfect, like always."

"Good. I think it's time we talked about your punishment."

I was stupefied. "You...my punishment?"

"Uh, yes," she said, as if I were a halfwit. "I've made a list of chores that need to be done around the house. I don't have time to do them myself; not that I should have to. If you had any kind of initiative, they'd have been done already. You'll do them for two weeks unless you finish before that. But you'd better keep in mind that whatever isn't done right you're going to have to do all over again."

I peered down at my journal.

"Understood?" she asked when I didn't respond.

"Yes," I muttered.

"Good. Start on them tomorrow. Good night."

I found the list on the kitchen table the next morning. My mouth dropped upon seeing the complexity of some of the work she expected me to do:

— Scrub kitchen, living room, bathroom floors

— Shake out rugs

- Dust

- Dust doors and molding

- Clean stove and refrigerator

- Clean Dad's study

- Clean Lucy's room

- Sweep porch

- Trim shrubbery and bushes in front of house

- Mow yard

- Repaint front porch, railings on steps at backdoor
  (I will get you paint. Do this last.)

With a heavy sigh, I set the list aside to get breakfast started for Lucy and me. I hated the fact that I had to do it, but at least once it was over, I wouldn't hear about it anymore from my mother.

I started on scrubbing the floors that day. It wasn't as bad as I thought it would be. Lucy—being the curious two-year-old she was—kept putting her hands in the suds and carrying off the funny sponges and scrub brushes. I changed her into an old pair of pajamas when she insisted on helping me. We moved to the kitchen, where she went behind me, using the brush on the spots I'd already scrubbed. Once, she even ran it through my hair before I could stop her. We worked hard, occasionally wiping the suds from our hands on each other's faces.

After buffing the kitchen floor, Amos' bathroom and part of the living room, Lucy started to whine, rubbing at her eyes. I put her down for a nap while I finished cleaning the floors. Once I was done with that, I shook out all the rugs, stopping for the day.

I was pleased when, after dusting over the entire house Friday, my mother actually complimented my work. Scouring the thin layer of grime off the trim in the kitchen, neither of us spoke as she ate dinner behind me.

"I suppose you're going back to that camp tomorrow," she said.

There was a hitch in my movements, though I continued scrubbing. It had sounded more like a curious statement than a question. "No. I've not quite regained my energy from when I was sick. All the cleaning has drained me. I think I'm just going to take the day to relax."

My chest felt tight. Why did I feel conscience-stricken now when I'd been stretching the truth the whole time? I had a valid reason for not wanting to go back; my prisoner told me I should die. Why should I feel guilty?

I watched the morning light brighten through my windows the next day, considering what the right thing to do was. If I didn't go back, there was no chance at all that I could help him change. Everyone else who had joined from our church was still going to the camp...

But no one else in that building was half-Jewish, much less had admitted it to their Jew-hating POW.

Still, I prayed for wisdom. Was it truly justifiable for me not to go now that I was scared he might try to hurt me? Or was I being a coward? My faith told me I was supposed to reach out to the lost even if it came at a cost to myself, but I had little confidence that me being a willing victim would be enough to change his mind.

There was no way I could get out of going to church that week. Pastor Gilbert beamed as he shook my hand at the door, the rest of the congregation heading out to their cars. "Cassie, it's good to see you. How are you feeling?"

I mustered my best smile. "I'm better now, thank you."

"We've missed you at the camp. Do you think you'll be able to make it Saturday?"

I stared at him, bracing myself for the answer I'd prepared the night before.

"Uh—no, not this weekend. My mom works a lot, you know, so—well, she's needing...she needs a lot of help around the house and I...she doesn't have time to do it all. So I'll probably have to stay home. I need to help...clean."

He nodded in response, though I could see the disappointment in his eyes. I could almost hear him thinking, *There goes the first one.*

"Well," he said, with a pat on my back, "give me a call if you change your mind."

I continued crossing things off my mother's list throughout the rest of the week. One day, while in the midst of scouring the stove, the phone rang. Lucy was coloring at the table and I took off my gloves, picking up the handset. "Hello?"

The phone crackled. "Cassie."

My heart jumped at the hushed male voice. I had a vision of him in someone's office at the camp. His palm cupped around the receiver, he cast a surreptitious look around to make sure no one was about to walk in and catch him.

I spoke in a breath. "Yes?"

"It's me. What are you doing?"

I lowered onto the couch, my chest heaving. "Donald?"

"Don't tell me you've forgotten me already."

I closed my eyes, sighing. Donald made much more sense. "No. Of course not. I'm just surprised you called me."

He chuckled. "Why are you surprised?"

"No reason."

He said something, but I was still recovering. "What was that?"

"I asked what you've been doing the past few weeks. Holly said you were sick."

"Yeah, I was. I had a bad cold for almost two weeks."

"That's no good. How's Lucy?"

I leaned back to see Lucy through the entryway, still scribbling at the table. "She's great. I don't know what I would do without her."

"I wish I felt that way about my little brother."

"You don't?"

"No. Most of the time I wish he would leave me alone. I used to tell him he was adopted." He laughed to himself. "He used to cry and get me in trouble."

"Oh."

The sound of his amusement faded as we both went quiet. He cleared his throat. "So, I was calling because I wanted to tell you something. I...I'm joining up in November, when I turn eighteen. I'm going into the Army."

I tried to think of something to say. For some reason, I was struck dumb.

"You're the first person I've told," he said. "Besides my parents."

I thought about Amos, remembering how his training seemed to have changed him. "That's...that's really great, Donald. Very brave and...honorable of you."

"Well..." His voice was soft. "I just wanted you to know."

I draped my gloves over the sofa arm. I wasn't sure what to say, but his silence told me he wanted something from me. He must have realized I wasn't going to speak.

"I...I was thinking maybe we could meet downtown at the soda shop on your way back from the camp Saturday. I have to be there, anyway."

I breathed out, wincing. "I'm actually not going to the camp this weekend. I got in trouble a few weeks ago and got grounded. I have to stay home to help around the house."

I braced myself, waiting for him to get angry; I waited to hear him sigh before asking me why I was lying; to ask me why I never wanted to meet him, why I didn't like him that way. I waited for him to get it so I didn't have to say it.

"Oh. Okay, I understand," he said instead.

A chair scraped in the kitchen, followed by a loud thump and Lucy's high-piercing cry. I gasped, seeing her on the floor. "Donald, I have to go. Lucy just fell out of her chair."

"Oh. Right. Okay. Talk to you some other time then?"

"Sure."

I hung up, running into the kitchen. Lucy cried as I looked her over, but it seemed it had hurt her pride more than anything else. I held her anyway, rocking her on the couch until she fell asleep in my arms.

My eyes fell on the phone. Why hadn't my first thought been Donald when I heard the male voice on the other end? Why had my thoughts automatically thought it was...him? He didn't know my number; why would he call even if he did? He'd forgotten me by now, pleased that the little half-Jewish girl hadn't had the audacity to return.

I rolled my eyes at myself. Why was I still thinking about him? He and I were from different worlds, and where he was from, I was detestable. He had made that clear. How could I associate with someone who was determined to hate me?

On Tuesday, after cleaning Lucy's room and putting her down for a nap, I headed down to my father's study. Feather duster, a rag and some wood polish in hand, I turned the doorknob to his office.

I half-expected to see him sitting behind the desk. The only time I ever went in there was when he was home, and that was usually only to be disciplined. I eyed the bookcases with dread, seeing the coat of dust from the door.

I dusted everything first. I was surprised at how filthy this room had become. None of us ever came in here except my father, and when he did, it would only be for a day or two. I could only imagine that my mother hadn't noticed how bad it had gotten since she didn't have much time to do a thorough cleaning of the house anymore. I cleared off his desk before applying the furniture polish and wiping away the clustered hand prints and condensation rings. Getting on my knees, I tried to clean the nooks and crannies along the drawers.

Reaching up to hoist myself, I paused as I noticed something dark, like a smudge on the underside of the center desk drawer. Pushing my father's desk chair out of the way, I sat on the floor, scooting under his desk for a better look.

I lifted the rag, preparing to polish it off before noticing it wasn't a smudge at all. Someone had penciled in numbers.

Something about them looked familiar. I studied them a minute before recognizing why; eighteen was for the day of my parents' anniversary. The number two was for the day of Amos' birthday and twelve was the day of mine.

Why would my father have written them in such a discreet place? Had it really gotten so bad that he had trouble remembering such important dates?

Bewildered, I pushed myself out from beneath the desk, my eyes falling on the safe.

The safe! *That* would be a good reason to hide numbers. Amos and I had never been allowed in the safe. The black and silver dial on the front beckoned me to try. I didn't expect to find anything that would interest me—maybe some of my mother's jewelry or important documents from my father's work. My curiosity was merely for the sake of being nosy.

Tossing the dirty dust rag aside, I crawled over to the corner. Dusting off my hands, I stared at the dial. It would be no different than opening my locker at school.

I turned the knob clockwise a couple spins before starting on the number eighteen. Turning it left until it stopped on the number two, I then spun it clockwise again, landing on the number twelve.

The door became ajar. Pulling it open, I peeked around inside. There were papers stacked throughout, just as I knew there would be. A small ledge on the upper half held a thin wooden box, containing my father's favorite, expensive

Cuban cigars. I didn't touch anything at the risk of him noticing someone had rummaged through it. Disenchanted with its contents, I started to lock it back when I spotted what looked like a brick in the darkened corner behind the papers.

My face fell with realization and I reached inside, pulling out a wad of hundred dollar bills.

Flipping through the leafy rectangles, I saw that they were all hundreds. I counted them, chortling as I did the math in my head. Two thousand dollars; I was holding *two thousand dollars* in my hands. That was two years' salary for some people. I'd never held that much money in my life.

Why had my father felt it necessary to hide such a large sum of money here? Surely it would have been more sensible to keep it in the bank instead of in a moveable safe in his house. He wasn't even here that often. Why would he stash two thousand dollars at home?

Pieces started to connect in my brain. The money—the numbers beneath the desk—weren't for him; they must have been for my mother. He could access the money in the bank quicker and easier than she could. This money must have been for emergencies. I leafed through the bills one last time before putting them back. I wished Amos were there for me to tell him I had discovered what was in the safe.

Thursday, I spent most of the day trimming the shrubs and bushes around the house. After putting Lucy to bed, I lay across my own, tired and achy. My arms, legs and face still felt hot from being out in the sun all day, my nose and cheeks feverish with summer heat. My shoulders and forearms were tender as I undressed, getting into the shower. The water was cool against my skin, once the burning on the sun-kissed parts had subsided to a tolerable level. I was careful not to let the fabric of my pajamas scrape against me too much as I pulled them on. As sensitive as my skin was, it wasn't severe and I hoped I'd begin to tan by tomorrow.

I sat in my window after rolling my hair. Moonlight glinted off the satin blades of grass in the fields below. Mr. Stewart's porch light was still on, visible in the distance.

Wanting my journal, I walked over to my desk. The record to "O mio babbino caro" was still on my desktop and I picked up the sleeve. I hadn't listened to it since before Friedrich had asked me about it. Remembering the way I'd bled out my sentimentalities to someone who was disgusted by me, I felt like a silly little child, closing the top to my record player.

I decided I didn't feel like writing tonight. Turning off my bedside lamp, I got into bed.

This coming Saturday would be the third week I'd skipped the camp. It made me nauseous thinking about it. As wounded as I had been, it didn't change how certain I'd been that this was something God had wanted me to do. I felt like I had not only let God down, but I'd failed Friedrich. My admission to him was reckless; it had been foolish of me to think he would've reacted any other way.

My routine was interrupted Saturday, preventing me from watching the clock as I had taken to doing. Mom got up early, saying she wanted to go into town for paint and some other things. Lucy and I went with her.

We left the car in the public parking lot, starting down Main Street near the bank. I played with Lucy in the lobby while my mother made a transaction. Afterwards, we headed to Crewe's Department Store to find some summer dresses for Lucy; the ones from last year were too short on her now.

While my mom walked around the toddler section with my baby sister, I was allowed to go to the junior section. I stopped to admire one of the styles on display on a mannequin. She was wearing a red plaid shirt, untucked, coupled with a pair of dark blue jean capris that had been rolled up. It looked very casual and comfortable, though I knew my mother would never allow me to wear it. She wouldn't be caught dead wearing that in public, and wouldn't let me either, if she could help it. My mother had come from a wealthy family, and my father's family had worked hard to rise above their impoverished means. My mother had had a conniption once, when I came home wearing one of Holly's socks and shoes. I told her it was a new trend and that everyone was doing it, but she fussed at me, telling me to have some pride for the Wyndham name.

I wondered what it was like to have some say over what I wore—over what I wanted out of my life. I'd find out when I got to California, after I turned eighteen and had access to my trust fund.

I smiled to myself at the thought.

My mother called for me down the aisle, motioning with her head for me to follow her rather than speaking to me. Taking one last longing look at the mannequin, I jogged to catch up with her as she started down the stairs with Lucy.

The hardware store was just around the corner from Crewe's. I held Lucy's hand as my mother stood at the front counter, when Lucy started jumping, pulling on my hand. "Look! See, Look!"

A shiny red tricycle with a chrome bell sat in the window. I picked Lucy up, carrying her over for a closer look. "You like that?"

"Yeah! See, I like!"

Her eyes were bright with wonder, causing me to chuckle. I kissed her forehead. "Maybe Santa will bring you one for Christmas—as long as you're a good girl."

She nodded her head. "Uh huh. I dood dirl."

I laughed as she kept an ambitious gaze glued to the tricycle.

"Cassie?"

I turned at the voice. Donald was standing at the end of one of the aisles. My cheeks grew hot, realizing I was in town after telling him I wouldn't be. I thought he'd be mad, calling me out in the middle of the hardware store.

Instead, he smiled, walking toward us. "I thought that was you."

"Yeah." I set Lucy down next to me. "My mother needed some things so we came with her into town. Right, Lucy-Goosey?"

Her jade eyes never left Donald as she hid behind my leg. Donald chuckled.

My mother was suddenly at my side. "They don't have the same color gray we used when we first painted it, so I had to get a pale blue." She looked at Donald. "Hello."

Lucy was yanking on my hands and I picked her up again, trying to appease her. "Uh...Mom, you...you remember Donald, right?"

"Of course," she said. "How's your mother? I saw her a few months ago at the hospital."

"Better," he answered. His eyes were sickle-shaped; they always were when he smiled. "She was standing on a chair to dust the bookshelf and fell. She broke her arm in two places," he explained to me.

My mother's expression was sympathetic. "I remember. I hope she's been taking it easy."

"If you know my mom, you'd know it would take more than that to stop her," he said. My mother gave him a polite smile. He hadn't stopped looking at me. "Well, hey, I was just about to head to the soda shop. Care to join me, Cassie?"

"Uh..." I looked at my mother, begging for help with my eyes. My mother looked between the two of us.

"You can go—as long as you take Lucy with you and don't go anywhere else," she said, checking her watch. "I still have some shopping to do. I'll come find you when I'm done."

I clenched my teeth. "Thanks, Mom."

Donald was beaming. I supposed I shouldn't have been aggrieved; between the two, I did prefer Donald's company over my mother's.

I held tight to Lucy's hand, using her as a barrier between Donald and me. The soda shop was just down the street.

"I thought you weren't going to be in town today," he said as we crossed the street.

"I...didn't think I would be. I'm just as surprised as you are."

"I thought you were just trying to get out of seeing me."

I gave a well-mannered chuckle in reply, squeezing Lucy's hand. She squatted, preparing to jump up on the curb, stepping onto it instead.

"So...how's your summer been?" I asked him.

"Good. My brother and I have gone to Washington a few times to show my Dad's horses." He put his hands in his pants pockets. "He won first place with Chavi in the first show and then I won second with Zephyr the last time we went. Dad'll sure be happy when he gets his letter."

"See," Lucy whispered.

She was looking up at me, open-mouthed, about to speak. Eyes flashing toward Donald, she bit at her forefinger. Donald grinned at her as he opened the soda shop door for us.

There were only a few people inside. A group of popular girls from the upcoming junior class were sitting in one of the booths. Their laughter and squirrel-like chatter filled the entire dining area. A couple of them recognized us, which made me uncomfortable. An elderly couple was sitting at one of the tables in the center of the room. Tommy Easton, who had played with my brother on the football team, was sitting with Minnie Brandon, a girl in my class. I could tell by the way they were looking only at one another and tittering that they were probably on a date. I led Lucy as Donald started for one of the booths.

Donald continued his story. "The judge said Zephyr was one of the most beautiful Arabians he'd ever seen. He's more my horse than Dad's, so it was a compliment to me."

Lucy was still scrutinizing Donald as she leaned against my side.

"I bet," I said. "That's great."

The waitress delivered me from the conversation, taking our orders. I ordered a Coke for Lucy and me to share while Donald got an ice cream cone. Lucy was standing on the booth seat, murmuring as the waitress walked away.

I kissed her cheek. "What did you say, baby?"

She was wriggling, fingers in her mouth as she looked at Donald across the table.

"What did you say?" I asked her again.

She whispered. "See, him prince?"

My eyes widened. I tried to laugh it off. "No. No, Sweetheart."

"What did she say?"

Donald was smiling at us. Lucy hugged my neck, hiding her face in my shoulder. "Uh...she asked if you were a prince. Probably because you were talking about the horses."

Donald laughed. "I wish I was a prince," he said to Lucy, though his eyes sparkled at me.

Lucy and I sipped from straws after the waitress brought our soda, chatting with Donald while he ate his ice cream. Lucy was slurping what remained out of the straw when Donald nodded toward the door. "I think she's ready to go."

Clutching paper packages, my mother was waving outside the window. I grabbed my purse, sliding out of the booth. "I guess we're going home, Luce. Mommy's outside waiting for us."

"Oh, no. Hey, I've got it," Donald said as I rummaged through my purse.

I glanced at him, fearing the implications. "It's okay."

"No, no, I insist." He laid coins out on the table before I could retrieve my change purse. I thanked him, reminding Lucy to thank him as well. I'd just have to deal with the repercussions later.

"Hey, Cass," he said as I walked away. "I'll call you sometime this week."

Or now.

I cast a quick look at the girls sitting in the other booth, hoping they hadn't heard. "Okay."

At church that Sunday, Holly sat next to me with her typical benumbed disposition. Pastor Gilbert began preaching, delaying the question Holly had persisted in asking me every week. It had been almost a month since my last visit to the camp; Pastor Gilbert no longer inquired when I might come back, but Holly still did. I tried to think up another excuse to give her this time.

"Have you heard anything from your brother?" Holly asked as we walked with the rest of the congregation out to the parking lot.

"A couple weeks ago. He's still doing combat training."

Eyes narrowed from the sunlight, she peered ahead. "Are you going to the camp this Saturday?"

"No. I wish I could, but I don't think I'll be able. How's it going for you?"

"All right. Egon doesn't take it very seriously, but it's something for me to do."

I stared at my feet. I wondered if Pastor Gilbert and General Turner realized yet, as I had, that this program was a waste of time.

"You went to the soda shop with Donald the other day," Holly stated.

I watched my mother put Lucy in the car. I couldn't place the strange tone in Holly's voice. "Yeah, Lucy and me."

"Are you guys going steady now?"

"No."

"He likes you."

I swallowed. "I know."

She stopped just before we reached my mother's car, facing me. "Do you like him?"

Discomfited, I looked around the parking lot. Anything I said could potentially harm one or both of my friendships with them. "I don't know."

She chuckled under her breath, surprising me. "How can you not know?"

"I just...don't. I've never really liked anyone before."

"You liked Jimmy Taylor."

My cheeks flushed. How could she possibly have known about that? I hadn't told anyone but my brother and only because he'd asked. Perhaps I'd exposed my feelings a little more than I realized. "I—well, sort of."

She raised an eyebrow, eyes dropping in thought. "Well, I should go. I'll see you next Sunday."

I nodded, confused as she walked to her parents' car and I headed to Mom's.

Seven

"Cassandra Anne Wyndham!"

I opened my eyes, rolling over. My mother was in her uniform, standing in my doorway. "This is the *second* time I've come up here. Get out of bed and come downstairs *this instant!*"

Sitting up in bed, I stared at the doorway as she stomped away. Yawning, I rubbed at my face; she was in one of her moods again.

I stretched, collapsing back into bed. The sun was blinding; I was surprised it hadn't awoken me. A bird chirped in the tree outside my window. I laid there listening to it, summoning the resolve to get up and cross out another humdrum day.

Waiting for the end of my final year in secondary school might as well have been an eternity. I could do my best to hide from Donald during the summer, but I'd have to face him when school started in the fall. I wanted so badly to gather the courage to tell him the truth, but the thought of it petrified me. It would be much easier if he figured it out for himself. I wasn't attracted to him in any way. He was a good person—that was evident—but I didn't have anything close to romantic feelings for him.

This thought led me to Holly. The only time she showed even a hint of emotion was whenever Donald came up in a conversation. I wasn't sure if that was because she was resentful of the fact that he apparently liked me, or if it was because she sincerely wanted us together.

The more I thought about it, the more annoyed I got. She never told me anything; she never talked about herself, never talked about her feelings. I always had to work to figure her out and even after the effort, I was still left empty-handed...

Just like I had been with Friedrich.

Her friendship fit me like a dress that was two sizes too small; it was uncomfortable. All this time, I'd told myself that was just the way she was—because if that weren't true, I'd have to confront her. I didn't want to fight with her; she was the closest thing I had to a friend, whether it was genuine friendship or not. I just didn't want to deal with it; I wasn't strong enough.

Everything about this place made me feel insignificant. Donald didn't even know the real me; he knew the me I felt I had no choice but to be. That wasn't necessarily his fault; it was mine for not having the confidence to be myself—if I even knew who that was. Still, wasn't there a part of him that sensed that I was holding back? That I was more than what I seemed? If not, then any relationship I got into with him now would be doomed, because one day, I was going to change. I didn't know when or how, but the real me could not remain chained up inside me forever. Then what would he do? He liked the fake Cassie.

And if he did have the feeling that I was concealing a part of myself, then why wasn't he seeking it out, trying to discover me? Because he was afraid of what he would find? I didn't want to be with someone like that. I'd always longed to fall in love with someone who could see the real me and love me for it. I dreamed that this man would see the part of me no one else did, not even myself. I had been so miserable up to this point in my life, that my only hope—the prayer that I clung to—was that there was a purpose for all of this pain. I could only continue to trudge through the years ahead if I knew that at some point, someone was going to be there to walk with me the rest of the way.

I blinked away the wetness from my eyes. This was stupid.

I ripped off my blanket. Unbuttoning my pajama top, I started toward my bay window, gasping.

Two large trucks were parked just in front of Mr. Stewart's barn. I recognized Mr. Stewart in the distance standing with two men dressed in Army uniforms. That didn't startle me as much as the image of his fields.

All three of his fields—the one closest to my house, the one behind the barn and the one on the other side of Mr. Stewart's house—were speckled with men, the large letters 'PW' written on their backs. One of them was on a riding row tiller, led by two horses, tearing up the ground. Some of the men had shovels. Others had seed bags draped over their shoulders. I watched them in curiosity until my mother's furious steps pounded up the stairs. I threw on a blue and white gingham dress, slipping on my shoes just as she barged into my room. I could tell she was about to yell at me, though seeing me ready brought her irritability down a couple degrees.

"Have you looked outside?" I asked.

She handed Lucy to me. "Yes."

"What...what's going on?"

"A guard came over this morning and said prisoners-of-war were going to be working for Mr. Stewart to get his crops growing again."

I looked toward the window. "With only two guards?"

"Apparently they're holding the men to the honor system." She adjusted the pins in her cap. "Besides, the guard said they have no money or anything of value to trade, not that anyone around here would do business with a German in the first place. It's a small town; I'm not worried about it. Are you starting on the lawn today?"

"I'd planned on it."

"Good. The grass is past my ankles." She bent to kiss Lucy. "Mommy loves you. Behave yourself."

I was speechless, watching as she turned to go. "Wait, you're...you're going to leave us here alone—with them?"

She sounded annoyed. "What else am I supposed to do? It's not like they're working in the house, Cassandra. There are guards watching them. Go down to Mrs. Williams' house if you want, for a little while, but that lawn had better be mowed before I get back."

Frozen with terror, I listened to her heels peter out down the hallway, holding Lucy a little closer. The front door slammed and I wandered over to the window to get another look. Besides the one on the tiller, the POWs still had a long way to go before they reached my end of the field.

I rushed through breakfast, Lucy having already eaten. Looking out the window as I cleaned my plate, I saw they were making little progress. There was a possibility I could be finished mowing before they were close enough to talk to me.

Gripping my hand, Lucy toddled out with me to the shed. None of the prisoners noticed us, too busy dropping seeds or digging up soil. Opening the shed door, I spotted the mower leaning against a shelf lined with tools almost right away. It was red, with a cylinder of blades between two wheels.

I preferred to pull the mower around the far side of the house, but they were going to see me eventually. I tried to remember what my mother said; that the guards were confident the Germans would keep to themselves. Though I didn't want them aware of my presence, there was no way around it. Sighing, I pulled the mower around the house with one hand, tugging Lucy along with the other.

A few of the Germans looked up and I was certain they saw me. Lucy paid no attention to the prisoners, running for the tire swing Amos had hung up for her before he left. It was on a tree near the driveway. That would keep her entertained until I had to mow around back.

I began cutting the grass next to the driveway, working my way over to Mr. Stewart's field. The POWs were still less than halfway across, buoying my hope to be at least on the other side of the house by the time they reached the edge of the field.

I continued to work, making sure to get as close to the side of the house as possible, leaving no patch of grass untouched. Lucy argued with me when I asked her to come with me while I mowed the side of the house, whining as she jogged after me. I pacified her by letting her push the mower a couple times. By the time I reached the backyard, the prisoners were halfway across the field, dropping seeds behind the tiller. They seemed to be working faster, having finally gotten into a routine. By the time the backyard was done, they were closer than ever, but I thought I could mow the final side of the house before they reached the edge of the field.

"Do you want to go back on your swing?" I asked Lucy.

"Yes!" She punched the air, jumping in place before running around the side of the house.

I knew it was going to happen before it happened. Lucy's legs were moving too fast for her little body. She lost her balance, hands out to catch her fall, but her face still smashed into the ground.

I dropped the mower. "Lucy!"

She screamed. Her fleshy baby face was red, glazed with tears. I knelt down, looking over the blood from the abrasions on her cheek, hands and knees. "Shh, shh." I soothed her as I picked her up. "It's okay. You're okay, baby."

She rested her head on my shoulder as she wailed, her howls carrying across Mr. Stewart's field. I tried not to think about it.

In the kitchen, I sat Lucy on the counter. She couldn't take a full breath for her sobs.

"Shh...calm down, baby. You're okay. Let's rinse your hands off, first."

She shrieked, yanking her hand away as I ran water over it. "No!"

"We have to, Luce. We have to get the dirt out."

"No!"

I didn't have a choice. Rubbing the soap to lather up suds in my own hands first, I forced each of her hands under the water, washing them off. For her cheek and knees, I used a wet rag. That was a struggle, too, and I wasn't able to get her knees as clean as I would've liked. I would have to scrub the stains out of her frock later.

She hiccuped. I held out my arms. "Let's go back outside now."

Still crying, she kneaded her eyes. "No. You hold me."

I wanted to talk her out of it—I had to get the yard done *now*—but she was ready to burst into tears again.

I carried her into the living room, sitting on the couch with her. I rested against the arm of the sofa, Lucy sniffling with her head on my chest. Chewing on my lip, my arms were fastened around her, but all I could think about was how much closer the POWs must have been getting.

"Do you want to go swing?" I asked once she'd calmed down. Whimpering, she nodded. I sighed in relief, carrying her out onto the porch.

The screen door slammed behind us. A wave of apprehension swept over me; the POWs were just feet away from the border of our yard. I swallowed, trying to appear unperturbed as I led Lucy down the front steps. Some of the prisoners knew I'd seen them; I hoped they would think I was unafraid. With any luck, it would dissuade them from trying to talk to me or from actually stepping on our property.

"Here." I lifted Lucy so that her spindly legs went through the center of the tire. "Hold on tight—"

"See, push me."

"I can't, baby," I murmured, peeping at the approaching Germans. "I have to finish mowing."

"Peez?"

That was one area where I couldn't fault my mother; she always enforced manners. Lucy looked so cute and pitiful —and had asked so politely. I couldn't refuse her.

I took hold of the tire. "Fine. But you have to hold on."

My focus was on her, though I watched the prisoners from the corner of my eye. Most of them had resumed digging or dropping seeds, no longer interested in a toddler and her older sister. One of them kept looking up at us every time his shovel hit the ground, but his gaze didn't make me nervous. He seemed more curious than anything else.

I tickled Lucy under her chin. She kicked her legs and I laughed. "Hold on."

"I will. I will hold on, See."

She swung back to me. I gripped the tire, preventing her from swinging forward. She seemed confused before I spun her around, keeping her safely pressed against me. I began to laugh with the same inhibition she had as I released her.

"See, dop!" she said, startled. Then she giggled. "Again!"

Her little body tensed as I twirled with her once more. I couldn't keep from laughing as she gurgled, overwhelmed with the thrill.

"Ah, *Hallo, Schöne.*"

My face fell and I hugged Lucy and the swing against me on instinct. Looking toward the field, I recognized Egon's dark hair and prominent cheek bones. He had paused, watching me.

Leaning against the handle of his shovel, he gave me a roguish smile. *"Du bist sehr schön. Darf ich dich küssen?"*

A couple of the men nearby glanced at him, some of them chuckling, shaking their heads. He knew English; he was either doing this to unnerve me (which was working) or else what he was saying was so inappropriate he didn't want to risk me understanding. I was grateful none of the others joined in. Instead, they all seemed more concerned with getting their jobs done.

Egon scratched at his upper lip as he glanced over his shoulder, probably to see if any of the guards were close. I thought of my father's guns upstairs in my parents' bedroom, no use to me all the way out here.

I whispered in my baby sister's ear. "Hold on, Luce."

Her grip tightened on the rope. I gave her an easy push forward, trying to think of what I would do if he tried to come near us; I had to think of Lucy first. I wouldn't have time to get to either the front door or the back door before any of them could get in. Running to hide in the woods wouldn't be best for us; these men had combat training in areas more dense than this. They could easily overcome an adolescent girl and a baby.

"Was machst du heute Abend? Ich will bei dir sein."

The men closest to him were sniggering. My skin tingled with fear. I was going to have to swing the mower upside his head; that was my only option.

Another one of the Germans was talking now, but I didn't think it was to me. I was shaking. Regardless of how it was going to look, I decided just to take Lucy into the house when I heard what sounded like arguing.

Egon was in a heated discussion with one of the others. The other men that I could see were sneaking peeks at them, making casual smirks and muttering to one another.

Egon looked at me. I could tell he was angry, but he clenched his jaw, taking up his shovel again, his eyes kept shamelessly flickering in my direction. I wanted so much to run inside and hide—to lock the doors and hide with Lucy under a blanket in a closet somewhere—but I was even more afraid of Egon knowing that he scared me. Just like at the camp, I was going to have to be brave.

I pulled Lucy out of the swing. "Come with Sissy. Sissy has to finish mowing."

I was glad she didn't protest, excited with the idea of helping me again.

We finished mowing the yard, though I'd stayed vigilant the entire time. All the POWs seemed to have forgotten about me, and I made it a point to appear as if I'd forgotten about them. Their guttural voices carried over the summer breeze and I knew it was unrelated to me. Using their distraction as an opportunity, I left the mower propped beside the house, heading for the front porch.

The moment I stepped inside, I shut the front door, locking both the door knob and the dead bolt. It felt unnatural with it being summer; the doors were usually kept open until we went to bed.

I carried Lucy into the kitchen, closing and locking the back door, too. I looked through the blinds over the sink. All the Germans seemed to be where they were supposed to be, none of them looking back at the house.

After lunch, Lucy and I stayed upstairs in my room for the rest of the day. It was a beautiful day, but we enjoyed it from my bay window where I kept a watchful eye on the prisoners. They ate their lunches near the barn before going back out into the field. It was almost five-thirty in the afternoon when they finally gathered their shovels and lunch pails, piling into the trucks in the distance. I sighed in relief knowing they would not be there overnight to hamper a peaceful sleep.

I took Lucy outside once they were gone, to put up the mower and to let her swing. I kept looking toward the field, which was now covered in dark brown soil with channels that gave the impression of an optical illusion in the distance. It was strange to think that there had been Germans walking around freely just yards from my house.

It was half past ten that night when I heard my mother come in. After the day I'd had, I hadn't been able to sleep knowing she wasn't home yet. It was late for her, since she was always home before eight-thirty. Hearing her coming up the staircase, I opened my bedroom door, peeking out into the hall. Pulling off her cap at the top of the stairs, her steps were sluggish; it didn't even look like her eyes were open.

"Hey Mom," I said.

She watched me for a second before disappearing into her room. Rooted in place, I was taken aback. Perhaps she hadn't heard me.

It was a moment before she reappeared, tugging her pinafore at the waist. A few sinewy strands of hair were sticking out around her face and she reached up to smooth them. "How was Lucy today?"

"Good. Why are you getting home so late?"

She didn't look at me. "My shift ran over into another."

"Oh," I said, finding this dubious. "Okay. Good night, Mom."

She opened Lucy's bedroom door without responding. I sighed as I shut my own. Turning off my lamp, I returned my journal to my desk, crawling into bed. The night air was serene, with the kind of calm that enticed one to take it all in on a blanket underneath the stars. It tempted me, but I didn't see the point in lying out there by myself. Lucy was too little, and it made me laugh thinking about asking Mom to do such a thing. The only one in my family who might have done it would have been Amos, but he wasn't here. Even with him, I couldn't imagine it being meaningful. I wanted to lay under the stars with someone I could connect with; a soul mate I could pour my heart out to while we gazed at the heavens—a best friend or a lover. I had neither.

I bolted upright as my door flung open. Squinting from the light pouring in from the hallway, my mother's shadow stretched across my bed.

She was shouting. "How the hell did she get those scrapes? They're on her face, her hands, her knees—"

"S-she tripped, running toward the swing."

"Were you not watching her?"

"Of course I was watching her, but I was mowing."

She scoffed. "If you were watching her, it wouldn't have happened! I am a damn idiot for thinking you could take responsibility for *anything*. She is a baby, Cassandra; you are seventeen years old! She'd be better taken care of if I left her here by herself!"

I gaped at her. "Mom, it was an accident—"

"I am working twelve hour shifts almost every day! My patients and my co-workers are the *only* people who appreciate me; they're the only ones who help me when I need help! I can't even depend on my own daughter to take care of what few responsibilities I give her!"

I was crying now. "Mom, I took care of her. I cleaned her up and held her until she stopped crying."

"You didn't stop her from falling though, did you?"

I buried my face in my knees, bursting into tears. I loved my baby sister more than I loved any other person in the world. To act as if I was careless with her struck a nerve. Just today, I had contemplated hitting a German in the head with a lawn mower to protect her. How could my mother possibly imply that I was careless with her?

"Stop that damn crying or I'll give you something to cry about!"

She slammed my door, leaving me in chaos. I sobbed into my pillow, burying myself under the covers to keep from being heard. I stood on the very precipice of hate, yearning for the release of tumbling over the edge, feeling the wind blowing in my hair as my body plummeted. And still, my feet wouldn't allow me to make that jump. When I was this close to giving up on her, it was a great source of frustration for me to try to understand what kept me hanging on. I knew the right thing to do was to forgive her, so I cried at the injustice of it rather than the fact that I felt incapable of hating her.

I woke up late the next morning, surprised that she had never come to wake me. I put on a brown and blue plaid dress with a peplum waist and an A-line skirt; it was one of my more informal dresses. I hadn't bothered rolling my hair the night before since I was going to spend all day today outside painting. Brushing through my hair, I wrapped a headscarf around it to keep it out of my face. It would be my luck to swipe a strand away and get a streak of paint that would only fade with time across my forehead or in my hair, incurring my mother's wrath.

I glanced out my window on the way out of my room. The prisoners had returned, scattered throughout the field. I tried to get a good look at the ones working close by. None of them had Egon's dark hair, so I assumed he must have been working in one of the other fields today.

I could hear voices on the radio on my way downstairs. Lucy was playing on the living room floor, my mother sitting on the couch in a regular dress. I stopped in the middle of the staircase, wondering why she was still home.

Mom was leaning forward, her head between her knees. It looked like she was crying. The closer I stepped toward her, the more discernible the voice on the radio became:

"...this very exciting day—this historic day—the day for which the world has waited: D-Day. The day, on which, the Allied armies gathered in England under the supreme command of General Eisenhower, have lashed across the Channel to bring the liberation of the peoples of Europe from their Nazi oppressors. Yes, it's the real thing...Thousands of Allied troops, paratroopers, are spearheading this invasion, dropping behind Nazi lines to knock out their first line of defense. Overhead, the skies are black with Allied planes, dropping their bombs on every likely target...Offshore are swarms of ships as far as the eye can see, acres and acres of ships; ships bombarding the coastal defenses, ships bearing troops and equipment to back up the assault..."

My mother sobbed to herself. Agape, I listened.

"...First, the early and unconfirmed reports from German sources; later, the first communique from the Allied Supreme Headquarters in London. That communique was broadcast direct at three thirty-two o'clock Eastern War Time this morning...We have a transcription of that historic message, which we're now going to rebroadcast. Here is the first word—the first official message—sent out to the world on the Allied invasion."

The radio became staticky, noisy with playback as another voice began to speak. *"This is Supreme Headquarters, Allied Expeditionary Force. The text of Communique Number one will be released to the press and radio of the United Nations in ten seconds...Under the command of General Eisenhower, Allied naval forces, supported by strong air forces, began landing Allied armies this morning on the northern coast of France..."*

I gripped the back of the couch, my legs shaking as I struggled to take a normal breath. "We...we invaded France?"

My mother shuddered. It only took a second for me to realize why she was so distraught.

I touched her shoulder. "We knew this was going to happen, Mom. This is what he signed up for; this is what he wanted—to defend our country."

She looked up at me, her emerald eyes red and puffy. "Do you not think I know that? Have a little tact, Cassandra!" She ran her hands through her hair, bowing forward again. "Just go away."

The man on the radio persisted in his commentary on the invasion. Lucy hadn't stopped playing with the little wooden people in her dollhouse, oblivious to our mother, oblivious to the monumental occurrence that was happening in the world. Knowing anything else I said would only incense Mom, I conceded defeat, retreating to the kitchen for breakfast. Taking a biscuit off the stove, I smeared it with jam, my appetite waning as I imagined my self-possessed older brother with dirt and blood on his face, shouting, with guns blasting and deafening explosions all around him, crawling and running around the maimed bodies of Americans. Feeling queasy, I scarfed the biscuit down just to get it in my stomach before getting the broom, some rags and paint supplies out from under the stairs. There was no use in worrying; not yet, anyway. Amos was clever. He'd been training for months. He could do this with the best of them.

I swept the porch, wiping down the railings. I was relieved that the Germans weren't on this side of the field today. From the porch, I would be out of sight for most of them. I began painting the railing first, before starting on the planks. The men on the radio were still talking about the invasion. It was evidence of how distressed my mother was, the fact that she must have called in to work today; she *never* called in.

I worked for hours when I was finally able to stand back in the doorway and admire my work; the front porch was done, which meant after painting the rails on the back porch, my punishment would be over. Checking the time, I ate lunch before going out back. The radio was off now and Mom and Lucy were nowhere to be seen. I made a sandwich, peering out the kitchen window. There were only a couple of

Germans working nearby, none of whom were close enough to accost me as Egon had done.

Eager to start the back railing and finish my sentence, I gulped what was left in my glass, picking up the paint and brush.

I faltered on the back steps. There was a POW I hadn't noticed earlier, right on the boundary of Mr. Stewart's garden. He was crouching down, burying seeds. I stared at my feet just as he looked up, wishing I'd checked the yard before coming out. Fists clamping around the brush and the handle to the paint can, I made my way down the steps onto the grass; I would paint fast. On my knees, I lifted the top off the paint container.

"Cassie."

I went rigid, slowly looking over my shoulder.

Friedrich eyed the back door before glancing around the field. I realized at the same moment he did that there was no one else was around.

He was frantic. "Cassie, I am sorry. I am so sorry. I expect you not forgive me; I am not deserving it. I know it is much to ask, so I am not, but I just...I have to...I just..."

My heart was pounding so hard it was making me dizzy. Eyes burning, I realized I was holding the wet paintbrush to the skirt of my dress.

He tossed a couple seeds down. "I am so angry with you. I hate that you lie to me, I hate what you are...but then I realize I am not mad at you at all; I am mad at me. I am mad at me because you are all I think about."

I blinked the blurriness from my vision. His eyes were the summer blue I remembered from before, but I was close enough to see the unrest in them. "I feel so...confuse; I want to know the truth. So I read my Bible like you always tell me; I read the worksheets from our time together, over and over and over. And what I realize—what I am understanding—damages everything I think I know."

It was hard to swallow. Shaking, I dipped the brush in the paint can again, too distracted to pull it back out.

"I watch and wait for you, hoping you come back," he said, his voice low. "Once I realize my mistake, all I do is hope—and pray—that you come back so I can tell you I am sorry; so I can tell you..." He grunted to himself in frustration. "So I can tell you one day is not passing where I am not wishing I can take back what I say. I cannot eat; I cannot sleep. You are like a ghost that is always in my dreams, haunting me when I am awake. I feel myself...I feel I am...like I am...*verrückt*...crazy," he said, remembering the English word. "I feel I am crazy."

My jaw quivered. I breathed out, wiping at the tears that were starting to fall before they could touch my cheeks.

His eyes were pleading. "You have a right saying no; you have a right to forget me. But I ask for a mercy I deserve not anyway: please, *please* come back. I need you. I have questions and many things to sort through and you are the only person I trust."

My tongue was rolled up and tied, my thoughts having evaporated from the torridity of his words. He wasn't paying attention to where he dropped the seeds anymore, his eyes on me for a reaction, for a response; for a slap or a smile. I had to say something.

Say something!

"Cassandra!"

My mother's voice echoed from somewhere in the house. She couldn't know; she could never know.

I got to my feet, aching as I looked at him. "I have to go."

Cheeks flushed from the summer heat and the avowal that was still ringing in my ears, I went inside. My mother was standing at the top of the stairs, Lucy on her hip. It was almost comical the way her expression went from unexplained misery to fury. I blinked, only then registering that she was yelling at me again.

"What?" I asked.

She was stomping down the stairs. "What is wrong with you? You are getting paint *everywhere*! Oh my God, Cassandra!"

I looked down, seeing the saturated paintbrush still in my hand, having left a trail from the backdoor through the kitchen and living room. I panicked, cupping my hand underneath it.

"Do you not use your head for *anything*?" she roared. "Look at your dress! Did you even get any on the porch?"

I rushed to the back door. "I'm sorry. I'll clean it up."

It was humiliating to think he could have heard her berating me, yet I hoped for just another sight of him—to be sure he was real, and that I wasn't the one going crazy.

To my dismay, he was gone, his back to me as he walked toward the barn with the other prisoners for lunch. I raked the brush on the side of the can, wishing he would turn around, wishing my legs might disobey my brain and run after him.

My mother bellowed out for me again and I ran inside to clean the paint off the floors.

I had to take Lucy when I returned to paint the railing on the back porch later, which would have prevented me from talking to him again, if he'd been in the same spot. But he didn't come back, and I wasn't sure which one he was in the distance. His declaration had caught me so off guard that I hadn't managed to give him more than a gaping, dead stare. I feared the impression I'd left him with, that his words had had no effect on me—because nothing could have been further from the truth.

I stayed outside with Lucy the rest of the day in the hopes of catching another glimpse of him until the prisoners loaded up in the backs of the trucks. I watched them drive away, wondering if he was experiencing the same gut-wrenching disappointment that I was.

After dinner, I took a shower, intent on reading for the rest of the evening in my window. Yet, my gaze was drawn out into the field, and all I could see was him.

My bedroom door opened, rattling me out of my reverie. Mom was all dressed up, with fresh make-up and her hair pinned. "I just put your sister to bed. I'm going out for a little bit."

At seven forty-five in the evening? I closed my book. "Oh. Do you have extra rations or something?"

Mom had always been adamant about not wasting gas rations. She stared at me before turning away. "I'll be back late."

My door clicked shut. Stupefied, I waited until I heard the front door close before creeping across the hall. Lucy sat up in bed as I entered her room.

Peering out the window, an unfamiliar black car sat in the driveway. My mother's silhouette passed through the headlights, getting in on the passenger side. I watched as it backed out.

I stood there in stunned silence, long after it had driven off down the road. Lucy's bed creaked, reminding me of where I was. I made her lay back down, tucking the covers around her and kissing her forehead. "Go to sleep, Lucy-Goosey."

Out in the hallway, I leaned against the wall as a disturbing notion swirled in the pit of my stomach. My mother was hiding something from me; quite possibly from my dad, as well. Perhaps I was jumping to conclusions, but the more I thought about it, the more sense it made. Despite her frequent irritable behavior, my mother knew the difference between right and wrong; she had made many difficult decisions in her life just because they were the right ones to make.

My father was away a lot, though—too much—and I'd always assumed my mother thought her previously noble decisions had betrayed her. My mother was giving up on our family just as my father had.

If they could have their secrets, I could have mine.

Eight

It hadn't even occurred to me to tell Holly I was going to the camp that Saturday. All I could think about was him; what he was thinking, what I was going to say. What if—because of my muteness during his profession in my backyard—he didn't even show up today, thinking all was lost? The prisoners hadn't been back to the farm since that day, so I hadn't placated him with a furtive, forgiving smile.

I pedaled faster. I didn't know what lay ahead for me at the camp, but I had to find out. Maybe we could just pick up where we left off, without referencing that fateful day. I'd rather pretend it hadn't happened than talk about it, making things even more awkward between us.

Some of the women eyed me in curiosity as I approached on my bike. That made me more uneasy than the idea of sitting with Friedrich did.

I parked my bike, hugging my Bible. Pastor Gilbert beamed at me, speaking with sincerity as he shook my hand. "So glad to see you, Cassie."

My whole body was tense as I stood separate from the rest of the group. The women were more comfortable than they'd been before, prattling on amid lighthearted chatter. Holly was talking—no, *smiling*—with Nancy and Sharon at the gates. We locked eyes for only an instant before I looked to my feet. Not once could I recall her ever showing enjoyment in a conversation with me. What was so wrong with me that made it so hard for people to be my friend? It made me question my own goodness. Maybe I was a worse person—a more *annoying* person—than my perception allowed me to see. Maybe it was just too upsetting to accept.

I stared down the road behind us that led away from the camp; I didn't want to cry here.

"Hey."

Holly was next to me now, close enough to see the water in my eyes. Her smile was gone, reverting to the same stultified expression she always wore with me. "You didn't tell me you were coming today."

I cleared my throat. "I know, I-I forgot to call."

She looked back at Nancy and Sharon, and I could see it wasn't her preference to be standing there with me. I wondered why she'd come over at all. Nancy whispered in Sharon's ear, glancing away from us, and I lowered my eyes, feeling self-conscious.

After putting our purses away and being searched over by the nurse, I felt stiff with uncertainty as I entered the mess. Maybe it was a mistake, coming back; maybe that had been his plan. Maybe he wanted to make a fool out of me—or worse.

I put down my Bible and worksheets, preparing to sit down when someone dropped their own belongings beside me.

Nancy, with her dark eyebrows and wispy, wheat-colored hair, stared at me as she sat down. "This is where I sit now," she said with a thick, country accent.

"Oh." I picked up my things.

"That's okay," Nancy said to me. It was as if I weren't even standing there anymore. Holly never looked up, though I knew she'd heard. Sharon sat at the table behind Nancy, also having moved from where she used to sit. She gave me a frail grin that I mirrored before moving down to another table.

I opened my Bible to a random page, smoothing out the folded worksheets. I kept my eyes focused there, afraid if

I looked up someone would see my tears, my exasperation. I supposed it was my fault; I hadn't been there in a month.

The prisoners entered. I could hear their voices, see them moving about from the corner of my eye. I didn't look up from the table until someone set down a Bible in front of me.

The wariness with which Friedrich regarded me made me doubt his motives less as he lowered into the seat across from me. "Are you okay?"

I nodded. "It's not you this time."

He chuckled under his breath, though his smile withered. "I think you are hiding from me after we speak in the field. I think I never see you again."

"No," I said, shaking my head.

"What makes you sit all the way down here?"

I heard the drawl of Nancy's vociferous voice and knew we were safe from being overheard. "She told me that was her seat now."

He followed my line of vision. "Oh. I think maybe you want to be alone with me."

He watched me with a timid smile. Perhaps I might have returned it before. My gaze fell to my clasped hands and I swallowed. "Did you—did you really mean everything you said the other day?"

"Every word."

My eyes brimmed again; this time, from something besides hurt. "Don't lie to me, Friedrich. If this is some kind of trick, or game, or—"

"I am not lying to you, Cassie. I swear. I am so sorry for what I say. Every time I think about how much I am hurting you..." He trailed off, looking down at the table. "I am an idiot."

"You're not an idiot. You just—you were confused. I'm not mad at you for that. For that matter, I...I'm sorry too. I shouldn't have taken you by surprise like that. I could've found a better way to say it, a better time—"

"It matters not when or how you tell me; I think I still behave this way. And why are you sorry? I am the one who makes a fool of me."

"Yeah, but, I shouldn't...I shouldn't have sprung it on you like that. Maybe it would've been better if—"

He leaned across the table, commanding my gaze. "I accept no apology from you. You are doing nothing wrong."

I had to look away. I tried to be discreet as I wiped at my cheeks, begging God not to let anyone notice.

"I promise," he whispered, "I am never making you feel this way again. I am the one who is sorry. You should not be sorry. Now please, *please* tell me you forgive me. Because if you cannot, I make one of the guards knock me out with his baton because I am not sleeping in weeks."

I grinned at him. "I forgive you."

His visible relief resembled someone who had been freed from a stockade. "Thank you."

His eyes twinkled as they had before and I felt my cheeks flush, handing him a worksheet. "Would you like to read the first verse today?"

"Certainly."

He finished the passage in Psalms before we read Pastor Gilbert's applicable questions.

Friedrich snorted. "I know God is hearing my prayers when I see you outside your house. Now, I see He makes sure I learn my lesson."

"What do you mean?"

He motioned with his head. "Read the first question."

I read aloud. "Tell of an instance where you didn't show compassion. Why not? What would you do differently if you could?"

"I want to answer this one," he said.

He'd never volunteered before. With a restrained eager grin, I nodded.

He fiddled with the pencil, eyes never leaving me. "One time, there is this girl. She is very sweet to me, very kind. Very compassionate. And one day, she tells me something about her—something to help me—and I use it as a weapon to hurting her."

I peered down at my hands.

"Why am I doing this?" he continued. "I am doing this because I am not knowing better. But this is no excuse, and I know it is not, because something inside tells me I know the truth: this girl is special, because she shows herself to me even though I maybe turn away from her."

My lips were taut as I fought a smile. I felt ridiculous as my eyes moistened again.

"And what would I...?" he looked at the question. "What would I do differently? I tell her it matters not. I tell her she is a wonderful person—a better person than me—and I tell her she is important to me. More than she knows."

We stared at each other from across the table. Words were racing towards my lips, filling my mouth, jamming at the tip of my tongue.

He gulped as he glanced toward Nancy and Holly. "I am sorry, if this scares you."

I shook my head, smiling, my mouth opened to speak, but still, no words came out.

He sighed. "You are not coming back next weekend, are you?"

I beamed at him before laughing. "I...Friedrich...no one's ever said anything like that to me before."

"Then no one knows what life is like without you. Your little sister knows, though. I see in her face her love for you. She..." He searched for the right word. "—*appreciates* you."

I paused, wondering when he could've seen me with Lucy. A realization snapped in place in my head. "It was you, wasn't it? You were in the field that day when Egon started talking to me."

He looked down the tables, probably at Egon. "Oh, yes. This is me."

"What did you say to him?"

"I cannot tell you this."

"Why?"

"Because I use words a man should never use in front of a girl."

I chuckled and his eyes crinkled just the way I loved. "Well...thank you."

"My pleasure."

We finished what we could of the Bible study. As dispirited as I had been, I was now so elevated that I didn't think I'd ever come down. An awareness seeped through my skin, straight through to my bones, that our connection had been healed; that no matter what happened from here, we would never be estranged again. I'd never felt such undeniable security in my attachment to another person before.

Pastor Gilbert called out the last five minutes.

Friedrich leaned closer on the table, whispering. "When am I seeing you again?"

I thought for a moment. "Next Saturday, I guess. Why haven't you been back to the fields?"

"We give the crops time to grow before harvesting. I am not back until the twenty-first."

This disappointed me. "Oh."

"You are coming to the concert on Wednesday?"

"What concert?"

"We make a concert here; Wednesday night at six o'clock thirty. Usually, it is just for us, but the commandant asks everyone from this program to come. I hear the guards talk about it."

I didn't even think about it. "I'll be there."

"Good. I look for you, Miss Wyndham."

We both smiled at one another. Pastor Gilbert spoke as if on cue.

"I have a couple announcements before we adjourn. Next Saturday we will not be having Bible study due to camp administration meetings that day. Also, for those of you coming to the concert on Wednesday, be at the gates by five forty-five. If you come any later, you won't be able to get in...Shirley." The church women laughed.

Friedrich and I stood.

"I see you soon," he said.

Our gazes lingered before we turned around, going to our respective exits. Holly and Nancy were giggling together, but I didn't notice them until long after I'd passed by. I kept hearing Friedrich's voice in my head, seeing the heartfelt regret every time he looked at me. Was that truly what he thought of me? He'd never spoken so openly before. I didn't know how to take it all in.

Maybe I rode home on a cloud; I wouldn't have known. My thoughts were so far away, left behind the tall pair of wooden gates behind me, that I almost couldn't remember the trip home.

I sat in my bay window that night, long after Lucy and Mom had gone to bed. It was tranquil in the darkness, the stars sparkling like champagne bubbles in the sky. My breath fogged the glass as I looked out over the fields.

I know he's a Nazi. I know I could never utter these words to another soul. They wouldn't understand; not now. Not with the war going on. That's why I can only talk to You about it. You won't look at me as if I'm crazy, or treat me as if what I'm thinking is wrong. You created him; I know You love him. Even though he has wandered from You, You can still see his heart—the real him. You can see that there is more to him than what everyone else sees. So I'm asking You, God, because I do believe there is a chance; is he good?

I could hardly stand waiting for Wednesday night to arrive. It was difficult to balance my internal reveries while exuding external indifference, lest my mother start to suspect something. No one—least of all my mother—would understand my fraternizing with a German. Sometimes, I couldn't believe it myself, but it was a harmless association; I was certain we weren't the only ones who found ourselves growing closer over the Bible study.

I had asked Mom on Sunday before church if someone could watch Lucy for a couple hours while I went to the concert.

"A concert?"

"Yes."

She brushed through the curls in her hair. "Why would you be going to a concert at the camp?"

"Because...I was invited," I said, unsure how else to answer.

"You've never mentioned anything like that before."

I realized then that she didn't believe me; she must have thought I was making an excuse to sneak off with that phantom boy again. "They've never asked us before. This is kind of a thank you for what we're doing at the camp."

She slid pins into the knot at the back of her head, patting her hair.

"It's only for a couple of hours. You can ask Pastor Gilbert if you don't believe me. I already asked Holly. She said her mom doesn't mind watching Lucy while we go. You could swing by and pick her up on the way home if I don't get out before then."

Reaching for her hat, she paused, twisting to look at me. "You already asked Holly's mother?"

"I wanted to make sure I could work something out before I asked you."

She scoffed as she slammed her hairbrush down on the vanity, jamming a pin through her hat to secure it. "I am tired after working all day, Cassandra. I just want to come home afterwards. This is all an inconvenience to me——"

"I'm really sorry, Mom. I just thought since you pass the Morgans' street on the way home, that would make it easier on you. It's just for this Wednesday night."

She glared at her own reflection as she put on her crimson lipstick.

I tried to smooth her over. "It'll be nice. They even have two dogs Lucy can play with; you know how much she loves dogs."

"And then I'll hear, 'Mommy can I have a dog?' for weeks after this and hear her cry every time I say no. Yes, that sounds great."

"I'll talk to her about it before I take her. I'll make sure she understands that we can't have a dog——"

"I didn't say yes, Cassandra."

I didn't speak for a moment; I couldn't let her stand in my way. Friedrich was expecting me.

I stiffened my back. "Okay. I'll just bring her home then——on my bicycle. I didn't think you'd want her out past her bedtime, but it's not a big deal——"

She snapped her lipstick cap, turning on me. "I didn't say you could go!"

"Mom, I'm sorry, but I've already told Pastor Gilbert that I'd be there."

Her lipstick case clattered as she threw it on her vanity, pushing herself up. "Fine. Just do whatever you want to do," she said, before muttering to herself. "Just like your father, you've never thought of anyone else before in your life, so why should you start now?"

She brushed past me out the door. I pivoted on the soles of my saddle shoes. "So do you want me to just bring her home, then?"

She took Lucy by the hand, grousing. "No, I'll get her."

I waited until she was out of sight before bringing my hands together in silent victory. She'd capitulated; it was only the second time in my life she'd ever surrendered to me, and both times had been for Friedrich.

Lucy sat on the handlebars of my bike Wednesday afternoon, her little feet planted in the basket. It slowed me down, making sure she didn't fall out, but I made it to Holly's house just in time. Lucy was shy at first, until Mrs. Morgan's cocker spaniel climbed in her lap, lapping her face with its wet, pink tongue.

Holly and I reached the gates to the camp ten minutes before we were supposed to be let in. Almost everyone was there, except Miss Fannie, Miss Jean and Shirley. I also didn't see Nancy, though Sharon was there, talking to Ruth.

At five forty-five——the exact minute Shirley arrived——the guards led us through the first gate and into the mess hall. I couldn't believe how different it looked once we were inside. The familiar tables were nowhere to be seen in the room. Metal chairs sat like soldiers in even rows, facing a makeshift stage. There were a few POWs in their military uniforms setting up the lights, positioning a piano and microphones about the platform. They peeked at us in curiosity as we walked in.

"The prisoners won't start coming in until six," Dennis said, unlocking a side door we'd never entered before. "We wanted to get you seated before they do."

We followed him up a couple flights of steps before coming out another door above, stepping out onto the balcony that encircled the entire mess hall. I'd always seen guards up here, keeping watch from above during our Bible studies; a few of them were pacing up there now.

The same metal chairs as down below were lined up against the wall. We each took one, scooting it closer to the railing to see. It wasn't long after we all got settled that the door the prisoners usually entered from opened.

The men that walked in were unlike any I'd seen at the camp so far. They weren't dressed in POW clothing; it was apparent by their proud gaits, their solemn visages, that they were officers. Their faded olive or greenish-gray uniforms were wrinkle-free and awe-inspiring. They wore peaked caps, their tunics adorned with patches on their arms and chests that probably revealed their ranks—I didn't know how to tell. Their black boots thudded on the concrete floor as they strolled with dignified grace to the chairs in the first few rows. A couple of them noticed us, but they didn't stare; they looked too proud to stoop to catcalling.

It was a few moments later when the door opened again, raucous voices and laughter wafting up to where we sat, announcing the arrival of the enlisted men.

It was astonishing to see them all in uniform, too. Some wore field caps; some didn't have hats at all. Some uniforms looked greenish-gray while others looked beige. As somber as their superiors had been, the enlisted men paralleled them with their energy. Most of them were laughing, their German boisterous as they spoke to one another. A few of them whistled upon catching sight of us, climbing over their comrades as if that might get them closer. Chin pressed to my chest to conceal my awkward grin, my hair fell forward as I looked at Holly. "This is uncomfortable."

She was observing our spectators, unenthused. "Not really."

I watched the prisoners, not caring what she said.

When the mess was full to bursting, the POWs began to find their seats. The ones who had called out to us were now talking amongst themselves, while the less abrasive ones considered us in silence. My eyes darted around for Friedrich. It was pointless to look for a blond man with blue eyes; over half of them fit that description. I tried to look into all the faces of the ones looking up at us. He might have been sitting there, waiting for me to spot him. I frowned. Unless I had skimmed over him—or if he was too involved in a conversation with one of the other men to look up—I didn't think I'd seen him.

The room darkened, and my shoulders drooped as the faces below us became indiscernible. Maybe he had at least seen me.

One of the prisoners walked onto the illuminated stage. His dark hair was slicked back and parted. He spoke into the microphone, his teeth gleaming as he made animated facial expressions. The prisoners below boomed with laughter and I couldn't help but chuckle, especially whenever he spoke in a falsetto. Everyone clapped, including the speaker as he introduced another prisoner who sat at the piano.

The pianist took off his cap. With a pompous expression, his back straight as the edge of a knife, his nimble fingers danced on the keys. As complex as the piece sounded, he made it appear effortless. After a grand finish, the prisoners erupted in cheers and applause. The POW stood, bowing before departing from the stage.

A string quartet came up next, with a cello, two violins and a harp. After that, a piano and clarinet duo played.

As gruff and serious as I had always imagined the Germans to be, it was somewhat fascinating to see them adept in fine arts. My eyes still searched the prisoners' faces in the light that ebbed over the audience, even though I knew I wouldn't find him. I wondered if he could see me, wherever he was. The thought of him watching me made me self-conscious, causing me to sit a little straighter in my seat.

The clarinet and piano duet ended. I joined in the applause with everyone else as they made their way off the stage.

Holly nudged me. "Isn't he yours?"

My gaze frenzied over the POWs. "Where?"

"On the stage."

The pianist who had played a solo had returned, making himself comfortable in front of the keys. Friedrich was standing on the other side of the upright grand piano in a beige uniform. His hair glinted like gold under the lighting as he positioned a sleek violin beneath his chin; he'd never mentioned anything to me about being able to play.

I leaned forward on the rail, the cold metal against my forearms as I sat enthralled. Lifting the bow, his eyes flickered toward the pianist, the signal to start.

My ears recognized the song before my mind even had time to register it. I became overwhelmed, breathless, at the sound of "O mio babbino caro."

The piano harmonized beneath him. With dextrous hands, Friedrich and the instrument were one, the violin responding to the caress of the bow across the strings. His eyes were closed, as if he were the only one in the room, the intensity of his countenance conveying the feeling that the violin was siphoning the song from his soul.

My eyes had filled with tears. Drawing out the diminuendoing last note, he looked straight at the balcony where I was sitting. I knew the stage lights prevented him from seeing, but I got the message. I couldn't look away from him even after the song had ended, and I was certain I had been the first in the entire room to clap.

"Wow," Holly muttered beside me.

I continued to applaud, clenching my eyes as a couple tears trickled down my cheeks. Friedrich and the pianist bowed before walking off behind the curtains. He had played for me. He had played my favorite song for me. In all my life, I could think of nothing that compared. It seemed unimaginable that someone would do such a thing—for *me*.

I sat through the rest of the concert, almost unaware of every act that followed. Keeping my eyes on the curtain, I waited to see Friedrich again. A small number of prisoners began to sneak through the door between acts, and I finally saw him enter the mess hall. He leaned against the wall opposite of me with a few of the other men who had performed. Though I couldn't make out his face, I kept my eyes on him from the safety of the darkness.

When the concert ended, the soldier who had opened the show returned to the microphone to close it. He spoke again, causing the prisoners to laugh a few times before shouting what sounded like a command.

All the prisoners stood, standing at attention as the officers exited the room. As they passed by, one of the enlisted men in the first row began singing what sounded like "Pack All Your Troubles In Your Old Kit-Bag" in ebullient German. His fervor was infectious, causing prisoners in each row to join in as the officers passed by. Every prisoner in the room was belting out the words with zeal by the end, even Friedrich.

We weren't allowed to leave until all the prisoners had left the mess hall. They were all lost in leisurely conversation with one another, even as the guards ushered them toward the doors. Friedrich was one of the ones that dawdled.

My smile wilted as I watched him. Maybe I was mistaken; maybe it was normal for it to be hard to breathe around a friend. Maybe it was innocent the way I was always thinking about his eyes, the curve of his lips, his imperfect English, the sincere timbre of his voice. Maybe it was just the romantic atmosphere of the night that had bewitched my heart into believing this was something it could not possibly be.

I could tell no one about this; not even him. No one could ever know. This feeling would surely dissipate by morning, and I would feel like a fool for having ever entertained such a notion.

And yet, though I knew it was wrong, part of me longed to wake up and find it was still there, out of my control, taking on a life of its own.

I looked up in time to see Friedrich cast a grin in my direction—subtle, uncertain—before following the other prisoners out the door. I gave a nervous chuckle, peering down at my hands.

For how long, I could not be sure, but I knew that smile was going to haunt me.

Nine

My feelings didn't go away as I thought they might after the night of the concert. If anything, they intensified. I fell asleep thinking of him, the way he played with passion, commanding the violin that serenaded me. I woke up, still seeing it all in my mind. I walked around the house in the following days, smiling every time I caught a glimpse of my reflection in the mirror. I'd laugh to myself, shaking my head, the other person in the glass doing the same. She was the only one who knew what I was thinking, what I was feeling; she was the only one who would ever know.

I floated on my airy wings until Friday morning, when I saw my mother's suitcases at the front door. There was movement in the kitchen and I lumbered down with caution. My mother was in her nurse's aide uniform, spatula in hand. She glanced at me over her shoulder. "Get some plates. I made omelettes."

Doing as she said, I tried to think of how to broach the subject as she portioned out the omelettes on each plate. It turned out I didn't have to.

"I'm going away for the weekend and I need to leave Lucy with you. There's enough food for you both until I get back, as long as you cook it right. I've already told Mrs. Williams. She's going to come check on you every day. Go to her if there's an emergency."

Lucy was sitting in her high chair, drinking from a cup of milk. I felt that familiar tug. A weekend trip? I tried not to remember my mother's late night venture in the mystery car a little over a week before.

"Where are...?" I cleared my throat. "Where are you going? Is it...something for work?"

I pretended not to notice as she glanced at me, turning away to wash the pan. "No."

I'd set her up with an explanation for my own peace of mind and she hadn't taken it. I wondered if she'd be truthful if I asked the blunt, abominable question I was dancing around in my head.

She removed her apron. "I'll be back Monday morning. I'll call you every night, so make sure you're by the phone."

Monday morning? "Don't you have to work?"

"I changed back to night shift."

I chewed, wondering why she never mentioned it until now. "And what if we need you? Is there a way I can reach you?"

"You can reach me when I call you."

I felt as if I couldn't move. Not wanting to alert her to my misgivings, I distracted myself by eating.

My heart sank to the pit of my stomach as she left. I didn't want to believe what she was doing. My father had no idea; how could he? Of course, what she was doing was wrong, but it was his own fault that he didn't know. It had almost been three months since his last visit. I wanted to condemn my mother for this, but in the depths of my heart, I felt bad for her. She was lonely; we were all missing him.

As much as I thought my father should know, I couldn't say anything; not yet, anyway. I had only assumptions—no proof. Second, it wasn't any of my business. What my parents did was their own to reckon with. If my mother was indeed having an affair, it didn't render my father faultless; even I would attest to that.

I was disappointed to not go to the camp that Saturday. I knew just being able to talk to Friedrich would lessen some of my angst. I wondered what he was thinking right now; what he was doing. Was he as eager as I was to see him again? This coming Wednesday was the twenty-first, the day he said he was coming back to Mr. Stewart's farm. I still hoped—or feared—that this was a feeble crush. Seeing him again would help me discern what exactly it was.

My mother returned home Monday morning, just as she said. I tried to detect any guilt radiating off of her, but found none. I wondered if she was repressing what she was doing in the back of her mind or else justifying it, just so she could live with herself.

I occupied myself with what remained of my mashed potatoes at dinner, the only thing on my plate that I felt I could manage with my lack of appetite. Lucy sat next to my mother, heedless of my disquiet and my mother's secretive behavior. It was not as simple as coming out and asking her. I had to tap around it, hoping to hit something. "Did you have a nice trip?"

She scooped up a clump of potatoes that had fallen from Lucy's spoon. "I suppose."

The sky was dark. The crickets through the screen door and our utensils scraping our plates were the only noises as we ate. I swallowed, thinking of what to say next.

"What were you doing?"

My mother sighed. "I just needed to get away for a bit."

She cut up the pork on her plate. I hoped the next one wouldn't tip her off.

"Is Daddy coming home soon?"

She paused in her cutting motion, her lips parting. I tried not to appear alarmed as I continued to chew, surprised to see a troubled look on her face.

The panic in her voice didn't soothe me. "Why are you asking me that?"

I stared at her. "It's been three months. I just wondered."

Her sights remained on me before falling away. Spearing one of the sliced squares of pork, she fed it to Lucy. "I'm not sure when he's coming home."

I watched her eat for a moment before laying my napkin beside my plate, pushing away from the table. "May I be excused?"

Mom eyed my plate. "You didn't eat much."

"I'm not feeling well." It wasn't a lie.

She consented with a nod and I sensed her watching me as I walked away. She might not have known I had any idea about what she was doing, but she knew now that I was keener than Lucy.

Tuesday went by uneventfully, except for the arrival of a letter from my brother. My mother was relieved at first until we saw its postmark was from the thirty-first of May. Though he didn't specify what he would be doing or where he would be, due to recent developments, my mother and I deduced that he was certainly in France right now.

"Maybe this is a sign that he's okay," my mother breathed. We had found out only hours before that Jimmy Taylor, my brother's best friend, was being sent back to recuperate after sustaining severe wounds during the invasion. It had made my mother fear for Amos even more, but she seemed to take his letter as a good omen.

I awoke with eagerness Wednesday morning. Hurrying over to my window, I shook with excitement to see the prisoners working in the fields. I searched for Friedrich; I thought I saw him in one of the rows closer to Mr. Stewart's end.

I played with Lucy down in the family room, sneaking peeks outside from the kitchen window until my mother came down around twelve. We ate a quick lunch, remnants of the previous night's dinner, before my mother asked me to put Lucy down for her nap.

"Never mind, I'll take her," she said as I started up the stairs. "I'm going to lay down again, too. Can you do me a favor and get my purse out of the car? I forgot it last night and it makes me nervous with those Germans out there."

I waited until my mother was at the top of the stairs before pushing open the screen door and speeding outside in the most nonchalant manner I could muster. Friedrich was close. He looked up, noticing me from the corner of his eye. Neither of us put on as if it were any more than a passing glance, though I had to bite my lip to keep from beaming at him.

Her purse was in the passenger seat. Sitting down on the driver's side, I leaned over to get it. A sheet of paper was laying on the floorboard and I picked it up, assuming it had fallen out of her bag.

'Jefferson Hotel' was in bold letters at the top and I stared at it, realizing it was a receipt for a three night's stay. I was alarmed before I even noticed what was in the background.

Ashes in the ashtray. My mother didn't smoke.

I hesitated, unsure of what to do before returning the receipt to where I'd found it. I didn't want her knowing I'd seen.

I was so upset that I forgot about Friedrich as I went back inside. My mother would've known she'd be recognized getting a hotel room around here. Richmond was further east, near the coast, too out of the way for a lone getaway—but it was the perfect place for a clandestine rendezvous.

I set her purse on the couch, in a daze as I mulled over my discovery. My gaze fell on the rotary phone on the end table. Maybe if Dad realized he was losing Mom, he'd come home—or maybe he'd just tell me I was reading into things. It wouldn't be a wasted phone call either way; at least I could hear his voice.

I backed away, deciding to mull it over. Grabbing a book off one of the shelves in my father's study, I headed back out onto the porch to watch Friedrich until he had to leave.

He was still there, dropping seeds into the soil, off to himself again. It seemed silly that I couldn't just walk over and talk to him while he worked, but the implications could jeopardize us both. So instead, I sighed, pretending we weren't even conscious of each other.

I flipped through the pages without even reading. He knelt to the ground, and I watched him drop a couple of seeds from his hand. With impressive aloofness, he turned his face toward me. I gave him a blushing grin.

He stood to stretch, examining his surroundings, and I lowered my book, reading something strange in his mannerisms. My lips parted, and I watched in disbelief as he moved toward the tree-line with a cavalier stride.

With one last look back at me, he disappeared into the shadows.

I stared at the spot where I'd last seen him. When he didn't come back into sight, I hurried inside.

Tossing the book on the couch, I started up the stairs to tell my mother I was going for a bike ride before halting. My mother would be furious if I awoke her. Besides, she was sleeping; she wouldn't even notice I was gone.

Heart pounding, I dashed back out onto the porch. None of the remaining prisoners were mindful of me, but I forced myself to maintain composure to avoid suspicion anyway, retrieving my bike from beside the house.

On the road, I didn't stop until I was completely hidden on the other side of the trees. Looking down both directions to make sure no one could see, I steered into the woods.

Wheeling my bike deep into the trees until it couldn't be seen from the road, I looked around. There was no way for me to know where he went or how near or far we were from one another.

My voice was muffled, afraid of being overheard by unwanted ears. "Friedrich?"

I walked farther into the woods when he didn't answer, straining my ears for his footsteps. "Friedrich?"

Emerging into a glade, the sweet scent of honeysuckle wafted in the breeze. A large tree had toppled over, jagged and lifeless. It looked like it had been there for a while. The stump's ragged edges made it seem as if the trunk had been ripped from it, though the rest of it was smooth and flat. My concentration broke then, as I heard rustling somewhere in front of me.

Friedrich had already seen me, making his way through the trees. I gripped my elbow as he surfaced, standing in the clearing with me.

As eager as I had been to see him, my skin prickled at meeting him this way. It was strange, though; I wasn't afraid of being alone with him—I was afraid because we weren't supposed to be.

He looked as unsure as I felt. Lifting the seed bag from around his shoulder, he rested it against a tree. "I want to talk you. I cannot wait until Saturday."

I gave him a timid grin. "Me, too."

"I see you at the concert."

Anxious again, I doubted if I had the fortitude to ask. "Did...did you...play that for me?"

"I think this is obvious."

I delighted in this, lowering my gaze to my shoes. "Well...you were amazing. You have an incredible gift."

He stepped closer, though he wasn't looking at me. "Yeah, this...this is what I hear."

"You say that like it's a bad thing."

"I suppose it is not. I remember not a time I am not playing. It is just something I am always making. It causes me much..." He seemed to struggle for the right word. "Humiliation. Music is such a feminine activity."

I shook my head. "I don't know who told you that, but they're wrong. They clearly have no grasp for talent. You were wonderful."

He chuckled as he crossed his arms. "I am glad you like it."

My cheeks grew warm. "I don't...I don't understand *why* you did it, though."

His gaze roved across my face. "Maybe I want to make you smile. Maybe I want to make friends with you again."

I gulped. Lowering onto the fallen tree, I gave myself a minute to think. "You don't have to do that, Friedrich."

"Yes, I do."

Elbows to my knees, I was suddenly feeling very foolish. "So...you're doing all this just to make up for what you said?"

"Kind of."

"What do you mean 'kind of'?"

Leaning against the closest tree, he seemed thoughtful. "I am not really knowing."

A crashing feeling came over me. I pushed myself up from the tree.

"Wait," he said, "where are you going?"

I paused, looking at him over my shoulder. "I'm going home, Friedrich."

"Why?"

I considered telling him, before realizing how destructive that would be. God had had a purpose in putting me at that camp; dishonoring that by letting my feelings get in the way meant putting my desires above God's intentions. I thought there had been a chance Friedrich felt the same way, but now I knew this was just to clear his conscience. It was for the best.

"You wouldn't understand," I said.

He took hold of my arm, and I didn't resist as he turned me around. "Please tell me."

"Tell you what?"

"What you are thinking."

This Friedrich was different from the one I'd gotten to know at the camp. His teasing demeanor was absent; he was serious, almost puzzled. "It is just...I am not understanding you."

"What?"

"I mean, I *think* I understand you. I think I know who you are; how to tease you, how to make you laugh...but you are not like what I think. I want to ask you something I wonder ever since the day you tell me about your mother."

He swallowed. "Why you are not telling? I think this is why you raise your hand, to tell the guard. When you say nothing, I think you are afraid and are waiting until I am not around; I think you are going to tell the pastor. I know you are hurt. I know you are angry. Why you say nothing?"

I wasn't sure I understood this. "Are you asking why I didn't tattle on you?"

He nodded. I could tell this had been something he'd thought a lot about. I wondered why it mattered to him.

I raised my shoulders. "That's just not the kind of person I am. Being spiteful to you wouldn't have changed what you said or how it made me feel." I stared at the grass at our feet. "It wouldn't have made you like me."

I couldn't bear the idea of him thinking I wanted him to feel guilty about it anymore. "It wasn't *that* bad. I was surprised more than hurt. And I understood why you said it. I tried not to blame you for it."

He was looking into my eyes, but it felt as if he were peering past them, into the depths buried deep inside me. Feverish, I became aware of how close we were standing to one another. I brushed by him, sitting on the broken tree again. Crossing his arms, he paced.

"Can you say something for me?" He stopped in front of me. "Tell me how you really feel."

"That...that is how I really feel," I stammered.

He shook his head. "I am not believing you."

"Well...it doesn't matter whether you do or not. It's over, Friedrich; I forgave you. Please, let's just forget about it."

"You may forgive me, Cassie, but you are not forgetting it. I see it in your face. You want to say it, but you are not. Well, *I* want you to say it. Stop being afraid you hurt my feelings. I am a bastard."

I covered a laugh with my hand. "You aren't a...that."

"I am. Tell me in your own words. I need to hear it as much as you need to say it."

"Friedrich..."

His eyebrows rose in expectation as he rested against the tree.

I tossed up my hand. "I don't...I don't know. I was hurt. I was...I was mad..."

I trailed off. His patience intimidated me and it made me wonder if I could hold out longer than he could. The last thing I wanted to do was talk about it; I didn't want him to regret asking me for the truth. Deciding to give him the watered down version of my feelings, I sighed.

"It's just...I trusted you." I picked at my nail. "I thought you were different. You certainly acted like you were."

I paused, surprised to hear the scornful tone of my voice. I tried to stop, but his silence beckoned me to continue. "I think that's why it bothered me so much; you were pretending. You were just like everyone else. I told you more about myself than I've ever been able to tell another person. I was honest with you because I thought you understood me."

A torrent of anger was building beneath my lids and I clenched my jaw. He was still leaning against the tree, arms crossed and eyes focused. I could no longer hold back.

"I trusted you!" I cried. "You made me feel so stupid, so...*worthless!* No one has ever hurt me the way you did. I'm tired of people treating me like I'm useless. I have feelings too, you know. I'm seventeen years old; I'm not a child anymore. I hurt just like everyone else does but no one seems to care. All they care about is that I'll hide it. Well, I'm done hiding it! I'm tired of boxing it all up and storing it away. Nobody cares...nobody..."

I sobbed into my hands. "Nobody cares about who I am. I'm a good person, Friedrich."

"I know you are."

"I'm a good person, and I did *not* deserve the way you talked to me that day."

"I know this."

"Then why did you do it? How could you?" I wailed. "Was the person I was, the person you knew, not enough to make you say 'no'? No. All you saw was a silly little girl who wouldn't do anything about it. Sometimes, I wish I would've just hit you."

I looked up at hearing him laugh. "Don't laugh at me."

"Sorry."

I hid my face from him again, sniffling as I felt the pressure of more tears. "I don't want to be weak like this anymore; I don't want to be a pushover. I don't even have any real friends. The only friends I do have are Holly and Donald. Holly's so bored with me that I don't know why she bothers, and Donald—Donald likes someone that I'm simply not. What is so unlikable about *me*? I try so hard to be a good person—I *am* a good person," I said firmly. "My mother acts like I'm the biggest burden she's ever had to carry and my father is content ignoring my existence."

Sniffling, I wiped at my face. "My whole family has secrets they don't want anyone to know. They don't care if *I* know though, because what am I going to do about it? Nothing. And they know it. My mother's having an affair, my father's miserable here, and my brother, the prodigal child, was anything but. I don't do anything like that. Why doesn't anyone see that? Why doesn't anyone see me?"

Noticing the pained look on his face, I looked away.

"What?" he asked.

"What do you mean, 'what'?" I asked irritably.

"What is this look for?"

My eyes felt sore. "I want to believe you, Friedrich. I want to believe that all of this isn't going to disappear, but I don't trust you anymore."

He sighed, sitting down beside me. "I know. What can I do?"

"What do you mean?"

"Tell me how I get it back—your trust."

The weight of my words bore down on me and I was ashamed of making him feel like he owed me something. "Friedrich, I'm...I'm sorry. I let my mouth get away from me—"

"No apologies. Be honest with me, Cassie. I do whatever it takes, for however long it takes, because you are worth this. Tell me what I must do."

I was sure I was worth something to my parents, but Friedrich had been the first person to ever say it. "I can't tell you what to do to change it. It's something that's just going to take time."

I occupied myself with the fabric of my skirt. "I keep thinking about something General Turner told us our first day at the camp."

"What? What is he saying?"

I hesitated, wondering whether I should tell him or not. "He said...he said the Germans can't be trusted because most of what you say is a lie. You'll say anything to get a person to drop their defenses so you can take advantage of them."

I was afraid he was going to get angry. Instead, he smiled. "Well, he is not wrong. We do this to the guards, Cassie. Not once am I doing this to you."

The warmth of his hands enveloped mine. "I do whatever I must for your trust again."

I struggled to catch a proper breath. If he was as wound up on the inside as I was, I couldn't tell. He was calm, his eyes searching my face, falling on my lips...

I pulled my hand away, feeling nauseous. I hugged myself at the waist. "What are we doing here, Friedrich? If I get caught, I'm dead and you...I don't even know what they would do to you."

"I know not, either," he said quietly. "I only know I want to be close to you."

He didn't turn away, though I was still too embarrassed to look at him. "This is hard for me," he said. "But since you are open with me——even if it is against your will..." I could hear the grin in his voice. "I want to be honest with you. Something is changing, Cassie. Every day is challenging what I am believing before. I become frustrate; I become relief. I become angry; I become comfort. I am hopeful; I am disappoint. It is so overwhelming that it is much easy for me to give up. If I let me return to my old ways, I am not having to think—just do. But when I am next to you, pieces start connecting. And each time I face these doubts, I feel more strong than before."

His voice softened as he looked at me. "Everything is clear when I am with you. You are the calm after a storm. No matter what damage there is, I believe you are here so I can pick up the pieces."

The musky scent of perspiration on his skin teased my nostrils. His eyes relaxed, and it was then that I realized our noses were almost touching. I straightened, struggling to regain my self-possession. He sat up, too, though I could see him watching me from the corner of my eye. As much as it frightened me to know how I felt about him, I knew it would be far worse if he knew it, too.

"I want not to scare you, Cassie," he said. "I hope...I hope the things I say—"

"I'm not scared of you, Friedrich. Not anymore."

"Then what is holding you back?"

"What do you mean?"

I tried not to think about how much bluer his shirt made his eyes—or how appealing his lightened hair was against his sun-kissed skin. He shook his head, his brow furrowing. "I know not. There is still something I cannot follow in you. I am not understanding why you say not what you think."

I shrugged. He considered me, eyes narrowing as he smiled. "You are a puzzle to me, Miss Wyndham."

I chuckled, and he held out his hand. "We should go back. I am not knowing how long I can stay before someone sees I am missing."

We stood. Blue eyes fixed on me, I wondered what he was thinking. "Today is a pleasure. I hope we meet like this again."

He brought my hand to his lips, kissing my knuckles. I turned as he did, the two of us heading in opposite directions, back to our incompatible worlds. The moment he was out of sight, I sighed, pressing the back of my hand to my cheek.

Ten

Friedrich hadn't been able to get away the rest of the week. I kept track of him, especially watchful whenever Lucy was down for her nap—the only time I could get away myself. When I wasn't outside, I sat in my window, reading or writing, or playing with Lucy. He kept his eyes on me, too, smiling at me when no one else was close enough to see. Catching one another's eye—possessing a secret that only the two of us shared—sent tingling sparks of euphoria throughout my being. I longed to be near him again; to hear the smooth, accented inflections of his voice, to breathe in the scent of his skin, to marvel inwardly at the contours of his face.

I grew clammy thinking of him this way. This was wrong; who we were, the situation we were putting ourselves in. If anyone ever picked up on how magnetic our eyes seemed to be, or the way his face softened when he looked at me, or the way I so easily blushed when he smiled, they would destroy us—both. It would have been wise for us to sever our attachment when we knew what catastrophic results it could yield. I continued to excuse it, to justify it, by acknowledging it couldn't go any further than this. We could flirt and be one another's confidant—but that was all.

In spite of this, I also knew that we had crossed a threshold far past the point of no return.

Friday afternoon, Friedrich—with watering pail in hand—watered over the channels with some of the other prisoners, when I heard my mother call me from downstairs.

"Cassie, you have a telephone call."

Hopping down from my window to take it, I remembered with a jolt who it must have been. Glancing at Friedrich outside, I sat back down, calling out for her to take a message.

After the POWs had gone, I sat down for dinner with my mother and Lucy that night.

"That was Donald who called earlier," my mother said from across the table.

"Oh."

She watched me as she chewed. "Is he the one who asked you to the movies?"

"Yeah," I said, cutting off a corner of meatloaf. "Why?"

She nodded, before swallowing another mouthful. "You can go with him—Donald—if you want."

Chuckling under my breath, I shook my head. "Thanks, Mom, but...I don't think so."

"Why not?"

"I just—I don't really like him like that."

"Well, he seems like a nice boy." She said this as if it was all that was needed.

"He is."

"So why wouldn't you?"

Why was she pushing a date with Donald? As far as I knew, I wasn't allowed to date. The last thing I wanted was her permission for someone I didn't feel attracted to.

"I think Holly likes him," I said, hoping to deter her. It seemed to work, because she didn't press the matter any further.

The next week and a half went by rather slowly. I spent most mornings with Lucy, pining for another moment with Friedrich. It seemed our secret assignations in the glade were ill-fated, though, as he hadn't been left alone long enough to sneak off since that day. It made me look forward to Saturdays even more; at least we had that guaranteed to us. We would make small talk before going through our Bible study with the usual repartees. Though I knew it was for the best, I hated how we pretended our convergence in the woods had never happened.

Monday morning, Lucy played in my room. We had been up there for maybe half an hour when my mother came up. I tried to appear casual as I stepped away from the window.

"Can you do something for me?" she asked.

"Sure."

"That raisin cake I made last night—will you take it and this over to Mrs. Williams' place?"

She held an envelope out to me. I could tell by the thickness of it that there was money inside. "Why?"

My mother sighed as she put her hands on her hips. "Carolyn from church just called. Mrs. Williams was robbed last Friday."

I gasped. "Robbed? At home?"

"Apparently they made off with almost two hundred dollars. I'm only giving her fifty; I didn't want to insult her by giving her more. I can't imagine how upset she must be, all alone, taking care of James. That was probably money they've been saving for a long time."

James was Mrs. Williams' son. He was twenty-seven with a mild form of mental retardation. He was capable of managing their farm animals, following the same routine his father, Mr. Williams, had performed with him from dawn to dusk for years before he died. James had never done it a different way.

My mother lifted Lucy from the bed. "That's all we need. First the Germans and now this. Whoever it was must've been desperate. Who would take from a woman and her disabled son?"

I found the cake stored on the first rack in the fridge. I put it and the envelope in the wire basket between my handle bars, rolling my bike toward the driveway. Friedrich did a double-take when he saw me, quickly going back to observing the water falling from his watering can. I chuckled, hopping onto the seat of my bicycle.

With longing, I surveyed the place where I'd snuck off the road to meet Friedrich, wishing I was going there now. The road curved ahead, beyond Mr. Stewart's property, and Mrs. Williams' fields were past that. The two guards that always accompanied the POWs were standing with Mr. Stewart on his front porch while he drank coffee. Mr. Stewart waved to me and I nodded my chin in response to keep from letting go of the handlebar. "Hey, Mr. Stewart."

Farther up the road, I saw Mrs. Williams' field, though I still had a way to go before reaching her driveway. Cows littered the pastures, the bronze Herefords with their sweet dispositions and the black and white Holsteins with their exotic appeal. I slammed on my brake then, seeing someone outside the Williams' barn.

For a second, my eyes had deceived me, and I thought Egon had somehow escaped. James had the same dark hair, the same build; it had been so long since I'd seen him that I hadn't realized how similar they looked. He tossed a square bale of hay over the paddock, pausing as he saw me. I waved to him, going on to the driveway.

Dismounting my bike, I pushed it up the gravelly hill. The house wasn't in good condition, the front porch old and rickety, the roof patched up in places. Even the screen door was torn. I knocked, looking around inside when no one answered.

"Why, Miss Cassie."

I followed the voice, seeing Mrs. Williams on the other side of the porch rails. Wearing a ragged apron, her skin was leathery and tanned from working on the farm all these years. Her dark gray hair was pulled into a bun on the back of her head. She was the kind of woman who looked formidable and when she smiled, you knew she meant it.

She was smiling at me. "Well, ain't this a surprise?"

I glided down the front steps. "Hi, Mrs. Williams. How are you today?"

"Right as rain. What can I do for you?"

I reached into the basket for the cake and envelope. "I'm actually bringing this to you for my mother."

She lifted the cloth over the cake. "Raisin cake. Looks delicious. We'll have it for dinner. Why don't you come in?"

I obliged, following her inside. The threadbare couch was an eyesore, along with the tattered sitting chair in the corner. An old wood stove stuck out from the wall, and a couple sepia photographs hung on the wall. Family heirlooms and handmade doilies were placed throughout the room.

"Would you like something to drink?" I heard her ask from the kitchen.

I paced the floor. "No, thank you."

A Bible that looked like it was falling to pieces sat perched on a stool that acted as an end table, a pair of wire-rimmed glasses on top. It was all so very bare and plain, but filled with love. Quite a contrast to our house, which had expensive, brand new furniture. The walls were painted and embellished with molding, and pictures and decorations had been strategically bought and positioned by my mother. We even had radiators in our rooms. Yet somehow, it always felt empty.

"What on God's green earth is this for?" I heard Mrs. Williams ask.

I stepped forward, meeting her in the kitchen entryway. She had opened the envelope, peering at me with wide, disbelieving eyes.

I couldn't tell if she was offended or not, unsure of what to say. "Mom heard about what happened last week."

Her hand rested against her waist as if she couldn't breathe. "There must be fifty dollars in there. I couldn't possibly accept this."

Hands behind my back, I stared at the exposed bills as she tried to hand it back to me. We had plenty of money; my mother wouldn't want me to take it back.

"Then, take it for James," I said.

To be such a stern older woman, it surprised me to see her eyes fill with tears. She hesitated before stuffing it in her apron pocket. "Your mother and her generosity. She is a wonder. Please tell her she didn't have to do that, but it is very much appreciated."

"We were both so sorry to hear it even happened," I said.

"Right in the middle of the day." She motioned toward the door and I started out with her. "I'd gone into town. They walked right into the house while James was out in the barn, found the money and took some of his clothes. The police investigated those POWs working for Mr. Stewart, and even notified the camp officials to search their belongings, but they didn't find anything. They think it was a vagrant; if that's the case, he's long gone by now. I'm just glad they didn't take my wedding rings. Thank heavens they didn't rob anyone else. It would be prudent to keep a sharp eye out, especially with you being home so often, alone with the baby."

This chilled me. Lucy and I usually slept in my parents' bed when Mom worked at night. Dad's guns were in there, but maybe I would begin propping a chair against the door while we slept from now on.

I got on my bike. "I should be getting back."

"Well, thank you again. Please let your mother know how grateful I am."

"I will for sure. Goodbye, Mrs. Williams."

I nearly crashed on the way down the driveway. The yard was too bumpy for my thin bicycle tires. The paved road was smooth, and I coasted back toward my house with ease.

It frightened me to think of someone robbing a house that close. What if the POWs had been working in Mrs. Williams' field instead of Mr. Stewart's? Our house would have probably been targeted. It didn't make me grateful that her house had been burgled instead of ours, but I was glad the Germans' presence reduced the chances; too many witnesses.

Mr. Stewart, along with the two guards, stared at me as I pedaled by. It unsettled me, and I turned my gaze ahead, wondering why they weren't watching the POWs work as they usually did. Turning into my driveway, I slowed down, coming to a stop upon seeing a taxi in the driveway.

Mr. Appleby, who owned the drugstore, was coming outside. He hesitated as he saw me, and I tried to pin down why he would be there. Remembering the black car—the Jefferson Hotel—I gaped at my misfortune, catching them under such incriminating circumstances. He was nowhere near as handsome as my father. How dare my mother send me down the street under the guise of charity when she was just trying to get me out of the house to see her lover.

Mr. Appleby frowned, putting on his fedora as he started down the steps. And then I heard my mother scream.

Throwing my bike on the grass, I ran past Mr. Appleby without so much as a word, flinging open the screen door.

Mom was at the bottom of the stairs, her knees bent beneath her as she wailed. Lucy was crying in equal volume beside her looking terrified, her soft, plump cheeks red and wet, her fingers hooked in her mouth. Disoriented, I didn't know what to do; I didn't understand what had happened, until the wadded up telegram fell from my mother's hand.

I couldn't breathe; I couldn't move. I wasn't even sure I was really standing there, that this was happening. My mother screamed, sobbing, her forehead pressed to the hardwood floor. Lucy had crawled over to her, her hand on my mother's leg for attention. She didn't understand.

I crouched down to pick up the yellow, unpropitious telegram. Tears I hadn't even realized I was crying leaked onto my hands as I spread it open, yanking at its edges to smooth it:

```
MRS. MIRIAM J. WYNDHAM
925 - MAGNOLIA LANE DR.

THE   SECRETARY   OF   WAR   DESIRES   ME   TO
EXPRESS   HIS   DEEP   REGRET   THAT   YOUR   SON
PRIVATE   AMOS   H.   WYNDHAM   WAS   KILLED   IN
ACTION   EIGHT   JUNE   IN   FRANCE.   CONFIRMING
LETTER FOLLOWS.

                    ULIO, THE ADJUTANT GENERAL
```

I shook my head. It had been almost a month; my brother had been dead for almost a month. I kept staring at his name, imagining his playful smile, remembering his jokes.

"Mom..." I fell to my knees, reaching for my weeping mother. "Mom, I...I'm so sorry."

"Don't touch me!" she shrieked, jerking away at the stroke of my hand. She pulled at her hair, rocking back and forth. "He's dead. My son is dead!"

Lucy howled as my mother did. I picked her up, holding her against me to comfort us both.

I didn't know how long the three of us sat there in the floor. My mother continued to moan, though Lucy calmed down once she was in my arms. Silent tears streamed my own cheeks, and I wondered if there had been some mistake; if maybe, a few months from now, he'd come back to us in the end, like in a film.

Lucy fell asleep in my arms. My mother reached for the crumpled telegram, standing as if she were drunk. She didn't speak to me, didn't even look at me, as she staggered to the kitchen, opening the door to Amos' room and shutting it behind her.

I kissed Lucy's damp head. I thought of Friedrich. I wanted to run to him; I wanted him to see me crying as I hurtled outside, finding a way to get to me out in the glade. I needed to talk to someone; someone who could console me, someone who could help me work through this in my head.

But I didn't. I wouldn't be like my mother, like my father; I wouldn't run from the people who needed me. Lucy was too little and my mother was too hysterical. Someone had to do it.

I carried Lucy over to the couch, laying her beside me. Hands trembling, I picked up the receiver, dialing the long distance operator. The switchboard operator at Wyndham Aero Industries transferred me to my father's secretary.

"Mr. Wyndham's office. This is Mary. How may I help you?"

I sniffled. "I need to speak to Mr. Wyndham, please. This is his daughter, Cassie."

"Of course. One moment, please."

The line clicked. I ran my fingers through Lucy's fine, blonde hair. I felt as selfish as I did selfless for calling. As much as I didn't want to say it out loud—making it real—as much as I didn't want my father to hear it, it felt like an anvil bound to my back. Telling my father wouldn't make it go away, but at least it might feel as if I weren't carrying it alone.

Able to see the fields through the window, I teared up. Friedrich would have sympathized; Friedrich would have asked me how I felt. He would have let me cry.

The line clicked again. "I'm sorry, Cassandra, he's in a meeting right now and can't be disturbed. May I take a message?"

I closed my eyes, the warm affection I felt for my father now scalding me with ire. "No. No, absolutely not. I don't care what he's doing or what important people he's talking to, I need him on the phone *now*!"

My voice had broken. Tears were streaming freely down my face. The line was quiet.

"I'll see what I can do," Mary finally said.

She put me on hold again. I could feel myself unraveling, unfamiliar with this degree of grief, overwhelmed by its strength. I didn't understand it; I didn't know how to handle it.

The line clicked.

"Cassandra?"

I burst into tears. "Dad, you have to come home. Please. You have to come home right away. I don't know what to do."

"Shh. Calm down, calm down, Sweetheart," he said. "What's the matter? What's wrong?"

I tried to suppress a sob, unable to contain it any longer. "Dad, Amos...He's...we got a Western Union today. Dad..."

I cried. There was no sound at the other end of the phone.

"Daddy, *please* come home."

It was a moment before he spoke in a subdued voice. "Hold on a second."

The line clicked, and I waited until it clicked again.

"Tell me what it said," he said.

I told him what I remembered. "Do you think there's a chance there was a mistake?"

Woeful, he sighed. I thought I heard a crack in his voice. "No. No, Sweetheart, I don't think there is. Where's your mother?"

I glanced in her direction. "She locked herself in Amos' room."

"How's Lucy?"

"Confused." I teared up, seeing how peaceful she was sleeping. "She doesn't understand. I don't either, Dad."

"I know, baby." He sniffed. "I don't either."

We sat in a reciprocal silence. I continued sniffling. "Do you want me to see if Mom will come to the phone?"

He breathed in. "No. No, just...just leave her alone. Let me, um...let me finish up some things here. When she comes out, tell her I'll be home by morning." He sighed. "I love you, Cassandra. Don't worry, okay? Everything's going to be all right."

"I love you too, Dad," I said, pinching off a couple of tears.

I sat there, watching Lucy as she slept long after I'd hung up the phone. She looked so innocent, so serene. I longed to switch places with her, if only for a second. I wondered if she would even remember him.

I cried into my hand at the thought. Shuffling with lethargy toward the front door, I lowered onto the porch swing, hugging myself. It surprised me to see Friedrich had moved much closer. He took into consideration the men closest to him before looking straight at me.

He hadn't even spoken; I could read the question on his face. I shook my head in response, to say that I was *not* okay, before drowning in another surge of tears. I tried not to imagine him—Amos. I tried not to conjure the images of what he might've seen last, or how others had seen it happen, or how they'd found him; bleeding, his lifeless green eyes aimless. I prayed with desperation to know he hadn't suffered. Every time I remembered his famous smile or one of his jokes, I broke down all over again. He was never coming home, his body covered and buried in some shallow grave in France. He was never going to make me laugh again. He wouldn't return as a war hero, finish college and take over Wyndham Aero Industries. I could only imagine their hopelessness, their despair, how bleak the Wyndham name now appeared, because my brother was dead.

I dreaded Wednesday night. Pastor Gilbert held memorial services for any member of the church that died in combat overseas. He had called my mother Tuesday morning after hearing the news through the grapevine. I wished he wouldn't do it so soon. Putting it off another week would have allowed me more time to soak in the reality of it all. I was beginning to understand that people's condolences or offers for prayer were more for us than for Amos. My brother was gone forever; sympathy and prayers couldn't bring him back.

My parents, Lucy and I sat through the service. It felt better having Dad there, though he would be leaving that night. It was the longest he'd stayed since Amos had left for training. I had cried when I saw him, hugging his waist as he held Lucy, too. My mother hadn't left Amos' room since going into it. I had sat on the couch while Lucy played, listening to my mother crying in the other room amid my dad's soft murmurs. I wondered if my brother's death and my father's presence might be enough to knock sense into her.

My father and I had no time to talk alone while he'd been there, though I doubted I would have mentioned my suspicions even if we had. It would have only caused more turmoil, and I expected my mother would be changed after this.

I kept my eyes glued to the hymnals on the back of the pew as Pastor Gilbert spoke. The black apparel everyone wore did nothing to lighten the mood, and I tuned out the sniffles around me. My mother was grave, deathly still beside me. A couple of times, lone tears would varnish one of her cheeks, but she held everything in. My father had reached for her hand once, and it shocked me when she removed herself from his grasp. It surprised me even more when my father acted as if he hadn't even noticed.

At the end, Pastor Gilbert left the pulpit first and we were to follow. I didn't look up as we passed by those who had come to remember Amos; those who had come to grieve with us.

They sang a song in the sanctuary behind us, giving us a few minutes alone with Pastor Gilbert. He talked with my parents, and I longed to go sit in the car rather than face all these people. Knowing how it would only further upset my mother, I remained by my family, unable to smile.

People hugged me and shook my hand. They told me they were sorry, that we were in their prayers and how good my brother was. I felt no comfort. I wanted someone to hold me. I wanted to scream; I wanted to cry. I wanted someone to say they'd stay with me until it stopped hurting.

I spotted Donald in line with Holly. Remembering how I'd never returned his phone call, I knew that right now, I didn't have to worry about him asking me about it.

"Hey." He hugged me. "I'm so sorry, Cassie. He was a good guy. He'll be missed. If you need anything, please let me know."

"Thank you."

Holly hugged me next. "I still can't believe it. I always thought if anyone..." She pursed her lips. "I'm sorry."

I nodded, tears welling in my eyes. All the great things Amos still had to do were left undone. The Wyndham name would die out, and the future of Wyndham Aero Industries was shrouded in mystery, just as the details of my brother's demise were. If the Army hadn't made a mistake in counting him among the casualties, and if God hadn't made a mistake in taking him, what did that leave us with? He hadn't even made it past the beaches; it wasn't supposed to happen like this.

Holly and Donald stayed with me, which I found I was grateful for; it kept me from having to talk to too many others. When they finally left, I didn't want to stand there anymore. Seeing it was dark, I decided to slip outside.

I didn't say anything to my parents as I left their side, skulking toward the door. I pushed on the door handle, feeling the cool night breeze slink in around me.

"Cassie." I turned to see Pastor Gilbert approaching. "Do you have a second?"

Glancing at my parents, who were still talking to congregants, I closed the door.

"How are you doing?" he asked.

I shrugged, trying to suppress my tears. "I don't really know right now."

He nodded. "That's to be expected."

I sniffed. "I'm trying to be grateful that he's where he is now instead of over there; that he doesn't have to suffer anymore. But it still doesn't take away the pain."

"It's just going to take time," he comforted.

Lucy was hugging my father's neck, refusing to look at anyone. She hadn't understood when Amos had left, and she cried out of incomprehension when my parents told her Bubby was in heaven with Jesus now.

"I know how difficult things are for your family right now," Pastor Gilbert said. "I want you to know that no one will think less of you if you decide not to return to the camp."

I looked at him. "Oh. I...I was planning on going back."

He looked uncertain. "I admire your enthusiasm, Cassie, but I'd prefer you really think it over. We love having you. I'm just concerned this could affect your attitude toward the prisoners."

If only he knew in my case, that was the last thing he had to worry about. "I've thought about it, Pastor Gilbert. I want to go back; I *need* to go back."

He gave a vague nod. "God doesn't overlook these things, Cassie. Your strength is going to reflect Him to others. If you have no comfort yet, then I hope you find some in that."

I stared at him a moment, though I diverted my eyes as they watered over. "Thank you, Pastor Gilbert."

I didn't pay as much attention to Friedrich the rest of that week. I hoped he didn't think I'd forgotten him, or that I now collectively loathed his entire race. It wasn't that. I was still so overwhelmed by the emotions the news of my brother's death garnered that I had little room in my heart for anything else. I couldn't eat more than a few bites at every meal before getting sick to my stomach, thinking of Amos. Sometimes, I didn't even notice Lucy talking to me, who, for the most part, was the only one carrying on as if nothing had changed. It was when she became aware of the far-off look in my eyes that she'd remember what my parents had told her. She'd stop what she was doing, putting her little arms over my leg to get my attention.

"What's the matter, baby?" I'd ask.

Sometimes, she'd say it right away. Other times, I'd have to ask her again before she'd answer.

"Bee not tum home?" she would ask.

I would cup her little face to kiss her, sometimes hugging her so she wouldn't see me cry. "No, baby. Bubby's not coming home. But he's always here." I'd point to her heart. I didn't want her to feel as lost as I did; I tried to be strong for her because I needed someone to be strong for me.

My mother didn't speak to us much at all. The only time a word escaped her lips was whenever Lucy asked her a question. She didn't really have a choice, because Lucy would repeat it, thinking my mother hadn't heard her, until she responded. Even then she was concise, austere. She kept from looking at either one of us, when she could help it. I knew she was keeping it all corked inside; it was just a matter of time before she popped.

Friday night, after another wordless dinner, I withdrew to the family room after clearing the table. Lucy was already there, sitting in the middle of the floor playing with her dolls. I sat on the sofa, cringing as she combed through their yarn hair. Unfolding the Bible study worksheet, I glanced over it before searching for the first verse in my Bible. I hadn't been doing this long when I saw my mother's form in the entryway from the corner of my eye.

"What are you doing?"

I looked at the frayed hair of Lucy's dolls before realizing she meant me.

"Oh." I turned the sheet to the next page. "I'm just looking over the material for tomorrow."

"What?"

I looked at her. "For Bible study tomorrow."

Her eyes widened, hands slowly rising to rest on her hips. "What do you mean for Bible study tomorrow?" She aimed her finger at me. "You're not going back to that camp."

She stomped away. My eyes fell on my sister, still playing with her baby dolls. That tone was just the tip of her iceberg. If I challenged this, I risked being sunk by the full body of her wrath.

I closed my Bible, setting it and the worksheets aside. In the kitchen, Mom was scrubbing at a plate with excessive force.

"What do you mean I'm not going back?"

"I *said* you're not going back and that's final," she said, her tone like the warning rattle of a snake. "End of discussion."

There were tremors in my hands, but I wasn't sure if it was from fear this time. "I have to, Mom."

The dish clinked heavily against the sink. "Don't argue with me, Cassandra. Not this time."

I made my way to the table. As much as I was used to conceding defeat, retreating into another room to sulk by myself wasn't an option to me this time.

My voice was steady and calm. "Mom, I miss him, too. I loved him, too. I looked up to him and...and I still don't know how I'm going to go on without him. But Mom, I can't ignore what God's called me to do."

I watched her jaw tighten as another dish slammed into the basin, my mother scouring it with tenacity. "Sometimes I think you misunderstand what God is saying."

"Then why else would I go?"

My mother shook her head. "You're not going back."

I clenched my fingers around the back of the dining chair. "I'm sorry, Mom. But I am."

"No, you're *not*!" The plate in her hands shattered at her feet. "They *murdered* him! They murdered my son! How dare you!" she screamed, yanking on one of the dining chairs. "How dare you! How could you even *think* about going back after what they've done?"

"Because this is bigger than me. It's bigger than you, it's bigger than this war. Don't ask me to choose between what you want and what God wants. You of all people should understand. You know who I'm going to choose."

"I'm asking you to choose your brother!"

"But they are my brothers, too."

My mother struck me with such force that I fell against the refrigerator, sliding to the floor. Shocked, I pressed my hand to my cheek as it pulsated.

"How dare you!" she bellowed. "You are a shame to this family and a shame to me!"

My eyes were watering. She was trying to subdue me, but the pain in her eyes belied her fury.

I began to cry. Not because I was afraid, not because my cheek was throbbing, not even because of my brother. I cried because I could finally see the devastation she had fought so hard to conceal, a black cloud behind her eyes.

I saw it all, but her wants and emotions were no longer allowed to supersede my own feelings. "I love you, Mom. But I still have to go."

"You don't love me and you certainly didn't love your brother."

"Yes I *did!*" I screamed. "This has nothing to do with Amos. I'm going back because it's what I'm supposed to do."

"Does it mean *nothing* to you that I don't want you to go?"

"It means everything," I cried, "but it won't change the fact that he's gone. It won't take away the hurt and it will not bring him back!"

"No, but it will make me feel better!"

"Then hit me again!" I yelled. "Hit me until you feel better, because I'm still going."

Her chest billowed as she breathed, speechless. I held back more tears, clamping my jaw shut, refusing to look away from her.

A little hiccup broke the tension. Lucy stood in the doorway, finger in her mouth as her lower lip stuck out. She rubbed at her eye with her little fist.

"Lucy," I whispered. I reached for her. "Come here, baby. I'm sorry. Come here."

Lucy burst into tears. Arms locking around my neck, she dropped into my lap. Her tears soaked my hair and I closed my eyes as I rocked her.

Ceramic crunched in front of me. I opened my eyes just in time to see my mother tramping into the living room. Her door slammed upstairs.

My mother had never struck me before. It was humiliating, and oddly gratifying. She hadn't hit me out of malice; she'd been frustrated by my noncompliance, my

171

boldness unnerving her. Despite what she believed, I hadn't done what I did to demean my brother's memory. I did it because I believed in something and I would honor it, even at my own cost.

My cheek ached, but I would suffer it without protest.

Because no matter what happened now, she and I both knew she couldn't stop me.

Eleven

I woke up the next morning with a tender cheek. My reflection showed it had discolored some overnight, small blotches of plum and pink indicating where her hand had alighted. I put on a little extra make-up, not caring if she noticed; I'd rather her notice the cosmetics than the bruise.

When it was time for me to go, I left Lucy in my mother's room as usual. Mom never opened her eyes or rolled over, making me wonder if she was still sleeping or ignoring me. I didn't care either way, grateful to avoid another attempt to thwart me.

As content as I felt riding to the camp, I didn't mean for the tears to come when I saw the concern on Friedrich's face. Though he tried to appear blasé, I detected the urgency in his steps. All my tension and anguish dissolved, if only for the hour, as he sat down across from me.

"What is happening?" he asked quietly.

I retained my smile even though it was an uncomfortable one now. "It was my brother."

"They take him prisoner?"

I knew he didn't believe that; he only hoped so for my sake. I shook my head, determined not to crumble so no one would see and think I shouldn't have been there. Friedrich slid his hand across the table before he balled it up, pulling it back.

"You are not knowing how bad I want to run to you," he whispered. "How much I want to be the one holding you and telling you everything is okay."

I pursed my eyelids shut, fighting back tears. How could what I'd needed all this time have been his first instinct? While I was hidden, invisible to everyone else, how was it that he had full view of the raw, bare person underneath?

His eyes flinched, his voice becoming severe. "What is this on your face?"

I must have wiped off too much of the make-up, revealing the bruise. I tried to hide it from him now.

"Someone *hit* you?"

His voice had raised, and I peeked around to make sure no one had heard. His jaw clenched, along with his fist on the table. "Who does this to you?"

I gulped. "My mother."

"Why?"

I made the worksheet my focal point. "She didn't want me to come anymore."

"And you come anyway."

I nodded.

His expression softened. "I wish I am as strong as you."

"You are strong."

He shook his head. "Not like you."

There was so much tenderness in his gaze that I wondered what it would be like to have his arms around me.

We did our Bible study, though with less zeal than we had in the past. My head was too overrun with everything at home. I would've felt guilty for my atypical lack of interest, but I spent most of the hour talking to God in my head anyway.

My stomach was in knots as Pastor Gilbert told us to wrap up our lesson. Not knowing if we'd get another moment alone before next Saturday, I yearned to make these last minutes stretch. I gathered my belongings with reluctance.

Friedrich had been watching me. "Your mother hits you because your brother is killed by one of us. Right?"

I lingered, hugging my Bible to my chest. "The world wants me to hate you, Friedrich."

He eyed me with such fondness that it seemed impossible that I'd ever feel sad or weak or scared ever again. "Then we are either perfect together or wrong together, because the world wants me to hate you, too."

I raised my shoulders. "So what do we do? What happens now that we've gotten ourselves into such a complicated mess?"

He watched me. Eyes flickering toward his Bible, he leaned towards me. "We love, in defiance of them all."

His eyes did not lose their solemnity, never lighting up as if it were just a playful nuance. Was he saying what I thought he was saying? I felt too stunned to even think, much less respond. He picked up his Bible, walking slowly toward the exit.

I couldn't sleep that night because I couldn't get him out of my head—I didn't think my spirits could ever be dampened again.

I had been wrong—quite literally.

It began to storm Sunday after church. I thought I could make it through a day without seeing him, but I hadn't counted on a week going by. It was as if the rain was never going to let up. It didn't stop for a break or slow down, keeping us under an almost constant downpour. I had convinced myself that the skies would surely be clear by Saturday afternoon, but they weren't. I called Pastor Gilbert Saturday morning to tell him I wouldn't be able to make it to the camp. Under different circumstances, I would've chanced asking my mother to drive me, but after what had happened the week before, I wouldn't dare give her the opportunity to revel in having that kind of power over me.

I was surprised my mother didn't say more regarding what had happened between us. Never before had she allowed my scarce mutinies to go unpunished. I doubted she'd forgotten; instead, I assumed she was so emotionally exhausted that she didn't want to trouble herself with me. She was always quiet, though the darkness that had been in her eyes was no longer there.

One day, I opened my door, headed down the hall to the bathroom. I heard her voice drifting up from the living room and paused, wondering if we had a visitor. When no one else spoke, I surmised that she was on the telephone. It was difficult for me to hear over the rain pounding on the roof, but I leaned over the banister to listen.

Her voice was low with intention. "Don't be ridiculous. Do you think I want a scandal? Especially now? Yes, but...yes...I know what I said, but I also told you I wasn't making any promises. It's just...I really need to be with you." I could hear her sniffling, my blood freezing in my veins. "No. I won't do that. I...I can't. We could meet somewhere again. You have to understand, nothing's changed. I just need someone right now and I want so badly for it to be you....Maybe someday it can be. Just not right now. I'm going to need more time."

I gripped the rail, heart pounding in my chest. She'd hung up the phone. At least she hadn't told him she loved him. She loved my father—or at least, I thought she did. This man was a dirtbag, a homewrecker that had no business talking to (or doing anything else with) my mother. As sympathetic as I'd been at first, the thought of my father working in Maryland, unsuspecting and unaware made me sick. He didn't deserve this any more than she deserved to live like she didn't have a husband.

As upset as it made me that he was never home, I still loved my father. The idea of him being hurt in such a way was unfathomable—especially when he'd just found out his son had been killed. I couldn't imagine his heartache if he knew my mother was unfaithful.

Worst of all, I feared if he knew, he'd never come back—even for Lucy and me.

Sunday night, the skies were clear. Beads of water dripped from the sleek, viridescent leaves on the tree outside my window. I woke up each morning, full of hope. It had been over a week since I'd seen him, but the prisoners were nowhere in sight. Every day, I bounded from bed, desiccated by the disappointment of finding the fields empty.

Anticipating yet another anticlimax, I rolled out of bed on Wednesday, slinking over to my bay window. My heart leapt into my throat to see the POWs back at work, Friedrich near the edge of the field by the tree-line.

By himself.

Dizzy with impatience, I sorted through dress after dress in my closet, none of them appealing to me. An old, navy, crepe one my mother had bought for me years ago hung forgotten in the back. I'd never worn it except to try it on once, my mother saying, on second thought, that the sweetheart neckline was too old for me.

I pulled it out, the material flowing like water over my fingertips. I smiled; surely, I had grown into it since then.

Slipping it on in front of the mirror, it was like looking at a different person. There were no puffed sleeves, no Peter Pan collar, no bows, and the skirt didn't flare out. The bodice hugged my waist, hinting at the shape of my hips as it draped to my knees. The layered side wrap was elegant, as were the notched, fluttery sleeves. The sweetheart neckline was either less offensive or more offensive—I didn't know which—now that the bust wasn't as empty as it used to be.

I rushed to take the rags out of my hair, pinning up the sides with bobby pins. I put on my foundation and blush, applying a little more of the latter since my mother hadn't noticed it after I covered up the bruise she'd left on my cheek.

In such a grown-up dress, my reflection felt lacking. Scrutinizing my face, I watched my own brow lift as my most daring idea yet crossed my mind.

Cracking my door open, I peered out into the hallway, straining my ears. I could hear Lucy's high-pitched voice downstairs, as well as the murmur of my mother's responses. Sneaking into my parents' room, I pulled open the center drawer to Mom's vanity, extracting the liner, mascara and lash curler stored there.

I'd never put it on myself, but I'd seen her do it enough times to get the gist. Still, I wasn't heavy with the liner, dainty as I traced the rim of my upper lid. Then, I curled my lashes, topping it off with the mascara.

Returning them to their rightful place, I stared at myself, agape. I'd never seen myself like this. Perhaps it was vain, but I couldn't believe how pretty I looked—how feminine, rather than juvenile. Many fights with my mother began to materialize on the horizon; after this, I didn't think I could go back to wearing just foundation and blush.

I tiptoed down the stairs, hoping to sneak out the door before she could see me. She and Lucy were in the kitchen.

I pushed open the screen door, calling out over my shoulder. "I'm going to go ride my bike, Mom."

"You haven't even had breakfast yet."

"I'm not hungry."

I pedaled down the driveway. Friedrich saw me and I gave him a meaningful glance as I rolled by.

On the road, I couldn't get to my entrance to the woods fast enough. Certain that no one was watching me, I deposited my bike where I'd left it before.

Smelling the honeysuckle in the air, I perched myself on the fallen tree and waited. My nervous fingers picked at one another as I sat, listening. I could hear the whisper of the breeze grazing the leaves overhead, accompanied by the trills of sparrows and blue jays. I hadn't been there long when I heard the crackle of footsteps in front of me.

I stood as he came into sight, propping the shovel in his hand against the tree.

"I was starting to think you'd forgotten about me," I said.

He chuckled. "I hope you know this can never be true."

I almost reached my anxious arms out to him, anticipating that his would encircle me. I was glad I hadn't though, as he stopped a few inches before me, hands in his pockets. He tilted his head. "You look very pretty today."

"For once."

"What?"

I looked up at him as I sat down. "I just—I've always pictured myself as kind of a plain-looking person."

"Well, believe me, I see many girls," he said, sitting down next to me. "You are not plain."

I wanted to say thank you, but I wasn't convinced. "I'm sorry I didn't get to see you Saturday. It was raining so hard, I didn't have a choice."

"I think this is why." He reached down, ripping a handful of grass from the ground. "I have to sit with Holly and Egon. It is the least interesting discussion I am having since this program starts."

I chortled. "What was this week's topic? I've forgotten."

"Family."

I watched him tear at each blade of grass, tossing the smallest pieces away.

"You've never really told me about your family," I said.

He snorted. "There is not much to tell."

"That can't be true. What did you mean that day when you said we had a lot in common but that we dealt with things differently?"

He glimpsed at me. "My father is a lot like yours, except he works at home. He is a farmer. I am afraid of him until I am about eleven, which is only a year before he dies."

This disturbed me. "Why were you afraid of him?"

"He is intimidating. And I can never please him."

"What happened to him?"

He sighed, flicking a couple shreds of grass away. "One of the horses startles. It kicks him in the head. Kills him."

"Oh, Friedrich..."

"I am not sure what is worse: my father dying in this manner, or my brother deciding this makes him man of the house."

I angled myself toward him. "Tell me about your brother."

He grinned to himself, as if enjoying some kind of inside joke. "Hans. He is older than me. He is the favorite of my father. I am the favorite of my mother—the *baby*. Hans considers it a sport, pointing this out at everyone; family, friends, girls..."

He leaned over, tearing up more grass. I wondered how many girls Hans could've said this in front of to upset Friedrich. "Where is he now?"

"Home. He works for the Gestapo—police," he clarified.

"How does your family feel about you being over here?"

"My mother is happy. I know she prefers I sit out the war than be shot at in Africa or France or Russia. She says Hans is happy, too, but I hear otherwise when I get home."

This surprised me. "Why?"

"Because I am a prisoner."

"Wouldn't he be happy? If Amos had been captured..."

I tapered off, thinking of my brother. It was still difficult for me to accept that he was gone. All I could remember was his smile, his laugh, the carefree manner of his speech. It was confounding to think that someone so alive could die in such a cruel, senseless way.

Friedrich's voice was tender. "I am sorry, Cassie. It is different for us. We are supposed to die before being a prisoner. When I get home, I expect Hans tells me this."

"Is your brother the one who makes fun of you for playing the violin?"

"Naturally. He never touches a musical instrument. He says a man's hands are for work. He is stronger than me, even though the last time we fight, I break his arm in two places. He is braver than me, even though I get an Iron Cross for my actions in Africa and he stays home to guard citizens. And he is the smartest, even though he thinks only of making fun of me. He is everything I am not."

I picked up a clover to tear off the petals. "Your brother's stupid."

Friedrich looked at me, snickering. He dusted the shards of grass from his pant legs. "He is. Enough about me. What kind of mischief are you making since I last see you?"

"Well, let's see: I eavesdropped on my mother talking to the man she's cheating on my father with. I think that counts as mischief."

"Really?"

I sighed. "I don't want to believe it. I didn't, at first. But there are too many things pointing to an affair. I just...I can't believe she'd do this, especially now, after finding out about my brother. She's so selfish. She only thinks about herself—which is ironic, because that's what she's always accusing me of."

Friedrich continued picking at the grass while I plucked another clover.

"What are you going to do?" he asked.

"I don't know. My dad should know. I just don't have the heart to tell him. I probably shouldn't anyway—right?"

"I know you want not to hurt your father. But I think it is of concern for you."

I considered him. "You think I should tell him?"

He made a sound in the back of his throat. "If she has an affair, the consequences of this are affecting your entire family—including you and your sister."

I stared at him. "What do you think I should do?"

"I know not. You must decide this." He snapped a twig in half, tossing one of the pieces into my lap. His blue eyes were impish as I chuckled at him.

"You look different today," he said.

"Bad different?"

"No. Definitely not."

I toyed with the dry twig he'd flung at me. "I'm wearing make-up today."

"You are not needing make-up," he said.

I was silent for a moment. "Do you really mean it when you say things like that?"

"I say nothing if I am not meaning it."

"It's just that...you say it a lot. I always thought...you know...you were just being mean, mocking the ugly girl."

He scoffed. "What?"

He'd paused, pieces of broken sticks in both hands, the amusement on his face causing me to look away. "For instance, the day we met, they called my name and one of the prisoners stopped you and said something to you. My hair was messed up that day and I'm not allowed to wear make-up so I thought—"

Friedrich threw his head back with laughter. Horrified, I peered toward the trees.

His fingertips were cool as he tugged at my chin to look at him. "You really are not knowing, are you? He is not talking about your hair, your make-up. He asks me what kind of friends I have, getting me the most beautiful girl in the room."

I was dumbstruck. "Are you...are you being serious?"

He laughed. "Of course!"

His hand hadn't left my face, and I closed my eyes as he caressed my cheek. I envisioned him pulling me in, imagining what it would feel like to have his lips against mine. The tip of his thumb brushed my chin and heat flashed through my body like an out of control forest fire. His eyes focused there and for a moment, I thought he might actually kiss me.

He frowned as he reconnected with my eyes, pulling his hand away. "It is wrong, you know, that you cannot see what I see; that no one tells you everyday how special you are —how beautiful."

The bark from the tree trunk we were sitting on dug into my palms. "Maybe that's because you're the only one who sees it."

"No." He shook his head. "No, everyone sees it. The problem is there are people in your life who are afraid of it. The day you catch on to who you really are, you are untouchable. It is intimidating."

I'd never had the impertinence to think of myself like that, but I liked the way he made it sound. It made me wonder if it could be true. "Then what about you? Why aren't you afraid of it?"

"I tell you, I am a fighter. I am made for such a challenge. I fight until I reach you or until I die; whichever comes first."

I contemplated him and he smiled, lobbing another twig at me when my mother's voice echoed in the distance. Uneasy, Friedrich looked in her direction.

"It's okay," I told him. "I told her I was riding my bike."

Another voice called out my name, and I looked over my shoulder in surprise. "That was my dad."

I turned to Friedrich as I rose. "I'm sorry, I've got to go. He's not usually back so soon."

"Wait."

Chill bumps afflicted my skin, his hand grazing down my arm as I went past him. "I see you Saturday?"

"As long as it doesn't rain." He was holding my hand. I couldn't bring myself to pull away from his touch, even as my body flashed with heat.

"I am not back here until Tuesday," he said. "I try and sneak away again, so watch for me."

I nodded. His thumb stroked my knuckles. It was an instinctive reaction for me to do the same.

"Be careful," I whispered, "when you go back out."

He simpered. "You too."

With one last long look at each other, we parted ways.

Intoxicated with bliss, I managed to find my bike somehow. Seeing my father's black Plymouth DeSoto in the driveway, I propped my bike against the porch. Friedrich hadn't returned to the fields yet, and I dashed inside.

Dad was playing with Lucy in the living room. She giggled as he lifted her, her little fingers curled around his wrists. My mother looked hostile, unsmiling as she observed them with crossed arms.

"Dad!"

He released Lucy to hug me. "Surprise."

"But it's a week day," I said. "How are you here?"

He looked cheerful, more than usual. "It's my company, isn't it? I missed my girls."

His bronze eyes wandered over to my mother. By the look on her face, I thought she was annoyed. I wondered if his unexpected appearance foiled the liaison I'd heard her planning with her lover.

Seemingly unimpressed with my father's reasoning, her eyes fell on me. She unhooked her arms, gaping at me. "What is that on your face?"

I ignored her, beaming up at my father. "Make-up."

It pleased me to see him smile, the unmistakable adoration in his eyes for me.

"You are *not* supposed to be wearing make-up, Cassandra," my mother said. "Go upstairs and wash it off right now."

"I just put it on for my bike ride," I reasoned. "And it's already on, so—

"*Now!* And change out of that dress while you're up there."

I wanted to hear my father tell me I looked pretty. I wanted him to tell my mother I was growing up and deserved this, just as he had done with Amos.

"Do as your mother says," he said instead.

I waffled before starting for the stairs. On the way up, a thought occurred to me. I turned on my heel, looking at my mother over the banister. "I guess this means you won't be leaving again this weekend since Dad's home, right?"

My father had heard, even with Lucy squealing, swinging from his hands. I got a thrill at seeing my mother's eyes widen as she glanced at my father. "No. I'll be here."

I nodded, trotting up the stairs with a murky grin. I didn't know if such an innocuous question would raise any suspicion in him, but I hoped I'd at least planted a seed that might sprout later.

After washing my face and changing into my gingham dress, I returned downstairs to see my father pulling on his jacket. "Where would you like to go for lunch?"

I paused. "We're going out?"

"Of course. It'll be a treat for you and Lucy. Besides, I'd say your mother deserves a break, wouldn't you?"

I was astounded by this, considering my father usually bolted himself in his study from the time he got home until he left. Dining together meant spending quality time with us.

Friedrich was busy, unaware that I'd even come out with my family to get in my mother's car. My parents were engaged in conversation in the front seat and I peered out the window, watching his form until he was out of sight. Forehead to the glass, I closed my eyes, reveling in the reminiscent brush across my chin, the clamminess of his hand gripping mine. If my parents had any inkling their daughter daydreamed about sharing a kiss with a German POW while they talked about where to go for lunch, I was certain my father would have swerved into a ditch.

My father took us to lunch at Giordano's, an upscale Italian family restaurant just outside of town. Lucy was the one who kept it from being uncomfortable. Not only was she the only one without any secrets, but she wasn't mindful of the deafening absence at the table. Though neither my parents nor I mentioned it, I knew we were all thinking about how—though we were all together—our family would never be whole again.

This awareness heightened during the newsreels that played at the matinee showing of *Once Upon a Time*, the new Cary Grant film my dad took us to see. Though we'd been chitchatting just before, the three of us went quiet as it played, showing images of American soldiers fighting overseas. I stared at the empty seat beside me, knowing that was where he would have been sitting.

Turning back to the screen, I tried to shut it out.

I had observed my mother's mannerisms toward my father the entire afternoon. Once, during lunch, her hand had been on the table. My father reached for it and she pulled it away—just as she had at church—tucking her hair behind her ear. My father didn't seem to even notice, going on about how he used to love Giordano's when he was younger. His obliviousness intrigued me while we waited in line at the theater. Every time he pressed his hand to her back, she'd step away, out of reach, crossing her arms. He'd just smile and joke around with Lucy and me as if nothing had happened.

Bringing Lucy out of the restroom and back into the lobby before the movie, it was almost embarrassing for me to see my father leaning on the concessions counter. He smiled like an adolescent boy trying to impress a girl, angled toward my mother, eyes glinting as he spoke. She shook her head, walking away. My dad remained in that position even once he was alone, in a daze as his jolly expression faded into something more grim. His eyes caught mine and he blinked, giving me a misleading grin before picking up the popcorn and drinks.

And that was when I realized that he knew.

Perhaps he was like me—without proof—but he knew. That was why he arranged a 'surprise' visit. He feigned ignorance for the same reason I did; to keep from forewarning her until he had the proper evidence.

My father spent little time in his study the rest of the weekend until he left Monday afternoon. After having spotted Friedrich nearby earlier that day, I had hoped for another opportunity to slip into the woods to meet him. I'd seen him on Saturday at Bible study, but we had to be reserved there for appearance's sake. Monday was ill-fated, however, since Lucy had gotten bored sitting with my parents as they talked in the kitchen. At my mother's insistence, I took Lucy outside to play, pushing her on the swing with Friedrich in view.

Tuesday morning, I ran to the window, seeing Friedrich just below, too close to some of the other prisoners. Biting my lower lip, I pushed my bay window open. I leaned on the seat in front of it, breathing in the summer air, praying he would meet my gaze.

When he finally did, I chuckled to see him pretend he hadn't. He continued pulling up radishes, slanting himself to get a better look at me. With reluctance, I left the window to get started on the day.

Lucy and I ate a quick breakfast before heading outside. I knew it would be a while before Friedrich and I could meet—if we got to at all. My mother would not be up for at least another hour or so and then Friedrich would go to lunch. Our only hope was the afternoon.

As the prisoners headed toward Mr. Stewart's barn for lunch, I took Lucy inside as well. They were just returning to work as my mother washed Lucy up at the kitchen sink. I took the opportunity to peek out the living room window, locating Friedrich near the corner of the field. I could hardly contain myself.

"I'm going to go for a walk, Mom," I called over my shoulder.

I sat on the porch swing, pretending to fix my shoelaces. Friedrich saw me, and I gave him a nod. If someone saw him going into the woods, I didn't want them to see me biking down the driveway, too. His movements were casual and calculated as always. I waited, adjusting my shoes as he disappeared between the trees. A vehicle was coming up the road. If I timed it right, I could be on the road after they passed my driveway.

Halfway down the gravel drive, I halted, the rusty, tomato-colored truck slowing, turning into our driveway.

My first thought was that it was my mother's lover. I felt an even stronger sense of dread upon seeing it was, in fact, Donald.

He smiled as he pulled up, parking next to me. "How do you like it?"

It backfired, the engine puttering beneath the hood. I made a quick glance toward the woods.

"It's nice," I said.

He turned off the ignition. "Thanks. My parents gave it to me. It's kind of an early birthday present—something for me to drive when I get back."

I nodded. I knew he wanted me to say something, but my mind was frantic, trying to figure out how to get rid of him.

"So what are you doing today?" he asked.

Think, I told myself.

"Oh, I...nothing really." *Just going off to the woods in secret to flirt with a German POW I can't stop thinking about.*

"I came over to see if you would go to dinner with me. Maybe see a movie afterwards?"

I almost said, *"I just went to the movies,"* but even in my irritation, I couldn't excuse being so rude.

"Uh—well," I said, thinking about how Friedrich was waiting for me, "My mom probably won't let me go. I'm kind of not allowed to...go out." I refused to use the word 'date.'

He nodded, getting out of the truck. "Let me talk to her."

My grip tightened on my handlebars. "You don't have to do that."

"I don't mind," he said, walking up to my front porch. I nearly choked on my tongue, setting down my bike to follow.

I could hear Lucy's high-pitched voice coming from somewhere in the family room as Donald knocked. My mother appeared on the other side of the screen door with Lucy on her hip. I motioned toward him as she opened it. "Um—Donald's here."

His eyes went semi-circular as he smiled. "Afternoon, Mrs. Wyndham. I hope you don't mind. My parents got me a new truck for my birthday and I wanted to stop by and show Cassie."

"Oh, not at all," she said. "A new truck? That's exciting. When's your birthday?"

"Not until November, but I'm enlisting then. They wanted me to have time to enjoy it before I leave."

She nodded though something flashed across her visage—a thought of Amos.

"I thought since I'm all the way out here, maybe I could take Cassie to dinner and a movie."

My mother looked at me. With eyes full of dread, I shook my head just enough for her to notice.

"That sounds like fun. Cassie needs to get out of the house more often. I'm off tonight, anyway. It'll be nice," she said to me. "It'll be good to get your mind off things."

I glared at her, suddenly regretting my remark to my father about her leaving for the weekend. Maybe this was retaliation.

"Great!" Donald didn't hide his excitement as he turned to me. "Do you need anything before we go?"

"I...um...yes." Keeping my eyes down, I brushed inside past my mom.

I was in a near state of panic once I entered my room, slamming my door behind me. Friedrich had been waiting for me for at least fifteen minutes now. I ran to my window, but he was nowhere to be found; he was still in the woods.

My reflection revealed that my already light foundation and blush had worn away throughout the day. My hair was tatty from having been outside so much that morning. I didn't even consider tidying myself up at the risk of Donald thinking I did so for him. Grabbing my purse from my bed, I paced, trying to think of a way to get out of this bind or at least let Friedrich know I wasn't coming. I couldn't yell out the window; I couldn't have Donald wait a moment while I went traipsing through the woods. Even worse, I couldn't think of a sufficient excuse to give Donald for why I couldn't go.

Swallowing with an abnormally dry throat, I had nowhere to go but downstairs.

"I'll make sure she's home by nine-thirty, Mrs. Wyndham," Donald said before his half-moon eyes met mine. I gave him a weak grin.

"Thank you, Donald. Have fun, you two," she said.

Lucy had her little forefinger in her mouth as Donald and I walked away. My mother gave me a grin as she shut the screen door. Part of me wondered if she actually thought she was doing me a kindness.

I was still gazing towards the woods as Donald opened the passenger side door for me. "Where would you like to eat?"

I got in, not even looking at him as he shut the door. "I don't know."

He walked around the truck, sticking the key in the ignition. "I was thinking maybe Shaker's, across from the soda shop. That way we could go straight to the movie after—unless you want to go somewhere else, of course. I'll go anywhere."

"Shaker's is fine."

My eyes were glued to the trees as he pulled out onto the road. Anywhere else would be further than Shaker's. I wanted to spend as little time with him as I could. I cringed as I began to comprehend that I was with him; that Friedrich was waiting for me in our secret place. I couldn't understand how I had let this happen, allowing myself to be bullied into going with Donald. What was Friedrich going to think? Was he going to keep sitting there, waiting for me? Was he going to be angry that I'd never come? Was he going to be insulted that I'd gone with Donald instead of coming to him? I wanted to cry.

If Donald noticed the space I kept between the two of us, he didn't say so. On the way into town, I tucked the strap of my purse under the cover flap so I'd always have something in my hands. He insisted on opening my door for me, helping me down. His hand lingered in mine before I pulled away, scratching at an imaginary itch on my forehead and opposite elbow. With both hands gripping my pocketbook, I followed him to Shaker's. I wished it was winter so I might've had pockets to stow them in.

We kept up polite conversation between ordering and eating. Detailed responses were harder than one word replies, but I did my best.

"So what movie do you want to see?" he asked as we walked outside.

The street lights were lit up all the way to the cinema. I tried to recall all the films that had been playing when my father brought us last week. Most of them had been mushy, romance movies—which I liked, but I didn't want to give him any ideas. I remembered the poster to one about a woman trying to depict her husband's murder as an accident to collect money from their insurance company. That, I could handle. "How about *Double Indemnity*?"

"Nah, I saw it a couple weeks ago," he muttered. "What about *Since You Went Away*? It came out last Thursday."

That was about a woman's struggles after her husband left to fight in Europe. I wondered if he had ulterior motives for choosing that one.

Weakly, I agreed.

He bought the tickets, and I recognized a few people we knew from school. My stomach twisted as I imagined them believing Donald and I were together. The sad thing was there was nothing wrong with him; he was a good person, very friendly and warm. There was just the simple fact that I felt nothing more for him than friendship—I didn't *want* anything more than friendship with him.

I was shivering as we sat down. I wondered if the cinema owners did that on purpose to get boys to offer their coats to the girls.

Donald must have noticed. "Do you want to borrow my jacket?"

"Oh. No, thank you," I said, preferring to freeze.

Skin covered in goose bumps, I leaned toward the empty chair on my left. Donald kept his hand open and settled on the armrest between us. Nestling into the seat, I warmed my hands between my knees, counting down the minutes until the movie was over.

Halfway through the movie, he yawned. My toes curled as he stretched, his left arm inching its way down behind me. My body remained in the same uninviting position, refusing to budge. There was no way I was going to lean closer to him, making him think I liked the way he was stroking my shoulder. I grew cross with telling myself it might hurt his feelings if I told him to stop. I didn't like him like this; if he had any self-respect, he'd want to know that.

But I still couldn't bear the thought of a confrontation. As the film ended, I jumped to my feet, fast, yanking my purse up from the chair beside me to occupy my hands.

Donald frowned, looking at his watch. "I guess we don't really have time for anything else."

"No. I have to be home by nine-thirty," I reminded him.

His hand rested between us in the dark the entire way home. It reminded me of a fisherman sitting in a boat, unsure whether the fish were going to bite or not, casting out on the off chance that they might. I wasn't going to.

I'd never been so happy to see my house as we pulled into the drive. The porch light was on, along with the light in the upstairs hallway. I couldn't wait to run inside and lock the door behind me.

He turned off the truck, and I didn't dawdle, opening the door. "Well, thanks for tonight Donald. It was nice to get my mind off of things. I'll see you around."

"Let me walk you to your door."

I slammed the heavy truck door, feet away from freedom. Feeling his hand against my back as we started up the porch steps, I tried to walk a little ahead of him. Sighing, I turned to face him as we reached the front door.

I didn't like the way he was looking at me, his eyes all soft and glossy. "I'm really glad you came tonight, Cassie."

"Yeah, it was fun." I gripped the door knob. "Thanks."

He studied me a minute before looking toward his feet. "Listen, I know this may seem a bit hasty, but it's something I've thought a lot about."

I stared at him, unsure if I wanted to know or not.

He swallowed. "Is there...is there any chance at all that you might wait for me...Cassie?"

I opened my mouth, trying to breathe lightly to keep from hyperventilating.

"I know we haven't even started going steady," he said with a chuckle, causing my skin to crawl, "but I really like you. I've always liked you."

He tugged at my arm, pulling me away from the door. "Things'll be different when I get back, whenever that may be. I already have a job waiting for me once I return. It won't be long after that and I'll be able to get a house."

My eyes widened.

"I know you're probably thinking I'm crazy, it's just—I know I want to marry you someday."

I stepped back. "Donald—"

"I know you don't want to right now, but maybe after I get back—"

I shook my head. "Donald, I really don't think you've thought this through."

"But I have," he said. "I think about it a lot. I think about *you* a lot. Haven't you?"

I wanted to be honest. I wanted to end this now before it got any more out of hand, but there was still a part of me that was afraid of upsetting him.

"No," I murmured. "Not really."

He stared at me. "Maybe it's not something you've thought about right now, but maybe afterwards—"

"Donald, I...I'm leaving Rockmont as soon as I graduate. I'm not staying here."

"That's okay, I've thought about that, too. We can wait until you're ready. I don't mind."

I was getting rankled, like an animal backed into a corner. "Donald, please understand me. I don't want to hurt you, but you cannot tell me something like this. I can't...I'm not..."

I couldn't say it. I opened the door. "I have to go. Thanks again for tonight and I'll...I'll talk to you later."

I shut the door between us, ear pressed to the door to listen. He didn't walk off the porch right away. Hearing the rowdy truck engine start, I dragged myself up the stairs. He had proposed to me—sort of. It wasn't even a proper offer. It was as if he were playing the fisherman again, seeing if I would take the bait.

Wait for him? He wasn't in any position to ask that of me. We weren't together and never once had I given him the impression that I wanted to be. The more I thought about it, the angrier I became. He didn't even know me—not really. It was like he wanted to skip all the important parts of a relationship—the pursuit, the vulnerability, the honesty. What kind of person did he think I was anyway? Some girl who wasn't looking for love, just marriage? I couldn't imagine my parents being happy about a match-up with Donald, even if I wanted it. It had always been expected that I would marry into a distinguished family. Since Amos' death, I knew that this had probably become of even more importance than before. My father would prefer to hand the company over to my husband—who would have experience in this type of business—than to someone who had no familial ties to him.

I tossed my purse on my bed. Changing into my pajamas and taking down my hair, I settled into my bay window. I wondered how long Friedrich had sat there, waiting for me to come. Had he thought I hadn't shown on purpose? Did he think I'd grown fainthearted, no longer wishing to put myself in such a precarious situation?

With a finger, I drew in the condensation from my breath on the glass. Friedrich was wrong for me; Donald was safe. If Donald and I were together, he would always be at my disposal. He would never challenge me to become something more, to look deeper inside myself to uncover the person I wanted to be. I could already picture a future with him. We'd live in a little white house with blue shutters in town. I'd wake up when he went to work. I'd clean house and cook dinner as I waited for him to come home at night. I'd live here in Rockmont for the rest of my life. Perhaps Donald could even be trained to fill my father's shoes at Wyndham Aero Industries. I'd forever be controlled by my parents because my husband wouldn't have the nerve to stand in their way, especially when it worked to his benefit.

Where Donald was harmless, Friedrich was dangerous in every way. He was a German soldier—a former Nazi. I knew the ideas that had been a part of his life for so long had not simply vanished. He could wake up one day and decide in an instant to go back to the way he was, everything we'd worked for having been for naught. As I sat there, thinking it over, I realized I couldn't even dream up a future with him. He would be sent back to Germany one day, once the war was over. When that day came, we'd have no choice but to go on with our lives, trying to forget this summer. Our worlds were going to change before we even knew it was happening.

And yet, even acknowledging this didn't dissuade me from wanting to be with him. Even if all we had was this time together before it all evaporated into nothingness, I had to take it. No matter how badly it was destined to hurt later, I knew I'd regret passing him by more than the inevitable pain.

Throwing on a weightless pink tea dress the next morning, it took me a moment to find him in the field. He was working, and the way he wasn't looking for me made me worry he was mad at me. I ate a quick breakfast with my mother and baby sister downstairs before excusing myself. "I'm going to go ride my bike."

My mother made a sound in the back of her throat before swallowing what was in her mouth. "Take your sister with you."

I halted. *Not today*, I thought. I needed to see him.

Lucy scoffed as I turned around. "No, Mommy, I not want to."

"Mommy has to do some things today. It'll be too hard—"

"I not want to! I wanna stay wif you!"

"Lucy, please, Mommy has a lot to do—"

"I not want to!" she repeated. "I wanna stay wif you!"

Exasperated, my mother waved toward her. "Cassie, just take her."

I thought fast, trying to come up with an excuse. Lucy went rigid, shrieking as I tried to lift her from her high chair. "No! *No!* I wanna stay wif you! I wanna stay wif you!"

I finally loosened her from her chair as she unleashed a high-pitched scream.

"Fine! Fine! You can stay with me. Sheesh." Mom put her plate in the sink. "Cassandra, do the dishes while I'm gone, will you?"

I kissed Lucy on the head before sprinting away. I had the gift of persuasion over my baby sister, but I had chosen to let her have her way today.

Getting on my bike, I made sure Friedrich had seen me before continuing ahead. Part of me wondered if he'd come at all, considering I'd left him waiting the day before.

I hid my bike a little further in than usual, just to make sure my mother wouldn't see it when she drove by. I rushed toward our clearing.

I sat on the fallen tree before getting up. I wasn't sure what I was going to say. It made me nervous as I imagined how he might react. What if he thought I didn't care about him? What if he thought I'd chosen Donald over him? Should I even mention Donald? I had no choice. Anything else would be a lie.

I had been waiting perhaps twenty minutes when I heard footsteps. He took off the seed bag from around his shoulder and I rushed to him before anything could be said. "Friedrich, I'm *so* sorry about yesterday."

He seemed surprised by my shameless embrace, though his arms were at ease around me, as if it was something he'd always done. "It is okay. Where are you?"

"What do you mean?"

"I mean yesterday. Where are you?"

I pulled away to see his face. "You aren't mad?"

His arms were still around me as he laughed. "No, I am not mad."

"I got sidetracked," I grumbled.

"How?"

I sighed as we separated. "I had a visitor. They insisted on taking me out."

"Ah, the famous Donald."

I stared at him. "What?"

"This is who takes you on a date. Right?"

"Yes. How'd you know that?"

He had begun to pace the glade. "You talk about him before."

I smiled, grazing my hand across the bark of a nearby tree, recalling my explosion of feelings during our first time in the woods. "I think 'mentioned him' is more accurate."

He shrugged.

"So, how is it going?" he asked in a jaunty tone my mother would've used if she cared.

I walked after him as we circled the clearing. "With Donald? It was awful. I didn't want to go in the first place, but he was persistent."

"Where is he taking you?"

"Dinner and a movie."

"Unimpressive."

I snorted. "Why do you say that?"

"Dinner and a movie, ice cream, carnivals—it is all too careful, too reliable." He glanced at me. "If it is me, I am doing it different."

I was delightedly curious. "What would you have done then?"

"First, where are we? Pick a place."

I thought for a moment. "I've always wanted to go to Hawaii."

"Then we are in Hawaii. First," he said, "I surprise you; I drive you to the beach. You are uncertain, asking me what we are doing here. I tell you I rent a boat for us. We get on, just the two of us."

"But I need a swimsuit, towels, and something to tie my hair up with," I teased. "You haven't planned this out."

"Everything we need is in the trunk. I hide it from you because I plan it out."

I chuckled.

"We spend the whole day on the water," he continued. "We get a little burning from the sun, we are tired from swimming, but it is a day we never forget."

"That sounds perfect."

"This is not all," he said on the other side of the glade. "After, we change and I take you to dinner—but not to an ordinary restaurant. This one sits on the shore so we can watch the sun go down. It is making a warm orange glow over the blue waters."

I leaned against a tree. He propped himself up next to me, plucking a yellow, trumpet-shaped blossom off the honeysuckle vine. "You laugh about something I say and I laugh at how you pick at your food. Then I take your hand," he said, his voice quieter as he did just that, "and I lead you onto the sand, where we sit between the dunes. I put a flower in your hair and admire the moon shining on your face as you look out over the water."

He tucked the honeysuckle floret behind my ear. "And then I kiss you, right out there where anyone can see."

For a moment, I thought he was going to act out this scenario. My breathing hastened, but he chuckled as he resumed his casual stride. We were quiet for a minute.

Hands behind my back, pressed into the bark, I looked at my shoes. "He kind of asked me to marry him last night."

Friedrich stopped, a wary, disbelieving smile teetering on his lips. "He what?"

"Sort of. He asked me to wait for him until he comes back from the war. He started telling me about how he's going to have a job when he gets back and that he'll be able to buy a house..."

I trailed off, hesitant to say anything else. It embarrassed me even to think about it. Friedrich didn't speak, though he had started walking again. "What are you telling him?"

"I told him...well, I tried to hint that I'm not interested. I was trying to be nice to him, but he kept talking about how he knew I wasn't ready now, but that I might be later. He said he'd wait until I was ready, but I...I don't think I'll ever be ready—not for him."

"Tell him this."

"That's mean. I couldn't say that to him."

Friedrich laughed. "So you want to marry him instead of disappoint him."

"I *never* said I'd marry him. I can't even imagine saying yes. I'm as wrong for him as he is for me, he just doesn't know it."

"Well," Friedrich said, "maybe it is time you tell him."

I gulped. "It's not that simple. He's friends with Holly, too. They're the only friends I have and I know if I upset Donald, Holly would cut me off. I'll be friendless. I'm not worried about it. He enlists in November; I can put him off until then. After that, I'm leaving anyway."

"You are always defending how you feel," he said. "There is nothing wrong with saying it; they should understand. Believe me, he is to be more upset believing you lie to him than if you tell him the truth."

I pushed away from the tree as he closed in on me. "I'm not lying to him."

Friedrich snorted. "You convince you that an indirect answer is still an answer; it is not. He is hearing what he wants to hear. You put him off if you want, but it saves you both trouble later if you are honest with him now."

Walking, I focused on the stylishly scuffed toes of my saddle shoes. I hated the fact that he was right. I found myself in a constant race away from every potential conflict. My heart always defiantly objected to this, but I could never follow through with expressing my feelings, as if I didn't have a right to them.

"You are quiet," I heard Friedrich say behind me.

"I'm just thinking."

"About what?"

"What you said."

Something tugged at my waist. I peeked behind me, the ties hanging down the back of my dress falling from his fingers. It made me feel as if there was a part of him that wanted to touch me, but he refrained.

I stopped, facing him as I leaned against another tree. "I know you're right. I just can't bring myself to do it."

"Well, if it means anything, I think you should."

I studied him. "Did someone hurt you like this?"

He rested against the tree with me. With the worn leather at the toe of his shoe, he dug at one of the exposed roots. I wasn't used to the way he kept his eyes from meeting mine. "Not exactly like this."

"Is she the one who found someone else?"

His eyebrows tightened. He opened his mouth to speak, but nothing came out. I heard him exhale as if he could think of no way out of an explanation. "My situation is more...developing than yours."

As in...they still associated with each other? I gulped. He and I were not a couple. I kept telling myself that in the hopes that it would make the jealousy inside me dwindle. It was a new and unfamiliar reaction; I wasn't sure how to reckon with it.

"Her name is Delana. I meet her when I am sixteen. She has this attraction that draws people in, like rats to poison."

I crossed my arms.

"She cheers me on when I fight with other boys. It makes me even more aggressive; I want to impress her. She hangs on my arm when she sees me, telling me how brave I am, how strong. She points at boys, saying she thinks not I can beat them—which is making me fight them and prove I can. She plays with me; one day pretending she likes me, the next ignoring me. When I am not figuring out why she acts this way, she is mad that I am unable. At first, I like it. Then it is irritating me when I find out she is mad because she hears another girl likes me—or something silly like this. We start getting serious before I enlist. She still plays these games with me, but I look over it—for reasons I am not admitting out of shame..."

I wasn't sure what this meant, but because of his sudden self-consciousness, I kept my eyes down.

"And so, before I leave for Africa, I ask her to marry me. She says yes. We celebrate with our families, plan to marry when I come home. We write to us every week. Then, three months I am here, in America, and my mother writes saying Delana marries someone else. She meets a *sturmbannführer* in the SS while I am away; before I even leave, though I am not knowing this then. She has no interest in a *gefreiter* in the Wehrmacht after this."

He kicked at a stone. I felt myself beginning to tremble. He'd been engaged; he'd been in love with someone.

"Losing her is a bad moment in my life. Everything she makes me believe disappears. I am not the strongest or the bravest or the smartest, and she finds someone who is. I am stupid believing she waits for me when she can have a fighting officer instead."

He scoffed. "She never even writes to tell me; the letters just stop. Before then, all she writes about is how happy she is; how she loves me. The whole time, she is dating this *sturmbannführer* when I am not there. It makes me look like a fool."

He didn't notice how uncomfortable I was. I wouldn't have been, if I hadn't had feelings for him. I was so immature compared to him, in many ways. How could someone like me ever be what he needed?

Pushing myself off the tree, I fidgeted. "I should probably go."

"Cassie..."

"I...they're probably missing me."

He stopped me. "I am upsetting you."

"No. No, you haven't."

He chuckled. "Yes, I am. Why are you so afraid to tell me what you feel?"

I knew what he meant by that, but my mind automatically thought of something else—the reason I dreamed about him, the reason I yearned to be next to him, to feel his touch.

His gaze was soft, and he pulled me closer. "Tell me."

Tears of embarrassment rose in my eyes as I stammered. "I don't...I don't think I can."

His Adam's apple shifted. I closed my eyes as he pressed his forehead to mine. "Please say it."

I tried to remember to breathe. There was a part of me that was desperate to tell him. I wanted him to know that it made me ache from the inside out knowing what I felt for him. I wanted to tell him how scared I was about everything that I wanted to happen between us; of everything that I was afraid would never happen between us. I worried my open heart would frighten him away.

Emboldened by a sudden rush of spontaneity, I wrapped my arms around his waist until there was no space left between us. "If I do, you have to promise you won't look at me differently—that you won't run from me."

"What makes you think I am not feeling the same?"

I focused on the white undershirt beneath his POW uniform. Was that encouragement? Was that his way of saying he knew what a struggle I'd been having, because it had been his, too?

I closed my eyes. "I've tried to tell myself that this is wrong; that you could never know how I feel; that I could never tell you that you're all I ever think about." I cringed at my frankness. "I've never met anyone who makes me feel like you do. You see something in me that I can't even see in myself. But hearing you talk about her...I'm not enough for you, Friedrich."

"No, no, Cassie." He lifted my face, palms warm under my jaw. "You misunderstand. I am not telling you this comparing you to her; it is more comparing her to you. I am always reaching for something I can never be with her. I know now what I need—what I am always needing—is someone who sees who I really am; the not so brave, the not so strong, the not so smart. You see me at my worst and it is amazing me how you continue looking beyond it. You see the person I want to be. You are more than anything I deserve. How am I ever wanting anyone but you after this?"

I gripped the fabric of his shirt. "You really mean that?"

"With all my heart."

My heart hammered in my chest. I was thrilled; I was terrified. How was this ever going to work? How was it even going to last?

My hand rested on the part of his chest where his T-shirt was exposed. The rhythm of his heartbeat quickened under my palm, the momentum of his breath accelerating. I began to quaver as he swallowed, leaning his face towards mine.

There was hardly an inch between our lips. I knew this from the way I could feel his breath and how I could already imagine the salty taste of his mouth.

Whatever caused him to waver won him over because he pressed his lips to my forehead instead. I stood there, breathing him in, my fantasies of being this close to him never having felt this wonderful. I'd been ready for him to kiss me, but I wasn't upset that he didn't; I wasn't sure I'd even know what to do.

So for now, I was content, safe and cared about in his arms.

Twelve

As troubled as I had been over my affections for him, I felt no remorse in admitting them to him now. My feelings were requited. Whether it was unacceptable or not had no relevance anymore. We had fallen into something neither of us had foreseen. There was no turning back; it was too late for that.

My euphoric demeanor was irrepressible. I almost felt like a different person. As I waited with the others to enter the camp, I didn't care who could see the exultation on my face—until Holly came up to me as we went through the gates.

"So what happened?" she asked.

I was still smiling. "What?"

"What happened on your date with Donald?"

I felt my face drop. "Mmm...I didn't think it was a date."

"Well, you went out with him, didn't you?" There was a sharp edge to her voice.

"Yes."

"What did you say? What did you tell him?"

I stared at her. "Holly, what are you talking about?"

"What did you tell him when he asked you to wait for him?"

My blood chilled beneath my skin. I didn't like how aggravated she sounded. "How did you know about that?"

I pretended not to notice as she rolled her eyes. "He told me he was going to ask. What did you say?"

"I told him no. I told him I wasn't ready for that."

She was quiet. "But one day you will be?"

I shook my head. "Well, I didn't tell *him*, but no. I don't look at Donald like that. He's just a friend."

"Just a friend?" Holly stopped, turning to face me as the other women passed us. "He's liked you ever since he met you."

We continued walking, but only because the hind guard was shepherding us along.

"How could you say no?" she continued. "Who else is going to ask you, Cassie?"

I gaped at her. She had never simulated interest in anything to do with me before. It infuriated me that she felt she had the right to do so now. I was glad I was clutching my Bible, keeping her from seeing the way my hands shook. "It doesn't matter what options I have or don't have. I can't be with someone I feel nothing for."

"If you hurt him, you can consider our friendship over," she threatened.

She hurried ahead of me, catching up with Nancy and Sharon. I couldn't even comprehend what had just happened. If she liked him, then why was she mad that I refused him? If she didn't like him, then why would it matter to her what my decision was? I didn't like the way it seemed Donald and Holly had conspired to get me to like him. I wrestled with the impulse to march up to her and tell her that it was okay with me if I never spoke to her again.

Between our meetings at the camp—where Friedrich and I forced ourselves to act as if we were mere acquaintances—we met in secret at our clearing. The times we had been able to sneak off together, I only found myself falling for him more. He began to open up, revealing his heart to me in a way he'd never done before.

"You know what Milo tells me yesterday?" he asked one day. Milo was one of the men who'd fought with him in Africa. I continued staring up at the sky, my head resting on his stomach, feeling the cadence of his inhalations. He was running his fingers through my hair. "He tells me something is not right with me."

I rolled my head to look at him. "What's that supposed to mean?"

"I react not to provocations anymore. Strange looks, irritable remarks, practical jokes—I use none of them as a reason to punch someone in the face."

I couldn't help but chuckle. "Okay..."

He tickled me under the neck.

"You are not understanding," he said. "I never let someone get away with such things. I challenge them. Now, I find their reactions funny. I laugh at them; sometimes, I walk away without saying anything. Sometimes, this is more intimidating to them. A few change bunks, afraid I get back at them while they sleep."

"And you're proud of this, are you?" I teased.

He shook his head, his eyes reflecting the sky. "No. It is interesting that they all see something changes in me. They know not what it is. They understand it not. This is why they are afraid."

I watched him a moment before looking up through the trees again.

"I think about if I should get angry or not," he said. "I think about situations and stay calm. I consider the consequences to my actions; I am not doing this before. It is how we are trained; my country wants no independent thinkers. But there is a voice I am aware of now, wanting me to be something I am not knowing I can be before."

My thumb caressed his as he locked his fingers with mine.

"You know not how hard this is," he said. "God is coming into my life at a very inconvenient time. I cannot reject my beliefs at my comrades, Cassie."

He was saying he couldn't tell anyone the truth—that his convictions were changing. It was strange to hear a hint of reservation as he spoke, especially when he was always telling me that I didn't have to justify myself to anyone.

"I am so confident about what I believe before. Now it is as if my principles are shattering and I sort through them, separating the poison thoughts from healthy ones. I know you should be willing to die for Him—and this is exactly what I am doing if I tell them I feel this way. If the worst I face is a fight, I can handle this. I take a beating if it means I can believe what I want. But it is not this easy. They kill me, Cassie; they make it to look like a suicide. This is what they do. If not this, they blacklist me and punish my family; I prefer they kill me instead of punish my family."

I closed my eyes at the word. I sat up, his arm wrapping around my waist as I scooted closer to see his face.

"I cannot serve both Nazism and God. I have to make a choice—and I make it. But I am afraid I never have the chance to live it. I am not there yet, Cassie. I walk a tightrope, wondering if it ever becomes a board, if it ever becomes solid ground. I am not sure how long I can do this. I worry I am not making it to the other side."

I stroked his cheek. "You're putting too much pressure on yourself. You're depending too much on your own strength. If you continue this way, then it's a certainty you'll fall. You have to trust Him, Friedrich. It's not as if in the moment you decide to live for God that He expects you to physically die for Him. He's preparing you for something—right now. Every step you take to get closer to Him is drawing in His strength. Don't give up."

He considered me a moment. Kissing my hand, he sat up, his face inches from mine. "And then there is you. I know not what happens, Cassie. I worry I am not able to doing this without you. Whether you go to school or I am sent back to Germany, we are going to be separate."

I bowed my head. It pained me to think about it, too. "I'm just one of your steps, Friedrich."

"No. You are more than a step. Even in my childlike faith, I see this. What is happening between us is greater than I think either of us understands. There is a deepness you have that makes me want to be where you are. It is not emotions that bring us together. I cannot explain it. Please tell me I am not the only one who sees this."

I stared at him, a tottering grin on my lips. "Do you realize you just compared yourself to a child?"

He seemed confused for a moment before comprehension dawned over his countenance. He smiled. "You are right."

His blue eyes roamed my face and I watched his expression fade with thought. He brushed back the hair that rested on my shoulder. "You know what else I realize?"

I didn't answer, entranced by him. His voice was soft and I almost melted from the way he was looking at me. "If it is real—if it is true—then you know it, too."

I could do little more than look at him, my mind going blank as a sheet of writing paper. I began to imagine the nerve-endings in my brain emitting frantic signals to each other, mystified as to the message they were trying to send me.

But they weren't trying to communicate with me at all. Those little sparks weren't from the launching of information; they were fireworks, celebrations of a most profound happiness. He was being coy. I wasn't going to expose my heart until he did.

"Well," I said, struggling to keep the smile from extending off my face. "I guess you're going to have to find out."

He drew me toward him. I rested my head on his shoulder as he embraced me, his lips against my head.

The following day, I woke up, spotting Friedrich near the center of the field. I was somewhat disheartened that he was so far off, but it was probably for the best. We took enough risks sneaking off as it was without doing it two consecutive days in a row. Sometimes we only managed it once a week, and we'd already used up our allotment for this one.

I played with Lucy outside for most of the morning. Friedrich tried to appear indifferent as usual, but it stirred up my heart whenever I caught him looking. I kept praying for a chance to be alone again, if not today then before the week was over. I would be starting my senior year Monday, limiting our windows of time to two hours in the afternoon. I wasn't sure if that would make it better or more difficult for him to get away.

My mother came down around lunchtime. Having put Lucy down for a nap, I was halfway down the stairs when I heard the phone ring.

My mother was washing dishes. "Cassandra—"

"I got it." I jogged over to the phone. "Wyndham residence."

There was silence. I stood there a moment, certain someone was on the other end.

"Wyndham residence," I repeated.

My blood went cold upon hearing a strange man's voice. "Uh, yes, could I speak with Miriam, please."

It sounded more like a command than a question. Speechless, I just stood there.

"Hello?" he asked.

I glanced toward the kitchen, muttering into the receiver. "Who is this?"

He didn't answer right away. "I'm sorry. I need to speak with Miriam."

I could feel the hair on my skin rising. It was him; I had intercepted his phone call. How foolish of him to call in the middle of the day. I didn't even know this man, but the detestation I felt toward him was unrivaled.

"May I—?"

"Listen to me, and listen to me closely," I growled only loud enough for him to hear. "I better not *ever* catch you talking to my mother again. Don't call her, don't meet up with her, don't be her crying shoulder or her confidant; she has my father for that. Speaking of whom, I swear to all that is good and holy that if I ever find out you contacted her again, I *will* tell my father. You're a slimy, despicable excuse for a human being. How dare you interfere with my family. Don't ever call here again."

I slammed the phone down, my whole body shaking with fury.

"Who was it?" she called out.

I felt dizzy, probably from my rampant breathing.

"Nobody important," I returned, starting for the front door.

I stepped out onto the porch, sitting on the swing, angrier than I'd been in a very long time. I had no regrets; that low-life deserved it. I wondered if he would tell my mother what I'd said. I hoped he did, and I hoped it made her furious enough to reprove me for it. They were both imbeciles if they thought I wouldn't educate my father on the matter after that.

A car had come up the road. I lifted my head, an unfamiliar black Chevrolet pulling into the driveway. As it parked, I stood, walking over to the steps. The driver's door opened first. It had been so long since I'd seen her that for a moment I forgot who she was. She was busty, with a thick waist and dark brown hair.

"Mrs. Taylor?" I asked in surprise.

"My, look at you," she said, as she shut the door. "It's been so long since I last saw you. You're quite the young lady now."

Halfway down the steps, I came to a standstill as the passenger side door opened and Jimmy Taylor stepped out of the car.

He was in a dark green dress uniform, a khaki tie and collared shirt visible just beneath it. A side cap sat on his trimmed, dark brown hair. He had an attractive cleft chin, with features that defined his heart-shaped face. He and my brother had always shared the same expressions and had the same lanky frame (though Jimmy had bulked up some), but I could tell something about him had changed. He seemed to have lost the carefree demeanor he had had in the days he ran around with Amos. He looked less like the boy I remembered and more like a man, and more handsome than ever. His nut brown eyes brightened when he saw me.

"Jimmy," I said, continuing down the steps. "What...what are you doing here?"

"Sent back against my will," he said, showing me his arm, which was in a sling.

His mother gave him a reproving chuckle. "It was for much worse than a broken arm. Do you know the first thing he said upon waking up and seeing me was, 'Tell the nurse to give me morphine so I can go back.'"

Jimmy was looking out over the German-scattered field.

Mrs. Taylor was shaking her head. "Bound to a convalescent bed, hardly able to move, and the instant he's conscious, he wants to go back and fight. Is your mother inside, dear?"

I led them up the porch. "Come inside. She'll be so happy to see you; both of you."

"I'm sorry I've not been by already," Mrs. Taylor said. "I wasn't sure when a good time would be, but once Jimmy was well enough, we both wanted to come over."

Jimmy gave me a wary grin over my shoulder. I wasn't looking forward to seeing the look on my mother's face when she saw Jimmy in the same uniform Amos would have worn if he had come home.

I called out for my mother, waiting with the Taylors as she came out of the kitchen. My mother rushed forward to embrace Jimmy's mom.

"How have you been?" Mrs. Taylor asked, sympathetic.

My mother only nodded, tears rising in her eyes. I could tell she wanted to speak, her lips clamped together to keep from bursting into sobs. Her emerald eyes flickered toward Jimmy, who had moved to stand next to me. He took off his cap.

"Jimmy," she said, her voice cracking as she hugged him.

"Mrs. Wyndham, I'm so sorry."

I crossed an arm in front of me, looking toward the floor. My family and I were moving on with the news the only way we could—with time. Some days were better than others; sometimes, we could smile without thinking about him, while other times, spurts of unexpected memories brought us to tears. This moment fell into the latter category.

My mother's voice was broken, looking at Jimmy with a fragment of the affection she had always felt for my brother. "At least you're safe and well."

"For today, anyway," he said.

"Come have a seat," my mother invited, starting for the kitchen. "I'm just finishing up something for lunch. You're both welcome to join us, if you like."

"As long as it's no imposition," Mrs. Taylor said, sitting down.

"Actually, I'm feeling a bit stiff. I'd like to take a short walk," Jimmy said, putting his cap back on. It surprised me when he looked at me. "Care to join me, *Cassandra?*"

My smile was irrepressible, remembering the way Jimmy used to poke fun at the way my family pronounced my name.

"Cass-ahhhn-dra," Jimmy exaggerated in a plutocratic voice, causing Amos to laugh. "You might as well be looking through a monocle while holding a glass of bourbon when you say it like that."

I followed him out the front door. It wasn't long ago that I would have done anything to have Jimmy Taylor want to be alone with me. It was odd the way he'd asked, and I got the sense that it was premeditated. I tried not to appear as awkward as I felt walking beside him and his gaze wandered over the prisoners again.

"It's something, isn't it?" he asked. "They started this, and now gardening is all they have to do until it's over. I wish blisters and sunburns were the worst the rest of us had to worry about."

I glanced toward the field. I was certain Friedrich had looked away a millisecond before our eyes would have met.

"It must be hard, having them so close after what they've done," he said as we strolled down the driveway.

"I try not to think about it."

Jimmy sighed as we stepped on the road. "How've you been?"

I contemplated how to answer, before simply saying, "Okay."

The truth was I had been an emotional train wreck the last few months. I had been as far down as I could go as well as high, but I didn't feel like going into detail over the grief of losing my brother or my attraction to a German POW.

"What about you?" I asked.

"Swell. Not exactly what I thought I'd be doing when I turned eighteen, but..." He gave me a winsome grin.

"What? Being a war hero?"

"I'm not a hero. Amos was a hero. I couldn't believe it when I heard. He was like my own brother, you know?"

I laughed under my breath. "I do know, actually."

"Yeah, I guess you would." He chortled. "He was my best friend. I'll never forget him."

We both went quiet, my mind riffling through memories of Amos, some including Jimmy. I had wondered ever since we'd gotten the telegram; ever since my mother had our blue star in the window turned to gold. I didn't even know if my parents knew, because I hadn't the capacity to ask. "How...how did it happen? Do you know?"

He looked at me. "You don't?"

"I've never been able to ask," I said. "I'm afraid I'll imagine it—see him like that in my head. But, at the same time, I want to know. It almost feels like it dishonors him not to."

In the middle of the road, I stopped as Jimmy did. "He stepped on a mine. But, Cassie—"

I burst into instantaneous tears, crouching to the ground. My brother—my sweet, sunny, perfect brother...I couldn't even imagine it.

Jimmy knelt down beside me, his arm around my shoulders.

"Did he suffer? Did he know what was happening?" I sobbed.

He seemed reluctant. "It happened fast."

This seemed to open another floodgate of tears for me. I knew Jimmy was uncomfortable, but he didn't say so. He merely kept his good arm around me while I cried. I kept seeing the expression Amos always had when he played football, countenance determined and focused as he weaved between the opposing team's players. He was athletic and strong, yet he hadn't lasted two days.

I wiped at my eyes, embarrassed to look at Jimmy. "I'm sorry. I didn't mean to do that. It's just hard to hear."

"I know," he said as we rose. He frowned. "We should probably head back. I'm sure your mother's finished cooking. I'd hate to upset her."

We started home. He was telling me about when he'd been wounded when I thought I'd heard rustling in the woods. I scanned around, certain I'd seen a flash of blue between the trees. I strained my eyes, hoping the shadows were playing tricks on me.

Lucy had woken up, sitting on Mrs. Taylor's knee when we walked in. She ran to me, giving me a hug and hiding behind my leg from Jimmy. We all sat down to eat, talking about my father's business, Lucy's success at potty-training and how the Allies were doing in Europe. I could tell by some of Jimmy's remarks that he despised the Germans. I understood why, and part of me felt like a hypocrite for not sharing the same opinion—but I couldn't; not when I knew Friedrich. Surely he wasn't the only one capable of change.

Mrs. Taylor lingered on the porch with my mother and Lucy after we ate. Jimmy's eyes strayed past me, in the direction of the POWs as I accompanied him to the car.

He leaned against the trunk. "It was good to see you again."

"You too. Take care of yourself, Jimmy. You better come home when this is all over."

"Don't you worry." He looked toward the field with visible loathing. "I won't let these Krauts lick me."

I chuckled. Jimmy cast a furtive glance behind him as his mother laughed. "Listen, I made up my mind to talk to you the moment I found out about Amos. I know you and I have never been close—nothing more than acquaintances really—but I want you to know I'm always here for you. If you ever need me to beat up some John who's breaking your heart—or if you just need someone to talk to when things are hard…" He nodded back at my mother. "I'll be your stand-in older brother. Amos loved you, Cass. You were his kid sister. I'm not trying to replace him. I just know it's what he would have wanted."

My eyes watered over. "Thanks, Jimmy. That means a lot."

He gave me a nod. "I'm heading back next week. Write to me. Letters from home are like sunbeams in the dark. It helps us remember what we're fighting for."

"Of course, I will."

Jimmy didn't take his eyes off of me. I wondered what he was thinking as he gave me a cautious grin. "Can I ask you something? I don't want to come across as a creep, but…you're the first girl I've seen in months who isn't my nurse and who I'm not related to. I don't know if I'll come back or not; it's just the way it is. I thought I was done for this last time. Sharing a kiss with a pretty girl before I go back would go a long way for me." He seemed to get lost in a daze. "Over there, you wonder if you're ever going to get to again."

My cheeks grew warm. I'd always wondered if Jimmy thought I was pretty. "You…you want me to…to kiss you?"

He regained his focus. "Just a little one. If you don't find it too inappropriate."

I bit at my nail, glancing first at my distracted mother. Friedrich was on his knees, pulling up onions.

"It might not be good," I murmured, blushing as I looked at Jimmy. "I've never…I've never kissed anyone before."

He shook his head, pushing away from the car. "Trust me. You can't go wrong with this one."

I held my breath as he lifted my chin. I wondered what it was going to feel like, what I was supposed to do, as he bent toward me.

I closed my eyes, feeling the soft warmth of his lips on mine. I had expected a simple peck, but he took his time. It was just a kiss—something for him to think about when he was in the black clouds of war. It was the least I could do for him after who he was to my brother, what he was doing for our country—what he had done for me.

With one last kiss, he pulled away from me with reluctance. His eyes remained closed, savoring it a moment longer. I tried to keep from laughing out of awkwardness as he hugged me.

"Amos would have killed me if he knew I'd done that," he said.

Over his shoulder, my mother was shielding her eyes from us in mortification, and Mrs. Taylor was tittering uncomfortably as they muttered to one another.

"I hope I didn't get you into too much trouble," Jimmy said, as gravel crunched under Mrs. Taylor's weight. "I know how she gets with you."

I gave a feeble shrug. "She'll get over it."

He opened the car door. "Bye, Cass. Remember what I said."

I waved to him. Mrs. Taylor's voice was melodious, causing me to chuckle, as she opened the driver's door. "Bye!"

My mother had huffed, the screen door slamming behind her as the Taylors pulled out of the driveway. Sighing, I strapped on gloves of resolve as I prepared to spar with my mom.

It was then that I heard a piercing clang come from the field.

I looked over, unsure of what could have made such a shrill sound. Friedrich had his back to me, stomping toward Mr. Stewart's barn while the other prisoners worked, jerking his gloves off with ferocity. A couple of the POWs closest to him were watching him stomp away, too. He must have thrown the trowel, hitting the metal basin of the wheel barrow. Obviously, he wasn't thrilled either. I felt a cold sweat come over me.

I guessed he had seen, too.

Thirteen

I had been right about my mother. She was appalled.

"That was *humiliating*!" she'd bellowed.

She was like a broken record, reiterating all the things she had already said to me yesterday afternoon after seeing Jimmy kiss me in the front yard.

"Have you *no* shame? You aren't married! He isn't even your boyfriend! God, right out there in front of Mrs. Taylor, too!"

I didn't look up from my book. Lucy was playing with her blocks, uninterested in the affairs of her older sister.

"What if this gets out? What if Pastor Gilbert finds out? How could you do this, Cassandra?"

I sighed with exasperation. "If we weren't in the middle of a war and they had come over for a visit, then yes, it would have been very inappropriate. But he asked me to, Mom. He was Amos' best friend. War changes things. You didn't grow up during a war, so——"

"Yes, I did! And I can tell you right now that I never, *ever* would have carried out such a blatant display of affection with some boy."

"He is not some boy and it was not a display of affection. And you were what, Mom? Seven, when the Great War started? It's not the same thing."

"We'll just see what your father has to say about this," she said brusquely. I shrugged before hearing her mumble to herself, "Amos *never* would have done something like this."

I couldn't help but laugh. "Well, I don't think Jimmy would have ever asked Amos, Mom."

Her heels clacked on the floor. She leered at me from the doorway. "I don't know what has gotten into you or where this attitude is coming from, but you'd better get rid of it and fast. You will not speak to me that way, young lady."

I stared at her until she was out of sight. Lucy was eyeing me in curiosity, and I muffled my laughter in my hand. She grinned, returning her attention to her blocks.

I hadn't realized the double meaning in Jimmy's words when he said he'd hoped he hadn't gotten me into trouble. It wasn't my mother I was worried about. I had decided the instant he kissed me that I didn't care what she said or thought.

It was Friedrich who concerned me.

He had ignored me for days now. I had tried catching his eye to persuade him to meet me in the glade, but he looked away from me each time, his garden tools shoved into the ground with unnecessary force. He wasn't even giving me a chance to explain. Knowing I was responsible for his outrage bothered me, but I still couldn't apologize for letting Jimmy kiss me. There wasn't any emotion involved; it was a simple act of kindness. I wished he would let me defend myself.

Then, one day, I grasped why he was so upset. It reminded him of Delana; he'd opened his heart to me, and my actions—no matter how innocent they may have been—dredged up old heartaches. I could only imagine his hurt, even his mistrust of me. That, I did regret.

My heart was heavy Friday afternoon. It was the last week day I had before school started. I'd been sitting on the porch, reading a book on Queen Victoria ever since Mom had woken up, taking over watch of Lucy. Friedrich was off to himself and I knew he'd seen me, though lately he'd made a great effort to show me he was pretending he hadn't. I dreaded tomorrow, having to face him at Bible study without rectifying this first.

I flipped the page, blinking up in his direction. I yearned to be close to him. If he still felt the same way once I told him the truth, I'd accept it. I didn't like him not knowing and refusing to even hear me out, though.

Noticing him move from the corner of my eye, I looked up. He stood and stretched as he often did, checking out the positions of the other POWs. My mouth parted as he glared at me, tromping forward into the tree line.

I threw my book down on the swing, bolting for my bike. Pedaling as fast as I could on the road, I swerved onto the grass, stumbling from the loss of balance as I careened through the trees. I dropped my bike, sprinting through the woods until I reached the clearing.

He was already there, arms crossed, his tools on the ground with his back to me. I stared at the faded white letters on his back, the friction between us billowing, headed for an imminent explosion.

I grabbed his arm, trying to turn him around. "Friedrich...Friedrich, I'm sorry."

He scoffed as he shook his head, refusing to look at me.

"What?" I asked. "Talk to me. You've been avoiding me for days."

"You know all these times you ask if I am mad and I say no?" His blue eyes pierced me. "Well, this time, I am mad."

"Let me explain—"

"Explain what? The fact you are *kissing* someone? You have not to explain, Cassie, since I am *seeing* it. Explain this for me: if you care for me so little, if you cannot give a damn what I think or how I feel for you, why are you spending the last six months making me believe you care? I tell you a long time ago that you cannot hurt my feelings..." He trailed off as he struggled to continue. I could tell he had so much to say that he didn't know what to say next.

"Who is he?" he finally blurted out. "Are you together?"

"No—"

"Then why are you going off alone? Why is he at your house?"

I opened my mouth to speak, but he interrupted, a week's buildup of indignation pouring from his mouth. "What is this? A game for you to find how many fools you can trick? Oh no, I know. You are afraid of hurting the feelings of someone. You cannot say no so you go until you can escape a fight. Well, this is not a game to me."

"It's not to me either, Friedrich," I cried in disdain.

"I am putting me at risk of severe punishment for you—"

"As I have you—!"

"And yet, you make a date with one idiot, kiss another in your front yard."

I gasped.

"Admit it, Cassie. I am not good enough for you. You can never have with me what you can have with one of them. You should say it."

His outline became blurry as tears filled my eyes. "You want to talk about someone pretending? Then let's talk about you. You fill my head with all this nonsense about us, but you don't really mean it. If you did, you wouldn't talk to me like I'm some kind of harlot. You didn't even hear me out first. You just want to be mad and hurt me."

"Hurt *you*? What about *me*? How you think it makes me feel seeing you kiss a man when a day before, you make me believe you love me?"

"I *do* love you!" I exclaimed. "I kissed him because he asked me to."

"Oh, it is this easy? Someone is asking you?"

"He was my brother's best friend, you *jerk*!" I sobbed. "I do not have to justify myself to you when you're acting like this. Even if he survives the war, I'll probably never see him again. If you have any sense of compassion about you, then you'd understand why I did it. And what were you doing spying on me anyway?"

"I am not spying on you. You kiss him where everyone can see. And everyone *is* seeing."

"I'm not talking about that. I'm talking about when I went walking with him. You were in the woods following us."

"No, I am not."

"I saw you."

He laughed in contempt. "Cassie, I am not following you, but maybe I should. If you can do *this* in front of so many people, I wonder what you make in private."

I gaped at him, staggered that he could even imply such a thing of me. After all, I was alone with him all the time.

"I'm sorry that I hurt you," I said. "Believe me. I didn't mean for this to happen. I didn't think anything of it because there's nothing between Jimmy and me. He doesn't know my heart; he doesn't love me. I just felt sorry for him."

My voice cracked. "But I'm not her, Friedrich. I am *not* her. The truth is that I really do love you. I love you so much that it kills me inside knowing this is as good as it's going to get for us."

From the corner of my eye, I watched him lower his hands. As much of a right as he had to be offended, he had betrayed me, fighting the only way he knew how, with spiteful, angry, razor-edged words to make me bleed.

I backed away. "I can't do this. I can't start to trust you just to have you yank the rug out from under me again."

"Cassie, please——"

"I can't stay here."

"Cassie, no. Please, wait." I felt him behind me. My eyes were closed from the pressure of my tears as he turned me around. He held my face, trying to get me to look at him. "I am sorry. I make it again. Please stay. I am not meaning to say these things at you."

He kissed my hair, my forehead, my nose. "Please, leave me not here alone. Please."

Our lips touched. I wasn't crying anymore, incapable of even thinking as he kissed me. He held me close, his hand tightening in my hair, the other at the small of my back. The skin around his chin and upper lip was coarse on mine, but I clutched onto him, imploring him not to stop.

I opened my eyes with uncertainty as my legs buckled, his arm under the crook of my knees. He lifted me as if I were weightless, sitting with me on the ground. His hand slid along my jaw, into my hair, pulling me close as his lips meshed with mine.

We were in a car that was driving too fast, on the downward cruise off the peak of a hill. He was a shooting star that had floated in through my bedroom window. Trickling handfuls of diamonds through the crooks of my fingers wouldn't have compared. I was certain that we were on the moon, just the two of us, far away from the rest of the world and in our own. We had to be. A phenomenon of this caliber could only happen in an extraordinary place.

He was more than just my introduction to romance. He was engrained in me, the fabric of who we were reduced to mere scraps without the other. We wouldn't be gambling our futures for the sake of hand-me-down feelings. We were doing so for each other's lives—mine for his and his for mine. I craved to be the person he saw hidden away in me; the person I was when he was near. He had claimed once that if God looked at him the way I did, he would be unstoppable; I don't think he realized that I found the same solace in the way he looked at me.

He was peering into my eyes. "I love you."

I smiled. "I love you, too."

It felt as if his arms had been crafted with me in mind. "I can hold you like this forever," he said.

"Can you promise me that? That no matter what happens, we'll find each other again?"

He leaned down to kiss me. "There is nothing in the world that can keep me away from you."

His kiss changed me the same way his heart had. My fear—having been a life-long partner in my decision-making—was overcome by a new empowering voice within me. I was tired of running; I was done negotiating with the things that had kept me in a shell all these years. Flying out of the walls I had allowed to confine me would do nothing to set me free, for even if I left, those walls would remain.

No. The only way to break the cycle was to bust through them, reducing them to rubble. Such an intrepid goal would have once sent me off to hide in a corner, but I was beginning to embrace what I was capable of. The unconscious intake of God's strength and Friedrich's love had brought me to a new place; I could never go back to the way it used to be.

I leaned against the school building as my peers streamed out the doors, out into the light of day. Feeling around in my dress pocket, I felt the folded up square of paper stashed there. It was a note Friedrich had slipped in my Bible Saturday without me noticing. I had been like the sun that day, impossible to keep from shining, and he had been the moon, reflecting me. If anyone had been observing us, there wouldn't have been any doubt that something more was going on between us.

I unfolded it, reading it quickly for the hundredth time since discovering it:

I cannot stop thinking about you. I think about your hand in mine, your hair falling around your face, your smile, the taste of your lips. You are perfect for me and so much more than I am worthy of having. You have my heart, and I swear on everything I am when this ends, I come back for you, mein Liebling.

I bit my lip, smiling to myself.

Donald stepped out into the sunlight, tossing his keys into the air to catch them. I started for him. "Donald!"

The color drained from his face. He slowed down for me to catch up, though he didn't look at me.

"How have you been?" I asked, walking with him toward the parking lot.

He shrugged, checking our surroundings. I thought he looked nervous. "Good. You?"

"Good." I took a breath, thinking over all the things I'd prepared to say days before. "Listen, Donald, I want to apologize for the way I acted that night. I'm sorry if I upset you. I should've been honest with you from the beginning."

"Hey, Cass, it's okay. You just want to be friends."

We rounded the corner. "Well—yeah. You're a great guy, Donald, so please don't take offense. It's just...I'm sorry, I just don't think I feel the same way you do."

His voice was chipper, though he still wouldn't look at me. "I understand. I kind of figured it out. It's almost been three weeks since you last talked to me."

I blinked toward my feet. "I know. I'm sorry about that."

He rested his books on the hood of his truck. "It's okay. But—now I suppose it's my turn to be honest with you."

My grip tightened on the handlebars to my bike. "All right?"

I could see his discomfort. "Well, I kind of assumed after that night how you really felt. But, then I heard you were with Jimmy Taylor and—"

"I'm not with Jimmy Taylor." It was a small town. Knowing my mother wouldn't have dared tell anyone about that kiss, I assumed Mrs. Taylor was the culprit. Through the grapevine, the facts had been misconstrued.

"You're not?"

"No."

He pondered on this information. "I just assumed since he was Amos'...and then Holly told me about how you used to..."

He scratched at his forehead in thought. It irked me that Holly had told him I'd once liked Jimmy. She hadn't talked to me in weeks and didn't even sit with me at church anymore.

He sighed, shaking his head. "Listen, Cassie. I don't know how else to say this, so—"

"Are you ready?" a sharp female voice asked behind me.

I looked over my shoulder, watching Holly as she marched up to Donald's side.

"Uh—yeah," Donald replied.

"Let's go then," she demanded.

My mouth fell as she stood on her toes, planting a prolonged, wet kiss on his lips. Wide-eyed, he went speechless as Holly stomped around me, getting in on the passenger side and slamming the door.

He rubbed at his chin. "What I was trying to say is that we're engaged, Cassie."

Though I didn't regret this, I couldn't hide my shock. "What?"

"I asked her yesterday. And...I'm sorry, but...we can't be friends anymore."

I could tell by the look on his face that he didn't want to say it. Holly had her arms crossed inside the truck cab, her jaw tight as she purposefully looked out the window away from us. I couldn't explain her disdain of me any more now than I could before.

I turned my bike around. "You're a really good guy, Donald. You deserve the best and if you think you've found it..." I glanced at Holly. "Well, then, congratulations."

He looked as if there was more he wanted to say. As I pedaled away, I never heard his truck door open and close. Passing the school building, I dropped my feet to brake, hearing Donald call out my name.

He was jogging toward me from the parking lot. Stopping in front of me, he was panting. "There's something you need to know, Cassie. I'm not telling you this to upset you and I'm not saying it to get revenge or something. In fact, Holly probably won't speak to me once she knows I told you. But whether she's my fiancée or not, you deserve to know."

I was engrossed. "What is it?"

He swallowed, unmistakable sympathy on his countenance. "Amos was paying Holly to be your friend."

Whatever I'd expected him to say, it hadn't been that.

"Sometimes it was money; sometimes he'd take her on dates. He worried about you. He said that...that you were awkward and couldn't make friends on your own."

I dropped my gaze, my cheeks scalding with heat. "How...how long have you known this?"

"She just told me a couple weeks ago. I swear to you, Cassie, I never knew. The only reason she told me was because he...he's gone now. She felt like she shouldn't have to do it anymore."

I hid my eyes in my hand as I tried not to cry. I had never been so humiliated in all my life.

"I just...I didn't want you to think it was the same with me," he said. "I don't think you're awkward. I was your friend because I wanted to be. It wasn't just because I had feelings for you, either. I liked you as a person; that was always why."

I felt guilty. Perhaps I'd never given Donald the credit he deserved. "Thanks, Donald. I know that wasn't easy, but...that's what true friends do."

This seemed to mollify him. He turned away, walking back to Holly and his truck. I shoved off with my bike, riding as fast and far away from the school as I could.

That had to have been one of the most demoralizing things I'd ever heard of. No wonder Holly always kept me at a distance; no wonder she always seemed dull around me. I began to comprehend that I'd never known Holly at all, just as she had never known me. It was a strange concept, considering she'd been my closest friend for a year.

Friedrich was in utter disbelief that someone could be so deceptive. Although he tried to be mild in his condemnation of my brother, I could tell it really troubled him.

"This is proof he sees not who you really are. He is not knowing you like I know you."

"At least Donald was honest."

Friedrich laughed. "Right. He is an idiot. He deserves what he gets if he is marrying her, knowing what she is capable of."

I punched his arm and he smiled, bending down to kiss me.

One afternoon after school, I went down to Crewe's Department Store instead of going home. Using what I'd saved from my meager allowance, I bought a make-up collection of my very own. This was my last year of secondary school; I would be eighteen in less than a year. If I bought it myself, I could keep it in my purse so my mother could never find it. If she tried, I'd just start leaving it at school. She couldn't stop me from leaving the house wearing it, since she was often sleeping from working most nights. I looked forward to the afternoons, when I would be coming home just for her to see I'd been wearing it all day.

I didn't know if it was the make-up, my new confidence, or the fact that it was my senior year, but I hardly felt the repercussions of losing Holly and Donald. I always sat down to lunch by myself, but I never ate alone. Some of the boys in my year—still not eighteen—who had been friends with Amos on the football team started approaching me. They usually initiated conversation by bringing up what a great fellow Amos had been, though that soon led into what kinds of things I liked to do and if I was free that weekend. Sometimes, I would even catch Donald casting longing glances at me from a distance (as he was always accompanied by Holly). I always smiled back, hoping she noticed.

After a rather ugly dispute with my mother over my refusal to stop wearing my make-up, she called my father in her wrath. She made me leave the room first and I wondered what truths she was stretching that she didn't want me to overhear. It was tempting as I imagined her face if I told him everything I knew about her affair—but that wasn't the right way for it to be revealed. I couldn't hurt my father just to get back at my mother.

As militant as I had become towards her, I still respected my father. My mother called me down from the living room and I took the phone from her hands with dignity. "Hello?"

"Hi, Sweetheart." He sounded weary. "How are you doing?"

I waited until my mother was out of earshot. "Fine. How are you?"

"Tired. Can't seem to catch a break these days."

I could've been wrong, but I thought I detected a meaningful undertone in his voice.

"Tell me what's going on, Cassandra."

"Mom doesn't want me wearing make-up."

"Right. And you're doing it anyway."

"Mmhmm."

"She says you've been very disrespectful for a few months now. What's going on?"

"I don't know," I said. I wasn't going to plead my case to him when I knew he was just going to side with my mother. He wasn't here to do anything about it anyway.

"Listen, Cassandra. I know things have been difficult—for all of us. Your mother's going through a lot. She's under a lot of stress and doesn't get near enough sleep. It wouldn't hurt you to take it easy on her."

I sat there, biting my tongue. He was defending her. If only he knew what she was doing.

"If she doesn't want you wearing make-up, then take it off before you get home. She doesn't have to know...and don't tell her I told you that."

"I won't."

"And it would take a lot of pressure off of her if you were a little more helpful with Lucy. She does a lot for you, Cassandra."

"Yeah." I refrained from saying more at the risk of saying too much.

"You don't have much longer with us before you go to college or get married. We don't have much time left with you. Let's try to make the time we have pleasant, okay?"

What time? You're never here. "All right."

"All right," he said, satisfied. "I have to go. I have a lot of things to do before I get to leave tonight. Give your mother and Lucy a hug and kiss for me, okay?"

"Sure. Love you, Dad."

"I love you, too, Sweetheart."

Nothing in that conversation had persuaded me to change what I'd already set into motion. As far as I could tell, the only thing I was guilty of was growing up. For years, I'd believed that to be a bad thing. Now, I was beginning to see that maturity was a natural process. Perhaps if my father had genuine concern for my behavior, I would've abided by his suggestions. I knew, though, that he was a puppet and Mom was the hand. It annoyed me that her nagging him was the only time I found myself on the phone with him. I could tell even then that he was too busy to talk about anything else.

In spite of my father's counsel, I refused to wash my make-up off before leaving school. I set my mind to hold out longer than my mother, even if she brought my father into it again. The first few days I came home with it on, she would roll her eyes and fuss. I would try not to argue, making my point by keeping it on until bedtime. By the end of that first week, her harassment turned to mumbling, and by the next, she ceased to say anything at all.

I looked forward more than ever to my time with Friedrich, whether it was at the camp, surrounded by others, or alone in the woods. I would spend the week exercising my new confidence—talking with the boys at school, defying my mother's absurdities—then replenish my strength at Friedrich's side. Being with him was like being at peace, a time I had to be refreshed and energized; it gave me the fortitude to face the coming week without fear.

The air was crisp and chilly during my ride home, though it didn't keep me from pedaling at a brisk speed. The sooner I got home, the better chance I had of being able to meet with Friedrich. It was the beginning of September and I was already bored with school. Often, I would spend most of my last hour in math class writing to Jimmy just to have something thought-provoking to do. I had tried to conceal it, at first, whenever I thought someone was close enough to see. It made me self-conscious thinking it would encourage the rumor that we were together. Then, I stopped trying to hide that I wrote to him at all, letting them think whatever they wanted; it would help distract from my rapport with a German POW.

I let my mother know I was home before telling her I was going for a walk. I peeked at Friedrich with indifference as I walked out. My steps were slow, casual, in stark contrast to the audible thumping in my chest. If it wouldn't have drawn attention, I would've fled from my house without even stopping for a breath until reaching our clearing. I had seen him last Saturday, as well as the Saturday before that, but it had been over two weeks since we'd been able to sneak off together. The moment I noticed Friedrich was far enough away from the others not to be noticed, I had to restrain myself.

I entered the glade a few steps ahead of him. My coy smile flickered to see his fierceness, as if he was angry about something.

I raised my hands. "It's not my fault, okay? I get home as soon as I can and sometimes, there are just too many people around for you to——"

He cut me off with a kiss. I forgot whatever it was I was saying, my arms entangling with his. His unruly mouth on mine frightened me while at the same time awakening a curiosity of what would happen if we didn't stop. I wanted to trust him, but his passion inundated me, and I floundered out of distress under its waves.

His hands were in my hair, his body pressed against mine as the bark of a tree scraped my back. As much as I wanted to keep kissing him, the lack of control daunted me.

"Friedrich," I whispered, unsure of where to put my hands. "Friedrich..."

I turned my head away when he didn't slow down, his lips landing on my cheek. His breathing was heavy; I could feel him trembling. We'd been apart for too long.

His voice was hoarse. "I am sorry."

I twiddled his hair with my fingertips as he held me, the two of us trying to recover. "I take it you missed me?"

"I am starving for you."

Brushing his lips against mine, he took me by the hand, leading me over to the fallen tree. Sitting down, I rested my head on him, cherishing his hand in mine.

"They say the war is over until Christmas," he said.

"*By* Christmas," I corrected him.

I'd heard the boys at school talking about that, too. Most of them were disgruntled that they were going to miss out on the fighting. Some of them had even decided to lie about their ages just to get in before it ended.

"By Christmas," Friedrich muttered. "This is not true, but...it makes me think a lot."

I perked up. "Really? You don't think it'll end by December?"

He shook his head. "Unless something big happens—for either side."

I wasn't sure how I felt about this. Of course, I wanted it to end. The sooner it ended, the sooner the world would stabilize—the sooner Friedrich and I could be together. Yet, I knew before that could happen, we would first have to endure an indefinite period of separation. Every time it crossed my mind, I tried to force it out. He was with me now.

Friedrich seemed lost in thought. "I cannot imagine what I am going back to. It is not the same place after this."

His hand was so warm in mine; so firm, so present. I blinked toward the sky, trying to keep the water out of my eyes. "It scares me."

He kissed the top of my head, putting his arm around me. "What scares you?"

"I don't want to be without you. I keep thinking, what if it's years? What if I don't know where you are and have no way to contact you? Worst of all..." My voice had cracked from the strain of emotion. "Worst of all, what if you forget about me?"

He rubbed my arm, chuckling. "It is not me I worry about. You go to college. You get out of this little town, get away from your parents; you experience true independence. There is going to be an endless line of boyfriends at your doorstep. If anyone forgets, it is you."

I sniveled, clinging to his neck. "That's not true."

"One day, you wake up and realize you want to be with an American war-hero, not some prisoner from the enemy country. When you are old and wise, you want not your family knowing about us. It is easy and appropriate if you marry an American."

I buried my face in his chest, using every ounce of strength I had to keep from weeping. I didn't want to talk about this, *think* about this. The truth was, I knew I was only seventeen. I still had a lot of growing up to do, a lot of the world yet to explore. As much as I wanted to believe that nothing would change—that my feelings for him would always be this strong and real—I was uncertain. My record of making hard decisions did not serve me well. I did what was easy to avoid confrontation or to make other people happy. I wanted to believe with my whole heart that I would continue being steadfast even after he was gone, but I didn't trust myself.

I pulled away, my hands on either side of his face as I cried. "I don't want to believe this is temporary. I don't want to look back and say that I was young and foolish and that I didn't understand love. I know I'm young, but I also know that there could not possibly be another person on earth who

looks at me the way you do, who kisses me the way you do..."
I kissed him. "Who loves me the way you do. Look at how
much we've changed. We've become better people because of
this, Friedrich. This is more than lust, more than convenience,
more than impulsive passion; you are the other half of my
soul. Isn't that enough to sustain us, even if we're apart?"

I wanted him to say he agreed; I wanted him to tell
me I was right, because the hope could only survive if we
both believed it. Wiping a tear away from my cheek with the
back of his hand, he studied my face as if to memorize it. "I
hope so."

I was glad when we moved on to something else. I
couldn't bear discussing this with him. It burdened my heart
that he thought I could forget him. If he believed that, did
that mean he'd vindicate himself by moving on without me
later, simply because he imagined I already had? It would be
like one of those sick, twisted, tragic romances, like *Romeo and
Juliet*. Love wasn't supposed to end that way.

"What are your plans for college?" he asked later,
once the conversation regarding our inescapable separation
was far from our minds.

"I want to go to the University of Virginia, but my
parents have always said they want me to be close—mostly
my mother," I said, thinking it over. "She wants me to go to
Mackerley. It's a local four-year institution. Most of the
people from my school that go to college usually go there."

"You are not wanting this?"

"Not really. The idea is if I go there, I can live at
home instead of a dormitory. That way I won't get into any
mischief. You know, because I won't get into any if I'm at
home." I gave him an ironic smile.

"Shows how little they know. I hope you go to
Mackerley, though."

"Why?"

"If you go to University of Virginia, how am I seeing
you?"

I stared at him a moment. "That's only if the war's
over by then. If not, I'll stay. I'd go to Mackerley for you."

He didn't look as pleased as I thought he would, lowering his eyes.

"It's just kind of...insulting that they want me to go there," I said. "They were going to let Amos go to Cornell. It's because I'm a girl. It's not practical for me to spend so much on school."

Friedrich looked puzzled. "Why? Is this not what the money from your trust fund is for?"

I felt uncomfortable about it now instead of resentful. I plucked up a dandelion. "They want me to have something I can give my future husband someday."

He chuckled. "What? In case you marry someone poor?"

"No. They've never had any intention of me marrying poor. The idea was always that I would marry into another affluent family. Now, I'm sure they'd like it to be someone who could manage my father's business someday, since Amos is gone."

"Why is someone like this needing your money?"

"They wouldn't. Not really. It's in case he needs some persuasion. Money will help."

His face hardened. "They tell you this? Like in conversation at dinner?"

"Of course they haven't; it's just been implied." I chucked the petals off the dandelion, tossing them to the ground. "And why wouldn't they feel that way? I'm not enough for them, so why would I be enough for anyone else?"

He gripped at my chin, forcing me to look at him. "If it is me, you are all I need."

His expression was unforgiving, though his eyes were soft. I looked away out of bashfulness, the idea of marrying him someday flashing through my mind. I could see us laughing, in awe that everything was just the way it should be at last. We had found one another again, with a love that time itself couldn't depreciate. In that instant, I prayed that it was not a dream, but a small glimpse of the future God had planned for us—an affirmation of unfathomable happiness, as long as we were both willing to wait for it.

He slid down the log onto the grass, holding out his arm to me. "Come."

I sat next to him, resting against his chest as he held me. I wondered if this would ever be my right, my privilege; if he might ever call me his wife. He rested his head against mine.

Blithe little birds chirped to one another overhead in the trees. The breeze was gentle, scented with the sweetness of honeysuckle, brushing through the limbs and tickling the leaves. The ambience was perfect, if there was anything that could be. I listened to his heart beating, counting each calm, soothing breath, as he murmured a song.

It was in German; I couldn't understand the words. It was beautiful in a haunting, heartbreaking sort of way. His silken tenor voice was captivating and I began to cry without even knowing why.

"Schumann," he said once he finished. "My mother sings it all the time."

I sniffled, hoping he didn't feel the dampness on his shirt. "What does it mean?"

"It is a love song. Kind of. It is about being apart from the one you love; dreaming of her, only to wake up alone; being in such torment that sleep never comes; how she is giving her heart to you so many times. I never can relate to it. I can now."

New tears leaked from my eyes as he kissed the top of my head. "But we aren't apart yet."

He didn't say anything and I was desperate not to think about it.

"Where will we go after you take me to Hawaii?" I asked, giving me time to correct myself.

"I know not. Where are you wanting to go?"

"How about China?"

"Why China?"

"Amos used to say he wanted to go there. He read a book once on the collapse of the Han Empire and was infatuated with China from that point on. It makes me think of him."

"Hmm. We can walk on the Great Wall. I want to see this myself. You are probably liking to see the panda bears. There is also a famous palace in the near of the Himalayans. You are probably liking this, too. But the real question is," he said, "what are we doing when I take you to Germany?"

My blood flashed with heat and I tried to curb my smile. "You want to take me to Germany?"

"Of course."

I laughed. "You'd have to marry me first."

My mutinous tongue had spoken before my brain even knew what happened. The idea of marrying him didn't scare me; it was that, for the seven months we'd known each other, everything from our unsuitable friendship to our indecent romance had been done in secret. I didn't even know if that was what he wanted.

Tense, I clenched my eyes shut. "What I...what I meant was——"

"I marry you today if I can."

This shocked me more than if he'd told me we needed to slow down. I sat up to see his face. "You would?"

His sincere expression didn't change. "Go get your Pastor Gilbert. I make it right now."

I erupted in delight as he smiled. "You would? Truly, you would?"

"Yes. You are wanting this, too? Right?"

I considered him, biting my lip. "If you asked me the right way."

"What is the right way?"

My little sister's voice rang in the distance, calling for me. I listened before kissing him, getting to my feet. "I have to go."

He pulled me back. "No, no, no. Tell me what is the right way."

My little sister screamed my name in frustration.

"Surprise me," I whispered against his lips.

He laughed before yanking me down onto his lap again, holding me tight. My fingers ran through his hair as he attempted to siphon from my mouth every secret I'd ever kept. With a ragged breath, I broke away before I got too delirious to remember my own name.

Lucy was on the front porch when I arrived, her little fists balled up as she yelled for me. "Sissy!"

"I'm here, I'm here," I said, jogging up the drive. "Why are you yelling?"

"Mommy wants you watch me."

"Why?" I asked, mostly to myself as I picked her up.

Approaching the screen door, I saw my mother's silhouette hurry into my father's study, slamming the door. In the living room I paused, hearing her muffled sobs on the other side.

"What's wrong with Mommy?" I asked Lucy.

She wasn't concerned. "I not know."

Leaning close to the door, I could hear her crying as if she was trying to keep me from hearing. I wanted to walk away, but she sounded as distraught as she had when we got the letter about Amos.

I made a couple light raps on the door. "Mom, are you okay?"

"Just go away," she answered tearfully. "Take Lucy outside and go away."

I adjusted Lucy on my hip. "Is Dad okay?"

"Dad is *fine*. Go."

Her bitterness was unmissable. I lingered by the door for only a moment before returning outside with Lucy. Starting for Lucy's swing, I stopped.

He must have told her; he told her I'd talked to him on the phone. Maybe that was why she spoke with such derisiveness to me about my father. Maybe the scum had told her he wasn't going to risk it anymore. She was in a difficult situation because she knew she'd done wrong, and she couldn't take it out on me for confronting him.

Not directly anyway.

"Sissy, we tan swing?" Lucy asked.

I picked up my steps. My mother wouldn't let me get away with this. There would be a reprisal, even if she didn't say what for. As long as she ended her liaison, I would deal with whatever else she might throw at me.

Fourteen

By the end of the week, I knew beyond a doubt that something had deeply agitated my mother. I couldn't remember a time where she could be set off so easily. I walked in after school one day to see her spanking Lucy for spilling milk on the floor. I had tried to intervene, pointing out that it was an accident, but that only incensed my mother further. I cleaned it up for her without speaking as she continued to berate me and scold my little sister. After Mom left for work, I held Lucy more for myself than for her; by that point, she had forgotten all about my mother's short temper. I knew it was only a matter of time before it showed itself again.

How accurate my assumptions had been.

I had come home and, upon seeing Friedrich in the center of the field in the midst of the other POWs, I knew we wouldn't be seeing each other that day. I played with my little sister outside until my mother called us in for an early dinner, a little more than an hour before the prisoners usually left. With one last pining glimpse in Friedrich's direction, I carried Lucy inside.

My mother was pensive and I stayed silent, with the exception of whenever Lucy spoke to me. I was grateful for this quiet dinner, considering my mother seemed on the edge of fury for the past week. At one point, I became aware of her watching me as she chewed and I braced myself for the onslaught.

She stabbed at her green beans. "Have you sent in your application to Mackerley yet?"

I took a deep breath. "No."

She seemed to frost over, fork in midair. "Why not?"

I glanced at her, pushing the lump of mashed potatoes around on my plate. "Because...I don't know if I want to go to Mackerley."

Her fork clinked against the ceramic. I kept my eyes down as I ate, hoping to keep from provoking her any further.

"I thought we decided that was where you were going."

I took a drink of water, giving her a slight shake of the head.

"Answer me," she barked.

I didn't want to lie to her; I didn't want to let her browbeat me, either. "That's where you and Dad decided I was going to go. I'm not so sure it's where I want to go."

Her fork clattered as she dropped it, leaning her face into her hand. "You've got to be kidding me. *Why* would you want to go anywhere else, Cassandra? Mackerley is close to home. You can get there on your bike, and I need you here to watch Lucy."

Hot flashes of resentment and cold chills of dread over this imminent clash of wills were coursing through my body. I wanted to concede to her just to avoid what was coming—but I knew I couldn't. This was it, me busting down the walls of my shell. "Well...I was thinking if you went back to working the day shift—or if the war ends—it wouldn't be a problem. The papers are already saying it'll be over by December. I could come home on weekends and—"

"Who said I was going to quit working even if it does end?"

"Why wouldn't you? Dad will be home more once it's over. I thought this was just you doing your part for the war effort."

She shook her head, jaw clenching as she picked up her fork. "I'm not leaving my job and I'm not switching back to day shift. You're just going to have to go to Mackerley so that——"

I slapped the table, shouting before I even thought to restrain my anger. "That is *not* fair! I'm not the one who decided that you should keep working, so why should I have to stay here? This is my life—*my* trust fund—and if I don't want to go to the college of *your* choice, I shouldn't have to."

"Don't you *dare* talk to me that way, young lady! Who do you think gave you the right to even have a choice? It wouldn't even be yours to make if——"

"Grandpa Robert is the reason I can choose," I roared over my plate. "What is so wrong with me wanting to go to the University of Virginia instead? You were going to send Amos to Cornell. That's why the money was given to me and that's the only thing I intend on using it for."

"It's a waste of money when you can get the same education here. It doesn't make any sense to go to the University of Virginia when—not only is it more expensive—but I need you here to help me, Cassandra."

"Mom, I am *this close* to being legally allowed to make my own decisions. Maybe I'll even go to Cornell. I'll look into all my options, but I can almost guarantee I'm not going to Mackerley."

My mother threw her fork and I shot up in my seat as it slid across the table. "You are so selfish! I should've known when it came down to this, you'd only think about yourself! We have given you *everything*, Cassandra, and all you do is take and take and take. You don't give a damn about anyone——"

"Mom——"

"*Anyone*, but yourself. Why couldn't you be more like your brother? Do you think he was worrying about what college he was going to when he turned eighteen? No. He was facing the possibility that he would give his life for this country."

"You want me to join up, then?"

"That is *not* what I said! Your brother could see the bigger picture. He wasn't behaving like a child, looking only at the present. Going into the Army was never in our plans for him or his own, but he did what he had to do and we're very proud of him for that."

"I am not Amos!" I screamed. The table shook as I sprung to my feet. "Who says you can't be proud of me, too? Who says I'm not looking at the bigger picture? You? Dad? What about *me*? I've thought about this; I've prayed about this. It may have not been right for Amos, but it's right for me."

She scowled, but her eyes were glistening.

I leaned on the table. "You want to know the truth about your perfect son? Almost every night after Amos turned sixteen, he spent sneaking in and out of the house— drinking, partying, messing around with his friends and girl friends."

Her lips parted.

"He wasn't studying or sleeping like a good boy in his bed; he was lying to you. And do you want to know why Holly doesn't talk to me anymore? It's because Amos had been paying her to pretend to be my friend. The moment she found out he was gone, she was off the hook. My brother didn't believe in me enough to think I could make friends on my own. I loved him, but that is one of the most crushing, degrading things I've ever heard of. What do you have to say to that, Mom? Are you really so bullheaded that you won't tell me he was wrong to do that? Or do you not believe I have what it takes, either?"

She stared at me in shock. Tears filled my eyes though I didn't cry, the dripping from the kitchen faucet the only sound between us.

I watched her swallow, her voice dropping several decibels. "I'd say you have the potential to learn a hard lesson here. Amos had the right idea, Cassandra. There's no such thing as true friendship—true love," she said with contempt. "Loyalty, devotion, faithfulness; those are the real fairy tales. That's just the way of the world. You can try until you can't possibly try anymore, but in the end, you're just going to end up alone. Friends are only around for what you can give them and men...the only thing that enraptures a man is money, Cassie."

She didn't look at me as she wiped her face, my vision blurring as I watched her. As aggrieved as I was, I pitied her now. She'd given up on everything that was good, everything that was true. Her heart had hardened because it had been battered and neglected by every person she'd ever let in. She didn't just believe the lies; she embraced them.

Those same lies competed for a foothold in my own heart, but now, all I could hear was Friedrich: *"If it is me, you are all I need."*

I shook my head. "No. No, I don't believe that. You're wrong. And one day, I'm going to show you just how wrong you are."

Her expression was blank, neither encouraging me nor mocking me. I took that as my cue to leave, stalking out of the kitchen.

Saturday couldn't come fast enough. I needed the rejuvenation I only found with Friedrich after most of my energy had been depleted by my mother. Once, he'd reached across the table, flipping my hair with his pencil in response to one of my sarcastic remarks. I laughed before wondering if anyone had seen. Another time, he had left his hand near the center of the table, and I flicked it with my finger. For a moment, I imagined taking hold of it—unconcerned with how many people surrounded us—before common sense dropped like an anchor in my brain.

My mother was making dinner when I got home. With Lucy playing in the family room, I skulked out the front door before my mother could stop me. Meeting Friedrich in the woods, I greeted him in what had become our usual way—with scores of various kisses. His gait was restless around the clearing while I sat down, watching him from the fallen tree.

I twiddled the hem of my dress between my fingers. "What do you think it's going to be like when it's over?"

"What mean you?"

"When you go home," I clarified. "Do you think anyone else has begun to feel the way you do? Do you think Nazism will still be as strong as it is now?"

I almost felt out of line asking such a question when I thought about how he'd once dedicated his life to it. I was relieved to hear him chuckle under his breath. "It is not like we can discuss if we are changing or not. I hear a few expressing interest in ideas from the Bible studies, but not enough to raise suspicion. I imagine there are some who feel like me, but we are all trying to understand."

"Understand what?"

He paused to look at me, lost in thought. "All of this, it is...it contradicts all we know, all we believe—all they are telling us. Living a life after Christ means making the choice. I, and perhaps others, make this choice. Now we try to understand why."

He stopped, leaning against the tree closest to me. I could see his apprehension, as if he knew what he was about to say wouldn't please me.

"I am not where you are, Cassie. This is new; a relationship with Christ is foreign. He always seems so distant and simple, a figurine on a shelf you look at sometimes. When I think back," he murmured, crossing one foot over the other, "it is as if God is always there, but I am not looking for Him; I am not seeing Him. Now that I am aware of Him, it is as if He hides from me. Well, I suppose He is not hiding—He gives me a reason to look for Him. It is what I want right now, but I wonder about later. What if I go back before I am sure I find Him? What if my hold on Him is not as strong as I hope? I cannot help but ask if He is able to keep me from letting go and walking away."

I thought and I prayed, unsure what God wanted me to say about this—if He wanted me to say anything at all. Maybe this was just something Friedrich needed to talk about out loud.

"Sometimes, I think about how you are strong," he said. "I wish that I can say I feel as much passion and conviction as you. But I am not. I want this, but...too many things need filtering out of my head and heart first. There are bad thoughts here, bad beliefs," he said, pointing toward his chest. "It is not like pulling weeds from a garden; it is like digging bones from the ground, with careful, steady hands. I am once so certain of what my responsibility to the world is and now, I know not. My design, I know, is serving God's purposes, but I know not what they are. Before, I can give you lists of all the things I am proud of in my life. Now, it is not pride I feel when I think back. I am trying still to comprehend who God is; I cannot think of what I am making that has pleased Him—if anything."

He stared at his feet. "I am sorry if this disappoints you."

I gave him a sympathizing grin. I walked over, wrapping my arms around his neck. "I'm not disappointed. You have to figure this out yourself in order to call it your own faith. If you simply believed because I did, then it would be superficial. You're sifting through and comparing your beliefs so that you'll see that God has no equal."

He hugged me, my cheek cool against the warmth of his chest. His voice was so feeble it made my eyes burn. "I am not ready to do this alone, Cassie. I need you because I need Him."

"You'll never be alone, Friedrich. And you really don't need me; you *just* need Him. We both know there's coming a time where we can't be together. He's the only thing that isn't going to change. He's always going to be with us—here in the woods, at home in Germany, away at college." My voice cracked. "You have to understand that. I can't be between you."

He lifted his head away from mine. His forehead crinkled in vexation and I traced his cheeks with my fingertips. "Going through Him is the only way we can be certain of anything. I need Him, for many reasons, but one of them is because I want to be with you. It's the only way I'll be able to trust that you'll wait for me—or that you're still waiting for me, or if it's time to move on."

A breath escaped his lips. "You think we are not being together in the end?"

I fought back tears, hiding my eyes from him in his chest. "I want to be with you—only you—but what I want and what God wants could be two different things. I don't know if what we have is only for a season, or if it's for life."

I had always trusted that God had a better plan whenever my dreams were derailed. I wondered if God was watching us now, grinning to Himself, already seeing me happier with someone besides Friedrich in the future. That was a heart-shattering thought, one that I felt conflicted by. I wanted Friedrich because he was the only one who had ever loved the real me. He was a perfect fit, as if our flaws and our strengths fused to reveal the whole persons inside of us. I didn't want to face the possibility—ever—that he was only here to prepare me for something better later.

Engulfed by my sadness, I stood on my toes, clinging to him. "I can't picture a future with you. But all I know is I still want you, even though I can't see it."

"I cannot imagine my future *without* you." His grip on me was firm, as if keeping me depended on his physical strength. "If there is anything I *am* certain of, it is you."

His lips moved against mine with the kind of gentleness only sorrow could cause, as if this were to be our last. Each simple brush of his lips lingered, allowing me to relish it, to feel a sense of intimacy I'd never experienced with another person. I was in love with him, unreservedly, unconditionally, unapologetically. It was fear that kept me from believing he was the one for me. I was afraid to chance the heartache, the mere thought of it giving me a taste of despair that was too overwhelming to swallow.

But he was here with me now. The incessancy of preventing myself from dreaming I'd be with him after the war was exhausting. For an instant—one glorious, beautiful instant—I shut the door to doubt, allowing the hope to roam freely throughout my being.

I smiled, my eyes still closed as his forehead pressed against mine. I was going to be with him again someday.

"Tell me you love me," he whispered.

I chuckled under my breath, as if I knew he really was mine for the first time. "I love you."

There was a chance this wasn't destined to become a long-forgotten secret, locked away in a sunken chest of memories:

Maybe its true purpose was to keep us from forgetting who we were to one another during an incalculable interlude.

It was getting harder for me to separate myself from him. We were always one of the last pairs to split up at the end of our Bible study sessions. Friedrich's time in the woods with me was lengthening. I knew we should care that every second longer he spent away, the more likely it was that someone would notice. He appeased me, telling me that none of the men would rat him out and the guards weren't vigilant enough to detect him missing.

Some nights, I'd look out my bay window from my bed, an incorrigible smile on my face. My love for him would burn in my chest and all I could think about was what it was going to be like when we found each other after the war.

Then, on other nights, I'd clutch to my pillow and sob, wishing it was him I was holding onto. There was no possible way what we had was going to go beyond Bible studies and covert trysts in the forest. We had failed to create a redeemable situation. The only thing we had succeeded in doing was setting ourselves up for inescapable heartbreak.

When I got home Monday afternoon, the POWs were on the end of the field near Mr. Stewart's farm, a rather disheartening sight for me. I had taken Lucy outside for a couple hours, until the prisoners piled into the trucks to be hauled away. I finished eating dinner, washing the dishes as my mother finished getting ready for work.

"Sweep the downstairs for me tonight," my mother said, positioning the cap on her head as she reentered the kitchen. "I also need you to dust your father's study. It's getting filthy in there."

I tried not to grumble. "All right."

"It should've already been done." Her tone was severe. "I get tired of telling you to do these things, Cassandra. You know I don't have time. It would be nice if you would do them on your own without me having to say so."

I made an irritable glance at her over my shoulder, dismayed that she wasn't paying attention to me.

She smoothed the front of her uniform with her hands. "I'm coming home a little late in the morning. You're going to have to be late for school."

I paused, the water running over my hands. "Why are you just now telling me? I could've told my teachers."

"I forgot. Goodbye, Sweetheart." She kissed Lucy on the head. "Mommy loves you."

Lucy didn't look up, scribbling in red on a sheet of paper. "Wuv you."

"Get that done tonight, Cassandra," my mother said before leaving.

I gave Lucy a bath before bed, her angel blonde hair darkening to look like gnarled, wet strands of hay on her head. She chattered nonstop as I combed out the tangles. Her baby arms were like a necklace around my neck as I tucked her into bed.

"Sissy?" I heard her say as I stood at the door to leave.

"What is it, baby doll?"

She looked at me as if she were trying to think of how to put into words what she was thinking. "I want a pony."

I couldn't help but laugh. "A pony? Why do you want a pony?"

"I will ride it and...and when Daddy is home, he tan ride wif me."

I chuckled. "Maybe so. Can I ride it with you?"

"Yeah. We will ride be-toz we are princess. You are princess and I are princess."

Her jade eyes twinkled in the dark. I told her good night, chuckling to myself as I shut her door between us. Perhaps my father never being home and my mother's constant bad moods didn't affect her like they did me. Maybe her pure outlook on life kept her from seeing things the way I did. I envied her for that.

Grabbing the feather duster from under the kitchen sink, I started for my father's study. Setting my sights on the bookshelf in the right corner, I noticed the safe before doing a double-take.

The door was half-open. My mother must have left it open by accident. On tenterhooks, I crouched down in front of it. She had to have gone in for the money. I suddenly felt sick to my stomach; she told me she'd be coming home late in the morning...

She was going to see her lover.

I swallowed a festering ball of anger as I pulled open the safe door. Pulling the cash out from the back, I counted through it once, twice, just to be sure.

The whole two-thousand was there and accounted for.

Bewildered, I stared at it before returning it to its place. I had been certain that at least a few hundreds would be missing, yet it was all there. If it wasn't for the money, then she must have been in the safe for another reason—but why?

I didn't want to snoop—perhaps it was all an overreaction on my part—but I peeked at the stacks of papers inside without touching them. There was a packet of paper-clipped paper on my father's cigar box that hadn't been there before. I picked them up, my mouth dropping as I read the cover sheet.

It was a requisition for divorce.

Frantic, I slammed the papers on the floor, skimming through one after the other. It mentioned the two children, Cassandra and Lucy, and one deceased son, Amos. It mentioned what my mother was entitled to and guaranteed my father would retain ownership of Wyndham Aero Industries. It mentioned how much my father was to pay in child support—a large sum I was rather surprised by—and from beginning to end, it stated that adultery was the primary motivation for the dissolution of their marriage.

My mother hadn't signed it. It wasn't until I saw my father's signature that the tears came.

This was not random. It was apparent that my parents had been discussing this for a while. They were this far along in the process and I still wouldn't have had any idea if I hadn't seen the evidence in the safe. How could they have kept something like this from me? How long had my father known? How recently had he signed the papers?

Shoving the papers into the safe, I slammed the door shut as hard as I could. I cried into my hands, leaning against the wall. So my father really had been aware of my mother's infidelity. I wasn't sure if I was happy for him or simply bitter about the entire situation. He was divorcing her. No one I knew had ever been divorced before. I was glad I would be starting college soon. At least I'd be considered more of an adult than a child and I wouldn't be judged for my parents' broken marriage. Poor Lucy was going to be starting school in a few years with split-up parents. Children were cruel, and they would especially be so to her if they overheard their own parents talking about what a disgrace the former Wyndhams were. My age had given me the capacity to handle the loss of our brother and the soon-to-be separation of our parents. It frightened me to think of how so many catastrophes in such a short span of time were going to affect Lucy's innocence.

This must have been why my mother was so determined for me to go to Mackerley and why she wouldn't quit her hospital job. My father was leaving her and she couldn't do it all on her own. Instead of taking responsibility for herself, she wanted to force me to help carry her burden.

I became more irate than sad by that point. Heading back out into the living room, I was too furious to even care about dusting or sweeping as she'd asked me to. I resented my father for not telling me what was going on, but I blamed my mother most of all. Her exploits had disassembled our already damaged family.

No longer was I able to stay silent. Tomorrow morning, when she got home, I was going to confront my mother.

Fifteen

It was difficult for me to sleep that night with my parents' divorce looming over my head. I awoke at six the next morning, before I even usually got up for school, in spite of getting only a few hours of sleep. I felt wide awake, readying myself for when my mother came home. Knowing Lucy would sleep for at least another hour or so, I got dressed and put on my make-up for school later. I watched the prisoners arrive at eight, when I would've already been gone on any ordinary day. Friedrich was walking up the center, giving me a look that asked why I was still there. I smiled at him before going into Lucy's room to get her up and dressed.

I was reading to Lucy in the family room a little after ten when I heard my mother's car pull in the drive. Kissing Lucy on the head, I laid the princess book in her lap, sending her into the kitchen.

She obeyed and I headed for the door. Almost crashing into my mother, she gave me a tired, unenthusiastic greeting. After kissing my baby sister good morning, she headed back towards me.

"Mom, I...I need to talk to you."

She was taking her cap out of her hair. "Not now, Cassandra, I'm exhausted. I already won't be getting much sleep with Lucy up."

I followed her up the stairs. "Yeah, I know and I'm sorry for that, but Mom, it really can't wait."

"Well, you're going to have to—"

"Why didn't you tell me you and Dad were getting a divorce?"

She halted, agape as she turned to look at me.

"I know about the affair," I continued. "I've known about it for a while actually. But I want to know why neither of you told me you were getting divorced."

She fiddled with the hair pins to her cap, speaking in an angry whisper. "Just how did you find out?"

"I saw the papers in the safe."

She looked incredulous. "The safe?"

"Yes."

"You had no right being in there. Everything in that safe is mine and your father's business—*everything*. How *dare* you poke around—"

"I wasn't poking around. You left the door open. I went over to close it and saw the papers. Why didn't you tell me?"

"Because you are a *child*, Cassandra. This is none of your business. You had no right looking in that safe."

"I am *not* a child, and considering I'm a member of this family, you tearing it apart is my business."

This rendered my mother speechless before she erupted. "Why am I always the bad guy? Why am I blamed for everything? Does your father bear no responsibility for this?"

"Dad's made his mistakes, but they're nothing compared to what you've done."

"You have always taken his side," she cried, jabbing a finger at me. "No matter what he's done, you've always loved him more than me."

"That's not true."

"Yes, it is, Cassandra! Do you think I'm proud of this? Do you think I wanted this to happen? I didn't mean...I wasn't..." She bawled into her hand. I felt only a pinch of guilt that I didn't feel sorry for her. "Nobody loves me.

Nobody. Amos was the only one who ever loved me. I wish he was here——"

She cut herself off, somewhere between a gasp and a sputter.

I tightened my grip on the banister. "You mean, instead of me?"

"Don't be ridiculous!"

"It's what you were going to say," I said, my eyes watering over. "It's what you've always wanted to say."

"Yes, because everything is about you, Cassandra. You are *just* like your father; the only thing that matters is *you*! It shouldn't surprise me that you love him more. You're nothing like me."

My voice shook. "Fine. Then, when this is final, I'll make it easy for both of us; I'll go live with Dad so you can pretend *I'm* the one who died and I don't have to put up with *you* anymore."

Her face was red, coated with tears. "You do that, Cassandra. Do whatever makes *you* happy. Just like your father, you do what you want and forget about everyone else."

She stomped up the stairs, slamming her bedroom door. I stood there, giving myself a moment to keep the tears from overflowing before going to Lucy in the kitchen.

Making glances at the clock while I colored at the table with Lucy, I debated on whether I should even go to school or not. As far away as I wanted to be from my mother, school felt like such a trivial thing today. The day was nearly half over anyway. My mother had stomped downstairs without looking at me after lunch, yanking Lucy up and taking her away without a word. By then, I had decided it wasn't worth going.

It wasn't until I saw the prisoners coming back from their lunch that I went outside. Friedrich was off to himself, but I knew it was going to take a few minutes for him to sneak away. Leaning my bike against what had become its usual spot, I strolled through the trees, a path I now knew by heart. I sat down on the fallen log to wait.

Our family was disintegrating. The only thing that kept me from being overwrought was knowing that I would be leaving for college in a few months. The distance that the University of Virginia would guarantee me meant that I could detach myself from the mess my parents were making. The only thing I worried about was Lucy. So many things in the world she had come to know had changed—*would* be changing. I knew I'd feel guilty for leaving her behind, but I hoped—despite how my mother would surely tell her that I didn't care about them—that one day she would understand why I had to separate myself from our mother.

My mother had better be wishing that the Germans stayed in Rockmont for a while longer, because Friedrich was the only reason I would go to Mackerley instead. I didn't even mind if my mother believed I went there for her as long as Friedrich and I knew it was for him. The possibility of the prisoners being repatriated before next summer made my heart heavy. I couldn't wait to find him again after the war, but the time apart wasn't going to be easy. There was no way to evade it; no matter which college I went to or when the war officially ended, we were going to be forced apart.

"You are much too beautiful for being so sad."

It surprised me to see Friedrich dropping his tools. He was grinning at me, and I slid onto the ground, holding my arms out to him. "Hold me."

He didn't speak, sinking down behind me with his legs on either side of me. He brushed my hair away from my forehead. "What is wrong?"

"It's just not a good day."

"You want to talk about it?"

I looked into his inquisitive blue eyes. I shook my head in reply.

"Why are you not at school today?" he asked. "Though I am grateful for time with you."

"Aren't you afraid someone's going to notice you're missing?"

"I am sure they already notice. But they are not saying anything. They probably think I find a way to escape."

I chuckled. "Yeah, so...aren't you afraid they'll tell?"

"It is not like we are children, telling on little Wilhelm so we can be a hero for the teacher; we are all on the same side. If someone can escape, we want it for him. It is the duty of a prisoner of war, no matter what side you fight for."

"What do you mean?"

"The Geneva Convention says it is legal. We cannot be..." He paused to think. "—*punish* for it. The worst that happens is they catch us, maybe put us in solitary confinement and give us bread and water for a week. Then, they put us back with the others, conspiring again."

I thought for a moment. "So why isn't anyone doing it?"

The blue in his eyes shined like glass. "It is not as simple as it is in Europe. Here in America, we worry about how they catch us making our way across the country, but we also have to get on a ship, go through France and cross the front lines. Only those who speak English without an accent have a chance of doing this. Then you worry about money, identification—in case someone finds you suspicious and stops you. But the truth is," he said, lowering his voice, "no one is wanting to leave. It is safe here. We are as ready for the end of this as you are. Most of us prefer working here than moving forward the war over there—though no one is admitting this. It is shameful."

"So, if it's the right of a prisoner of war to get away, then what about you? Will you ever try?"

"I might have once—for fun. But not anymore."

"Why not?"

He laughed. "I think you know this. I am not afraid they catch me. I can never leave you like this; I worry the whole time. It is not worth it."

"Worry about what?"

"That they discover you know I am getting away," he said. "They call you a collaborator and charge you with treason because you know I escape. I tell you."

My face went lax as I faced the trees ahead of us. "I think we're a little too far past that to concern ourselves with it now."

"No. No, we are not," Friedrich said, shaking his head. "I tell you, I am not leaving; you are not helping me in any way. We meet in secret, and there is nothing saying they can punish us for falling in love. We make nothing wrong, Cassie. It is because of the war this is unacceptable. If you and I meet before the war, no one cares."

I outlined the muscles of his forearm. "It sounds like you've thought about this before I even brought it up."

"I am. Because I cannot live with me if I know they punish you because of me, or if I ruin your life. If someone comes through the forest right now and catches us, you are in more trouble than I am."

I went stock-still, craning my neck to look at him. "You're not going to stop meeting with me, are you?"

The longer his eyes stayed on mine, the more disturbed I became. His voice was soft as he looked away. "No. But I think about it. I want not any problems for you. The only reason I continue seeing you is...I pray about it. I realize it is the world that wants us apart, not God. He sees my heart for you is blameless; He sees what we have is real. But it is not changing the fact that I never forgive me if they catch us."

His expression was meditative as he rocked with me. I laid my head against him. "I love you. You really are the most fascinating person I've ever known."

Heat rushed to my cheeks from the endearing way he was looking at me. I watched him turn serious with thought. "I think there is a breakout soon, though. I notice some of the others acting odd. Distant. Secretive. I think not it is a mass escape—maybe one or two—but they need help getting the things I tell you, and like I say, they have to speak good English."

"Do you think you know who it is?"

"It can be any of them."

"Are you going to say anything?"

He smiled at me. "What? Inform on a comrade? No. I tell you. If someone has the chance, we let him take it. Most of them know they are not making it out of town. It is more like a game; make adventure for the guards."

I curled against him, the two of us watching the clouds move in the sky.

His lips were next to my ear. "What is bothering you?"

It was too exhausting thinking about the divorce and the words I'd had with my mother. I was already thinking of something else. "I think I'm going to go to Mackerley."

"Why?"

"Not because they want me to," I said, in a daze. "And I won't go the whole four years. Just until you leave."

I waited for him to speak. I had expected him to be excited, but his silence was foreboding.

I sat up as he pushed away to face me. "Cassie, no. I should not say this about hoping you stay. It is not fair to you. You should go to the University of Virginia."

I felt a cold chill sweep over me. "Friedrich, we don't have a lot of time left together. I want to spend every minute I can with you."

"I wish it can be this way, too, but you cannot stay here. Your mother, your father...they make you feel empty. You have to get away."

I had decided as long as he was there, I was going to be, too. "I've already made up my mind. It's fine. I'll transfer to the University of—"

"No, it is not fine, Cassie. This is not what you want and I am not being the reason for it. Promise me you are not going to Mackerley. If you come home on weekends, I see you at Bible study."

I shook my head, but he continued. "I prefer seeing you once a week with people around us than know when I leave, you are here alone. Besides, I may return to Germany in the spring and you make the choice going the university anyway."

My eyes were swimming. "Why are you doing this? I appreciate what you're saying, but Friedrich, I can't stand the idea of knowing you're here and I'm not. We don't have much time left—"

He cupped my face. "I know."

"Well, then, aren't you afraid?"

"It is terrifying me. All I think about is how you meet someone who is giving you all I cannot; not right now, no matter how much I want."

"Friedrich, no—"

"I cannot stop thinking about what you say to me—about putting you not before God. Well, I cannot put me before you either, Cassie. I want you to go to the University of Virginia because it is best for you. As much as I am afraid that you meet someone else, I take this chance. I have faith one day we have all the time for us we dream of. I believe in it, Cassie. This is why I am willing to let you go."

Tears fell from my lashes. Despite how I knew what he said was right and how much I wanted to believe him, I didn't want to hear it. I didn't want to be all the way in Charlottesville when I knew he was still close enough to talk to; to touch, to kiss. My chest felt tight with reluctance, and yet I felt comfort in hearing he believed we would be together again—once we were both free.

I sniffed, hugging his neck. "I wish there was a way I could just take you with me."

"You can keep me in a shoe box under the bed."

I couldn't help but laugh, despite how bleak I felt. "It's kind of sad that you and my little sister are the only things I'll miss."

"This is not such a bad thing. It is part of growing up. If you love everything here, you never leave."

I hated when he said things like that. It seemed to delineate how much more grown up he was and how far behind him I must have been. Right now, he either didn't mind or didn't notice that I wasn't on the same maturity level. I wondered if his feelings might change when he finally realized it.

I closed my eyes, focused on his breathing as I nestled my head in his chest. "I wish we didn't have to wait. I wish we could be together now. That's what I want more than anything."

"Well, if we find a lot of money, an ID for me and street clothes, and as long as we are okay being outlaws forever, we can."

My eyes bolted open. I gripped his arm, mouth wide open.

He spoke in a panicked whisper, scrutinizing the tree lines. "What?"

It was all coming together in my head. I couldn't believe I'd never thought of it before. A quiet laugh floated from my lips as I thought of how uncharacteristic it would be of me to do such a thing—as I thought of not having to wait to be with him.

"Cassie, what?"

I looked at him. "If I told you there was a way; if I told you it was possible…would you consider running away with me?"

He was staring at me. I took hold of his hand, on my knees in front of him. "Listen. My parents have two thousand dollars stashed away in their safe. I have the combination. I could bring you some of my brother's old clothes to change into. We could plan it out so that by the time they notice you're gone, we'll already be hours away. And no one will even know I'm missing until after school lets out."

Stupefied, he listened.

"I could tell my mother I'm going to school, but come here instead. If what you say is true, the others won't think anything of you missing. We could meet here, first thing in the morning. I'd have the money, you could change and we could leave—together. You wouldn't have to worry about identification. You'll have something the others couldn't possibly have if they escape—an American accompanying you."

He jumped up, rubbing a hand down his mouth as he began to pace in front of me.

My excitement was mounting. "We could head for the mountains; we could go to Mexico for all I care. We don't have to be apart, Friedrich. We don't have to wait and wonder and worry for only God knows how long. We can be together right now."

"Cassie, what...what if they catch us?"

I beamed at him. "What if they don't?"

I could tell there was a game of tug-of-war going on in his head. I stood, bracing his face with my hands. "This has to be available to us for a reason. We can do this. Run away with me, Friedrich." I kissed him, breathless. "Run away with me."

Something burned with desire in the pit of my stomach. I kissed him with an undisciplined intensity that I'd managed to keep suppressed until now. He matched my fervency, his hands forceful on my hips as he guided me backwards, pressing me against a tree. My whole body tingled to feel him so close. The path to our future was suddenly paved, unobstructed, and I was ready to give up everything in my present to walk it with him.

He pulled his head away, his voice hoarse as I kissed along his jaw. "This is not like you, Cassie."

My hands were all over him. "Maybe it should be. Maybe I'm tired of being good. I want to be with you now, Friedrich. I don't want to wait."

I opened my eyes as he gripped my arms, holding me in place as he stepped away. "You want not to wait because you are afraid. If we do this, you regret it."

"I doubt that."

His demeanor was a lot more placid than mine was. I tried kissing him, but he kept me pinned at arm's length. "Maybe not this day, or the next; maybe not even a week or a month later, but eventually, you regret it. It is spontaneous. You are a good person, Cassie. I know you are not believing this is the only way for us. The idea—it is tempting, but it is not right."

I jerked free from him. "Why does it have to be about right and wrong? I thought you wanted to be with me."

"Act you not...do not act like this. You know I want to be with you."

"Then why are you saying this? I can't bear the mere *thought* of being without you. I don't know if I can survive without you. This is our chance—"

"No."

I cried in painful desperation. "I don't want to spend my life waiting just to find out you've moved on."

"This is not what is happening."

"You don't know that! There is no way you can promise me you'll wait for me and mean it. What if I die? What if *you* die? What if you go home and find someone else? What if it gets too hard, waiting, and it's easier just to let go and forget about us, forget about me, forget that we ever happened? You don't know what's going to happen."

"No, but I tell you what I know. You are the only good and pure thing in my life—past, present and future. I wake up everyday wondering how I deserve you, because I am not. Nothing I do or ever do makes me worthy of keeping you. You are the last hope I have. You are the only thing that keeps me from believing God hates me. You know not what I see, what I think, what I do." His eyes filled with tears. "But He knows. And yet, for some reason, here you are, asking me to run away with you. I want to be with you, Cassie; if only you *know* how bad. So forgive me for refusing, but I want not to taint you or what we have."

Bereft of speech, I stared at him; never had I seen him even close to tears. His watery eyes stayed locked with mine. "When we are able to being together, I want it to be right. If we run, we are always running. Telling us we are together is a lie. Everything is as uncertain as it is now. We always wonder if they watch us, or follow us or find us. You are the only good thing—the only *right* thing—in my life, Cassie. I never want to ruin this."

The rims of my sight turned gray from breathing so hard. The bark of the tree was rough against my palms as I lowered to the ground. Neither of us moved, neither of us spoke, though I glanced at him a few times, trying to detect what he was thinking.

"Are you upset?" I finally heard him ask.

Playing with the skirt of my dress, I smoothed it out unnecessarily on my knee. "No. Just embarrassed."

Once more, I wanted to bury my head under the ground knowing he'd been the one to make the mature, responsible decision. "I...I'm sorry I acted that way. It's true. It's not me; the escaping or the way I almost persuaded you."

He snickered, still tense as he held out his hand to me. "It is fun while it lasts."

He pulled me to my feet. His fingers skimmed the inner surface of my hand as he lined his up with mine. Holding me close around the waist, he guided me in an unhurried sway. I learned his face by heart, every outline and shape, the color of his eyes, the bow of his lip. I wanted to engrave it into my memory, keeping him like this forever. Even as he sang me his German song, I watched the way his lips moved, the emotion in his eyes as he caressed me with his voice.

His hand squeezed mine. "I feel I think back on this day and regret it."

I laid my head on his chest. He continued to lead me and I closed my eyes as they stung. "I would go anywhere with you."

"I know." He chuckled under his breath. "So seduce me not again or I have no choice but to surrender."

Sixteen

Although we had come to the conclusion not to run away together, I still enjoyed imagining it. It made me want to plead my case to him again whenever I envisioned us living in some remote cabin deep in the mountains. We could find a little country church somewhere with a pastor who would marry us. For sustenance, we could tend to our own little garden, canning food for winter and raising our own livestock, unnoticed by the rest of the world.

And each night by the fire, I could fall asleep in his arms.

Maybe he was right. Maybe I wouldn't regret it right away—but as long as I was with him, I didn't think I'd regret it at all.

Other times, I ventured to consider the alternative. I was only seventeen; he was twenty-two and an enemy to my country. If we were caught on the run, we'd have an infamy comparable to Bonnie and Clyde's. They would all say I had been beguiled and used by this German. No one would believe that he really loved me, or that it was anything other than misguided infatuation that I felt for him. I would be expected to renounce my feelings in shame, blaming my youth for what I had done.

And after that, no matter how we found one another again, we would always be haunted by that notorious label.

Our story would not be one of two people falling in love, but of a stupid girl whose weaknesses she allowed a German man to prey upon.

That cheap perception of what we had disturbed me more than the idea of waiting for him did.

My mother hardly spoke to me after our face-off regarding the divorce. I avoided her as much as I could, barricading myself in my room or outside until she left for work. Her perpetual grimaces told me she was loath to even look at me. It was dumbfounding that she believed she was entitled to be offended; her affair had instigated the divorce. She had no one to blame but herself.

I wanted to talk to my dad about it. As usual, whenever he did call, he never asked to speak with me. I suspected he continued calling for the sake of appearances. It would take a great lack of finesse for me to phone him and strike up a conversation about the divorce—not that he had time to say much more than 'I can't talk right now' to me. I wasn't sure if my mother even told him that I knew. It had been almost three months since he'd last been home, and I feared the divorce would only prolong his absence—if he came back at all.

Though I had yet to receive a response from Jimmy, I enjoyed writing to him. It was heartening to think that what I had to say was comforting and meaningful to him, even if it was a simple boring report of my daily thoughts and routines. Despite the attention I'd been getting from some of the boys at school, none of them endeavored to be my friend. Most of them were just looking for a date before they went off to war. Besides Friedrich, it was nice having someone to talk to who cared.

Going to church with my mother was unbearable. She responded to my questions with sharp, curt replies. We both would sit stiff in the pew with Lucy between us, my mother donning a halfhearted, forced smile that her eyes didn't share when other church members greeted her. Once, while my mother conversed with Mrs. Webb, I caught Holly eyeing me from the opposite side of the sanctuary. Locking eyes with each other, her hateful expression flinched as she blinked away. I liked visualizing a confrontation with her over being a false friend and even worse, a fake person, but as quick as my tongue seemed to be in my head, I knew it would not be so in reality. So instead, I passed her in the lobby without so much as a turn of the head.

For almost two weeks, the Bible studies were the only moments I had with Friedrich. Each day after school, I'd do my homework in my bay window just to be able to see him working in the distance.

I was in the living room playing with Lucy when my mother called for me, her voice cutting as usual. I groaned as I pushed myself up from the floor. Tersely, I answered from the kitchen entryway. "Yes?"

She continued scrubbing the stove top, never looking at me. "Can you get the mail?"

I didn't respond, heading out to the mailbox. The prisoners were working, the periodic clanking of their tools and occasional voices and laughter pervading the air. Friedrich was on his knees tending to the vegetables, too far away to notice me.

Opening the mail box, a white paper package lay inside, along with a couple of envelopes. I pulled them out together, pausing upon seeing it was to me from the University of Virginia.

I gaped at it. Running to the trunk of my mother's car, I laid the envelopes down as I tore open the packet, pulling out the cover sheet:

We would like to inform you that you have been accepted to attend the University of Virginia...

I covered my mouth, laughing. Desperate to share the good news, I stared at Friedrich longingly in the distance, knowing it was too far for me to even make eye contact.

I couldn't let my mother know—not yet. Hurrying back inside, I was grateful she didn't look up as I tossed the mail on the table, grabbing Lucy and rushing back up the stairs.

Shutting my bedroom door behind us, I locked it. Lucy entertained herself with some of the knickknacks on my nightstand while I skimmed through the packet. It contained everything; cost of tuition, listings of undergraduate and graduate studies, dormitory options, cost of books. Doing the math, I could still live off my trust fund for years after I finished school if I wanted to.

I imagined myself walking across the green of the well-manicured campus, carrying my books to my classes, laughing with new friends along the way. I bit at my thumb with excitement. There was no doubt; I *had* to go to the University of Virginia. I belonged there. I could feel it. Being with Friedrich was of the utmost importance to me, but pursuing my dream of getting away from my mother and doing something meaningful with my life would make the time apart a little easier.

Through the window, I watched him work from afar, and I smiled. Somehow, I found myself accepting that it was okay for me to focus on other things during our interlude. It wouldn't mean I was letting go of him or moving on; it meant I was living. It was good, it was healthy, and it was necessary. All that I needed, in order to endure the coming time without him, was in Charlottesville.

Through the first week in October, a few of the boys in my class stopped coming to school. Michael Davis and Charlie Cantrell had both turned eighteen near the end of September. Michael had been absent that Friday, though Charlie had been out of school the whole last week of the month. Artie Pickett was another who just disappeared. I knew his birthday was a few days after mine in April, which made me assume he had lied about his age to get into the military. Dalton Burch came to school in his uniform on Monday, saying goodbye to his girlfriend and friends before he shipped out that afternoon. Realizing how many boys had already left (my brother included), as well as the ones who were preparing to, gave our senior year a strange feeling. I could only imagine how most students my age and under different circumstances discussed what they were going to do after school, what college they would attend, what their dreams and plans for the future were. Even the girls like me who were going on to college didn't chat about things like that. Everything revolved around the war.

For a second, I was glad I didn't have the worry most of the girls in my school had—falling for some boy who was heading off to a vague future. Some of them rushed into marriage, while others avoided it as if it were a contagious disease. Their only choices seemed to be to walk away from him or risk a great heartbreak. I was grateful not to be in their predicament...

Until I realized I was. Just in a very different way.

I had been looking forward to Saturday's Bible study so I could tell Friedrich I'd been accepted at the University. Instead, my heart nearly leapt out of my chest when I got home Friday afternoon. I hadn't even parked my bike yet as he slinked toward the tree line. My feet couldn't move fast enough as I propped my bike against the porch, charging up the steps and into the living room.

"I'm home," I called out. I jogged up the stairs to put my things away. "I'm going for a quick walk, though. Today was a hard—"

"Cassie, wait."

I paused mid-pace to see my mother in the kitchen entryway, holding something behind her back.

I stepped down. "What is it?"

A smile teetered on her lips. "You got something in the mail today. Here. Open it."

It was a large white envelope like the one I'd gotten from the University of Virginia. I took it from her, sullen upon seeing 'Mackerley College' in the upper left corner.

Lucy hopped down from sitting at the kitchen table, scampering towards us. Mom picked her up. "What are you waiting for?"

Carefully, I tore at the sealed flap. Pulling out the letter inside, I read the first line, wishing it said otherwise. "I got in."

Lucy giggled as my mother shrieked, swinging Lucy from side to side. "That's marvelous! Oh, I'm so relieved. Sissy won't be leaving us for school! She's staying home!"

I stared at her in horror as Lucy gasped, beaming at me as she clapped her hands, fueled by my mother's delight. I clenched the envelope in my fist. As much as I longed to contradict her—to tell her right then and there that I'd gotten accepted into the University of Virginia—I couldn't shatter Lucy's elation, and she knew it. "I uh...I'm going to go put my stuff upstairs."

My mother was dancing with Lucy in the living room as I went up to my room. Despite this unfortunate development, my steps were light as I remembered Friedrich waiting for me out in the clearing. Laying the Mackerley information on my desk and pitching my purse on the bed, I pulled out the envelope from the University of Virginia hidden under my mattress. Extracting the acceptance letter, I returned the package to its secret place, darting out of my room.

The air was comfortable outside, as long as I kept my sweater on. I had known it was going to be a beautiful day from the moment I woke up. The sky had been a lucid blue, the sun bright overhead. The light autumn breeze added to the exquisiteness of the day. It played with my hair, causing dark strands to tickle my cheek and forehead as I entered the woods.

Friedrich was sitting against a tree. I ran to him, greeting him with a kiss.

"Finally," he murmured.

I chuckled, pulling out the letter from my pocket. "I couldn't wait to tell you."

He looked at it before glancing at me, taking it from my hand. He whipped his head up as he read. "You get in."

Simpering, I nodded. He kissed me, spinning me around. "*Das ist toll!* I am so proud of you!"

I was certain I was blushing as he handed the letter back to me. "Thank you."

"Are you telling your mother yet?"

I dimmed. "No. I'll tell her once she calms down about me getting into Mackerley."

His eyes widened. "You get into Mackerley, too?"

"Yes. Don't look so impressed; I wasn't. They take pretty much anyone."

"You apply anywhere else?"

I shook my head. "I've only ever really wanted to go to the University of Virginia. Now that I'm in, nothing else really matters."

He held both my hands in his. "Then I cannot be happy for you."

I burst with laughter, having to explain to him why.

"Happier," he said to himself. "I cannot be *happier* for you."

"I'm not sure when or how I'm going to tell my mother," I said as we walked over to the toppled tree.

"Just tell her and finish with it."

I snickered. "How is it that you always give me the answer I'm trying to avoid?"

"Because our hearts are connecting in such a way that I am able to see your thoughts."

He looked smug. Chortling, I kissed him.

"You should tell her," he said. "What can she do? Tell you 'no'? So what? She cannot stop you now."

"Maybe I'll shout it from the taxi as I drive away." I thought this over. "I said that as a joke, but that's actually a good idea."

This amused him. "What about your dad? Can you talk to him?"

"I doubt it. He wants me to go to Mackerley, too, though I think it's just because my mother does. Not only that, but he never has time to talk to me."

Friedrich sighed beside me. "I understand this not. How can anyone not have time for you? Someday, I tell your parents what they miss all these years."

I brushed his nose with mine. "Is that a promise?"

"It is a solemn oath," he said, though his expression was nothing less than delightful.

I narrowed my eyes at him. "You seem awfully happy today."

"It is a beautiful day. I am here with you. You get into the university. What have I not to be happy about?" He was smiling as I gripped his hand. "I get a letter from my mother yesterday. This can be part of the reason. They endure many bombing raids, but she is okay. Every time she comes home from the bomb shelter, something is broken; a vase, a lamp, part of the ceiling..."

"What about your brother?"

He waved his hand. "He is fine."

Of course he cared for his brother, but I could tell Hans being alive was the only detail Friedrich cared to know about. Dragging his hand into my lap, I traced his fingers. "Do they know about me?"

"They know *of* you. But they are not knowing *about* you."

I pretended to pout. "Why not?"

"Because, while I mind not my mother knowing I am in love with a sweet American girl, I want not the American censors who check our letters knowing. She only knows there is a girl making a Bible study with me every Saturday." He elbowed me. "I tell her you are nice, if this means anything."

"I'll take what I can get." I flipped over his hand, outlining his knuckles. "Do you think your mother would like me?"

"She is adoring you. I think about this; about you meeting my family. My mother is loving you, not only because you are beautiful and charming, but also because I am her favorite."

I laughed.

"Hans is insulting me in front of you, thinking he is funny, trying to prove he is more of a man than me."

"I know better." I wouldn't admit to him that I'd already thought up retorts to his bullying older brother from the scenarios that had played out in my head. Just as Friedrich longed to take on my family, I found myself wanting to face this Hans character in his defense.

He kissed my hand. "Since you choose a college now, what are you studying for?"

"I don't know."

He bumped his knee against mine. "Yes, you know. Tell me."

I breathed in. "I'm considering History...or Literature...or Art. Maybe. I can't seem to decide on anything."

He shrugged. "What is your passion?"

"That's the thing. I'm not really keen on taking any of those things. I think they're interesting, but I can't see how I'd use them for anything besides teaching. I don't want to be a teacher." I sighed. "Maybe I should just major in Home Economics. Maybe I should just take classes that prepare me to be a good wife. At least that's something I'll know I'm going to use one day."

He chuckled to himself, shaking his head.

"What?" I asked.

"Not long ago, I agree; you should only focus on what makes you a good wife. But Cassie, even if you take all the right classes learning how to fold towels, or how to make a dinner party, or what direction to making the brush move when you clean, it matters not; your husband still defines you. It should not be like this, especially not for you. You are special. No matter what course of study you choose, it should be for you."

I admired his face for a moment, soaking in these sentiments. No one had ever taken that approach with me before. It felt as if a door I hadn't even known existed had been opened.

"I've been asking God to reveal to me what I'm supposed to do—what I'm made for," I said. "But I just don't know. It feels like my prayers aren't getting through the ceiling. I want to do something meaningful, Friedrich."

He gave me a supportive grin. "I am sure this feeling is here for a reason. Maybe you find out as you go. Maybe you are not supposed to know yet."

"Maybe," I said, halfhearted. "What would you go to college for?"

"I think not about this. The courses I take at the camp teach me these things."

"Yeah but, if you did go to college, why would you go? What are you passionate about?"

"You." He bumped me with his shoulder before looking toward the trees. "Maybe music."

I lit up. "Really?"

He looked at me as if to be sure I wasn't mocking him. "Yes."

"Why do you always act like that's something to be ashamed of? I was at the concert, Friedrich. You're not the only one with musical talent. The other men weren't embarrassed. Why does it bother you so much?"

I could tell by his expression that he was struggling in his refrain to give me an actual answer. "I think you enjoy Art more than the others. I have a good feeling about you and Art."

I pretended he'd succeeded in distracting me. Hugging his arm, I rested my head on his shoulder. "Well, at least one of us has a feeling about it. I'm nervous. I know it's almost a year away, but I'm worried I won't know how to handle myself."

"You are fine. It is not taking long for you to get comfortable. You decorate your dormitory room, get familiar with what buildings your classes are in. Then, you have inside jokes with your roommates, meet up with new friends after classes, plan study sessions with people in your Renaissance Art class...see a film with some guy what is nowhere near good enough for you..."

I hit his arm as I sat upright. "It sounded good until the last part. I couldn't, Friedrich. I'd be thinking of you the whole time. And what about you? You're going to return home, find some German woman who's going to make you ashamed of the fact that you had a secret meeting place with a juvenile American girl."

He gave an exaggerated gasp, forcing me to kiss him. "What you say."

"So don't try to convince yourself that I'm going to be the one who moves on first," I continued, afraid he might have really believed that. "I'll only find someone else if I know for a fact that you are unavailable by your own choice."

He kissed me again. "Listen to you. You talk crazy."

"And look at *you*. You aren't taking me seriously. I mean it, Friedrich." An unavoidable giggle escaped me as he pressed his lips onto mine. "You have to know that I won't go on without you. The only way I will is if you let go first."

"She is delirious. This is worse than I think," he said between pecks. "I think I have to put more effort into this."

Before I could even speak, his fingers hooked in my hair. He kissed me so slowly, so softly, so deeply that I moaned, melting like cream in his arms. His hand was on my knee and I didn't shy away from the impropriety of his touch; all I could think about was being close to him. We both forgot we'd even been joking, the heat between us rising with his hand. I didn't know what was happening—what could still happen—but whatever lay beyond his kiss, I wanted it.

He pulled away long enough to look at my face, as if to gauge my reaction. My skin prickled beneath his palm and I gasped in alarm, shoving away from him and leaping to my feet.

Egon stood on the edge of the clearing, watching us.

Seventeen

My face burned in mortification, in terror. I wondered how long he'd been standing there, but he looked more confused than intrusive. Neither of us moved as Egon considered the two of us, connecting the pieces himself.

He stepped closer, stuffing something inside the front of his shirt. "Well, well, well. What is going on here?"

I hadn't even realized I'd stopped breathing until Friedrich rose. Egon brushed a lock of dark hair from his forehead, his hands a shade darker than the rest of his skin. I didn't like the way he looked me over. "I am not surprised. I would pick her, too."

The veins in Friedrich's arms bulged as he clenched his fists at his sides. "Why are you here?"

"I could ask this of you." Egon circled Friedrich, ogling me with a feral smile. "Both of you."

His hands swung at his sides, an odd brick-red tint to them. I could've been wrong, but I was beginning to think it was blood, not dirt, that stained them.

"Interesting," Egon mused. "Here, I catch you both. But I can do nothing. I am also caught. Causing trouble for you makes trouble for me."

I tried to decipher him, wondering if he was saying what I thought he was saying—that he would leave us alone as long as we didn't report him.

Friedrich didn't seem as optimistic. He spoke in rapid German, his tone threatening.

"My friend, relax." Smiling, Egon patted Friedrich's shoulder. "I do not want a fight. I make an observation."

"What means this? That you are blackmailing us?"

Egon shook his head. "No. I swear, I will tell no one about what I have found here."

Friedrich was too fixed on Egon to notice the dark stain in the shape of Egon's hand that remained on his shirt. Egon followed my line of vision, looking over his fingers. He laughed. "Damned blisters. When they heal, I already have new ones. I should be on my way. If a guard comes, it will be trouble for all of us."

He gave me a mock bow. "*Fräulein.*"

With a snigger, he mumbled something to Friedrich in German, slapping Friedrich on the back. I waited until Egon was out of sight and out of earshot before scrambling for the log. My eyesight was failing and I gripped at my chest, hyperventilating. "Oh my...oh my..."

Friedrich hadn't moved, entranced as he looked at where Egon had last stood. My whole body was shaking and I burst into tears. "Friedrich..."

He seemed to snap out of it, taking my hand and lifting me to my feet. "Go home."

"What are we going to do?" I felt like I couldn't breathe.

"I talk to him. Worry not. I take care of this. I let nothing happen to you, okay?"

I was paralyzed. He held my face, kissing me. "I love you. I let nothing happen to you, Cassie. I swear, okay?"

I could only nod, frozen in place.

"Go home, *mein Liebling.*"

I stared at the washed-out white letters on his back as he went after Egon. My heart was still racing long after he'd gone. I wasn't sure how long I sat there, trembling with such violence that I knew I couldn't hide it from my mother. Wringing my hair in my hands, I tried to compose myself, spluttering between repressed sobs. It had been nearly two weeks since I'd last seen Friedrich in the woods. Why couldn't Egon have gone for a walk on one of those days? Why did it have to be today, at this very moment?

Traipsing up the driveway, I hugged myself, hoping she wouldn't be able to tell that I had been crying. Friedrich was nowhere in sight, making my stomach lurch. Kneeling on the ground, Egon yanked up a radish as if he'd never left. He leered at me, looking down as I noticed him. Gulping, I plodded up the front porch steps.

Lucy was playing on the floor. My mother had the phone up to her ear, beaming over her shoulder as I entered. "Cassandra, I was just telling your father the news. He's very excited."

I held onto the banister for support. "Okay."

She scoffed. "Why are you acting like this?"

I hesitated, hardly registering what she said.

Slumping against the couch, she sighed. "Apparently, Mackerley isn't good enough for her. It's as if...where are you going? Cassandra!"

I hadn't realized she was talking to me, stopping again. She looked miffed. "Where are you going? Dinner's almost ready—"

"I know. Thanks...Mom. I...I really don't feel like eating right now."

She stared at me, grunting before grumbling to my father. I didn't know if she was more annoyed because I didn't want dinner or because she thought I was mopey over the acceptance into Mackerley. At the present, Mackerley was the least of my worries.

I leaned against my bedroom door as it shut. The sky was open and clear through my bay window. Skulking towards it, I peered down below at an angle, careful not to draw attention to myself. Friedrich and Egon were crouched down close to one another. Though attempting to appear inconspicuous, it was obvious to me that they were talking.

There was still a chance—a small, but worthy chance —that Egon wouldn't snitch. Whatever he had been doing, maybe it meant as much to him as I did to Friedrich. Maybe it was more important to him to keep his activities hidden than it was to inform on us.

I lay on my bed, having accidentally dozed off by the time my mother came up to tell me she was leaving. Seeing the coming darkness outside, I knew I'd missed the prisoners leaving. Mom wasn't in any sourer of a mood than usual, so I knew none of the guards had come over with an interesting story while I slept. She kissed Lucy goodbye before heading out to her car, and I watched from the living room window as she drove away.

Lucy talked about puppies and kitties as I carried her up the stairs. After brushing her teeth and changing her into her pajamas, I tucked her into bed. She gave me a sloppy wet kiss on my cheek that I didn't wipe off until after I'd shut her door between us. Starting down the hall, I paused.

A dull banging resounded from downstairs. Someone was knocking on the door. Tiptoeing to the top of the staircase, I pulled back the curtain.

My blood froze. A black car sat in the driveway, the words 'City of Rockmont Police' in white letters on the side. I let the curtain fall back into place, trying to subdue my heaving lungs, unable to impede the tremors in my hands. Why else would they be here but to arrest me over my association with Friedrich? My whole body quaked as I imagined the cold steel handcuffs snapping on my wrists. They would drag me away into their car, and someone would take Lucy until they could contact my mother.

My mother—what was she going to say? What would she do when she found out? If I had ever been in trouble before, it wouldn't compare to what I was in for now.

I gave a jolt at hearing them knock on the door again. Swallowing, I clenched my fists to try to keep them still. Taking an intentional deep breath, I trotted down the stairs.

Two men stood on the porch when I opened the door. The one in the black police uniform was alert with roving mocha eyes. He looked young and eager, as if he hadn't been a cop long and it was all new and exciting to him. The other was older—my father's age perhaps—in a trench coat, charcoal suit and fedora. Patches of gray were visible in the soot colored hair behind his ears. He had a stern expression that only put me more on edge. Nervous, I looked between the two of them.

"Evening, Miss." He was no-nonsense, showing me the badge clipped inside his coat. "I'm Detective Wilcox, this is Officer Summers. I was wondering if we might have a word with your father."

"My father?"

"This is the Wyndham residence. Correct?"

"Yes, but...my father works and basically lives in Maryland." I closed the door slightly. "I would invite you in, but my mother's working at the hospital."

"There's no need." Detective Wilcox pulled out a notepad and pen from his inner coat pocket. "I only need a few minutes of your time. May I have your name, please, Miss Wyndham?"

I crossed my arms. "Cassie."

I watched him scribble, hoping they wouldn't notice the goosebumps on my arms.

"Do you mind telling me what you were doing between, say, three o'clock and five today?"

I scolded myself for allowing my eyes to widen; I had been in the woods with Friedrich. Hopefully, this wasn't some kind of trick question. "Well...I came home from school a little after three. Then, I went for a walk down the street."

Officer Summers looked at Detective Wilcox in a way that frightened me. Detective Wilcox narrowed his eyes. "For a walk, huh? In which direction?"

Mr. Stewart would have seen me on the road if I'd walked towards the Williams' house; he might tell them I was lying. The next house past ours was a couple miles down. I motioned towards it. "That way."

"Do you always take walks by yourself?"

My entire body quivered. "Sometimes."

He didn't remove his gaze from mine. "I see. How long would you say you were gone?"

"Umm..." I tucked my hair behind my ear. "A little more than an hour, I think."

He wrote this down. "During your walk, did you see anything unusual? Anything that you would consider out of the ordinary?"

I swallowed, pretending to think, though all I saw was Egon watching Friedrich and me from across the clearing. "Not that I recall. May I ask why you're asking?"

Detective Wilcox continued to write. "Just a few more, please, Miss Wyndham. Have you seen any vagrants lately? Maybe someone who looked like they didn't belong around here?"

I recollected my many bike rides home. As far as I could remember, they had all been the same—uneventful. "No. Never."

He studied me, lowering the pad and pencil. "Miss Wyndham, you must be aware of the prisoners of war working over here. Now, Mr. Stewart next door told me that the prisoners don't switch fields; they always work in the same areas. I would assume that maybe a few faces have become familiar to you. Has there ever been a time where you might have thought that one of them was missing?"

I stared at him, my skin becoming damp as I realized I was about to lie to a police officer. "No. Actually, I'm...I'm not often home while the prisoners are here. I'm usually at school until three. And they don't work on the weekends. If one were to wander off, the only time I would notice would be if I was watching for it between three and five."

Officer Summers snorted. Detective Wilcox found nothing comical about what I said.

"You said your mother is home most of the day?" he asked.

I nodded. Detective Wilcox tucked his notepad away, his eyes never leaving mine. "Very good. We'll stop by sometime tomorrow to talk to her. Summers." He motioned toward the car with his head.

"Wait," I said, causing both of them to turn around. "I'm sorry. What's going on?"

Detective Wilcox gave me a patronizing grin. "I don't much like the idea of telling such things to young girls, Miss Wyndham."

He turned to go.

"I'll be eighteen in a few months, if that makes a difference," I offered.

Detective Wilcox gave Summers the kind of self-satisfied look my father gave my mother when Amos and I asked for presents they'd already bought for us in secret.

He pocketed his hands. "Are you familiar with a James Williams?"

"Yes."

"He was murdered."

I felt the blood drain from my face.

"His mother came home, found him dead in their barn."

"There was blood everywhere," Officer Summers added. "The shovel was still laying there but you can't even tell what he looked like before——"

Detective Wilcox elbowed him. Summers cleared his throat.

"I apologize for my colleague's lack of sensitivity. He's new to the force. Don't you worry, Miss Wyndham," Detective Wilcox said, severing his gaze from Summers. "We're going to catch whoever did this. They took everything he had on him. Money, his identification...if he uses it, we'll find him. For the time being, I'd keep my doors locked."

I barely nodded in response. Detective Wilcox pulled out a business card, handing it to me before tipping his hat. "Let us know if you remember anything. Tell your mother we'll be stopping by to talk to her tomorrow. Have a nice night, Miss."

Shutting the door behind me, I stared at the card in my hand, trying to swim through my turbid thoughts as I slid to the floor.

The missing clothes; Mrs. Williams' missing money; James' missing ID:

All the things a POW needed to escape.

The blood on Egon's hands hadn't come from blisters; he'd killed James. I couldn't have been the only one who noticed how similar they looked. They were both about the same height. Both had dark, almost black hair and blue eyes. Egon's cheek bones were a little more prominent than James', but they looked enough alike that Egon could get away with using James' ID without adhering his own picture to it. Anyone outside of Rockmont wouldn't give the photo a second look or recognize the name. He could pass himself off as James Williams and no one would stop him. But why had he killed him? There was no point.

Unless James had resisted.

This entanglement was spiraling out of control. I became aware of how much I was rocking where I sat. I wanted to vomit, remembering how nonchalant he had been. It was James' identification and money he had been stuffing into his pockets. He couldn't have crossed us more than a few minutes after killing him.

I clutched at my hair. This changed our entire situation. Perhaps I could've stayed quiet if money and identification were the only things he'd taken, even if it meant Egon making a clean getaway.

But he had taken a life. All I could think about was Mrs. Williams. She had lost her husband only a few years ago. James was her only child, the one she depended on to look after the farm. I imagined she was in turmoil and as of right now, I alone held the knowledge that could give her some peace and her son justice.

I had to talk to Friedrich. As far as he knew, the only thing Egon was guilty of was strolling through the woods. I couldn't imagine him approving, viewing the murder as collateral for a mere escape attempt. If I was going to tell, then I needed to know he was going to stand by that decision, too. I couldn't do this alone. We had to come up with an alibi for when Egon would inevitably fink on us. The likelihood of Friedrich and me not being revealed in the process was improbable. I yearned to go back, wishing we hadn't gotten involved in this, but that couldn't be changed now. If only we'd parted ways minutes earlier, or if Friedrich hadn't had the chance to sneak away, this wouldn't have happened...

But then Egon would have gotten away with killing James.

I felt sick to my stomach as I woke up the next morning. I was still hoping it had all been a horrible nightmare. I didn't know what Friedrich was going to think about what I'd discovered. I couldn't let this go, even though the cost of it was going to be colossal and the repercussions unimaginable. All I knew was I couldn't live with this information just to protect myself; to protect us.

My mother was up earlier than usual. I could hear her ferreting about in the kitchen while I got dressed. She was scarce all morning as I played with Lucy, at one point even closing the door to my father's study. Perhaps I would have tried to listen in on whatever conversation she wanted to have in private, but I was too busy watching the clock with dread in the living room. When it was time to go, I braced myself for the unknown future that lay before me as I took Lucy by the hand, knocking on my father's study door.

My mother sniffled. "Come in."

She was wadding up a tissue when Lucy and I walked in. I released Lucy's hand, urging her forward. "I have to go."

Mom didn't look at me. I watched as she set Lucy on her knee. She had been so happy yesterday about Mackerley; in fact, I couldn't remember a time where she'd had such glee for me. "Cassandra, we need to talk when you get home."

"Okay. Is everything all right?"

She didn't look at me, sniffling. "We'll talk when you get home."

I didn't have time to pry into this. I had much bigger problems than my mother's melancholia at the moment.

Pulling on my sweater by the door, I peered into the mirror on the wall, unable to tear my gaze from my reflection. I was jealous of the girl on the other side. If mirrors were indeed an alternate reality to one's life, like Lewis Carroll's Alice had so discovered, then what I wouldn't have given to switch places with her for a while. Perhaps in her world, there was no war. Perhaps in her world, her father was always home and her mother loved her. Perhaps in her world, her brother was still alive. Perhaps in her world, she wasn't about to lose everything.

Perhaps it was only in such a fictitious world that I could ever be with Friedrich.

As discomposed as I was, my mind stayed blank the entire ride to the camp. Sitting at our usual table, I tried to remain calm as the prisoners came in. Friedrich's eyes met mine from across the mess hall. He didn't greet me with the warm, crinkle-eyed smile I was used to, and his somberness did not reassure me.

I whispered as he put his Bible on the table, sitting down across from me. "We need to talk."

He nodded. I surveyed the others around us to make sure we couldn't be overheard as I laid his worksheet in front of him. "Did you talk to Egon?"

His eyes were on the paper, but he wasn't reading it. "He swears he is not saying anything."

"But you don't believe him?"

He shook his head. "I trust him not."

"He's the one who's going to try to escape, isn't he?"

Friedrich didn't answer, lowering his eyes. The other pairs all seemed to be caught up in their own conversations. Holly and Egon's table was empty. Unnerved, I scanned the entire mess hall, hoping they'd moved. Instead, Holly was standing next to Pastor Gilbert near the front door.

"Where's Egon?" I asked a little louder than I probably should have.

"I know not." Friedrich was looking around, too. "I am not seeing him all day. One of the guards take him away this morning."

Arctic water could have been doused over me. Like the other prisoners, Egon had never missed. There was nothing to say that he was going to tell or even that anyone knew about Friedrich and me, but alarms were clamoring in my head. "Friedrich, I have to tell you something."

He was scraping his bottom lip with his teeth as he looked at me. "What?"

"I know what Egon was doing. He didn't just go for a walk."

"I can tell you this," he said, combing his fingers through the front of his hair.

"No. Listen to me, Friedrich. He...he killed someone. That's why there was blood on his hands."

His eyebrows pulled together. He seemed to ponder on this, leaning closer over the table. "Wait. How know you this?"

"The police came to my house last night. They asked me what I'd been doing between three and five, asking if I'd seen any suspicious people or activity lately. One of our neighbors had been found dead in his mother's barn, beaten beyond recognition with a shovel. His money and identification had been taken off him, too."

Friedrich stared at me.

"The same neighbors got robbed a while back. Whoever did it then took two hundred dollars and some of the victim's clothes. They did it during the day," I emphasized. "And what's more? The victim could have passed for Egon's twin. They look just alike, Friedrich."

He stroked his chin, peering at the others up the table. "Maybe you are wrong. Maybe it only looks this way. Maybe it is not him."

"He was stuffing papers into his pocket when he caught us," I murmured through my teeth. "I know it all seems circumstantial, but it fits. Why would someone—a drifter—walk in and take only money and a couple shirts when there were plenty of other things he could've used along with it? There was *blood* on Egon's hands, Friedrich."

He seemed to consider this.

I continued to whisper. "We have to tell someone. If all he was going to do was escape, I could keep quiet about what I know. But he killed someone; someone who didn't even have the mental capacity to defend himself properly—and we have to do it before he realizes that we know."

Friedrich rubbed at his eyes. I watched him a moment before looking around, hoping no one was aware of the seriousness of our conversation.

"We have to come up with something," I continued. "Whether they believe us or not, we have to have an explanation for why we were together yesterday. What do we say?"

He sighed as he shook his head, his blue eyes fixed in Pastor Gilbert's direction. "I know not. This is getting too complicated."

I hoped his perceptible regret was over Egon and not us. "I know. But that doesn't matter anymore. None of it does. I wish it hadn't happened either, but the fact is that it did and we're the only ones who know what he's done. Remember...?" With a furtive peek at those around us, I lowered my voice. "Remember when we talked about running away and you said you didn't want what we have to be tainted? That's how I feel right now. If we ignore this just to preserve ourselves, it will be a stain on our lives—on *us*— forever. I can't live like that. *We* can't live like that."

His eyes stayed on me, peering over his clasped hands. There was a hesitation in him I couldn't interpret, but I sighed in acceptance of my own conclusion. "There's still a small chance that they won't find out about us. When they find out he's a murderer, they'll be less inclined to listen to anything he has to say."

"Maybe."

Downcast, he kept watching me over his hands. I pulled my worksheet closer, pretending to read it out loud. "What reason should we give them for why we were out there?"

"Cassie..."

I looked up. His gaze was engaged with mine as he gulped. "I need to say what I come here to say today; I am sorry. I let this continue long enough. I want not to see you anymore."

For an instant, it felt like I was somewhere outside of my body. It was a strange sensation, as if the sudden ache in my chest was too much for my spirit to handle, leaving me a living carcass. My breath became shaky, my tears of confusion heavy as I tried to absorb these words.

"It is a mistake," he murmured. "It is always a mistake. I let you believe this is more than it is. It is just a game to me——"

I felt like I couldn't breathe. "Stop."

"I am not feeling the way you feel. I never am. It is a bet; this is all. I let it continue much longer than I should. You tell me about your family and I feel sorry for you. This is all."

It didn't hurt like it should have. He knew my heart; he knew how to damage me, if he wanted to, and these words should have broken me. What he forgot was that I knew his heart, too.

I peered at him through tear-soaked lashes. "Tell me you don't love me."

He opened his mouth, but no words came out.

"Tell me I mean absolutely nothing to you." My lip was quivering. "Tell me you aren't terrified of dreaming about me just to wake up in an empty bed; of being so haunted by us that you can't sleep. Tell me it means nothing to you how many times I've given you my heart."

His eyes glossed over. I sniffled, looking around. "Tell me you want to keep me safe, Friedrich, but don't do this. Don't you dare try to convince me it wasn't real."

With a shaky breath, I tried to be discreet as I dabbed beneath my eyes with my shoulder. "We should do our study."

The first question asked what one must do to become a disciple of Jesus, though neither of us read it out loud.

His voice was soft. "I start."

Sniffling away what remained of my tears, I heard, though found myself incapable of listening, as he read the first passage, trailing off.

He went quiet. Though I feared seeing his face might cause me to lose my composure, I was surprised to find he wasn't even looking at me. He looked uneasy, his eyes following somewhere behind me.

Two guards, one of them Dennis, were walking along the wall with intent. Dennis was looking right at us.

I slowly turned my head. Friedrich's wary eyes connected with mine for only a second. The heaviness had left my heart, replaced by a sickening, fluttering feeling in my stomach as Dennis and the other guard flanked him.

Dennis put his hand on Friedrich's shoulder. If I didn't know better, I'd have thought he was reluctant. "You need to come with us, Friedrich."

Friedrich's voice was steady, his solemnity impressive to me. "Is something wrong?"

The other guard put his hand on his baton. Friedrich noticed this, too.

"Let's not do this the hard way," Dennis said in an undertone.

Friedrich stared at him. I was helpless as he laid down his pencil, pushing out his chair. Despite our circumstances, despite how suspicious, how unseemly it would look, I fought the impulse to run to him; to hold him, to kiss him. There was a part of me that sensed they already knew anyway; they just didn't want our guard to be raised.

Friedrich didn't spare me a second glance as they led him away. I turned, willing myself not to watch as he walked out the doors I usually came in from. The letters in my Bible clouded in my vision. It was more difficult for me to blink them away this time, the paper crinkling from where my tears fell.

He had forgotten his Bible. Closing it, I pulled it towards me, running my hand over the leather-bound cover. The spine was creased. I imagined him in a bunk, reading from a dull light while the fog of cigarette smoke stung at his nostrils, the others laughing and playing poker around him. Whether that had been how he had studied, I didn't know, but that was the way I imagined it.

I lined up our Bibles side by side. His was newer and wider, while it was evident that mine was older and timeworn. The gold along the pages had faded to a light brown color, whereas his was still shiny. Some of the pages to mine had grooves from where I'd folded them. I'd gleaned so much from this book, reading out of requirement during Pastor Gilbert's sermons and other times in the privacy of my room, through tears of desperation to know that I was loved and treasured by someone. My Bible had been so involved in my life that it felt as if there was a part of me in it; I sensed the same quality radiating from Friedrich's.

Folding up the worksheets, I placed them with their respective Bibles. There was something intimate about owning what he had used to draw closer to God with; something that, every time I read from it, would also make me think of him. I could only hope he might feel the same way.

I gathered my belongings. While the other pairs talked and chuckled amongst each other, I walked up the aisle, looking for Pastor Gilbert.

There was a chance I was overreacting—that Friedrich had been called away for something else. Perhaps someone had even ratted Egon out and they were curious to know if Friedrich had any information. Maybe in a few days, I'd think trading Bibles had been a drastic move.

But if this was the last time I was going to see him, it comforted me to think he would have something to remember me by.

Pastor Gilbert was nowhere in the room, another anomaly I noted. I started for the guard by the door instead. He was one of the older ones, probably in his sixties, with wire-rimmed glasses and graying hair.

"Hi," I said. "My prisoner just got taken away. He left his Bible. Could you please make sure he gets it back?"

"What's his name?"

"Friedrich Naumann."

He held out his hand for it. I stared at my Bible, somewhat hesitant to put something of such sentimental value into someone else's hands. There was no way for me to know that he would actually give it to Friedrich.

I gave it to him with a weak smile. "So, what do I do since I don't have a prisoner?"

"That girl over there doesn't have one today, either. You can either sit with her or one of the other pairs."

Following his line of vision, I saw Holly sitting at a table by herself, picking at her fingernails.

"Uh...I'll sit with someone else," I told him. "Thank you."

I felt awkward sitting with one of the older women. I didn't know Ruth Howard all that well, and there was no way I was going to sit with Nancy Claremont. The only person I felt semi-comfortable about sitting with was Sharon Nichols. She might have been Nancy and Holly's friend, but she wasn't like them. She was more approachable.

Neither Sharon nor her prisoner looked up as I approached. "Excuse me?"

Sharon's nut brown eyes sparkled as she gave me a pleasant smile. "Hi."

"I was wondering if I could sit with you for the rest of the time. My partner's not here."

"Oh, of course," Sharon said brightly, moving her Bible and worksheet aside. "Cassie, this is Helmut. Helmut, this is Cassie."

Helmut was burlier than Friedrich. He also looked older, perhaps in his late twenties or early thirties. I gave him a bigger smile than I probably would have if I hadn't been so alleviated by her kindness. She'd even done the polite thing and introduced us.

I sat with them, nodding in interest and voicing mild opinions as they progressed through the worksheet. Sensing no attraction whatsoever between them, I began to see how our Bible studies were supposed to go. Their discussion was methodical and basic. Friedrich's and mine were always relevant, but we were more in depth into one another's lives. There was a fire between us that I was beginning to see wasn't commonplace. Perhaps it was for the best, or else love affairs would be epidemic.

Sharon looked at her watch, bringing me out of my contemplation. "Whoops. I guess we should start packing up our things."

The clock on the wall said it was a little after three. Pastor Gilbert was still nowhere to be seen. We had all gotten so accustomed to his five minute warning that no one had been paying attention to the time.

I waited as Sharon said goodbye to Helmut before walking with her to the door. I was glad Nancy hadn't rushed to her side as usual. Instead, Nancy linked up with Holly behind us, probably gossiping about how audacious I was to sit with one of their friends.

"You graduate this year, don't you?" Sharon asked me.

"Yeah, I do."

"What are your plans?"

She was harmless. It wouldn't get back around to my mother from her. "I'm going to the University of Virginia."

"Really? That's great!"

I smiled at her genuine excitement. We stopped in line behind the other women who were waiting to leave. I tried to maintain my presence of mind though on the inside, I was writhing; I wanted to know if he was okay. I wondered where Pastor Gilbert had gone as one of the guards led us out of the mess hall.

Sharon peeked at me. "I...I never really got a chance to say how sorry I was about your brother."

I gave her an uncomfortable grin. "Thanks."

"Teddy was so upset when I told him. He always thought Amos was going to be famous."

I smiled. "We all did."

Squinting from the sunlight, I scanned the compound in the hopes of seeing Friedrich. There were prisoners outside the barracks, but none of them were him. I couldn't shake off the disquiet expanding inside me. I didn't know what to do. I hadn't gotten a chance to make a plan with him about Egon.

My purse was where I'd left it at the desk in the Visitor's Reception building. Pastor Gilbert was still nowhere around while we retrieved our belongings.

"Cassie Wyndham?"

Startled, I turned at the sound of my name. A guard I hadn't seen before had come in behind us, standing at the front of the room. Though he regarded me with no condemnation, I could think of no other reason why he would be singling me out. Something was definitely amiss.

"Your presence is required in the conference room," he said.

The room had fallen silent. Swallowing, I didn't look back at the others, too disconcerted to meet their inquisitive gazes. I didn't look up from the ground until I was walking alone with the guard—away from the others.

His shoes squeaked on the tile. My breathing shuddered as I began to tremble. "What...what's going on?"

I feared he would laugh in contempt, but he didn't look at me. "Someone will inform you when we get there."

A cold sweat came over me and I hugged Friedrich's Bible tighter.

We passed another guard in uniform as he stomped in a rush down the hall. He didn't even give us a fleeting glance. This didn't feel right. There was tension in the air, as if we were on the brink of chaos. I stayed close to the guard escorting me as he opened the door to a room I'd never seen before, and I hesitated in the doorway.

Detective Wilcox stopped mid-pace. Pastor Gilbert was sitting on the edge of the conference table, though he got to his feet upon seeing me. The front of his pepper hair was disheveled. Grim, he motioned toward one of the chairs. "Have a seat, please, Cassie."

Detective Wilcox pulled his hands out of his jacket pockets, and I felt bare under his probing gaze. Crossing the threshold into the room, I noticed another guard and Officer Summers there, standing by.

The door shut behind me. Timid, I could feel their eyes on me as I lowered into one of the chairs, setting my purse and Friedrich's Bible down in front of me.

Pastor Gilbert sat down at the head of the table. "Cassie, this is Detective Wilcox. I've asked to be present for this as an advocate for you. First of all, you aren't in any trouble——"

"We'll see about that." Detective Wilcox approached the table. "I'll take over from here, Pastor. Miss Wyndham and I are already acquainted. Isn't that right?"

I shivered, but the room was warm. Detective Wilcox took off his fedora as he sat down, reaching into his pocket. "I need to know the nature of your discussions with Friedrich Naumann."

My heart plummeted into my stomach. He knew. "Umm——"

Holding a cigarette between his lips, he lit it. "Particularly if he's ever alluded to any intention of making an escape."

I shook my head. "No. Never."

Both he and Pastor Gilbert stared at me, Detective Wilcox clicking his lighter shut. "I need you to really think about that before answering, Miss Wyndham."

"He's never said anything like that."

Smoke swirled from the tip of his cigarette as he scrutinized me. "You seem oddly confident."

It was because I was the only one who had ever suggested it; he had never wanted me embroiled in a scandal.

I hugged myself, clearing my throat. "I'm...I'm sorry. Why are you asking me about Friedrich?"

"Did you know Friedrich Naumann was assigned to the work detail by your house?" Detective Wilcox asked.

Pastor Gilbert looked at him. I was mute, staring at Detective Wilcox.

"We have reason to believe he was involved in the murder of James Williams," he continued. "And since you've worked with him one-on-one for the last eight months, we also believe you may have information that could help substantiate the claims of others."

The hair on the back of my neck stood. "What do you mean? What...what 'claims'?"

Detective Wilcox tapped his cigarette on the ashtray. "Another prisoner came forward this morning with suspicions. A few of the others assigned to Naumann's work unit attested to his frequent disappearances. The commandant of the camp ordered a search of Naumann's effects and found blood stains on one of his shirts."

I covered my mouth, shaking my head.

"He must have been tipped off about the investigation. By now, what he stole has already been passed along to someone else in the camp for the same purpose. There's no way for us to know who possesses the items now."

"No." Tears welled in my eyes. "No, there's been a mistake. Friedrich didn't do this. He wouldn't."

Detective Wilcox's eyebrows fell as he cocked his head, dropping the hand with the cigarette. "He confessed to it."

I froze. "What?"

"He told us everything, down to what was taken and what Williams had been killed with——"

"Ye...but...no, that doesn't...that doesn't mean anything." I'd told him all those things myself. Hands shaking uncontrollably, I ran them through the front of my hair, leaning on the table. "This...this doesn't make any sense."

Detective Wilcox's cigarette went unsmoked. I felt Pastor Gilbert's hand on my shoulder. "Cassie, this isn't your fault. It wasn't anything you did or didn't do. You can't blame yourself. He just wasn't open to this. Is there anything you can tell us that can help?"

I hid my face from them, peering down at Friedrich's Bible. Why would he do this? Why would he tell them he'd done it when I knew he hadn't? He was saying a lot of things out of character today...

I caught my breath, his motive like a beacon through the hurricane in my brain. Egon was responsible for this. Perhaps he hadn't meant to kill James——perhaps he had——either way, his reckless crime was detrimental to his chance at freedom. He'd stumbled upon more than just our secret that day; he'd stumbled upon a scapegoat.

"I love you. I let nothing happen to you, Cassie..."

I knew it. Egon knew it. That was why he'd pinned the murder on Friedrich.

"Miss Wyndham?"

Our stars were falling. My dreams were in flames, burning on the horizon, their smoky remains eclipsing our sun. But as the embers lingered and glowed around me, I saw the beauty in my destruction; he had never wanted this for me. He was giving me the ability to walk away from all of it unscathed. I knew that's what he wanted me to do, to choose my reputation, my future, over the ashes.

But I chose him. I would always choose him.

My tears ceased. I blinked them away, meeting Pastor Gilbert's growing alarm and Detective Wilcox's acute suspicion in the eyes. "Where is he?"

Detective Wilcox had put out his cigarette at some point. He was a professional. I knew he could see I wasn't innocent; I wasn't even trying to hide it anymore.

He was curt. "Solitary."

I rubbed my neck on both sides, my eyes on Friedrich's Bible. "And what are they going to do to him? What will be his punishment?"

"Cassie——?" Pastor Gilbert sounded worried.

"He'll be court-martialed. They'll ask for the death penalty."

My face scrunched up from tears that I managed to fend off. With my face in my hands, I willed myself not to sob to the point of rendering myself incapable of speech. I was feeling so many things; brokenhearted, angry, shattered, cornered...

And overwhelmed with so much love for him that I thought it might kill me.

I thought of that night on the balcony over the mess hall. Friedrich had his violin, playing "O mio babbino caro." He had given me a glimpse into his soul that day. He played with passion, not only because of his love for music, but out of his love for me. The reason his brother's torment of his talent embarrassed him so was because that was who he was. Music was engrained in him. He needed it like the air he breathed; he loved it in the same way he loved me. It was what Egon had counted on; what he hadn't counted on was my love for Friedrich.

His love was a song, and I was a caged bird who was about to sing.

"Miss Wyndham——"

"The confession is worthless. He's lying," I burst. "He's just trying to protect me."

Pastor Gilbert wasn't moving. Detective Wilcox regarded me less as a witness now and more like a perpetrator. "Protect you from what?"

My hands were clasped over Friedrich's Bible. Calm in the eye of my own storm, I drew strength from it, surrendering my future, watching it sink like a slippery diamond beneath the waves.

"The reason for Friedrich's absences in the field is because he and I..." I closed my eyes, bracing myself. "We would meet in the woods by my house. We've been doing it ever since he started working there. Yesterday...yesterday, while we were together, Egon caught us. He was stuffing papers into his shirt and there was blood on his hands. The blood on Friedrich's shirt was because Egon touched him. I know Friedrich didn't kill James because he was with me when it happened."

Pastor Gilbert was gaping at me. Summers and the other guard were so still they could have been statues. Detective Wilcox studied me, and though I couldn't be sure, I got the impression that he believed me. "If what you're saying is true, then how did Naumann know details about the murder? How did he know what the victim looked like?"

I swallowed. "I came here today to tell Friedrich we had to tell someone what we saw. I told him what you and Officer Summers told me yesterday and that I figured out Egon must have done it. I told him James and Egon looked just alike. He knew all of this because of me."

The reality of this conquered me with tears. "He's lying about the murder because he's trying to protect me. He knew he'd still have to explain his absences. He always said if we were ever discovered, it would be worse for me than him. He told you he killed James so I wouldn't get hurt. Egon knows that, too. That's why he's framing Friedrich."

I gave Detective Wilcox a pleading look. "Friedrich didn't do this. He didn't."

I didn't care what happened next; I didn't care what they called me or how they might chastise me. All I wanted to know was that they believed me.

Detective Wilcox got up without even putting his hat and jacket back on. "Take her statement. She does *not* step out of this room until I say so."

The door opened and closed. Pastor Gilbert was in such shock that he was dumbstruck. I cried into my palms, powerless as Friedrich's fate balanced on the point of a needle. What if they searched Egon's belongings and found no proof? If that were to happen, all they would have was Friedrich's bloodstained shirt and my word. They might punish him for Egon's crime anyway, citing a lack of evidence against him.

I took a chance, God. I'm trusting You. Please don't let them kill him. Please don't let him die. Please, God, I'm begging You. I will accept whatever punishment they see fit to give me, just please don't let him die.

"Excuse me," Pastor Gilbert murmured, pushing himself up from his seat.

Leaving his Bible and his other things behind, the guard held the door open for him. Summers was already sitting down to talk to me. I repeated everything I'd told the detective while Summers wrote it down.

Then I crossed my arms, laying my head on Friedrich's Bible to wait.

I couldn't believe it had been me. After all the time we'd spent being careful not to draw attention to ourselves, I was the one who unearthed us. There was no longer a point to keeping it secret when his life depended on it; saving him was worth more than my reputation. I only hoped it hadn't been for naught.

I could still see his smile in my mind. It was only a matter of time now before my few friends, my family, the whole town knew what I'd done. It was too much to hope the camp officials and Detective Wilcox would keep this hushed; we were involved in a murder case. Everyone wanted to know the details.

Though engulfed in dread, I was ready. I loved him and he loved me; that was one truth they couldn't take away from us. Despite this being the end of my world, I realized this was the moment I'd been waiting for my entire life. My parents were about to see the real me.

I imagined Friedrich in a cell; sitting down, pacing, gripping his hair in his hands. I wondered if they had gone to him yet to verify what I claimed or if they'd simply released him. Hadn't he expected me to tell the truth?

Had he not?

Did he even know that by shielding me he had condemned himself to death? Another onslaught of tears flooded me at the thought. If he hadn't known, would it have made a difference to him if he did? I would've given anything to see him, to talk with him, even if only for a minute. We hadn't even had a proper goodbye. Some of his last words to me were that he didn't want to see me again; that he had never really loved me.

Summers and the other guard didn't speak. I didn't start getting impatient until I looked up at the clock to see that it was a little after four-thirty. I could just imagine the verbal beating I was going to receive from my already enraged mother for being so late.

My trepidation escalated with each strike of the second-hand, each rotation of the minute-hand.

Five o'clock.

Five twenty-five.

Five forty-seven.

Five after six.

My mother must have been furious, already dressed and extremely late for work. What was my father going to say? I cried thinking of him. He had lost Amos and was probably already distraught over my mother's affair and the divorce. When he found out about this, he would never want to see or talk to me again.

I could only imagine what kind of bedlam was going on outside the walls I was trapped behind. What was going to happen to me? Had Egon taken Friedrich's place in solitary yet? My leg bounced with nervousness as I lay my head on the desk. Maybe they had forgotten about me.

The door swung open. General Turner marched in, followed by a guard and Detective Wilcox. Pastor Gilbert trailed in last and I could tell he was making an effort not to look at me.

General Turner paced for a moment in front of the big desk below the chalkboard before sitting down. "I must say, Miss Wyndham, in all my years, I've never dealt with anything like this. You want to tell me why?" he snarled. "What empty promises did he make to persuade you to sneak around with him?"

"He made no empty promises," I answered.

He slammed one of the desk drawers closed. "Oh no. I'm sure they were all true."

"I didn't mean it like that," I said.

Detective Wilcox was putting on his coat and fedora. General Turner ignored me, writing something down on a notepad on the desk. I peeked at Pastor Gilbert. He was motionless, arms crossed and surly.

General Turner asked me something, but I missed it. "I'm sorry?"

"How *long* was this going on?" he barked.

I gulped. "A few months."

With a dark chuckle, he shook his head. The others were silent as he scribbled on the notepad.

I looked between the three of them. "Where is he?"

Pastor Gilbert raised his head. Detective Wilcox peered at me over the cigarette in his mouth before taking hold of it and lowering it.

General Turner glowered at me. "Do you have any idea how much trouble you're in, young woman?"

I fidgeted with the corner of Friedrich's Bible. "I'm sure I'm in a great deal of trouble. I would just like to know where he is."

General Turner shook his head as his eyes darkened. "Well, wherever he is, you needn't worry about seeing him again."

"What does that mean?"

I jumped as the general roared. "You are *not* in a position to be asking me questions! Your abominable actions are on the brink of treason and now you must face the consequences—foolish girl!"

My eyes watered over. "I am *not* foolish."

"He is German!" he bellowed. "You were consorting with the enemy, hiding him in a time of war!"

"Hiding him from what?" I cried. "The only thing we were trying to hide was what we felt for each other. Friedrich did his job—he worked in the fields. We didn't even see each other every day. It was innocent."

"I'm sure you'd like us all to believe that, Miss Wyndham, but no one involved in this muddle is innocent."

"We did nothing wrong."

"Nothing wrong? You were having secret meetings with a Nazi!"

"I was having secret meetings with a person! This wouldn't even matter if he wasn't German."

General Turner's face was tomato red. "Maybe so, but the simple fact remains that he *is* German; an obvious truth that you deliberately ignored and under the worst circumstances. For that, you must be punished."

"For what?" I asked in frustration. "I wasn't hiding him; he didn't run away. If there is any law against us that is constant, existing even during times of peace, then I wasn't aware of it."

"You didn't break any law, Miss Wyndham," General Turner said. "What you did is far worse. You defied a code of morality."

I clenched my teeth. "There are times when God's will surpasses the preferences of this world. My conscience is clear."

Pastor Gilbert hung his head, squeezing the bridge of his nose. He didn't see God anywhere in this situation.

"Then your view of God is questionable." General Turner continued to write. "Nonetheless, you are no concern of the government's. They have more important things to reckon with than the wiles of a capricious little girl. In this case, you are your parents' problem. I have faith in the patriotism of this country and believe you'll get what's coming to you. As I understand it, you recently lost a brother to these men. That's going to help me sleep better tonight, when I think about how your parents know you've been trifling with one of his murderers."

Squeezing the tears from my eyes, they splashed on the black cover of Friedrich's Bible.

General Turner threw his pen on the desk. "Your mother is currently waiting outside the gates to pick you up. It goes without saying that you are forbidden to ever set foot on this property again. Now, get her out of my sight."

The guard stepped forward, though it was Pastor Gilbert who came toward me. He grabbed his things off the table, heading for the door. Detective Wilcox stayed behind, and General Turner kept his eyes on the notepad he had been writing on as I passed by.

I walked in silence behind Pastor Gilbert down the hall, hugging Friedrich's Bible as I pinched off my tears. So my ruination had begun. This was just the pinnacle of a downward slope; it was going to be a long, painful way to the bottom.

The sun had almost completed its descent, the stars peeking through the periwinkle sky overhead. I resisted looking back towards the barracks, as if he would have even been there. I still didn't know what had become of him.

My mother's Ford was parked on the road as the gates opened. I kept my eyes down as I passed by the guards, hearing the clinking of the gates shutting for the last time behind me. Pastor Gilbert's steps faltered as my mother stepped out from the car.

The wrinkles on Pastor Gilbert's face were more pronounced as he frowned. "The guilty are receiving their just punishments."

I tried to discern whether this was a roundabout way of imparting Friedrich's fate to me, or a cruel way of implying Friedrich deserved Egon's sentence. Holding his Bible and paperwork to his side, Pastor Gilbert peered off into the distance. "I never would've expected this from you, Cassie."

The disappointment in his voice made me tear up. I wanted to apologize, I wanted to explain—but he walked away before I could speak. I watched him for a second before remembering my mother waiting by the car. Mustering what courage and self-esteem I had left, I started toward her.

I had expected a shouting match; I had expected to see hate in her eyes for me the way I'd seen it in the general's, having full knowledge of my secret life. Instead, she cringed as Pastor Gilbert drove past, regarding me as if I were a stranger trying to get into her car.

Gripping the door handle, I suddenly remembered my bike. It was propped all alone against the stockade office.

"Leave it." My mother's eyes were wide as I turned back to her. "You won't be needing it anymore."

For the first time in my life, my mother's disdain of me was nonexistent. She always wore her emotions on her sleeves, but I couldn't read her now, and I found it unsettling. I was glad Lucy wasn't in the car, but at the same time, it didn't make the ride home look promising.

She revved the engine as I sat in the passenger seat beside her. Shutting the door, I held onto the door handle as she went quickly in reverse, peeling out as she headed out of the camp. I stared out the window, the camp gates growing smaller in the side mirror. It didn't matter what lay ahead; my greatest loss lay behind me.

I leaned against the glass window as my mother spoke the only words she said to me the entire drive home. "What have you done, Cassandra?"

Eighteen

I laid on my bed, fingers clasped across my waist. It felt surreal, like a traumatic event that occurred in the haze of a dream. I could hear the crickets outside, the chilly October wind creeping in and causing a draft around my windows, fogging up the panes. I knew this was just the beginning. I was safe and secluded in my room for the time being, but I wouldn't stay this way forever.

I wasn't sure what to make of my mother. She'd parked the car, the two of us getting out without a word. Though it had been dark, my gaze had fallen on the spot in the tree line he always entered from. I felt the urge to run for it, to vanish into the darkness, before remembering he wouldn't be there.

Eyes burning, I followed my mother inside.

I could tell from the stillness of the house that we were alone. My mother was slipping off her shoes, leaning on the back of the couch. Her voice had been low, strangled. "Go to your room."

Swallowing, I had tiptoed up the stairs, looking over my shoulder once to see she hadn't moved, head inclined as if in prayer. Her lack of a reaction to this made me uneasy. I knew I had yet to grasp the severity of the fallout that was to come, but I also knew it wasn't at all how everyone must have assumed.

That had been half an hour ago. She had yet to come up.

The silence in the house was unnatural, almost as if it were waiting, like a band of soldiers preparing for an ambush tactic of the enemy's. I rolled my head, seeing Friedrich's Bible on my nightstand.

What was he doing right now? What was he thinking? Was he angry about what I'd done or grateful? I tried to imagine him, an effort to soothe the dull pang that had begun to throb in my chest. A black mist obscured him in my mind. I couldn't see him anywhere; I couldn't picture him in solitary, I couldn't see him amongst other POWs as he lay in a bunk, I couldn't see him resuming the boring routine at the camp he always complained about. There was no doubt that he, too, would be reprimanded, but I didn't know how. What was the appropriate punishment for falling in love with a girl from the country his country was at war with?

Unless they'd left him with Egon's rightful sentence.

The hands that once caused my skin to tingle were bound with rope behind his back, the morning blue eyes that looked upon me with such tenderness concealed behind a dirty, black blindfold. The bow-like lips that left their imprint on my own quivered as he respired forcefully, standing at attention as the command rang out: "Fire!"

I gripped my stomach, skin clammy as I rolled over onto my side. *Please, God, tell me he's okay. Please tell me he won't be held responsible for Egon's sin.*

My separation from Friedrich had begun. Whether given Egon's sentence or not, he wouldn't be back to work in the fields after this. The lousy part of this was that we hadn't done anything wrong. Girls were doing the same thing with American boys going off to war; Jimmy had asked for a flagrant kiss and my mother was the only one who had judged me for it. They were splitting Friedrich and me up because of how it would look if they didn't.

Biting my lip, I tried to keep my cries inaudible. I'd never needed him as much as I needed him now.

I sat up as my door opened. My mother barged in, her chariness from before having transformed into a tempestuousness I was all too familiar with. She glared at me for only a second before marching toward me, hitting me, smacking me, slapping every part of me her hands touched. "What is *wrong* with you?" she asked through her teeth.

I grappled with her for only a second before shoving past her, running around to the opposite side of the bed. "I am almost eighteen years old! I'm almost an adult! Punish me however you want, but you will *not* do it like this!"

My jaw was trembling and my eyes were overflowing with tears, but I was enraged.

She pointed at me. "You are *not*——!"

"Yes, I am! I'm not a little girl anymore!" My voice ripped through my throat. "Do you think I'm stupid? You never would've done this to Amos! I have never been good enough for you! You've never loved me like you loved him!"

Emerald eyes unblinking, she matched my volume. "Don't you *dare* try to act like a victim. You have——"

"This has just given you an excuse to beat me for all the other things you hate me for!"

She gawked at me. "I don't *hate* you——"

"Yes, you do!"

Hands on her hips, she paced.

"You'd prefer to just come up and *hit* me rather than *talk* to me! Not that it even matters! You wouldn't listen to anything I have to say, anyway——!"

"Are you still a virgin?" she yelled.

I stared at her, my cheeks burning at such an insinuation. As fearless as I was feeling, this made me want to hide my face from her.

My mother's eyes glistened. "Did you let him touch you, Cassandra?"

His hand had been under my skirt, on my thigh when Egon caught us. With everything that had happened, I hadn't given it any more thought.

But I wasn't going to tell her that. "The fact that you would even ask me that shows how little you know me!"

"Stop trying to turn this around on me. Do you not realize that whether you did or not, everyone is going to assume so?"

"Then *let* them! Do you think it bothers me that they'll all say I've disgraced myself? I've been a disgrace to you my entire life! And what right do you have to say *anything*, even if I had?"

"I am your mother! That is what gives me the right!"

"You're an adulterer!" I screamed. "You are the *last* person who has any right to say *anything* to me, especially when I haven't done anything wrong! I hate you! You are a liar and a bad mother! If today was the last day I ever saw you, I wouldn't even care!"

My mother seemed too stupefied to respond. Moisture shimmered in her eyes, but I wasn't sorry.

Her lower jaw jutting forward, she reached into her pocket, extracting a folded sheet of paper. She yanked it to flatten the creases so I could read it. It was my acceptance letter from the University of Virginia.

"It was on the floor when I got home this morning, dated September twentieth. Looks like you've made a habit out of keeping secrets lately."

I must've dropped it sometime after showing Friedrich. "Only from you," I replied viciously.

My mother crossed her arms. "You think you'll make this better by getting cute with me? You think you can assert yourself and we'll all just accept what you've done and move on? I don't know where your father and I failed in teaching you that there are consequences to your actions, but I can assure you we will mend that mistake today."

She tore the acceptance letter into pieces. "There's no need to worry about telling me you're going to the University of Virginia instead of Mackerley. You won't be going to either. The money's been taken out of your trust fund. You have *nothing*."

I could hear my heart beating in my ears. My hopes of getting away and starting over receded from view, just as the camp had in the side mirror of my mother's car. Her voice never rose above a menacing whisper.

"Do you think *I'm* stupid, Cassandra?" she asked, using my own words against me. "Your ability to make good decisions is severely lacking. If you hadn't thought about using it to run away with him yet, you would have sooner or later, whether voluntarily or from being coerced."

I gripped at my hair, shrieking. "How could you? *Never* did I consider using my money—*my* money for *my* education—to escape with him! He never would've...he wanted me to go to college! You can't do this!"

Her arms were crossed. "It's already done."

I sobbed, my hate for her searing like fire through every fiber of my body. "Dad won't let you! He would *never* agree to this. I want to talk to him right now!"

She shrugged. "Who do you think emptied your account? Wasn't me. I'm not the trustee."

I couldn't breathe, my legs giving way. I sunk down on the edge of my bed. My door creaked as she grabbed the door knob.

"I can't handle you anymore, Cassandra. All this—the lying, this ghastly behavior—I don't know what to do anymore. Your father is looking into other arrangements."

My hand rested across my throat, as if that might bring my voice back. "You're sending me away?"

"It's clear that I can't control you. Maybe if your father were here..." she trailed off, sniffling. "But he's not. You can hate me all you want to, Cassandra, but you have no one to blame but yourself."

She started to close the door before opening it again. "You're not to leave this room except to go to the bathroom. I'll bring up your food."

Without a second look, she slammed it like a jail cell door behind her.

Entranced, I sat stock-still in my prison. My eyes filmed over with hot tears and I clenched them shut. When I made my admission to Detective Wilcox, I knew things were only going to get worse. I had such certainty about mine and

Friedrich's relationship, though, that I thought I could handle the aftereffects. I'd known, those days in the woods with him, that we would be together again someday.

But knowing I could lose everything was completely different from actually losing it. My escape, my ambition to make something of myself by going to college, now lay in slivered ribbons on the floor. I no longer had the security of knowing that after college, I'd have years of money—if I wanted—to live off of before a job became a necessity. My prospects were grim; now, six months away from my eighteenth birthday, I was either going to live with my parents until I died, or find a job with the soiled reputation I was soon to have.

I fell back on my bed, hugging my pillow as I sobbed. I couldn't stay in this town—I couldn't stay with *her* forever. Luckily, no one was going to want to marry me when they heard about my relationship with a German during my youth. Maybe that had been God's intent all along; maybe that was how He was going to keep me waiting for Friedrich until we could be together again. Being single might keep me home for a longer stretch of time, but this incident would keep my parents from being able to pressure me into a marriage.

But what if Friedrich never came back for me? What if we never found each other again? I'd become an old maid, living with my mother, watching my baby sister live the life I'd always dreamed of, wishing my life away on second chances...

No. I would never regret Friedrich. I'd gambled my future because, win or lose, I believed in us. I had always been so sure that God wanted us to be together; that the two of our names being matched up as partners at the Bible study group had been coordinated by God's own hand.

But the casualties of my decision to tell were mounting. I'd also believed God wanted me out of Rockmont and now I was trapped here. Where had I gone wrong? Where had I misheard God's will for my life? Had it been college? Had it been my plans for the use of my trust fund?

Had it been Friedrich?

No. Not Friedrich. Never Friedrich. Even with my losses, he was the most sure thing I'd ever known. No, what we had was real. This was simply my first test to prove it.

Everything I've dreamed of has been shattered and everything I've ever wanted has been taken away. I want to trust You—I have to trust You, but I'd be lying if I said I wasn't scared right now. I thought You led me to him. I thought college was supposed to be my way out of here. Why did you lead me here, God? If this is the way it ends, why would you let my heart be filled with false hope and risk every chance I had at creating a good life for myself? Even if this isn't what You had planned, can You still use it? Can You even still use me? Please don't let this be for nothing. Please, God. I'll wait if I have to, as long as I know I'll be with him in the end. I just don't know what to believe anymore.

I wish you were here, Friedrich.

My mother didn't go to church. It was the first time she'd skipped in years; I couldn't even remember the last time she hadn't gone. She didn't have to tell me why—she was humiliated. By now, the news of my actions had spread beyond the camp fences. If not through gossip, then everyone had found out through the papers.

Whether she'd left it there on purpose or not, I wasn't certain, but I'd found the local newspaper on the counter in the bathroom one day. The anarchy at the camp had made the front page. I locked the bathroom door, sitting against it as I read the article. For the bulk of it, it stated what I already knew: that Egon had blackmailed Friedrich in order to keep the camp authorities' focus on him so as not to deter his long-anticipated escape. It mentioned my name, twice, as a local girl who had been convening in secret with Friedrich Naumann for months. I had come forward to prove Friedrich's innocence by disclosing our run-in with Egon in the woods.

It was in the last three sentences that I found the balm for my heart:

Wulf has been detained and is currently awaiting a court-martial. Naumann is being relocated to another camp facility in Texas. Miss Wyndham has been unavailable for comment.

I leaned forward, tears of relief dripping onto my knees. They were sending him far away from me, but he was going to live. This was what I wanted, solid proof that it was true; that he was all right. For now, that was all I needed.

My father never asked to speak with me after my mother told him what had happened. If all he had were words of anger and confusion, it would've been better than his silence. Not even hearing that his daughter had been involved with a German POW was enough to affect him. He didn't care. Maybe he preferred to distance himself from our family; maybe because of what my mother did, he was appalled by everything that reminded him of her. It didn't matter that Lucy and I were our own persons, or half of him. We still had a part of her in us, too.

I woke up each morning at the same time I always did for school. It was strange watching the time go by, knowing everyone there knew why I was absent—that Holly, Donald, all the boys who had started approaching me knew about Friedrich. I hadn't even found myself capable of sitting in my bay window as I had always done, knowing the prisoners were working below—knowing he was gone.

My mother brought up my dinner one night, telling me it had been decided that I would go to a girls' boarding school in Alexandria, over an hour and a half away. I would arrive by train on Friday afternoon, no doubt be paired with a roommate who had already been there since school started in August, and I would start classes on Monday. It made me nervous; these girls were all familiar with each other. I'd be coming in to find previously formed cliques. I would be the new girl who didn't belong anywhere. Despite what my mother thought, I wasn't like them. This was a school for troublesome girls—girls with much more serious issues than I had. They would realize right away that I wasn't like them. Already, I imagined what it was going to feel like having another girl's fist clobber my face. How was I ever going to adjust with girls like that when I couldn't even fit in with normal students in Rockmont?

There was antipathy in my mother's voice as she told me she had quit her job. Just as my birth had done, my monumental exploit had broken her. I wondered where this would leave her after the divorce. Without a job—with me at a boarding school until I was eighteen—she'd only be getting child support for Lucy.

Speaking of whom, Lucy was confused about what had brought on the new changes in our household. One night, I heard Lucy talking to my mother in the hall before bedtime.

"...but I lite peent more dan blue," Lucy commented.

"You do?"

"Yes, Mommy. Do you?"

"I suppose so."

"I not doe in Sissy's room 'toz Sissy's sitt," I heard Lucy say. I stared at the door.

"That's right," my mother answered.

"When Sissy is all better, she will pay wif me outside!"

"I'm sure she will. Go on, hop in bed."

I heard Lucy's bedroom door shut. The sky was almost black through my windows, tiny dots of silver beginning to appear within it. She'd told Lucy I was sick. She didn't tell her it was because I was being punished or because I was bad. Maybe she'd done so to keep from having to answer inquisitive questions. Lucy was bright; she might not understand the gravity of my actions, but she would understand them, nonetheless. There was also a slight chance my mother hadn't told her the truth so that Lucy wouldn't become disillusioned by me. If so, I could only presume that was for Lucy's sake and not mine.

I woke up jittery Friday morning. I got dressed before double checking my bag to make sure I had packed all I wanted and needed to take with me. Besides necessities, Mom let me take one of Lucy's baby pictures. I'd stored it safely in the cover of Friedrich's Bible, next to the note he had written me. I unfolded it, just to read the last line one more time:

You have my heart, and I swear on everything I am when this ends, I come back for you, mein Liebling.

My smile was absent, despite how these words had always had the power to make me giddy, and I put the note back in place. I looked myself over in the mirror before heading out the door.

Beaming, Lucy ran to me from the kitchen as I descended into the living room, wrapping her arms around one of my legs. "Sissy, you feel better!"

My mother was drying a dish with a hand towel, peering through the entryway as she watched us. Sitting down on the stairs, I pulled Lucy close, squeezing her against me. "I missed you, sweet girl."

"I missed you too, Sissy!" she exclaimed, playing with the hair that rested on my shoulders.

Lucy insisted I sit with her in the backseat for the ride. My mother drove us there without speaking. I tried to act happy, remaining as wrapped up in conversation as I could with Lucy. Whenever she thought of me, I didn't want her to remember me fighting with our mom. I didn't want her memory of me while I was away to be sad, or make her wonder in her little girl mind if she'd done something wrong to upset me.

I experienced déjà vu as we got out of the car, remembering the day we came to drop off Amos. Mom carried my suitcase as I propped Lucy on my hip, her little arms around my neck as we entered the station. "When we are home, you tan pay wif me!"

Mom's eyes met mine over her shoulder. Swallowing, I spotted an empty bench to sit on, standing Lucy in front of me. My eyes were burning, but I wouldn't allow myself to cry in front of her. Her wide, jade eyes considered me in curiosity as I took her little hands in mine. "Listen Lucy-Goose. Sissy won't be coming home with you today."

Her mouth parted as she nodded. I wasn't sure she understood.

"I have to go away for a little while. But while I'm gone, you have to be a good girl for Mommy. You understand?"

My mother was looking around, still holding my suitcase. Finger hooked in her mouth, I picked Lucy up. She hadn't lifted her head from my shoulder as I followed my mother out onto the platform.

People were goggling at us. The ones that weren't noticed, finding out quickly why my mother and I were such a spectacle. One severe woman standing nearby regarded us with an unwelcoming grimace. "Excuse me?"

"Miss Wilson?" my mother asked.

Hair the color of graphite and in a tight bun that could have been carved from it, Miss Wilson's glasses were perched on the tip of her nose. Everything about her was sharp. She was probably in her late fifties or early sixties and couldn't have weighed more than ninety pounds. I thought she was from town and was about to accost me for my behavior, which she'd read all about in the paper.

Her lips were thin, unsmiling as she extended her hand to my mother. "So you *are* Mrs. Wyndham." Down her nose, her steely eyes centered on me. "And you must be Cassandra."

"Cass-ahn..." I glanced at my mother. "Yes, ma'am."

Hankie in hand, the woman's fist was clenched against her waist. "I'm Miss Wilson. I'll be your escort to Puckett's Boarding School for Girls in Alexandria. I do not tolerate cheek, sarcasm or cursing. You will do exactly as I say without fuss until we reach the school. I will give you a short time to say your goodbyes," she said looking at my mother, "after which you will get on the train with me and we will discuss the rules and expectations at the school. Is that clear?"

My mother was looking at the ground.

"Yes," I said.

Miss Wilson cocked her head. "Yes what?"

I almost answered with *Yes, I'll get on the train with you* before realizing that wasn't what she was asking for, though it would've given her insight to the sarcasm I was capable of. "Yes, ma'am."

I was beginning to think her scowl was permanent as she lifted her chin. "Very good. Say your goodbyes."

My mother gave a polite grin though her eyes remained vigilant as she watched Miss Wilson march toward the doors of the train. Lucy had never once raised her head. I hugged her tighter before letting my mom take her.

"Your father said to be careful and behave yourself," Mom said quietly.

I shook my head, staring at the train. Hearing her say it was my father's wish made me want to do the opposite. He should've been here; he should've talked to me. He had been there to see Amos off, though Amos, of course, had never disappointed him. It hurt less for me to believe he was embarrassed of my purported transgression than to believe, as always, that I just wasn't as important.

Tears rushed to my eyes as I tried not to think about it. "This is ridiculous. I'm going to be eighteen in six months. Why are you doing this?"

"Don't do this, Cassandra. Not right now. Let's just say goodbye."

Glaring at her, I seized my suitcase out of her grasp without saying anything at all. She didn't move as I walked around her. I couldn't ignore my little sister's evident broken heart as easily, though. Her eyes were watery on my mother's shoulder and her nose was runny as I brushed her hair from her face. "Lucy, please look at Sissy."

Whimpering, she rested her chin on Mom's shoulder. I memorized her face, making an effort at a comforting smile. "I love you."

Her little voice cracked. "Wuv you, too, Sissy."

I tucked strands of her blonde hair behind her ears. Giving her one last kiss on the forehead, I turned for the train. Miss Wilson was already a couple steps up, reaching down to take my suitcase from me.

Lucy burst into tears behind me. My mother fought to keep a hold on her, slowly lowering her to the ground as she flailed.

Miss Wilson was stern. "This way."

Lucy was screaming, her little face red and wet as she reached for me, my mother struggling to restrain her. I tore my eyes away from the sight to go, seeing Miss Wilson trooping up the aisle, when I made out what Lucy was saying.

"Sissy not tummin' batt! Sissy not tummin' batt!"

I hesitated, my eyes filling with tears. Noticing I wasn't behind her, Miss Wilson's uptight shoulders drooped in disbelief. "Miss Wyndham, come here this instant. That is an——"

"My baby sister."

It was all my mother could do to keep Lucy within grasp. People on the car were listening; people on the platform were watching. Miss Wilson's eyes were wide. "I don't care if it's Franklin Roosevelt himself, you come here this instant."

My little sister's voice was ringing in my ears. I was indeed intimidated by this woman, but I couldn't bear the thought of Lucy believing I'd never come home again. I looked at Miss Wilson. "I'm sorry."

I rushed down the steps and back onto the platform. My mother looked helpless as I hurried toward them and I held out my hands for Lucy. Lucy was sobbing so hard that she couldn't breathe. My mother was crying and she didn't hinder me as I took my little sister.

"Miss Wyndham!" Miss Wilson shrieked from the train. I ignored her.

I carried Lucy a few steps away from anyone else, paying no attention to the unwelcome stares and Miss

Wilson's squawking. I knelt down, setting Lucy in front of me. "Luce, what's wrong? Everything's going to be okay."

Tears streamed down her puffy face. "I not want you to doe!"

I braced her face, sniveling in spite of myself. "I know, baby. But I have to. I promise, I'll be thinking of you the whole time. I'm going to miss you so much."

Her little voice was muffled in my shoulder as she blubbered. "Bubby."

"Bubby? What about...?"

I suddenly comprehended why she was so hysterical. I held her tighter as the train whistled. "Oh, sweet girl, listen to me. Sissy's not going where Bubby went. Okay? You don't have to worry. Do you trust Sissy? Do you believe what Sissy says?"

"Uh huh," she answered pitifully.

I wiped the tears from her cheeks. "I promise you that I'm coming back. I have to go away for a little while, but it won't be forever. I would *never* leave you forever. You are very special to me, Lucy." I buried my face in her hair. "Every time you feel sad, every time you feel scared, just remember that. I love you."

"Wuv you, too, Sissy," she cried.

I rocked her in my arms, unable to keep from crying anymore. Besides Friedrich, Lucy was the last ray of sunshine in my life. She was the only other person in the world that I trusted with my heart.

Someone's hand rested on my shoulder. I could see it pained my mother to separate us, but I didn't care. It was her fault I was being sent away; it didn't have to be this way.

"Sissy has to go now," I whispered, kissing Lucy's temple.

With reluctance, I handed her huddled form back to my mother. I heard Mom tell me she loved me, but I pretended not to hear, wiping at my face as I walked away. It was too little, too late for that.

Miss Wilson was fuming. I ignored her too as I brushed by, charging down the aisle of the car. I slumped into one of the booths toward the back.

My feet felt of lead, and my heart didn't have the might to go a step further. I hadn't thought there would be anything more painful than being torn away from Friedrich, but leaving my baby sister on that platform rivaled it. Something other than my own will was keeping me glued to that seat on the train; I wanted to run.

Miss Wilson adjusted my suitcase overhead. "Such blatant disrespect does *not* make your future at the boarding school look bright."

I didn't respond. Nothing seemed hopeful anymore.

"You will learn quickly, Miss Wyndham, that such behavior will not be tolerated. It is obvious that you have no respect for authority."

"With all due respect, *ma'am*," I muttered, unable to conceal my acidic tone, "the train has yet to leave the station and my little sister was overwrought. I would think that one might have some compassion—"

"Do not flash your temper at me, girl. I can already see you're going to fit in nicely at the school—with all the rich, spoiled young girls who run rampant because their parents never raised a hand to them..."

I looked at her.

"You'll find at Puckett's that your parents can't save you anymore; you're on your own. There, you will take responsibility for your actions and you will accept the consequences."

I chuckled in disdain to myself as the train began to move. It sounded like home to me.

The train ride was long and boring, especially with Miss Wilson droning on about the school's rules and regulations. I tried to appear in rapt attention, though really I only noted the important parts.

Obedience was the number one priority at the school. I was to answer with 'Yes, ma'am' and 'No, ma'am' when prompted, never to speak unless invited to by a teacher first. I would receive a school uniform upon arriving; the skirt was never to be more than an inch above my knees, the shirt always tucked in, and the tie smooth and in place. Letters were always allowed, but phone calls were only for birthdays and holidays. No male visitors, with the exception of fathers and relatives (which was of no concern to me), and they were only permitted during visitation hours in the afternoons. There were to be no cigarettes, alcohol or anything else unbecoming of a virtuous young woman on the premises. The dorm rooms were subject to random searches if any suspicions arose. If my roommate was found to be hiding an item of a dubious nature, I, too, would receive repercussions.

Miss Wilson had brought a copy of what would be my strict day-to-day routine. I was to be out of the room for breakfast no later than seven-thirty and in class by eight. Being with the senior class, I would have Home Economics until nine before going on to English and Literature. Behavior and Etiquette was a class exclusive to the boarding school, which I would take from ten to eleven before sitting in Social Sciences until lunch time. The senior girls were given an hour after lunch for reading before heading to Arithmetic and finally Art class. I was glad the schedule didn't seem any different from the one I'd had at public school, though I took into account that I had yet to meet the students or teachers. Four to five was to be study time and dinner was from five until six-thirty. We were then allowed personal time until bedtime at nine.

I found myself more nervous about personal time than anything else. I'd feel most comfortable staying in the room by myself, probably for the duration of the year. There was no telling what kind of habits my roommate had already acquired. Perhaps she and all her friends hung out in her room since she had been by herself so far. Or maybe she always went to someone else's room in her spare time, which would leave me to myself. I would consider myself lucky if that was the kind of person she was.

Miss Wilson finished her monotonous monologue, and I kept my attention outside the window. I began to imagine Friedrich riding on a train like this one, accompanied by guards on his way to Texas. I smiled to myself at the idea of us being on the same train. Perhaps he was in one of the cars in front of or behind me. I knew that was ludicrous—Alexandria and Texas were in opposite directions—but it was still interesting to imagine. I leaned my head against the window.

Miss Wilson admonished me. "No, no, no. Mrs. Hammond requires that all of her girls have excellent posture. Sit up straight, cross your ankles and rest your hands in your lap."

I stared at her, doing as she said. "Who is Mrs. Hammond?"

Her lips thinned and I could tell I somehow hadn't shown due reverence. "Mrs. Hammond owns the school. I will be handing you over to her once we arrive. She will give you a tour before showing you to your room."

I reflected on this, returning my now perfect gaze outside.

The ride was shorter than I would've liked. Holding my suitcase in front of me as I prepared to exit the train with Miss Wilson, I realized just how isolated I had become. I knew no one. To the administrators, I was just another mischievous girl, and to the wayward girls already in attendance, I would be a punching bag.

My mother had me right where she'd always wanted me; out of her hair and out of her life. My new surroundings didn't affect my father in the least. To him, being at home or being sent to this school didn't make a difference. It was unlikely I'd ever hear from him at either place.

I couldn't even think about Friedrich without my chest getting tight, my throat becoming dry, my eyes stinging. The recollections of my days in the forest with him was all I had left. I became frantic to recall every word—every detail—by heart, fearing that over time, the memories themselves would become as washed out as the letters on the back of his shirt.

I trailed after Miss Wilson through the tall, iron gates at the front of the school, walking up the long, semi-circular drive. The building was made of brick, large and looming overhead. It was only two stories, though what it lacked in height, it made up for in width. The building looked symmetrical from the front, with rows and rows of windows on each floor. It could have been a prison, were it not for the unabashed feminine accents on the landscaping. Shrubbery and patches of flower gardens adorned the front of the school, wrapping around the entire building. There were apple trees placed at random in the courtyard, along with sporadic park benches. I saw a girl—wearing the mandatory charcoal wool skirt, white collared blouse, brick-red tie and jacket—sitting on one of the benches, eating an apple as she read from a book. A few other girls dotted the courtyard. They all seemed to be studying, casting occasional merry glances at each other. They looked comfortable and well-behaved—incompatible with my original expectation and the rigid standards Miss Wilson had informed me of on the train. A few girls had noticed us, watching me with interest. I tried to keep from making eye contact.

A large, forest green, metal door was at the top of the entry steps. Miss Wilson pushed it open and I stepped inside the school behind her. A desk sat immediately to my left, directly across from a grand staircase with a landing. A group of chattering girls were coming down, dressed in the proper attire. They seemed oblivious to me as they turned at the bottom, books held to their chests as they started down the hall. One of the girls—with a freckled face and ice blue eyes—gave me a kindhearted grin, and I offered a feeble one in return.

Miss Wilson was conversing with the woman at the desk. "Inform Mrs. Hammond that I am here with Miss Wyndham."

The woman disappeared behind a pair of large wooden doors behind the desk. Miss Wilson faced me, her back stiff as she pursed her lips.

Worried that Miss Wilson was the standard personality around here, I tensed up as the secretary returned with another woman—presumably Mrs. Hammond—steps behind her. She was tall and slender, probably in her late fifties. A prominent patch of white behind her right ear gave character to her dark-chocolate hair. She wore an elegant bun, accented by the large pearl earrings in her ear lobes.

Her eyes crinkled. "Welcome, Cassandra. We're so glad you're finally here."

She extended her hand and I shook it, ennobled by the fact that she had pronounced my name correctly.

"I'm Mrs. Hammond, the Headmistress here at Puckett's. I'll be taking you around to show you where your classes are, as well as the other areas of the school that you'll frequent. I trust Miss Wilson has already familiarized you with the important details about the school?"

I looked at Miss Wilson. "Yes, ma'am."

Miss Wilson smirked with satisfaction as Mrs. Hammond motioned in the direction the group of girls had gone in. "Wonderful. Now, if you'll follow me."

Mrs. Hammond gave me a sincere smile as we started down the hall, inspecting me as if I was someone she couldn't wait to learn all about. "This is Central Wing. My office, as well as the student study room, is down this hall. It's where most of the girls in your class go during their free hour. Some even come here for the evening study hours, though you are welcome to study in your room, if you wish. It doesn't matter where you go as long as you utilize your time appropriately."

There was a pure, caring quality to her voice as she spoke. She was talking to me as a person, not a hoodlum.

"Central Wing connects to North Wing. This door," she said, motioning toward the gray door labeled 'Staff Only' at the end of the hall, "is the kitchen. You'll have no need to go in there, but I like to point it out to make you aware. Let me show you the dining hall."

Her heels clacked on the tiled floor, the sound echoing off the walls. "There are classrooms in North Wing and also down West Wing, but those are mostly for the lowerclassmen. The hall you'll primarily be using is East Wing. I'm sure you've been overwhelmed with information today, but rest assured, you'll grow accustomed to our school here in no time."

I gave her a shy smile. "I'm a little nervous. I'm not really...I'm not..."

She draped an arm around my shoulder, accompanied by a warm smile. "Don't be nervous, dear. My school does indeed specialize in behavior modification, but my methods are different from most institutions. I like my girls to be the young ladies they are. You aren't here to be changed, Cassandra. My school provides many opportunities for you and the other girls to showcase your individuality, which is something you should be proud of. All I ask in return is that you are respectful and kind, not only to other people, but to yourself."

She pat my shoulder. My eyes pricked.

"This is the dining hall," she said, having led me through one of the doorless entries ahead. "Breakfast is from six-thirty to seven-thirty, and you usually have the options of oatmeal, eggs and either ham or bacon—depending on rations—and muffins or biscuits. The junior and senior classes eat again at twelve. Food is not permitted in the rooms, but you are welcome to come down between classes for snacks, if you find yourself in need."

It was a large room, with two long rows of rectangle dining tables. I was certain at least a hundred girls could fit in here at once.

"Were your parents unable to come?" Mrs. Hammond asked.

I thought this odd considering she must have known why I was there and that my parents were in a hurry to send me off. "My father's busy. He owns an airplane manufacturing plant. He doesn't have a lot of time since the war started. And my mom...I'm not sure why she didn't come."

I refrained from saying what I thought—that my parents just didn't care—knowing Mrs. Hammond would have corrected me out of benevolence.

"Parents are always welcome," Mrs. Hammond said. "Preferably during visitation hours, but we do make allowances."

We both halted as a pretty blonde girl came whizzing out in front of us from Central Wing. Her hair was up in a messy bun and it was evident by her tense honey brown eyes that she was flustered.

"Marilyn," Mrs. Hammond said in a reprimanding tone. Marilyn's steps faltered, her mouth parting as she saw us.

"Sorry, Mrs. H, I didn't realize what time it was."

"It's strange that seeing Cecilia leave for class wouldn't induce you to do the same."

Marilyn's eyes flickered toward the wall. "I got lost."

I bit at my lip to keep from smiling, slowly looking up at Mrs. Hammond from the corner of my eye. Mrs. Hammond's gaze was stern, though I detected the hint of a smile on her lips. "Go to class."

Marilyn raised her eyebrows at me. "Fresh meat, huh?"

"You'd better hope Mrs. Evans lets you off as easily as I did."

"Of course she won't. That's why I love you, Mrs. H." Marilyn broke into a sprint, disappearing around the corner.

"Marilyn is a senior like you," Mrs. Hammond said, as if I hadn't just seen her let a girl get away with being late to class. "She's going down East Wing."

Mrs. Hammond led me down East Wing, showing me the doors to each of my classes. The only one of my classes that wasn't in the hall was Art class, which she explained, in her opinion, was better taught outdoors in the courtyard. After asking me if I had any questions, to which I answered no, she led me up the grand staircase.

"To reiterate what I'm sure Miss Wilson already told you, you are permitted time after dinner to yourself, but we have a strict lights out policy at nine. That means no moving from room to room with friends. You may leave your room for bathroom emergencies only."

She led me down a long hall with doors on either side, pulling a ring of keys out of her pocket. I couldn't help but notice how quiet the floor was. I was glad everyone else was downstairs in class.

She turned right onto the connecting short hallway. "There are two restrooms available around the corner there. They should never be so full that what you need is inaccessible, but just in case, there is also a bathroom located downstairs on West Wing."

I stood behind her, my skin damp as she inserted the key and opened the door to room 221.

She stood aside to let me in. The room was musty, no doubt due to its age, though the scent was overpowered by a mix of perfumes. Scanning the room, I saw there were three beds; one next to the door with a light blue blanket, another in the far left corner with a yellow quilt and one that was naked on the opposite wall. I cringed; two roommates was worse than one.

"You will be sharing a room with Kate and Anna," Mrs. Hammond said from the doorway. "I think you'll find them both helpful in getting you adjusted here at the school."

I eyed their belongings in curiosity. Everything had a place; the pictures, lamps and writing utensils on their desks; their books from morning classes; where they hung their sweaters. This area was theirs. I was coming into territory where I didn't belong.

"Your uniforms have been ordered. They should be here tomorrow. Be sure to stop by the front desk to pick them up so you'll have them for class on Monday."

"I...I will. Thank you," I said anxiously before adding, "ma'am."

Mrs. Hammond grinned. "Go ahead and unpack. Make yourself comfortable. The girls will be up after Art class. You can use the time until then to settle in."

Mrs. Hammond shut the door. I tried to fight tears as I lay my suitcase and bag on the bare mattress.

Motionless, I stood next to my new bed. My jaw began to quiver and squeezed my eyes shut as they became too misted over to see. I didn't want to be here. I hadn't had a choice in coming here, and Mrs. Hammond's geniality was like an unwanted sign telling me to make the most of it. Marilyn's boldness had intimidated me—a girl like me wouldn't fit in with a school full of girls like her. I'd be ignored because I was too quiet to make myself known. I'd be picked on, made fun of, left behind.

I needed a distraction—anything to keep me from thinking about this stupid school and the stupid girls and the stupid headmistress; anything to keep me from thinking of how much my parents disliked me; anything to keep me from seeing Lucy in my head, crying on the platform...

Anything to keep me from thinking of him.

I opened my bag on the bed, removing a few items on the surface before pulling out my sheets and purple patterned quilt, the familiar scent of home emanating from their threads. Lowering the suitcase and bag onto the floor, I set my make-up bag on my desk. Making up my bed, I looked around, my eyes falling on the room's only window. I could already imagine myself falling asleep this way, my sights set on the night sky beyond my reach.

I opened my suitcase. As I started rummaging through what clothes I had packed, a cold realization came over me, causing me to burst into tears.

I didn't have my pillow.

How could I have forgotten? How did I neglect to remember something as necessary as a pillow? I buried my face in my quilt, clinching it in my fist. How dense would my roommates think I was when they saw? I had no way of going out to buy one or having my mother bring it to me. I was going to have to improvise, balling up a sweater to sleep on or something. For six months.

Tears cascaded down my cheeks as I took the rest of my belongings out of the suitcase in slothful motions. There was nowhere to hang my dresses, only drawers to store things beneath my bed. I put Friedrich's Bible and the few hair pins I had in the drawer below where my pillow would've been, along with my hygiene items.

I brushed my hair and touched up my make-up before sitting on the edge of my bed. I wasn't sure how I wanted to appear when my roommates arrived—eager and chipper? Bored? Angry and resentful? I tried to tell myself to just be me, but I was having trouble figuring out who I was at the moment.

Without thinking, I reached into the drawer and pulled out Friedrich's Bible. The leather was cool against my fingertips. I lay down, propping my head up with my hand, flipping through the pages before closing it.

He used to care so little for it, dropping it on the table as if it were a schoolbook. Then came the subtle changes; his fingers tightening in the way he carried it, as if it were something of value that he feared dropping. It began to glide onto the table rather than falling on it from above. Laughing with me over an inside joke, I'd watched him smooth out a wrinkle from one of the pages in an absentminded manner.

Maybe I could pretend like I did after Amos died— that right now, Friedrich was back at the camp. Or maybe, I could imagine I was coming out of a deep slumber, ready to bound from my bed at home and dash to the window to see him working in the fields from my bay window. If I laid there long enough, if I cleared my mind, I could go back:

I could make him real again, if only for a droplet of time.

Nineteen

In a haze, I opened my eyes, greeted by a ceiling I didn't recognize. For a moment, I thought it was a dream. I lay like a fallen scarecrow on this foreign bed, images of Miss Wilson's scowl, Lucy's tears, and Mrs. Hammond's pearls inundating me like water from a busted dam. This was indeed a bad dream; one I wouldn't be waking from anytime soon.

I'd dozed off on accident, and now the door knob was jiggling. I sat up with only a second to spare, running my hands over my hair as the door swung open, banging against the wall.

"Darn it."

It was the girl with the freckles and ice blue eyes. She became aware of me, her arms full of books as she froze in the doorway. "Oh...hi."

I gave an edgy chuckle. "Hi."

Her cheeks flushed as she shut the door. "I'm so embarrassed. I'm so sorry. I don't usually say that word."

She shut the door with her foot, walking over to the closest bed—the one with the blue comforter.

"What word?" I asked.

Her eyes flitted toward me in discomfort. "The 'D' word. It's just that my key gives me trouble and the door always slams against the wall. It's maddening."

She began storing her books away in one of the drawers beneath her bed. A girl who was embarrassed for saying a bad word that wasn't really a bad word? Either she was jesting or not all the girls who came here were Marilyns.

She took off her jacket, smiling as she untucked her shirt. "I'm Anna, by the way. What's your name?"

"Cassie."

"Nice to meet you." She loosened her tie before pulling it over her head. "I knew you were coming. It still startled me, though."

"Oh...sorry."

She smiled. "Have you met Kate yet?"

I shook my head. "No."

"You'll like her. Our personalities are a little different, but it works. So what do you think about——?"

"I couldn't *believe* it when she said, 'What did I just say?'" a boisterous voice said in the hall. "She should have known better than to ask *me* that."

"I still can't believe you asked her why she expected you to know when *she* wasn't even paying attention," a second voice spoke before laughing.

I tensed up as a dark-haired girl with bright brown eyes and a soft face walked in, followed by Marilyn. They both paused in the doorway upon seeing me.

"Oh. Hi, there," the brunette said.

Anna glanced at me, unbuttoning her shirt. "Kate, Marilyn, this is Cassie. She's our new roommate."

Marilyn gave me a smirk that was full of impishness, plopping down on Kate's bed. "Yeah, we met earlier in the hall. So anyway, she made me write 'I will pay attention in class' a hundred times. You know how she is."

Kate laughed, putting her books in a drawer under her bed as Marilyn tossed a key into the air, catching it. "Robles is soft." Kate took off her jacket. "If it'd been Evans or Olsen, they'd have strapped you. I got strapped by Olsen today."

"I know, and Evans got me for being late," Marilyn said.

"Strapped is where they take a ruler and slap your hand with it," Anna said. I realized she was talking to me. "It's the primary form of discipline here. Mrs. Robles is the only one who doesn't use it."

"And as the resident delinquent, I have made it my life's work to be the one who breaks her," Marilyn said.

Kate paused. "Hey, I'm a close second."

"Ha! Don't kid yourself," Marilyn said. "Mrs. Hammond said I'm the first to reach triple-digits. You're not even close."

Kate growled. "Well, that freshman, Alice, has nearly as many straps as I do and she's not even been here as long. She'll beat your record."

I looked between the three of them. "You...you *try* to get strapped?"

Marilyn sat up. "Sure. Puts us in control."

Kate laughed as Anna shook her head.

"What? That's my logic behind it," Marilyn said.

"You have no logic, Marilyn," Anna said, pulling a day dress over her head. "Only whimsical reason."

Marilyn pointed her key at her. "Not true."

"Is Miss Wilson a teacher here?" I asked. Kate and Marilyn laughed.

"Heck no," Marilyn said.

"That woman is evil," Kate said, pulling on a blouse. "I don't know why Hammond keeps her on staff. She does all the odd jobs around the school; picking up new students, substituting, janitorial work...she's always around, but for the most part, you'll be lucky enough to sidestep her."

I breathed in relief.

Marilyn continued pitching the key into the air. "So where do you hail from, new girl? And what brought you here?"

My fingers fidgeted in my lap. "Um...well, I'm from Rockmont."

Kate finished zipping her skirt up before folding her uniform and putting it away.

"Right, and your reason for being here?" Marilyn asked when I didn't continue. Anna was the only one looking at me. I was glad the other two were too preoccupied to see how uncomfortable I was. "I...well...my parents...I was too much for them."

Marilyn chuckled, gripping her chest. "A girl after my own heart. In what way are you too much for them?"

"Geez, Marilyn, give her a chance to breathe. She just got here." Anna must have noticed my reluctance; I was beginning to really like her.

Marilyn blew raspberries, jumping off Kate's bed. "I need to go change, anyway. Meet you downstairs?"

"Sure," Kate answered.

"See-ya, Anna. Bye, new girl."

I gave a polite grin as she shut the door behind her. Kate sat on her bed to fix her make-up and Anna walked over to me, leaning on my wooden bed rail. "Don't worry about Marilyn. She's just curious. She's actually really nice. Usually we all study from now until dinner—"

"Or *you* do," Kate interrupted.

"But since it's Friday, we just go down to the courtyard and relax," Anna continued.

"It's been chilly the last week or so, though," Kate added, snapping her compact shut. "You'll want to bring a sweater."

"Do you have one?" Anna asked.

I slid off my bed. "Yeah, I do. Thanks. Actually...I don't know if either of you know what I could do, but I kind of forgot my pillow—"

"Oh, that's no big deal," Anna said. "There's a supply closet down the hall. It's got all kinds of stuff like that in it. We'll just have to tell Miss Barlow. She's one of the underclassmen teachers who's on site nights and weekends. She's not married, so she lives in a private room here at the school."

I was relieved. "But there are spare pillows?"

"Absolutely. Mrs. Hammond makes sure we always have whatever we might need," Anna said.

I walked with Anna and Kate out into the hall. Marilyn was waiting with another girl at the bottom of the stairs, hugging a large blanket. She had changed into a pair of rolled up jeans and a plaid shirt. "Cecilia and I were just talking. Did Evans really assign six pages for homework?"

"Yeah. It must've been before you got there," Kate said, as the group of us walked out the front door.

"Cassie, this is Cecilia," Anna said, introducing us. "She's Marilyn's new roommate."

Cecilia's hair was more like cotton than honey, as Marilyn's was. She had a pretty, girlish look to her, even with the noticeable gap between her front teeth.

"Are you new, too?" I asked.

"No," Cecilia answered. She had a light and airy voice. "She's talking about how Marilyn had to move in with me."

"Oh. Why?"

"Kate and Marilyn used to be roommates," Anna said, "but Mrs. Hammond says they're like a flame and dynamite together—"

"I'm the flame! She's the dynamite!" Kate and Marilyn said in unison before bursting with laughter. I couldn't help but chuckle.

"Mrs. Hammond had them separated after Marilyn snuck a couple boys into the school. They got caught—in the room—by Miss Barlow. It almost got them expelled. They moved Kate in with me and Marilyn in with Cecilia because her roommate was leaving. You know," Anna said, looking over at Cecilia, "I still don't know how they snuck those boys in."

Cecilia smirked. "I do."

"How?" Anna asked.

Kate tittered as she helped Marilyn spread the blanket, the five of us lowering onto it.

"Well, first, I tied carrots to these two sticks to get them to follow me home," Marilyn said, laying on her back. "Boys are like dogs; you feed them once and they just keep coming back."

Anna smoothed her skirt out, sitting on her heels. "Feed them what?"

Kate snickered. Marilyn pushed out her lips, pinching Anna's dappled cheek. "You are so precious. Don't ever change."

Cecilia gave a feathery laugh and Anna's brow was furrowed. "So that night you were caught, that wasn't the first time they'd been here?"

"Hell no, it wasn't," Marilyn said. She rolled onto her side as Cecilia tossed her an apple. "That night we were being too loud. They brought some drinks and we just got too rowdy. If Kate hadn't fallen off Dean's lap and caused us all to start laughing, we'd still be roommates."

Anna gawked at Kate. "You were sitting on his *lap?*"

"Yeah. Why not?" Kate said. "He was cute and I think he was starting to like me. Don't tell me you've never sat on a boy's lap before."

"Well...no..."

Marilyn chortled. "Sweet St. Anna. You have so much to learn from us. I'm sure even Cassie here's sat on a lap or two, haven't you?"

She nudged me with her elbow. I gave a shy grin, meeting Anna's disconcerted gaze.

"Ah, come on," Marilyn prodded. "Have you, or are you too much of a cold fish like Anna?"

"I'm not a cold fish," Anna said.

I only shrugged, too embarrassed to admit that I had.

"You have!" Marilyn said with a mouthful of apple. "Or, wait...was that because you're afraid to confess that you haven't?"

"Enough about boys," Cecilia said, inadvertently saving me from having to respond. "I'm tired of them."

"I never get tired of boys," Kate said.

"Cecilia's just sour because hers hasn't written her back yet," Marilyn said, chewing.

"It's been two days longer than it should have been."

"At least you have a boy," Kate said.

We sat outside until dinner, and I spent most of the time talking to Anna. Though I liked all the girls—and as different as Anna probably thought she was from me—I felt something of a kindred spirit with her. There was still one way she was different from the rest of us, though; her father was a chaplain in the Army. Her mother died giving birth to her and since she had no close relatives, her father had had to send her away for the war. She wasn't here for behavior modification, but for convenience.

Kate's family had sent her away because she was too much trouble. Kate liked boys—a lot. On more than one occasion, she had snuck out of her house with different ones, sometimes not coming back until the next night. She also had trouble getting along with her three siblings. Her father had left for the war, and her mother had given her the same reason my mother had given me for why she'd sent me away; she couldn't control her.

Cecilia had a boyfriend in the Army, but I didn't know why she was at the boarding school.

Marilyn's story was vague. The only thing I learned was that she lived with her grandparents. The way she skirted around the details with witty remarks made me think her past caused her discomfort.

By the time five o'clock took rolled around, I felt I'd had enough interaction for the day. I wanted to go upstairs and be alone for the rest of the evening. My appetite had suffered due to my circumstances anyway, but I appreciated being included in their conversations too much to leave. Hiding away in my room wouldn't help me start getting used to my new environment, either. Deep down, I knew it was best if I stayed with the girls.

Having to walk alone into a dining hall would've caused me to head back upstairs and starve for the night. It helped to be in Anna, Kate, Marilyn and Cecilia's company. I didn't get the feeling that everyone in the room was staring at me. To an outsider, I looked like I fit right in with their group.

"Mmm, meatloaf. My favorite," Kate murmured beside me. She gave me a look that said otherwise and I tittered.

Anna was scooping vegetables onto her plate. "You do have a choice between green beans and broccoli, though."

"I'd stick with the broccoli," Marilyn muttered to me on the other side of Kate. "I think they put something in the green beans—like some kind of behavioral sedative. Look at Anna compared to me. She always chooses the green beans."

"She also chooses how she behaves," Anna said, dumping some dry mashed potatoes on her tray.

"I love being a senior," Marilyn mused once we'd all sat down. "We still have all the same rules, but I feel less inclined to follow them than before."

"Since when did you ever *try* to follow the rules?" Cecilia asked.

Marilyn paused, cocking an eyebrow. "Touché."

Kate was pulling out the empty chair on the other side of me.

"To hell with social graces," Marilyn said, tossing a piece of bread in her mouth. She dusted off her hands. "I'm about to demonstrate the difference between me and our sweet little Anna."

Anna became alert. "Oh dear..."

I watched in shock as Marilyn pulled out her chair, using it to step onto the table, careful not to tread on our trays. Cecilia and Kate muffled giggles. The entire dining hall went silent as Marilyn sauntered down the table, singing "I'm Just Wild About Harry" at the top of her lungs.

"Oh, Marilyn." Anna hid her face as all eyes turned in our direction. Some girls began to whoop and holler while others laughed. The commotion only intensified as Marilyn unbuttoned her shirt, wearing only her camisole as she swung her top like a lasso, throwing it to the other table. She kept singing, even while Miss Wilson ran up the aisle after her, the woman's commands drowned out by all the cheers and cackling. I couldn't help but laugh as Miss Wilson reached for her and Marilyn dodged just beyond her grasp, shouting, "I'm not done yet!"

Tears were streaming down all of our faces from laughing as Miss Wilson looked around in a panic, pulling a silver whistle from her dress pocket. The high-piercing shriek only added to the pandemonium.

Marilyn made her grand finish at the end of the table, just as a couple other women (who I assumed were teachers) barged into the dining hall. Everyone erupted into applause as Marilyn was led away from the cafeteria, blowing kisses and waving all the way.

"Does that happen often?" I yelled over the noise in Anna's ear.

"What do you think?"

"I can't *wait* to see what she gets for this," Kate shouted, clapping.

Marilyn still hadn't come out of Mrs. Hammond's office even as we returned to our room upstairs. When she finally did come up, she and Cecilia stayed until it was time to get ready for bed.

Lying in my bed, we still had fifteen minutes until lights out. I tried to read from Friedrich's Bible, tuning out the conversation between Kate and Anna. They continued to talk even after the room went dark. I rolled over, facing the wall.

Long after Anna and Kate had said good night to me and the room had gone quiet, I wasn't sure how long I laid there. I hugged his Bible against me, doing my best not to make any noise, my new pillow absorbing my tears. As much as I was grateful for Anna's kindness and the warm hospitality of the other girls, the darkness served only to remind me of my seclusion.

Tomorrow would be one week since my confession, one week since I'd seen Friedrich; a lifetime since I'd heard his voice, since his lips last touched mine, since his fingertips grazed my skin. Every moment of those fateful two days seemed to play like a film in my head. I could still see his face, hear the pain in his voice, feel the grief throbbing in my chest. If only I'd known then that it would be the last day I would see him.

Nobody understood; nobody would *ever* understand. How could they? These girls liked me, but that was because they didn't know what I'd done. Anna's father was in France warring with the Germans right now. Kate's father and brother were fighting in the war. I could only assume Marilyn had someone overseas; Cecilia had a boyfriend. Once they knew, they'd keep their distance from me. I had stepped over the bounds of loyalty. My actions betrayed more than just my family; I'd betrayed my country.

All I have is You now.

He was the only one who could see the truth at the core of my heart. He knew Friedrich was not an act of rebellion or an offense with treacherous intent. He was the only one who could hold Friedrich at the same moment He was holding me.

Please tell me You're still holding him.

I wondered what Friedrich was doing. Was there any chance he was lying in his own bed, saying the same type of prayer I was? Was I crossing his mind at all? Was everything he promised me still true now that our goodbye had begun? I buried my face in my pillow to keep my sobs from waking the others.

I love him, God. Please show me he still loves me. Promise me that this pain won't last forever, but the resolve will. Don't let me die without him. Please don't let the truth go untold.

But most importantly, please don't let me be alone tonight.

Twenty

I awoke the next morning, my arm draped over Friedrich's Bible. Sunlight poured in from the window, my skin damp under the blanket. The ache in my heart from the night before remained, but I'd made it through the first night. I didn't even remember falling asleep. I took that to mean God had heard my prayers, having mercy on me in my suffering.

I was glad I hadn't come to the school in the middle of the week. The weekend gave me time to prepare and fortify my relationship with my acquaintances. (I wouldn't call them friends yet.)

Anna looked at my schedule and told me that I was going to be in the first senior group. I was thankful; Cecilia was in the second group, but I much preferred to stay with Anna, and even Kate.

We spent most of Saturday out in the courtyard. Anna enjoined Kate to come study with her until dinner. Marilyn laughed at the idea, though I followed my roommates upstairs.

"You'll get all your books on Monday when you go to your classes," Anna told me, browsing through her Arithmetic book.

"Are you doing your six pages of homework now?" I asked.

Kate groaned with dread.

"Yes," Anna answered.

I got down from my bed. "What other homework do you guys have to do?"

"Well, we have about twenty pages of reading for Social Sciences..." Anna started.

"And that essay for English," Kate said.

I looked at Anna. "Do you mind if I read from your Social Sciences book until you're finished with Arithmetic?"

Anna's face lit up. "Oh, sure! Go ahead!" She handed me the book. "I already labeled the start and finish pages."

"Wait," Kate said as I walked back to my bed. "You're going to do the homework?"

I shrugged. "What else am I going to do?"

Kate scoffed. "Well...I don't know, but you're not going to get in trouble for not having the homework done on your first day. I would take advantage of that."

I flipped to the first page. "It's all right. There's nothing else for me to do while the two of you study. I might as well see where you are in your curriculum compared to my old school."

I could see her shaking her head from the corner of my eye. "Okay, now I see what you mean about Marilyn and me being just alike," Kate said to Anna. "Looks like you finally found yourself a twin, too."

I heard Anna chuckle.

"Maybe now you can drag *her* up here to study with you so I can stay out in the courtyard with Marilyn."

"If you wish to share Marilyn's grades, be my guest," Anna said.

Kate bit at the eraser on her pencil in thought. She slapped her book. "You know, Marilyn doesn't do you justice. You can be just as sassy as she is when you want to be. And no, you're right; I do *not* want Marilyn's grades," she murmured.

After dinner, we returned upstairs. I tittered with Kate and Anna from our doorway as Marilyn and Cecilia snuck their mattresses, blankets and pillows down the hall into our room.

I whispered to Anna to keep Kate from overhearing. "Aren't we afraid we'll get told on?"

"No," Anna answered in the same quiet voice. "They do this all the time. After lights out, no one checks the rooms. Miss Barlow only comes out if we need her, and Mrs. Gregory, the night-watcher, isn't familiar with us enough to notice when one girl's coming out of a room she shouldn't be in. Don't worry."

Having Marilyn and Cecilia in the room turned out to be more fun than I thought it would be. They put their mattresses in the floor between my bed and Kate's and we sat in our pajamas, listening to music on Kate's gramophone. Marilyn brought sweets and Coca-Colas her grandmother had brought her recently to share with her friends. I only listened as they talked about boys. Anna said she had only ever liked a boy but had never gone steady with anyone. Cecilia's current boyfriend had been her only one, and he was fighting the Japanese in the Pacific right now. I was glad when Kate and Marilyn began to argue over which one of them had dated the most. It kept them from turning their attention to me. Marilyn, Kate and Cecilia soon got into a pillow fight over it, while Anna and I laughed. It seemed comical when the lights turned out at nine; we were all wide awake.

"I can't wait until my birthday. The moment I turn eighteen, I'm outta here," I heard Marilyn say.

"You're not serious are you?" Cecilia asked.

"You're going to leave us?" asked Kate. There was silence for a moment.

"Well, no," Marilyn finally replied. "I won't leave until school ends. I just like saying it."

I was glad Anna wasn't always piping in. It kept me from feeling awkward for not having much to say, either. I was also glad it was dark. I had Friedrich's Bible under the covers, hugging it as usual. I didn't want them to find me odd. Even more so, I didn't want to explain it to them—the way I felt the need to have it next to me at night.

Kate's covers rustled. "I don't know what I'm going to do when I turn eighteen."

"You're going to go back home to the farm," Marilyn answered with a thick country accent, "find you a right nice boy to settle down with, have yourself a houseful of young 'uns and cook in your bare feet at the stove."

"You say it like it's a joke, but that's probably what I'll end up doing."

Silence.

"You think so?" Marilyn sounded alarmed.

"Pfft. No," Kate said. They both laughed. I smiled to myself, toying with the ribbon bookmark on his Bible as I closed my eyes.

"Where are you going?" I heard Cecilia ask.

Marilyn's voice was somewhere near the door. "To the bathroom. I'll be back."

Light from the hallway spilled into our room as Marilyn opened and shut the door. Kate and Cecilia kept chattering and I tried to shut them out. I wasn't tired; I just didn't feel like talking anymore.

The door opened and shut again. I heard a thump.

"Hey!" Anna exclaimed. Marilyn's exaggerated, maniacal laughter in the darkness made us all snicker.

Kate sounded like an exasperated mother. "Marilyn, what are you doing?"

"Are you asleep?" Marilyn asked Anna, I presumed.

"Not anymore."

Marilyn made her way back to her mattress. I waited to hear her get back into her bed when something heavy fell across my legs.

"I don't want you to sleep yet, either," Marilyn said, sitting across my shins. "Tell us, new girl. Give us thy damning feat so that we might make merry and converse over it."

Kate chuckled. "What?"

"What are you here for?" Marilyn simplified.

"Don't bother," Kate said. "She won't crack."

Marilyn emitted a sigh. "Well, I could always break into Hammond's office, read your file and find out that way. That's how I found out Cecilia was sent here for repetitive stealing."

"Shut up, Marilyn. You only wish you were as complicated as I am."

"My point is," Marilyn continued, ignoring her, "I can find out the hard way—and I will if I have to——"

"She will," Kate declared.

"Or you can keep me——*us*——out of suspense, spare me another strapping as well as an extra week in detention hall, and just tell me."

I gulped. Anna was either sleeping or pretending to be so she could hear. In fact, everyone was quiet. As comfortable as I was beginning to feel around them, I knew the risks if I told them the truth; they'd hate me. They would avoid me, look at me as if I had small pox. Then, it would only be a matter of time before the whole school knew.

Marilyn gripped my leg through my quilt, shaking it. "I'm waiting."

I took a breath. "Okay. I'll tell you. But I'm not going into details."

"Fair enough. Just give us something."

I held Friedrich's Bible closer under my blanket. "I fell in love."

Cecilia gasped. "Oh my goodness, how romantic! And they sent you away? Oh, it's just like a movie!"

"I bet he was handsome," Kate speculated. "Was he handsome?"

"Isn't your dad rich?" Marilyn asked, though I had no idea why.

"Umm...yes, yes, and I suppose," I said.

"Who was he? Someone who worked for your father?" Marilyn asked.

"Was he a farmhand?" Kate asked. "My mother always told me that if she ever caught me sneaking off with Angelo, our farmhand, she'd disown me."

"No," Cecilia said in her dreamy voice. "He was a childhood love, someone you grew up with but he had no hopes of reaching your financial status so your parents separated you."

I chuckled to myself. "Uh—no. No to all of those. My parents are probably wishing it was one of tho..."

I trailed off, afraid I'd said too much.

Marilyn nearly choked. "Whoa, what kind of paramour are we talking about here?"

"He must've been a troublemaker. You seem like a good girl," Kate remarked. "They didn't want you messing around with a troublemaking boy so they sent you to a school full of troublemaking girls, right?"

"He was too old for you," Marilyn surmised. "He was one of your father's business associates—"

"Eww. No." I gave a disgusted laugh.

"He was a prisoner you were writing love letters to," Cecilia said, sending a chill up my spine, "and your parents intercepted one and grew furious."

"Maybe he's a foreigner," I heard Anna finally contribute.

I didn't respond, my gaze undirected in the dark. No one else had spoken and Marilyn squeezed my leg. "Someone said it, didn't they?"

"What?" I asked.

"Which one is it?"

"I said I wasn't going into details."

"Come on!" Marilyn pleaded through her teeth. "You know why the rest of us are here."

"I don't know why *you're* here."

"After what I did in the dining hall yesterday, you expect me to believe that? I think it's obvious why I'm here."

"I bet it was one of her father's co-workers," Kate said.

"I still think he was a childhood love," chimed Cecilia.

"Which one is it?" Marilyn asked.

"Yeah, tell us," Kate said.

I squeezed my eyes shut. "He was German."

Marilyn's hand stayed on my leg, though she stopped moving. I could've been the only one in the room due to their sudden speechlessness. Cecilia's silhouette sat up as Kate's rolled over, propping her head up with her hand.

"He was a prisoner-of-war and he was German."

In spite of the enveloping shadows, I could feel their eyes on me. Marilyn's profile looked toward Kate's side of the room as she slipped off my bed. "Well...out of all the answers I expected to hear, that definitely wasn't one of them."

"Agreed," Kate murmured.

My whole body was tense as Marilyn got down on her knees on her bed. "There's only one thing left for me to do now." She lay forward, stretching her hands over head. "I hand my title over to you. I will be your humble servant, for you are the ultimate bad girl."

Cecilia laughed, hitting Marilyn with her pillow.

"I-I'm sorry," I stammered. "I know...I know what you all must think, but—"

"That it took you long enough to tell us?" Marilyn asked, getting under her covers.

"That I'm bad."

Marilyn laughed. "Well, hell, darlin', what in the world do you think the rest of us are here for?"

Kate laid down. "You are *so* lucky. I wish my mother had sent me away because of a boy."

"I know," Cecilia said, "instead, when people ask me why I'm here I have to say, 'Oh, it's because I pick locks'— even though I'm not a thief. I'm really not."

"What was his name?" Anna asked.

"Friedrich."

"Friedrich," Cecilia repeated. "That's a romantic name."

"So how did it happen? How did you meet? How did they find out?" Marilyn asked.

I swallowed, my eyes beginning to burn. As relieved as I was that my revelation hadn't turned them against me, I wasn't ready to discuss it any further. I couldn't talk about him. Not yet. I couldn't bear the thought of them thinking he had been a mere dalliance. "That's all I can give you for now."

"Yeah, but—"

To my surprise, it was Kate who interrupted. "Marilyn, back off. You got what you wanted."

"What *we* wanted," Marilyn corrected.

"Well, whatever. That's all we need to know for now. She'll tell us before it's over, wait and see."

I laughed to myself, the warmth of a tear trickling down from the corner of my eye.

Cecilia, Kate and Marilyn whispered to each other even after Anna and I withdrew from the conversation. I couldn't tell if they were talking about me or not. Either way, I didn't care. I was done feeling like I had to explain myself, especially when no one really cared anyway. I was just ammunition for gossip; that was all Friedrich and I were worth to anyone. No one wanted to hear about the change we'd made in one another's lives because it didn't align with their perceptions. He was German; he had once been a Nazi. No one wanted to believe any good could come out of him after that.

My first day in classes was somewhat daunting, but I was over it by lunchtime. All my teachers had been impressed that I'd completed the homework assignments—except Mrs. Evans. By the end of the day, I knew she was going to be my least favorite teacher. She was strict, critical and had no sense of humor.

I wrote a letter to my baby sister that night. I told her about my roommates, as well as Cecilia and Marilyn, and how my first day went. I told her how much I missed her and couldn't wait to see her. I never mentioned my mother.

I appreciated being in a new environment. Anything customary, where I would have been stuck in a familiar routine, would have given me too much time to dwell over

Friedrich. I thought about him anyway, but it was easier for me to be distracted.

It was after classes that I had too much time to think.

Even while I studied, I'd cross a word that triggered a memory, or led me on a path of thoughts that took me straight to him. Sometimes, while the other girls carried on lively chitchat at dinner, I'd brood, pretending to listen as I picked at my food. I never had much of an appetite whenever I thought about what happened.

I missed him so much. Sometimes, I wondered if it had happened at all. Friedrich had been cut out of my life in such a way that it was as if he had never existed. The only real proof I had was his Bible.

On one exceptionally bad day, it had felt impossible to make it through my classes without crying. After Art, I ran to the room while Kate and Anna studied downstairs with Marilyn and Cecilia. The moment I locked the door behind me, I burst into sobs. I screamed into my pillow. It wasn't fair. None of it was fair. Who were any of them to tell us we couldn't be together? Like my mother, the general, Pastor Gilbert, and these girls had never made a mistake before; like they hadn't been in love before. I wanted to hate all of them. If only they could've seen into our hearts; if only it weren't for this stupid war.

Friedrich's Bible rested on the windowsill. It was easier to reach there. I glared at it now.

You've never abandoned me before, God.

So why was it so hard to fight a feeling of betrayal from Him?

I want to be mad at You. I want to hate everyone involved in our separation.

But I couldn't. As much as I wanted it, if I let the hate in, it would take over; I'd cease to be myself. It would cause me to forget how I used to be good and how there was still good that could come out of this. It would have me seek vengeance; not peace, not forgiveness, not hope. Giving up my self-control felt easier than forcing myself to take another step, another breath; to accept a punishment I didn't deserve, to keep going even when I felt like God had deserted me. I had followed my heart, where I believed He was leading me, and He was leaving me to face the ramifications of my actions alone.

So why do I still want to trust You? Why am I still trying to figure out what You want me to do from here?

Emotionally, I distanced myself from the girls who tried to be my friends. They would only judge me. They wouldn't understand the profound connection between Friedrich and me. They would think I'd been bewitched, too. I could already imagine them referencing him the way they did countless other boys, as if he were a box to be checked, a toy to be tossed aside, a phase to endure. But he wasn't. I was drawn to Friedrich because of who he was; because of who I was when I was with him. No matter how much the girls said they believed in true love, their logic would kick in, telling them my good sense was faulty. It was foolish to think that a seventeen-year-old could recognize her soul mate, but I knew now it wasn't foolish at all. I didn't need their voices in my ear, telling me to move on. He was it for me. If I ever stopped believing that, it had all been for nothing.

They never ganged up on me again, but I still had to evade their occasional prodding questions. Marilyn was curious about how we'd been able to see each other. Kate wanted to know if I'd kissed him. Cecilia's were more specific, but less relevant; she always asked if we had ever got caught in a rainstorm and kissed, or if he'd ever beaten up another guy who liked me. They all sought answers, but I gave them none.

The only one who didn't pressure me was Anna. She had to be as curious as the others, but she never accosted me with awkward queries. I knew if I ever did decide to tell anyone about Friedrich, it would be her. She wouldn't rush to inform the others; I didn't have that kind of confidence in Kate, Marilyn or Cecilia.

I begged God each night, and sometimes throughout the day, to tell me what to do to relieve the strain; to dull the unending hurt.

I know You say You'll carry my burdens, but why do I feel like I'm on my own? What do I have to do to make it stop? To get You to show Yourself to me? What am I supposed to do? Why aren't You here with me?

My frustrations swelled against the girls. My unresponsiveness did nothing to make them relent. It wasn't until one Sunday—after our weekly chapel in the dining hall —that the seams of my forbearance ruptured.

"Marilyn's going to get it," Kate said as we walked together out of the dining hall.

"I tried waking her," Cecilia said. "She knows they take roll. It's her own fault."

"Missing chapel is two days in detention hall," Anna muttered.

Kate laughed. "That's nothing to her. She's served two months before."

"Marilyn *is* a mystery," Anna said.

Kate elbowed me. "Much like Cassie and her German are."

A feverish heat flashed over me. I kept my eyes ahead.

Still, Kate persisted. "What is it with you and this suffer-in-silence martyrdom? It makes me wonder if he was even real. Maybe you made him up because the actual reason you were sent here is much worse. Are you a murderer?"

"Or maybe he was hideous and she doesn't like remembering him," Cecilia joked.

"I bet he had a great personality," Kate teased.

I tried to fight it off; I tried to subdue it. My anger came to a boil, the bubbles pouring over the top. I broke away from them, standing on the stairs. "Or maybe, just maybe, the reason I won't say anything is because none of you take it seriously. You all act like it was meaningless—like it's some kind of joke."

Kate's typically playful nut brown eyes had gone smooth. "Cassie, we didn't—"

"Well, it wasn't. I'll tell you when I'm ready to tell you. Why can't you just leave it alone?"

The three of them were staring at me. I hurried up the stairs before any of them could stop me. I slammed the door to my room, tossing Friedrich's Bible on my bed as I paced the floor. I wanted to hit something. I wanted to scream. Instead, all I could do was walk it off.

I was embarrassed when Anna and Kate came up later. I'd worried I'd only caused tension between us, and it astonished me when they both apologized. I told them I was sorry, too.

After that day, none of them asked me about Friedrich again.

For some reason, it made me feel worse. I wanted them to care. Their lack of interest made me feel even more isolated, as if what I'd done really had been wrong. Waves of devastating melancholy pummeled the shores of my desolate being. My Friedrich was far from me and there were days where I cried because I feared I was forgetting what he looked like.

I hadn't heard from my father since long before I'd arrived at the school. I'd been there almost a month and I had yet to hear from my mother or receive a response to one of the countless letters I'd sent to Lucy. It was as if they were glad to be rid of me and wanted to pretend I had simply disappeared out of their lives.

It became harder for me to start my days. Sleeping was the only escape from the despair; the only escape from pretending I was okay. Though never tardy and never having missed any classes, I waited until the last possible minute to get up each morning.

On one particular day, I sat in English class, chancing peeks at the dreary sky from the window. We'd waited for it to rain all day. Instead, the clouds seemed content to stay gloomy, keeping all the raindrops to themselves. I peeled my eyes away as Mrs. Olsen asked us to turn to the next chapter.

Thumbing through the pages, I lingered over one I hadn't seen before. At the end of each chapter was a page showing the ways other languages had contributed to English. A poem from eighteenth-century Germany, "Wenn ich ein

Vöglein wär," had been written in an Old English font on the backdrop of an unfurled scroll. Reading the German, I was surprised that it seemed to come naturally to me.

My heart almost stopped.

I'd heard it before; it was Friedrich's song. I read the translation:

If I were a bird and had two wings, I would fly to you. As that cannot be, I have to stay here.

Even though I am far from you, in my sleep I am with you and speak to you. When I wake up, I am alone.

Not an hour passes in the night but my heart wakes and thinks of you, and that you have given me your heart so many thousand times.

I covered my mouth to hide the smile that stretched across my face. Was there any way at all this was God's way of reminding me He hadn't forgotten about me? Or could it be that He was letting me know that Friedrich's feelings hadn't changed?

I mouthed the words, hearing the melody in my head.

"Do you find my lesson humorous, Miss Wyndham?"

I went rigid in my seat, along with every other girl in class. "Uh...No, ma'am."

"Either you find my lesson to be a joke or you aren't paying attention in class. Which is it?"

For a split second, I almost asked, *Well, which one will get me into less trouble?* before responding with a much less incendiary, "Neither, Mrs. Olsen."

I got my first strapping that day. Marilyn put her arm around me after class. "You're officially part of the group now, new girl."

"I bit my lip until it bled to keep from laughing when I heard 'Miss Wyndham!'" Kate said, mimicking Mrs. Olsen's nasally voice.

"Cassie's been part of the group since she got here," Anna said. "Besides, she wasn't *trying* to get strapped. It was an accident."

"I definitely wasn't trying to get strapped," I asserted.

"Doesn't matter. You're one of us now," Marilyn said.

Anna adjusted her books. "I've never been strapped and I'm part of the group."

"We took a vote and gave you an honorary membership," Marilyn said.

Anna didn't look amused. "I hope you're joking."

Marilyn and Kate looked at each other. Then we all laughed.

Though getting strapped had done nothing to cause the girls to look down on me, it still embarrassed me. Kate and Marilyn reminded me of it every once in a while, but it wasn't something I was proud of. In fact, I was keen on never letting it happen again.

One night, after finishing my homework, I opened my English book to the German poem. "Say, has Mrs. Olsen ever taught from these *Marks on English History* pages?"

Anna was writing at her desk. "Not that I can recall."

"I'm glad she doesn't," Kate proclaimed. "It's just a bunch of useless knowledge—more information than we really need to know."

"Do they check books at the end of the year?" I asked. "To see if any damage has been done to them?"

"No," Anna said.

"There are too many students," Kate supplied. "Besides, we get new books every three to four years."

"What if, hypothetically," I began, "they find out you *deliberately* defaced a book? Do you think they'd punish you with a strapping or detention hall? Or maybe make you pay to replace the book?"

Anna looked up at me.

"I don't know," Kate said from her bed, reading. "That probably depends on if they see you do it or not. It could've been an accident, for all they—"

I ripped the poem from the book.

Anna gasped, a wavering smile on her lips. "Why'd you do that?"

I folded it in half, placing it in the cover of Friedrich's Bible, alongside his note and my only picture of Lucy. "I need it."

"Need it?" Kate asked. "Why would you *need* one of those historical pages?"

I looked at her, glancing at Anna as I put Friedrich's Bible in my drawer. "I'm going to get ready for bed. Either of you want to come?"

Anna still seemed uncertain of me. "No, I'll go in a few minutes. I still have a little more reading to do."

"Yeah, me too," Kate said as I got my pajamas and toothbrush. She watched me as I crossed the room. I was halfway to the bathroom before I turned around. Kate was almost to my bed when I opened the door.

"No snooping!"

Kate turned, fiddling with the curtain. "I wasn't...It was just so bright in here that I wanted to block out the light."

Anna didn't look up from her desk. "Kate, the sun sets in the west. We're facing north."

"You are not helping," Kate sang as she scurried back to her bed. I couldn't help but laugh as I shut the door.

Finding Friedrich's song—whether it had been a divine accident or a mere coincidence—put a little bounce in my step. Finally, I had another connection to him, to the days when we were together. It became one of my nightly rituals to write a letter to Lucy, read from Friedrich's Bible, and read the poem. I read the German until I'd almost memorized it, hearing him sing it to me as I dwindled to sleep.

For one glittering moment, I thought I'd passed the valley of my sorrow to begin the upward slope, until one Friday after Art class.

"Oh, Cassie, Marilyn asked for some help with arithmetic for our finals," Anna said as I started up the stairs. "I told her I would. Do you want to come with us?"

"I'm going, too," Kate said. "Mostly just to watch. Marilyn never asks for help with homework."

I chuckled. "No. That's okay. I'll wait for you upstairs. I need to write another letter to Lucy. Do you want me to take your books?"

"That'd be great," Anna said as she and Kate handed me their Art books. "Meet us down here for dinner if we aren't back before then."

There were letters in the small box outside our door when I got there. (Miss Wilson always sorted the mail, putting them in our appropriate boxes.) I grabbed them before going into the room.

I wouldn't have even bothered to see who they were addressed to if I'd had only one roommate. My first few weeks here, my heart would float high above me with anticipation whenever I saw letters in our box, only for it to pop and whiz to the ground; I had yet to receive mail from anyone. Today, however, as I divvied up letters between Kate and Anna, I paused to see one addressed to me.

I stared at it, flipping it over as I leaned against my bed. There was no return address, so it wasn't from my parents. I tore it open, an intriguing thought entering my mind:

Friedrich.

Perhaps he had written me from a camp somehow. Since they checked all the prisoners' mail, it wouldn't be sentimental or detailed, but even the plainest words from him would be more than enough. I pulled the letter out with eagerness.

To the German's whore. Your dirty, shameless behavior has done nothing but pervert the Word and will of God. There is a place in hell for you and your German. I pray that you get what's coming to you, that Jesus in his righteous wrath will take His brutal vengeance out on you. You deserve death for what you've done. Don't come back. You are no longer welcome here. In Christ's sweet and holy, precious name.

My soaring heart plunged to the earth, crashing into the soil. I stared at the ferocious words before crumpling the letter up, throwing it across the room.

My hands were trembling as I sunk to the floor. This person didn't know me—and I knew none of what they said was true—but it upset me that someone believed this about me, using Jesus as a weapon.

Or was this another one of those signs God wanted me to see, like I believed the German poem had been? Was there *some* truth to this letter? I sobbed, rocking back and forth.

God felt as far away as Friedrich did. The words in that letter were venom, seeping painfully into my heart. This couldn't be the only person who felt this way—the only person who hated me. As if I needed another reason to not want to go home.

But where else could I go? I had no money; my parents had taken it all. I had no one, because no one cared. They had succeeded in removing me from everything I knew and loved, leaving me forlorn and starving for affection. How could this be good? How could this be the will of God?

"It's not," I said to myself, crying on the floor. "It's not."

I knew He loved me. There had to be another purpose for this pain. Perhaps this was all to prepare me for something that I couldn't see yet. That letter, my parents' total ignorance of me—these were not of God. Even though I couldn't feel Him, I knew He was still there.

"You are all I need," I whispered. "You are all I need. You are all I need. You are all I—"

"Cassie?"

I shoved myself up, feeling someone's hand on my shoulder. It was too late to even pretend that I wasn't distraught. Anna was kneeling in front of me, her crystal blue eyes showing grave concern. Kate stood frozen in the doorway. I gulped.

Anna's voice was gentle. "Cassie, are you okay?"

I looked back up at Kate before avoiding both their gazes. I shook my head.

"Do you want to talk about it?" Anna whispered.

I didn't answer. All I could do was stare at that abominable letter rumpled up next to Kate's bed. It was screaming at me. It was telling me I was all alone. I couldn't tell them because they wouldn't understand; they wouldn't care. They were just like everyone else. I was bad and that was why no one loved me.

"Okay." Anna was still speaking in whispers. "We'll leave you alone. Okay?"

I had been calling out to Him all this time and He had been answering me, but my vision had been too obstructed, too deceived to realize it. He had not compelled that person to write that letter because He had been there in the forest with Friedrich and me. He knew the truth.

And the truth was He didn't want me to be alone.

"Wait," I blurted through my tears.

Kate and Anna hesitated, looking at me over their shoulders. I watched them for a moment, wiping off my cheeks. They hadn't reacted negatively to finding out about Friedrich. They were willing to listen—they *wanted* to listen.

"I want to talk about it," I whimpered. "I *need* to talk about it."

I feared they would scoff, informing me that I'd missed my chance and that they were no longer interested. Instead, a guilty grin came over Kate's face. Anna stepped back into the room, shutting and locking the door behind them.

Twenty One

Before they would even let me talk, Anna insisted that
I calm down. I asked why they had come back up so early and
she said that Marilyn decided she'd rather wait and study
tomorrow.

"Do you want anything? Maybe a snack or a glass of
water?" Anna asked, regarding me with honest worry.

It made my eyes watery again. "Yes, please."

"Kate, would you——?"

Kate jumped to her feet, sprinting toward the door.
"On it! Don't you dare start without me!"

Anna watched me as the door slammed shut. "Would
you rather just talk to me? If you feel more comfortable that
way, I can talk to Kate. You don't have to say anything in
front of her if you don't want——"

"It's okay." I dabbed beneath my eyes. "Thank you,
though."

Kate returned with a cup of water and a variety of
snacks from Marilyn's room for all of us and I told them my
story. Neither of them interrupted unless it was for
clarification. I held nothing back, letting every little detail flow
out of me. I told them about the day I cried in the rain. I told
them about his violin. I told them about Friedrich's song,
showing them the poem. I let them read his note. I showed
them his Bible. I showed them the vile letter I'd received in

the mail. By the end of it, I couldn't believe how light my spirit felt. It was almost as if the letter had had no effect on me at all.

"Well, one thing's for certain." Kate tossed a couple raisins in her mouth. "Your mom's a real bitch."

Anna gasped. "Kate! That's inappropriate."

"Come on, Anna. Even you can't argue with that."

Anna glanced at me. "Well, I don't think she's been unselfish towards you, Cassie, or behaved like a mother should, but...but I wouldn't call her that."

I reached for the raisins. "I've wanted to. A few times."

"Believe me, she has *no* idea what trouble is," Kate said as she chewed. "I guarantee if I was her daughter for five minutes, she'd be begging to have you back. For that matter, if my mother met you, she'd adopt you."

I smiled at her, though it quickly faded. "Do you think I was wrong? Knowing everything that I've told you— do you think we shouldn't have done what we did?"

Kate and Anna looked at each other. I couldn't read either of their expressions, though a small grin came over Kate's face. "I don't think you can call it right or wrong. It just happened. Maybe it was supposed to, maybe it wasn't...but it did. The circumstances might've been—mmm —inconvenient. But wrong? I don't think I believe that."

"If you really felt like God was involved, that His hand was there guiding you both, then it can't be wrong," Anna said. "Your relationship may have been unacceptable to some, but God's will doesn't always make sense; it doesn't have to. There are things that we can't possibly know or see yet. If God wanted this to happen, then it was right, Cassie. Everything else is inconsequential because He does have a plan. You just have to wait and see what it is."

My eyes filled with tears. "But what about the letter? Someone really thinks that about me. How could I have been doing God's will if someone sees me like...well...you saw."

"What, this?" Kate asked, holding up the wrinkled paper. "It's nothing but words, Cassie." She tore it up. "A fire-starter, literally and figuratively."

"Do you honestly think God's pleased with whoever wrote that?" Anna asked. "It's more than evident that they know nothing about sharing the love of Jesus."

"And look at the cowardice. They throw all these words at you and don't even put a return address on the envelope. Why? Because they're spineless. They said all that because they can remain faceless and nameless to you," Kate said.

"And Cassie," Anna spoke with tenderness, "I'm not saying this to upset you or make you think your parents don't love you—I'm sure they love you very much. But..." She exchanged looks with Kate. "We're not blind. You've been here almost two months and this is the first letter you've received. You write to your sister almost every day; that's not something a bad person does. Your parents are just...I don't know. I don't think they realize what they're doing to you."

I buried my face in my knees to cry, but not out of sadness. I couldn't believe that they noticed.

"I mean," she continued, "I know you said your father's busy, but my father's in France, in the middle of fighting, and I get letters from him every other week, at least."

"Yeah." Kate nodded. "And I'm the least favorite in my family and my mother still sends me sweet letters; even gifts, sometimes."

For the first time, outside of Friedrich, I felt seen. "I don't know what to do. It's been this way for so long that I don't know how to make it stop. When Friedrich came along, he said the same things you're saying. He made me see myself in a way that no one has ever allowed me to before. I wish so much that other people would look at me the way he did."

"Well," Anna said with a smile, "I see you that way. Kate sees you that way. You're not a bad person, Cassie; you're a very good person. You just got caught up in something at an untimely moment."

"Yeah, and honestly, in another year or so, people won't even remember this," Kate said. "The war may be over by then, anyway. It just won't matter anymore."

Anna reached out to rub my arm. "You just have to wait and see what happens."

I smiled at them through my tears. "Can I hug you?"

Anna laughed. "Of course!"

I wrapped my arms around both of their necks. "You all are the best friends I've ever had. I mean it."

Anna pat my back.

"We love you, Cassie," Kate said. We all chuckled.

"I love you, too."

My sense of desertion and self-pity became extinct. Friedrich was gone, but I realized now that I wanted to be around Anna and Kate, too. My heart warmed toward them even more once I discovered they hadn't told Marilyn or Cecilia; not that I would've minded by that point, but I appreciated their discretion.

By the middle of December, I hardly even remembered what it was like not to be open with them. The three of us—Anna, Kate and I—had become very close. I knew everything about them, from each impish deed of Kate's pre-boarding school life, to Anna's strict studying routines and well-concealed quirks. I looked forward to our talks after lights out. Our best conversations seemed to happen in those hours.

I'd been sent here to learn a lesson, to be reprimanded and punished. But I didn't feel like I was being transformed; I felt like I was becoming more myself. It made me curious about whether my parents would be happy with how I'd turned out once I left here (if they would even be in the same house; I'd bitterly imagined them moving without telling me). Thinking it over, I didn't care which me they preferred. I would be eighteen when I left the school. I could be who I wanted to be.

It'd been less than a month since I'd gotten the hate letter in the mail. I had yet to hear anything from my parents, but since it was getting close to Christmas, they couldn't ignore me much longer. Through their own eyes, that actually *would* make them bad parents.

Kate had gotten the mail from our door. "Uh oh."

"What is it?" Anna asked as she folded her uniform.

Kate held up one of the envelopes. "You got another letter, Cassie."

I groaned. "It doesn't have a return address on it?"

"Oh no, it does. Looks like a...Jimmy Taylor," she said, reading the front as Anna took it from her grasp. "Do you want us to open it?"

I froze before getting up. "Wh...Jimmy Taylor wrote to me?"

They stared at me as I took the letter. His name and unit information was written in the corner. He'd never written me before, even in Rockmont. Remembering his visible detestation of the Germans and how close he'd been to Amos, I dreaded the vilification that was bound to be inside. Surely his mother had told him.

I held my breath, holding the letter out to read it:

Cassie,

I asked my mom to get your new address from your mother. I hope you don't mind.

How are you? Why haven't you written to me anymore? I'm sorry if it's because I haven't written back. It's not because I didn't enjoy your letters. I enjoyed them very much. It's hard for me to write as often as I would like. Please don't think I don't want to hear from you anymore. It always gave me something to look forward to.

I don't know what your reasons were for doing what Mom says you did, but I don't need to know. It doesn't matter. I meant every word I said to you back in August. If I could see you now, I'd tell you the same thing.

As for me, it's getting better and it's getting worse over here. It's getting better, because we advance a little further each day. It's getting worse because I'm losing friends faster than I can make them. Over half the men in my company weren't in it from the beginning. For some reason, I'm still here, so I'll keep fighting until my last breath. But maybe the war will end before that happens.

It won't be the same, being home without Amos there. I think about him sometimes, along with the others. Their sacrifices will not be forgotten, nor are they in vain. Whether I live to see it or not, we are going to win this war because of men like them.

I hope I hear from you soon. A letter from you is the light in my day.

Sincerely yours,

Jimmy

I was smiling to myself, my unease mitigated. Jimmy didn't hate me. Even though it sounded like he knew about what happened between Friedrich and me, he still wanted to hear from me.

"I take it by that smile that it's a good letter?" Kate asked with a smirk.

I folded it, returning it to the envelope. "Yeah."

Kate purred, laying across her bed as she spoke in a Queens accent. "Who's Jimmy Taylor? He sounds interesting."

I laughed at her as I put his letter in my drawer. "He's a friend. *Just* a friend." I sighed, returning to my bed. "He wants me to write to him."

Slipping off her shoes, Anna paused. "You're not going to?"

I was surprised, thankful even, that he didn't hate me like everyone else seemed to. But the moment he returned, he'd ignore me, no matter how much effort I put into writing him now. A decent guy like Jimmy—who would return a war hero, no less—would not want to associate with a girl everyone knew had been caught with a German POW. It was too embarrassing. "I don't think so."

"You should, Cassie." Anna spoke with caution. "No matter what, he's...he's still a soldier. Letters mean a lot to them. Knowing that someone's thinking of them keeps them from giving up."

I only looked at her. Somewhere deep inside, I knew she was right; somewhere deep inside, I wanted to write to him. But I couldn't. Not now. He pitied me, and I would write out of the hope that he would still be kind to me when he returned. "Maybe he'll find someone else to write to him. But I can't anymore."

I could tell by the grooves in Anna's forehead that she didn't like this, but she didn't argue.

I was ecstatic that I wasn't the only one staying at school over Christmas. Anna's father was still in France. Kate's family lived in Pennsylvania; both she and her family wanted her home for the holidays, but they couldn't afford the trip for her. Without her father or brother there to manage the farm, her mother and sisters were living off much less than before. The money they did have, they were saving for her return trip home in May when school ended.

Cecilia's mother didn't have enough money for her to come home, either, not without her father's income. The only one who went home for Christmas was Marilyn. She had told us all that her grandparents were making her come home and that she didn't have a choice, but Cecilia told us she'd read the letter Marilyn's grandmother had sent without her knowing. Marilyn's grandmother had written to say how much they missed her and if she wanted to come home for Christmas, they'd go shopping together, pick out a Christmas tree to decorate, volunteer at a nearby soup kitchen together and go Christmas caroling. I stored this away in my brain, Marilyn becoming even more of an enigma to me.

Classes ended after our finals and Kate squealed upon seeing a package left at our door as the three of us got to our room. They were just as shocked as I was to see my name in bold letters on it. It was from my mother.

It was filled with Christmas presents. There was a pair of rather stylish knee high socks (no doubt for the cold weather) that I couldn't wait to wear, a couple pictures of stick figures that Lucy had drawn for me (one in particular was the likeness of me holding her hand), a stationary pad and pencil, a box of candy canes and a case of Coca-Colas.

Beneath it all was my pillow. Despite the hard feelings I had towards my mom, that almost made me cry.

There was also a letter at the bottom. She told me briefly that she and Lucy were doing well and that my father was coming to stay the entire week and that they would call me on Christmas. As much as I thought hearing from them after so much time would only inflame my resentment, it mollified me. They hadn't forgotten about me; they hadn't moved without telling me. Maybe they loved me after all—in their own way.

Christmas Day finally came. The morning didn't start the way it always did at home, waiting on everyone else to wake up to rush downstairs and open presents. Instead, the day began for us as it would any other day, though the three of us wished each other a Merry Christmas upon waking.

The only chaperones we had were Mrs. Hammond, Mrs. Robles and Miss Wilson. This was enough, since there were only fifteen students staying over the holiday. The rest of the staff had gone to spend Christmas with their families, so even for a normal day, it was lax. At dinner, Mrs. Hammond hosted a show some of the girls had signed up to perform. There were skits and singing, along with music that played in the dining hall. It reminded me of the night I went to see the concert at the POW camp.

I became aware then of an affinity Friedrich and I hadn't had before. I was sent here against my will; he had been captured and shipped to America to be contained until the war was over. For both of us, what was supposed to be our prisons became our safe havens.

The cafeteria workers served hot chocolate, with our preference of coffee cakes, fruitcakes, custard pies and semi-sweet chocolate cookies with walnuts; treats for Christmas. Mrs. Hammond provided us all with craft supplies. None of us had any gifts to give one another, so we decided to make presents for each other. I made an Indian teepee, complete with a small orange construction paper fire out front for Cecilia. Kate drew Anna a unicorn running on a rainbow (we were all impressed). Cecilia gave me a paper flower with multi-colored petals, and Anna gave Kate a construction paper gift box, filling it with tiny paper hearts.

While we were still in the dining hall, Miss Wilson came to tell me I had a phone call. She'd been delegated to police the phone, making sure all calls were no more than ten minutes to ensure other families could reach their daughters, too.

Feeling a little nervous, I picked up the receiver. "Hello?"

"Cassandra?"

I didn't feel anything upon hearing my mom's voice. "Hey Mom."

"Merry Christmas."

"Merry Christmas," I returned. "Thanks for the gifts. It was really nice of you to do that."

"You're welcome." She sounded unemotional, as businesslike as I did. "How have you been?"

Wrapping the cord around my finger, I leaned against the front desk. "Well. Actually, I've been *really* well." It came out as a taunt.

"That's wonderful. Well...we miss you."

"You, too."

She didn't say anything for a second. "Um...Would you like to speak with your father now?"

"Yeah."

"Okay." Her voice was low. "I love you."

I swallowed, tempted to pretend I hadn't heard as I had at the train station. I sighed. "Love you, too."

I could hear scuffling as she handed the phone to my dad. "Hey Sweetheart."

My smile was irrepressible as I heard the sincere warmth in his voice. "Hey Dad."

"How are you doing? How's school?"

"Great. I'm doing great, the school's been great. I've made some really amazing friends."

"Really?"

"Yeah."

"Well, that's wonderful. Your grades are good, I know. In the report Mrs. Hammond sent to us, all your teachers had only nice things to say about you."

My brow tightened. I didn't know my parents were sent reports.

"Of course," he continued, "I would have expected no less. You've always done well in school."

With a frail grin to myself, I ran my finger over the rotary dial. "Thanks, Dad. I'm sorry I wasn't able to get you all anything for Christmas this year."

"Don't worry about it, Sweetheart. The best present we could have is hearing your voice."

I stared at a spot on the wall, my eyes suddenly burning. Why hadn't I gone home for Christmas? My parents hadn't even asked me what I wanted to do. I wasn't even sure I *wanted* to leave, but I would have appreciated being asked.

The anger rose inside me again. "Yeah well, seeing you would have been nicer. But at least I have friends to spend Christmas with. The best part is Amos isn't paying any of them off this time."

He gave an uncomfortable chuckle. It was a shame I was mad at him now.

"Well...I love you, Cassandra. Uh, looks like Lucy wants to speak with you."

Happy again. "Okay. Love you, too. Put her on."

Miss Wilson tapped her watch and showed me three fingers. I nodded.

"Sissy!"

My smile was automatic and she giggled as I spoke. "Lucy-Goosey! How have you been, sweet girl? Sissy misses you so much."

"I miss you, too, Sissy! Merry Tristmas." I could hear Mom coaching her in the background. "Sissy, I dot...new baby doll... and I help Mommy mate Tristmas toot-tees, and dot a new book! When you tum home, you will read to me?"

"Of course I will. I miss you so much, Luce."

"I miss you, too, Sissy. Sissy, when...when you will tum home?"

"Soon. Okay? It's going to be a little while, but I'll be home before you know it."

"Otay," she said. I snickered before seeing Miss Wilson motion for me to hang up.

"Okay, listen Luce. Sissy has to go now."

"Otay."

"But, I miss and love you so much. Can you please give Mommy and Daddy big hugs from me?"

"Yes."

"And can you give yourself a big hug from me?"

"Yes, Sissy. See? I do it right now!" She grunted.

"Good. I'll talk to you next time, Lucy. I'll send you another letter soon, okay?"

"Otay."

I closed my eyes. "Bye, baby."

"Bye, Sissy."

I waited for the line to click before hanging up and returning to the dining hall with my friends.

Regardless of the tension between my parents and me, and the way my heart ached as I hung up with Lucy, I realized this had been one of the best Christmases I'd ever had. I didn't feel sorry for myself; this year, Cecilia, Kate, Anna and I were each other's family.

Cecilia slept in our room that night. I closed my eyes, trying to sleep once we all fell silent. I couldn't seem to keep them closed for long. The curtains were open and the stars glittered like diamonds behind the falling snow.

It was always in the quiet that it became difficult for me to escape thoughts of him.

I'd enjoyed today so much that I'd given myself little room for any sadness. He did not make me sad, but the fact that I couldn't be with him—that we had been forced apart—did.

It was so hushed, so peaceful outside. I longed to lie out in the snow and gaze up at the stars. I wondered what he was doing now; how he was celebrating Christmas at the camp in Texas. I wondered if he was asking himself the same thing about me.

What a Christmas gift it would've been to hear how he was doing, to catch even a glimpse of him; to fall asleep in his arms.

Alone in my bed, I somehow felt close to him, as if tonight was such a special night that the strength behind our wills, the passion in our prayers, were no longer elapsing one another, but aligning with the other. My heart whispered, asking God to let it be real—to let this be a shared moment for both of us. I hoped I wasn't imagining it. If he was pining for me as much as I was for him, then surely the power of such emotion could almost become tangible—and it was Christmas. If there were ever a time it could happen, Christmas night would be it.

I nuzzled into my pillow, trying to pretend he was holding me. Perhaps at this very moment, he was closing his eyes, wishing with all that he had that his arms were around me. Maybe tonight, if we concentrated hard enough, God would let the pieces fit as they should, even if we were the only ones who felt it.

Twenty Two

Marilyn came back a few days before New Year's. Though I was glad to see her, it also weighed on my holiday spirits. Her return meant it wasn't long before classes started again. We only had a few days left of freedom to roam the halls and throw snow balls at one another. That cheered me.

They left the lights on an extra hour on New Year's Eve, not that it mattered. We were never asleep by then anyway. The three of us cuddled into our beds, still in conversation.

"So what are you going to do once you turn eighteen?" I heard Kate ask. "Where will you go?"

Anna didn't answer right away. "I don't know. I suppose I'll just go home. There's always a chance my dad will be home by June."

"But what if he isn't?"

"I don't know, Kate," Anna said with slight frustration. "I'm trying not to think of the worst or the most difficult scenarios. I'm trying to be positive. Even if my father isn't back by my birthday, I think I could live at home by myself. I'll be an adult."

Kate sighed. "I don't know what I'm going to do. My mother wants me back on the farm."

"You don't want to be?" Anna asked. Kate was silent.

"No," she murmured.

"Are either of you going to college?" I asked.

"No," Kate said quickly.

"I want to," Anna said. "Are you?"

"I *wanted* to," I said with contempt. "I don't know how I could now."

"Because of what your parents did with the money?" Kate asked.

"Yes."

"I can't imagine them not letting you go if you have the opportunity. It's not like you can use it to run away now," Anna pointed out.

I didn't reply. Sighing, I rolled over. Hearing our door open and close, I thought one of them had left.

"Um—hello," I heard Anna say.

"Who is it?" Kate whispered.

"It's me."

Anna sat up. "Cecilia?"

"Yeah," Cecilia whispered. I sat up, too, as she glided toward the window. "Why are you in bed? It's New Year's Eve."

"Well, what else are we going to do?" Anna asked. "What are you doing here, anyway?"

Cecilia raised our window. "I'm making your New Year's memorable, the way it should be."

There was a sudden suspiciousness in Kate's voice. "Where's Marilyn?"

"On the roof. She's waiting for us," Cecilia answered matter-of-factly.

I snorted with laughter. "What?"

"She climbed up the other side out of Mary and Patricia's room. The ladder on this side of the building is next to your window."

"You've got to be joking." Anna threw back her covers, hugging herself as she got out of bed. "It's got to be twenty degrees or less out there. Are you insane? On the roof?"

"Why not?"

Kate looked uncertain as she stared at Cecilia.

Cecilia paused, straddling the window. "If you three want to waste your New Year's snoring Auld Lang Syne at midnight, be my guest. If not, put on some good climbing shoes, warm underpants and sweaters, bring your best blankets, and follow me."

With that, she disappeared. Neither Anna nor Kate spoke. They were as hesitant as I was.

Kate was the first to move. "Well...on the up side, we'll probably have to serve so many detentions that we won't have to attend classes until we graduate."

Anna sighed, opening a drawer under her bed. "Why am I not surprised?"

"So I guess we're going?" I asked, to which the two of them gave unenthusiastic consents.

I climbed on my desktop to peer out the window. Cecilia's legs vanished overhead onto the roof. The cold air pierced my pajamas and I shivered. The metal ladder was freezing to the touch, but I was glad I didn't have to stretch to reach it. I imagined the ground was a lot farther down than it appeared.

I followed Kate and Anna's lead, slipping warmer clothes over my pajamas. "What if we get caught?"

"If we get caught, then we were meant to get caught," Kate said. She was wearing a heavy gray sweater, slipping on her penny loafers. "Mrs. Gregory and Miss Barlow are gone until school starts. No one's going to notice."

"And I suppose spending New Year's freezing on the roof together is better than being comfortable and warm in our beds alone," Anna said. I chuckled. Sometimes it was hard for me to tell when she was being serious and when she was being sarcastic.

Once we'd all dressed in our warmest clothes and grabbed our blankets, we followed Cecilia's trail out the window. Kate went first. I went after, the rungs of the ladder feeling like icicles beneath my grip. Reaching the top, I dusted off my hands, shoving them as far as I could into my coat pockets.

"Come on," Marilyn rasped.

"Over here," Cecilia directed.

The two of them were sitting against what looked like a brick shed in the middle of the roof. I helped Anna up the rest of the way. The three of us started towards them, careful that our steps weren't too heavy.

Marilyn had wiped away the dusting of snow, laying a quilt out for us. "Have a seat. Get close. It'll help us keep warm."

"Let me guess. This was your idea, right, Mar?" Kate asked as the three of us huddled together with them.

Cecilia handed bottled drinks out to us. "I couldn't have come up with something like this."

I inspected the bottle extended to me, unable to see any kind of label. Anna seemed to be experiencing the same indecision. Marilyn laughed.

"Don't worry, you goody-goods," she said. "They're orange pops. My grandmother gave them to me before I left. She told me to share so, I am."

Anna took a sip. She nodded and winked at me in approval.

"This," Marilyn said, pouring liquid from a larger and darker bottle into Kate's cup, "is for the big girls."

"What is that?" I asked.

"Poison," Marilyn rasped.

Kate began to cough as if it had gone down the wrong pipe. "Cider?" She licked at her lips. "Marilyn, what have you been reduced to?"

"Okay, so it's not the strong stuff, but I couldn't get away with sneaking anything out of the liquor cabinet. Poppa would've noticed," she said, pouring herself a cup.

"I really hope we don't get caught," Anna muttered, looking over her shoulder.

"Don't worry," Marilyn said. "They won't find us. Not tonight. I could hear Hammond's snores from the top of the stairs. She must've fallen asleep in her office."

"Yes, but Wilson's still unaccounted for," Kate said, slurping from her cup.

Marilyn paused. "You make a valid point, Miss Warren. Wilson's just ratty enough to scurry up the side ladders to confirm the legitimacy of a funny feeling, too."

"So maybe this isn't such a good idea," Anna said over her shoulder again.

"Well, none of my ideas are exactly virtuous, but here we all are—might as well exploit this one before we go to bed. The New Year is only thirty minutes away, anyway."

Anna didn't reply, but she didn't get up to leave, either.

"Mmm." Cecilia swallowed, sitting up on her knees. "We should make a toast."

"It's not midnight yet," Kate said.

"Kissing is for midnight. Toasts are for anytime," Cecilia said.

Marilyn brought her knees up. "She's right."

"Kissing," Kate said with a sigh. "I wish we had boys here. What good is midnight on New Year's without boys?"

"We could say what our New Year's resolutions are," Anna suggested.

"Agreed," Marilyn said, "but let's do a toast first. I'll start: to good-looking guys, strong liquor and the end of childhood."

"I'll drink to that," Kate said as our glasses clinked.

We each took a sip from our drinks. Cecilia held up her bottle next. "To boyfriends, the coming of the end of the war, and pretty flowers."

"Pretty flowers?" Marilyn repeated as our bottles touched.

"My turn," Kate said. "To delicious, memorable kisses, Christmas vacations and..." She stared at her bottle. "This sublime apple cider."

"Here, here," Marilyn said.

We drank, and all eyes turned to me. I thought for a moment. "To true friends...true love..." I glanced around at them. "And hope."

"Aww," said Marilyn.

"Don't patronize," I said.

"Okay. Me?" Anna asked. "To good grades, loved ones that we can't be with right now, and undetermined yet bright futures."

Kate laughed.

We spent the rest of the hour talking, laughing and shivering, watching our breath materialize in front of us. At midnight, fireworks went off in the distance and we hugged each other while Marilyn sang Auld Lang Syne just loud enough for us to hear. Though we were enjoying ourselves, more snow began to fall all around us and I could no longer feel my ears. Saying goodnight—and feeling rather jovial—we returned to our rooms. Before closing my eyes, I asked God to help me through the following year; if I wasn't meant to find Friedrich in it, that He would give me patience and endurance to make it through to the next. My New Year's resolution was to stay true to me; to not forget the cost of gaining that knowledge.

As uncertain as my future was, tonight, it didn't frighten me; tonight, I found myself trusting Him—that I'd done everything I was supposed to do. No matter how complicated my life had become, He still had a plan for me; He still had a plan for us.

Weeks went by without another word from my parents. I'd started my last semester of school—ever—and I had no letters, no phone calls wishing me luck or even one simply asking how I was doing. Cecilia's mother came to visit her at the beginning of February and I didn't fail to notice a twinge of jealousy. She had run to her mother, embracing her with the carefree manner of a little girl. Though that would have been the very last reaction I'd have toward my mother if she had decided to drop in and surprise me, part of me wished I could sprint to her like that, if I wanted to.

I got another strapping, though in Mrs. Evans' class this time. She'd caught me daydreaming out the window, something I'd been doing a lot lately. I wasn't worried about school anymore, really. My grades had been perfect and it wasn't as if I was going to college anyway. Besides, with all that had occurred in my life in the past year, school seemed unimportant.

One night, Cecilia and Marilyn came to do their homework in our room. Anna had already finished hers, writing a letter at her desk, and I read on my bed after finishing mine. Cecilia, Marilyn and Kate talked, the conversation somehow moving from the homework to how babies were made.

"That's not true!" Anna said, gripping the back of her chair to look at them. "Marilyn, don't be disgusting."

Marilyn gaped at her. "How do *you* think babies are made, then?"

Anna tapped the back of her chair with her finger, glancing at me for support. "Well...the man...the *husband*...and the wife sit on their bed...and they pray. They ask God to give them a baby and hope that He does."

Marilyn and Kate started howling. Cecilia's face was buried in her hands as she shook her head. I couldn't help smiling at their reactions, turning the page to my book.

"Oh my..." Marilyn was gripping Cecilia's shoulder, tears streaming down her cheeks. "I can't...I just...I can't..."

Kate was rolling around on her bed. "I can't breathe!"

Anna wasn't smiling. Her freckled cheeks flushed as she turned back to her letter.

"Cec..." Marilyn struggled, "Anna thinks she was immaculately conceived."

Kate was wiping under her eyes. "Geez, Anna, who told you that?"

Anna didn't look up as she wrote. "My father—after I asked him if he hated me for killing my mother."

Their humor ceased. And I wasn't the only one who lowered my eyes.

"He said they'd spent so long praying for me at their bedside, asking God to give them a child, that they didn't stop praying, even when they found out the pregnancy might end both our lives. He said even though God took her, he was grateful He let him keep me."

She sniffed, though she wasn't crying, looking at the others over her shoulder as she folded up her letter. None of us spoke as she sighed, stowing the letter in her desk drawer. "So—though I know I'm going to regret this—where do babies come from, then?"

Hilarity ensued as Marilyn began drawing diagrams, with Kate's help. Cecilia didn't provide any information, though she observed with interest, and even I laughed as Anna hid her face in a pillow.

"That is *not* what happens!" Anna yelled in disbelief, her voice muffled in the fabric.

Marilyn chortled. "Yes, it is."

Giggling, Kate reached down, pointing with her finger. "Hey, Anna. See this part? This is where the baby comes out."

Anna's face was so red I wondered how it would ever return to normal. They all busted with laughter as she hid her face again, murmuring, "Oh my gosh. Oh my gosh. Oh my gosh..."

I closed my book, getting down from my bed. I knew enough to get the gist, simply because Amos and Jimmy used to talk, sometimes forgetting I was there, but I still had questions. "Let me see that."

Eyes sparkling with mischief, Marilyn handed the paper to me, watching my face.

"Did you know how babies are made, Cassie?" Kate asked me, though I heard the underlying question. They were all looking at me, even Anna, peeking over the edge of her pillow.

I handed the paper back to Marilyn. "No."

"Yes, you did!" Kate argued, pointing at me. "Look, she's not blushing like Anna and Cecilia are."

Marilyn smirked as I returned to my bed. "Cassie, it's okay. I did. Kate did. We're not going to say anything."

Opening my book, I looked at them. "I didn't."

"You had a secret romance with a German soldier," Marilyn said, as if that proved I was lying.

"It...it wasn't like that." I felt my cheeks growing warm now, peering down at my book. "W-we didn't..."

I peeked at them from the corner of my eye, unable to face them directly. "We only ever kissed."

Kate blew raspberries.

"And what did you do the rest of the time?" Marilyn asked.

"We just talked."

Kate and Marilyn cackled.

"Now I know you're lying," Marilyn said.

Anna appeared sympathetic and I turned back to my book, my nose nearly touching the pages. There was no point in trying to explain it. Besides, a new question had sprouted in my head, diverting my attention:

Would we have? I hadn't understood all the particulars then, but even as his hand caressed my thigh that day, I'd known it was wrong. I wanted to believe we wouldn't have let it go that far, but somehow, I sensed I would have let it happen before realizing what it was. Knowing that made me feel as guilty as if it *had* happened.

I looked forward to Friday. Though I was with my friends all week, I enjoyed the freedom we had on the weekends. I almost got strapped in Mrs. Evans' class again, but I diverted my focus to the board as she turned around. She narrowed her eyes, unsure whether I'd done anything wrong or not.

Kate, Anna and I went straight to our room after Art to change out of our uniforms.

"I'm so glad it's the weekend," Anna said, putting on a different skirt.

"Are either of you going to start on Mrs. Olsen's essay tonight?" I asked.

"No, I think I'll wait until tomorrow," Anna said.

Kate was putting on a dress. "Me too."

Anna burst with a laugh. "Yeah right, Kate. You'll start it Sunday night and stay up until you finish it."

Kate paused from folding her uniform shirt. "Yeah, I'll do that instead."

Anna shook her head and I snickered as someone knocked on the door.

"Come in," Kate called out.

I finished putting my clothes away when they knocked again.

"For goodness sake, Marilyn, I said come in!" Kate threw open the door and we all froze to see Miss Wilson standing there.

With her critical gaze, she formed conclusions about the three of us before landing on me. "Cassandra Wyndham, you have a visitor," she said in her typical snappish manner.

I gaped at her.

"A visitor? Were you expecting anyone?" Kate asked me before turning back to Miss Wilson. "Who is it?"

Miss Wilson's hands rose to her hips. "I don't know and even if I did, I wouldn't tell you, young woman."

Kate's eyebrows rose as she pursed her lips over her shoulder, trying not to laugh at the woman's unwarranted hostility.

Miss Wilson stormed away. Anna grabbed my arm. "Do you want us to come with you?"

"No. It's okay. Thanks, though."

I passed Kate in the doorway. Halfway down the hall, Anna called out to me as she and Kate rounded the corner. "We at least want to wait for you at the top of the stairs."

"Yeah, what if it's one of those fruitcakes, like the one who sent you that letter?" Kate asked.

I gulped. "You think it could be?"

Anna shrugged. "You weren't expecting anyone, were you?"

Light came up from the main staircase, the dampness on my skin giving me a chill. "Maybe it is a good idea for you to be there."

"We'll stand out of sight until we know for sure," Anna said.

I set off down the steps, looking back at them for reassurance. On the landing, I hesitated. A man in a khaki trench coat had his back to me. He turned around and my mouth parted. "Dad?"

He chuckled, his bronze eyes crinkling as he held his arms open for me. "Cassandra!"

A second later, I bounded down the stairs. Tears filling my eyes, I jumped, throwing my arms around his neck. "Why are you here?"

"I just saw your mother and Lucy and thought I'd stop by on my way back to work."

I pulled away, able to see the adoration in his eyes for me was still there. I felt ready to forgive him for everything.

He ushered me toward the door. "Let's take a walk."

There weren't many girls outside because of the temperature. I hardly registered it as I goggled my father in amazement.

He gave me a smile. "How have you been?"

"Great. I like this school a lot better than my old one. I wish I'd come here sooner."

He laughed. "I don't know whether to be happy about that since you being sent here was for disciplinary reasons."

I grinned at him, still too surprised to speak.

"How's work?" I finally asked.

He glimpsed at me. "We're at the highest production rate we've ever seen. I had to buy out two more manufacturing hangars here in Virginia."

Even with my coat on, I hugged myself for warmth. "Wow. That's great, Dad."

He looked pleased by my approval. "I like to think so."

We sat on one of the benches between two sleeping apple trees. The courtyard was quiet and lifeless, with the exception of us. My father adjusted his coat, fiddling with his fedora between his knees.

"How's Lucy?" I asked.

He chuckled to himself. "She's well. Misses you, though. It amazes me with how intelligent she is for her age."

Lost in the thought of her sweet, angelic face, a silence fell between us. From the corner of my eye, I could tell he was studying me. "Aren't you going to ask about your mother, Cassandra?"

I sniffed from the cold, hugging myself tighter. "No."

He stopped fidgeting with his cap, scratching at his temple. "Sweetheart, I know I'm not around as much as I wish I could be, but...it seems to me that you have a lot of undue animosity toward your mother. Now, I'm not here to scold you," he said, flashing his hand at me as I started to protest. "I don't want to stain today with a disagreement. I'd just like to know where this has come from."

"Where did it come from?" I repeated, my anger stirring in its slumber. "Do you want me to start from the time I was born, or would you rather I begin with after Amos left?"

He frowned. "No one can claim to be a perfect parent, Cassandra. Your mother's made her mistakes, and so have I, but she's always taken care of you. She's given up so many things to make sure you and your brother and sister didn't go without. She's one of the most selfless people I've ever known."

"Selfless with everyone but me." My fury became taut. "Maybe you haven't noticed because you're never there."

My chest heaved. I'd always thought it, but never would I have expressed it before. Rather than implode with faintheartedness, I felt emboldened.

"Cassandra..." He trailed off with a heavy blink before sighing. "Let's not talk about this. Okay? I'm sorry, I shouldn't have brought it up. I don't want to spend this time on unpleasant thoughts—"

"I want to come live with you."

He looked at me.

I touched his arm. "I want to come live with you in Baltimore. Dad, I've thought about it. I'll be eighteen when I leave here; I'll be an adult. You won't have to worry about making sure someone's there to babysit me; it won't even interfere with your work. We could have breakfast and dinner together every day. It would be nice; it could be just the two of us."

I smiled at the possibility. He puckered his lips in thought. "And what would you be doing the rest of the time, Cassandra?"

"I don't know, I...I want to go school. I'll...I'll get a job and pay my own way," I said. "I just...I can't go back there, Dad; to that town, to *her*. I won't. I want to live with you."

His brow crinkled. My good spirits faded as he shook his head. "Sweetheart...as wonderful as that sounds, it's just not possible."

"Why not?"

He sat upright, straightening his pant legs. "Because, adult or not, you've shown you can't be trusted. Besides, your mother needs you." He shrugged. "In time, everyone else will forget about what happened, but that's just something you're going to have to face until they do."

"You think I don't want to go back because I'm embarrassed?" The venom in my voice surprised me. "I don't want to go back because that town—because my *mother*—drains the life out of me. You're probably right. One day, they'll all forget about it, but I won't. I'll never forget him, I'll never regret it, and I'll never deny that what we had was real."

His face hardened the way it did when someone was trying to take advantage of him in a business deal. "I don't want to talk about this and I *don't* want to hear about it. It's done. One day, you're going to realize it was a mistake; a youthful error in judgment. Nothing more."

"And you'll punish me until I do, right?" I asked. Tears trickled down my cheeks. "I will *never* stop loving him."

"Did you know twice now, someone's thrown bricks through the front windows at home?" my father asked, eyes blazing. "Your mother won't even let Lucy outside to play out of fear that someone will try to hurt her because of this—because of what *you* did. Or, what about the way your mother couldn't shop in town for weeks because she felt threatened? Or the way everyone stares at her at church? She can't walk down a street without someone recognizing who she is."

"Why doesn't she just *leave* and live with you, then?"

He blinked. "That's not realistic, Cassandra. And it's not her fault things are like that."

"It's not my fault, either—"

"Yes," he said, severe. "It is."

Eyes burning, I slammed my hands down on the bench. "Fine. It's my fault. It's my fault people are cruel. It's my fault people don't understand. It's my fault that I've been here for four months and neither of my parents have bothered to write me a single letter."

"And why do you think that is, Cassandra?" he snapped. I wiped at my cheeks, trying not to cry. "Why do you think we sent you away?"

"Because Mom can't control me."

"No. That may have been what she told you—what she wanted—but I sent you away to protect you. Four months, and you still don't grasp the magnitude of what you've done. Your mother doesn't send you letters because we don't want anyone knowing where you are. Mrs. Hammond even has your letters sent in another envelope under a different name. This was for *you*, Cassie."

I replied with a disdainful chuckle. "Well, someone knows where I am because someone who actually *did* write me told me to burn in hell. And while that may justify why Mom isn't writing me, it doesn't explain why *you* haven't."

This left him speechless. He bowed his head. "I can't say that's not fair. I could have been writing to you; I *should* have been. I'm sorry I haven't."

This caused tears to spill over. A couple of girls in coats and scarves were giggling, walking arm in arm in front of us. "Why do you defend her?" I asked. "Why are you *still* defending her? After everything she's done—"

"She's your mother, Cassandra."

"And I'm your daughter."

I could tell this conversation was upsetting him, but he tried not to show it. My voice broke as I began to cry. "Dad...I know why you didn't write me. You forgot about me. I don't know what I did...I don't know what Amos or I either one did that made it so hard for you to be home."

"Cassan——"

"I don't know why we've never been enough for you," I sputtered. "I know it must hurt to look at me; to look at Lucy and see her. But...but there's a part of you here, too. I don't understand why that's not enough. When she betrayed you, she betrayed all of us."

He sat his hat aside, face in his hands. I swiped at the tears that continued to pour down my cheeks. I imagined him bringing me into his arms, holding me and telling me I was right. That was what I wanted him to do—probably the only thing that could've dissipated my anger towards him, too.

The wrinkles around his eyes had smoothed when he raised his head. His jaw was clenched, as if he were making an intense effort to keep the water in his eyes from turning into tears. I dropped all my defenses as he took my hand in his.

"You know...I remember holding you right after you were born. Just like it was yesterday. Your brother was special and so is your sister, but you? You're my little girl. You've always been my little girl."

I hung my head, crying.

"And whether I meant to or not, I've tried to keep you that way. I don't want to admit to myself that you're growing up; that you *are* grown up. That you're old enough to talk about adult matters."

He swallowed, blinking up at me. "I was unfaithful to your mother, Cassandra."

To say my mind went blank would have been an understatement. My tears ceased in my shock. This couldn't be. It didn't fit; I'd misunderstood.

"It didn't mean anything," he continued quietly. "It was nothing you or Amos or Lucy did; it was nothing your mother did or didn't do. I did not love this woman, not like I love your mother. I wish I could say it was an accident. I wish I could say it never happened…but I can't. Your mother—once she realized you thought it was her—didn't correct you, because she loves me and because she loves you. You and I have always had a better relationship. She didn't want to ruin that."

I was shaking my head, trying not to sob. This was my dad; my favorite, my hero. "No. No, there was a receipt for a hotel in Richmond—"

He closed his eyes. "Your mother hired a private investigator who gave her proof. She arranged to meet me in Richmond to confront me over it."

"But the man I spoke to on the phone—"

"Was her lawyer," he finished for me. "He was calling to tell her I'd been served the divorce papers."

I sniffled, trying to absorb this. "But…they were signed. I saw your signature. If you love her, why…?"

"I signed them because it's what she wants. There's nothing I can do about it now."

I hiccuped, stewing in this. A revelation came upon me, one that felt foreign; impossible, yet impossibly true. My mother and I were more alike than either of us even knew. She'd rather sacrifice her own reputation and character than see the man she loved suffer.

I shoved myself up from the bench. "What she wants is for you to fight for her! That's all we've *ever* wanted from you! This isn't about you doing her a favor and making the process easy, it's about you not having to give up what you *really* want."

"You think I want to lose your mother? You think I want to lose you and Lucy?"

"Losing us is easier for you to accept than giving up your work! You've chosen it over us so many times that you don't even know your own family anymore. If we're this easy for you to walk away from, then you don't deserve me, you don't deserve Lucy, and you certainly don't deserve Mom."

He yanked his hat off the bench as he stood. "Obviously, me coming here was not a good idea."

"But at least you did! You didn't even talk to me after it happened, Dad. You just let Mom deal with the hard stuff while you kept doing what you wanted to do. Did you think I'd be like you and just pretend that everything's okay? Like I haven't been wondering this whole time whether my parents still love me or not?"

He settled his hat on his head. "I do love you, Cassandra. I'm sorry. I'm going to go."

"Dad——"

"I promise I'll do a better job of writing to you."

I clung to his waist. "Dad, please——"

"I love you," he said, his voice cracking as he made a halfhearted attempt to pry me off.

"I'm still me. I'm still your Cassandra."

"Cassie, stop." He forced me away from him. "It's time for me to go."

He left me there, drowning beneath my own weeping. I wanted to sink into the ground, sobbing until I dried out. I watched his blurry form walk away from me, and my scorn overpowered his rejection. With a surge of determination, I ran after him.

He was almost to the front gates when I blocked his path. "Do you want to know why I love him, Dad? Because for the first time in my life, someone finally saw me for who I really am. Someone finally understood me. Someone finally loved me enough to forfeit everything, even his life, for me. For once, another human being made me feel loved and special. I'm too much for Mom and I'm not enough for you, but I was enough for him; I was more than enough for him. So you can pretend it didn't happen. Mom can punish me any way she wants and the rest of the world can judge me, but the truth is, he still loved me as I loved him. And no matter where you hide or where Mom displaces me, it will never change the fact that the wounds he helped to heal were put there by both of you."

His eyes were wide. I didn't quail at my own brazenness. "And never once did he turn his back to me when I said I needed him."

This time, it was I who turned away.

"Cassandra!" he boomed behind me.

I broke into a jog, bolting past the few girls watching in the courtyard, rushing in the front doors. My peers ambled the hallway and still, I sobbed, running up the stairs. I wasn't even worried about my father coming back to have the last word, as my mother would have; I knew he wouldn't follow me.

I thought I passed Cecilia on the way to my room, but didn't stop to see. Slamming my bedroom door behind me, I screamed. I picked up my spare pillow, hitting my bed as hard as I could before dropping to the floor.

I kept thinking about my mother. There were so many ways I thought she had wronged me, but I found myself scrutinizing the past year under a microscope. There were so many things I'd said, hell-bent on hurting her when really, my father was at fault. No wonder it felt like she hated me.

And my father had known she was taking the blame for him, but somehow, he'd silenced his conscience enough to not think it mattered for me to know the truth.

I don't know how long I sat there on the floor. I wondered what Amos would've done. Would he have exploded like I had? Would he have reeled from the abrupt loss of respect for our father as I was now? Would he have picked a side, as I found myself doing? The irony was, it wasn't for the parent I'd always preferred.

I would've given anything to be able to apologize to my mother right now. I loved my father; my mom had been right about that. Even considering his general passivity, I had been partial to him.

But today, my image of him had been shattered. He wasn't who I thought he was—who I'd hoped he was. He was selfish, self-absorbed and an inactive member of our family. The sad fact was that he'd always been this way; only now did I resent him for it.

And after today, I wasn't the only one whose perception had been crushed. My father could no longer pretend I was a pretty little doll to be admired, left to herself in a corner. I had found my voice; no longer would I be ignored, no longer would they maneuver my arms and legs according to their own whims. The next time I saw my father, he would do as he'd always done, going on as if our confrontation had never happened. I wasn't sure I could go along with that anymore.

I used to look to Amos to defend me; as the one who had sway over my own opinions, being my older brother. But Amos wasn't here. I had no one to look to but myself. That was more power than I had been ready for.

Well, I was ready now.

The door cracked open. A pair of ice blue eyes peered through. With tentativeness, Anna opened the door the rest of the way. "Hey."

I stroked my hair in an absentminded fashion. "Hey."

"Cecilia said she saw you in the hallway. Are you all right?"

All of the drawers under Kate's bed were open at varying degrees, per usual. I was still thinking about the course my conversation with my father had taken. "I am now."

Crossing her arms, she took a couple steps toward me. "You don't look okay."

I snorted out of a rancorous sense of humor. Stretching out my legs across the floor, I rested my head against my own drawers. "There's this dream I've had since I was a little girl. I'm in this big, scary house. The wallpaper's torn, there are holes in the floor; there are no lights on inside and it's dead quiet. It's haunted. I'm alone, and I'm always running, trying to find a way out. I come to this long hallway lined with doorways and in my heart, I just *know* that behind one of them, someone's going to be there to save me—someone's going to get me out of there. But every time I reach the door knob, it turns into a mirror and I realize it's all just an illusion; there is no escape."

Anna quietly lowered down beside me. I swallowed. "This dream has haunted me, Anna. I've been running down that hallway my whole life; I've been waiting for someone to save me *my whole life*. But one night a few months ago, I just got angry. I touched the door knob only for it to turn into a mirror as it always does, but instead of running to the next one, I acknowledged my reflection for the first time. I realized it was me; I was standing in the doorway. The next thing I knew, I was out of that house. And then I woke up. All these years, I had the power to save myself, but the thought never crossed my mind until then." I looked at her. "Isn't that sad?"

She hugged her knees, sitting beside me. "No. I think it's beautiful."

I chuckled to myself in reply, lowering my eyes in thought. "He told me once that I was the purest thing in his life. I realize now he was the purest thing in mine."

I smiled at her. "Until I met you all. The same way I know that you and Kate and I will always be friends is the same certainty I have that Friedrich and I are going to be together again someday. I used to think that everyone in this world was just out for themselves." I lifted a shoulder. "Maybe they are. But for all my pain, I've also learned that true friendship and true love is real. That's the truth, and I have it. That alone means everything to me; that alone makes me willing to give up everything and everyone else to keep it."

Anna hooked her arm through mine. "With Kate and me, you never have to give up anything. And if Friedrich were here, I bet he'd tell you the same."

Twenty ~ Three

I tapped my pencil against my arithmetic book, trying to focus. Mrs. Evans had assigned homework for us to do during the period, an intermission while she graded papers. Keeping my head low, I peeked around the room.

Naturally, Anna was writing with undeterred tenacity. Across the room, Kate seemed to be working hard as well, though she'd often hesitate, leaning back in her chair and staring into her book while she nibbled on her pencil. I peered out the window.

If I could convey only one truth to my parents, it would be that I hadn't changed. This was who I'd always been; I'd just grown into myself. I imagined a horse being raised in the confines of the barn she was born in, never once allowed to set foot outside. Would she cease to be a horse the instant she was set free? Or would she be more herself than ever, hooves pounding as her mane flew in the breeze behind her?

I always think of Friedrich when this crosses my mind. I've finally caught on to who I really am. Sometimes, it's intimidating and I worry I'm going too fast; that liberation is best administered in small, manageable doses.

But I realize that's ludicrous. Besides, I like the feel of the wind in my hair.

Chin resting in my palm, I looked at the back of Anna's head before stealing a look at Kate. I don't think I could've gotten this far without them. Being ripped away from Friedrich had left me in a vulnerable state of recovery. I thought being sent away would destroy me, but I see now that it had been meant to revive me; to mend my heart and spirit into an even stronger condition than they'd been in before.

I smiled to myself, turning back to the window.

I wish I could tell you how much I miss you. I wish you knew how tightly I hold to my memories of you, drawing strength from each one like the lifesaving sip of spring water across parched lips. I wish you knew how, when I remember you, I can't help but smile.

And when I think of us together, we're happy. We made it through the trials that still lay before us to find each other waiting at the end. They can tell us that what we had was a delusion, that severance and time will do their jobs well. Love, though, knows nothing of indeterminate measures of absence.

But I suppose that'll be our little secret until the end.

"I would've *thought*, Miss Wyndham, that I made myself clear at the beginning of class."

My classmates went stiff in their seats. Kate lowered her face into her hand to muffle what sounded like a sneeze. Even she hadn't been strapped twice in one day by the same teacher before.

Mrs. Evans raised an eyebrow at me. "Do you need another reminder that arithmetic class is indeed for arithmetic and not for bird-watching from the window?" she asked. She was always trying to be a smart aleck.

And what the heck. Why not?

"Yes ma'am, I do," I answered.

Anna gawked at me. Kate burst with laughter. Marilyn snorted. The other girls all tittered in their seats as Mrs. Evans' eyes darted around the room.

"Belligerence is two straps in itself, Miss Wyndham," she said, her tone demanding silence. "Approach my desk this instant."

She retrieved her ruler, and I smiled as I pushed myself up from my desk.

I understood now what Kate and Marilyn told me my first day here at the school. Strappings had become something of a game to me. I told myself that it was to prepare me for what was to come. I could let my surroundings control me, or I could learn to control how I responded. This indefinite amount of time was going to hurt, but it wasn't going to break me.

Because each step I take, I take toward you. Each ache and sting means I'm one lesson closer to you. I can handle the pain; I can wrestle whatever is thrown at me because I know now how it's all going to end:

With you.

Yes, I've been here for five months, one week and four days. In less than a month, I will finally be free...

And I will fight for you, Friedrich. I will fight for you until they see who I really am:

I am yours.

Excerpt from

Love Story (Liebesgeschichte) (Captive Heart Trilogy, #2)

They came from adversarial worlds. The requital of his love for Juliet Capulet was as unlikely as wearing their ill-fated stars on a ring adorning her finger. Hostility abounding, they crossed the lines drawn in hate by their forebears. Every sweet word that left her lips, every soft stolen kiss, disproved a lifetime of inculcated animosity Romeo had been exposed to. Their love was pure, its thriving existence made all the more sacred by the brutal circumstances in which it defied. It had the power to render the offending sin between families obsolete; it had the power to heal wounds beget by hate. On a street in Verona they stood, the Montagues and the Capulets, where noble Romeo offered love in place of vengeance.

"Yes," shouted his beloved's cousin, Tybalt, unsheathing his sword, "but are you willing to die for her?"

One

Winter 1945 - Spring 1946

Le Havre or Southampton. In anxious whispers, the men on Friedrich's transport speculated upon which harbor they were destined for. The opinion that the British would be more agreeable to work for than the French was unanimous. But short of swimming across the turbulent English Channel, being relocated to an island off Continental Europe would only postpone the return home.

Some of them preferred the idea of Great Britain; the further they were from Germany, the better. Hints had been dropped, in tones of deadly desperation, that they'd kill themselves before going back to that mess.

Others were uneasy about the prospect of mooring in Southampton. If docked there, it could be months, years even, before they found themselves back in the Fatherland, back with what remained of their families. Which of the two Friedrich preferred...

Well, he wasn't sure.

The journey across the Atlantic had been quite monotonous, especially since he'd had to leave his violin behind in America. As an enlisted soldier, his bag had had the weight limit of thirty pounds, forcing him to choose between necessities and luxuries. From a personal viewpoint, it wasn't fair; to the American War Department, it was. Many of the men had complained as their belongings were rifled through and particular items confiscated; anything that was in short supply for the Allies was taken.

For whatever reason, their American captors didn't inform them of their destination until their arrival. Either by gross misfortune—or divine intervention—it was French soil on which Friedrich stepped upon his disembarkation.

Despite how much closer he was to home, there was no way of knowing when he was actually going to get there. He and his fellow POWs were on a loan of sorts to the British, the French—even the Russians—as well as to Holland, Belgium, Luxembourg, Yugoslavia and Greece. He could work for months rebuilding France only to be sent to one of the other war-damaged countries later. Ludwig—one of the men who'd been in the initial work force Friedrich had been assigned to—had told him he'd come with one of the first American transfers back in November. Though the minimum requirement of help from the Germans was supposed to be three months, Ludwig was no closer to leaving now than he had been in February.

Through winter, Friedrich had been placed in a group working as truck drivers, hauling rubble and debris to local drop-off sites. One chilly, late morning, the bearded Frenchman who'd been overseeing their work pulled him aside. Speaking in German, the foreman scribbled on a clipboard. "Naumann, you're being relocated."

Friedrich pulled off his gloves. "What? Why?"

"You're being transferred to a farm outside of town. As to why, I think that goes without explanation." Nose in the air, the foreman sauntered off towards the other men, reading off names.

It was disheartening to find himself assigned to yet another farming post. Some days, he thought with a sigh that it was his destiny to be nothing greater than a farmhand. Seeing where he had come from in Germany, the Americans at Camp Rockmont had put him to work in victory gardens in

Virginia. Now, with a background that testified to his farming experience in both Germany and America, the French relocated him to tend to their own fields in the spring.

Never had he wanted this; to wind up just like his father. Though his father had been a member of the Party, he'd done little besides voicing his opinions while hoeing his fields. When the time came, Friedrich swore his allegiance to his Führer with fervent readiness to do all that was asked of him. His lineage and body measurements proved that pure Aryan blood coursed through his veins; young, healthy and virile, the possibilities in the new Germany were endless. Doors to a superior future opened wide before him. Farmer's son or not, the Führer gave him value as a human being of the highest quality. Because of this, he vowed to fight for the Führer without conscience, to die for the Führer without regret.

Upon his enlistment, they'd shipped him off to fight in Africa. Serving under the great General Rommel's command only escalated his fervor, bolstering his commitment to the Führer's grand purpose for him. The road to his future forked ahead, with only two possible destinations; victory or death. There was no other option.

He would help build the foundation for the Thousand Year Reich with his own hands, covering it in his own unpolluted blood if he had to. And someday, when the Führer adorned his tunic with medals of bravery and service to the Fatherland, he would scoff at his humble beginnings, having accomplished more in his young life than his father ever had.

He still believed in this, even when he was captured by the Americans in 1942.

He still believed in this, even when he found himself right back where he started—skin browning beneath the scorching sun, sweat rolling in beads down his back, stiff fingers afflicted by excruciating blisters. It was beneath him to be reduced to such menial labor, and still, the promises of the Führer echoed in his mind, telling him he was meant for greatness.

Until one rainy, life-changing Saturday afternoon when his fate forked again. It happened in an instant, leading him to the most devastating, obscure choice he'd ever made: to stop living a life in pursuit of his own desires and those of the Führer's...

And, instead, to live a life in pursuit of her; to live a life in pursuit of the desires of God.

Here in France, it was nearing spring, and Friedrich had come to terms with his predicament. His budding faith stubbornly insisted God must've had a reason for putting him back on a farm—just as He'd had a reason for Friedrich being sent to a POW camp in Rockmont, Virginia. That was why it confused him even more when the French farmer who oversaw his work unit stopped him one damp April afternoon. "This will be your last day. The Americans believe you'll be of better use in Germany."

Friedrich's lip twitched. "They are sending me back to Germany?"

The corpulent farmer shrugged, scratching his groin and grumbling to himself as he walked away.

Friedrich had kept the thought of returning home—of repatriation—at a comfortable distance, wary of the questions it provoked. The mail in Germany had stopped; it had been over a year since he'd heard from his mother. Hans would have been sent to fight. Friedrich could be all that was left of his family.

The sense of being a person rather than a soldier—rather than a prisoner—struck him as he got on the train that would take him to the American headquarters in Wiesbaden. The pieces of his broken life that he had begun to collect in America were a start, but seeing the destruction around him reflected the damage that had been withstood within him. It was going to take years before these cities became whole again.

And the spark of hope he allowed—but didn't rely on —that he would find his mother or Hans began to dwindle more and more the further he ventured into Germany. He peered through the windows, as did the other repatriated men, with a sense of foreboding; with a sense of responsibility for the decimation of their homeland.

There was nothing left. Houses and businesses had been flattened. Roads and bridges were but crumbled, dusty blocks of cement and broken, splintered beams. Germany was a mere skeleton of what she had once been.

And the silence. There was nothing but silence. No one in his train car even spoke anymore upon catching sight of their once proud Fatherland. The occasional whistle of the train and the rumbling on the tracks was the only proof that there was still life among the ruins. That, and the people who crowded the platforms, the doorways, calling out names of their fathers, of husbands, of sons whenever the train stopped. Friedrich imagined finding his own mother this way; it was the only comforting thought he had about home now. Somehow, he knew she wasn't going to be there when he finally made it back to Köln.

Wiesbaden had scars from the war just like any other city, but at least it hadn't been demolished. Here, Friedrich began the long and arduous task of gaining his repatriation.

The Americans had set up an assembly line in a former *Luftwaffe* hangar. Friedrich filled out so many questionnaires that he groaned under his breath every time they handed him another. A few of the questions seemed repetitive, obvious tools to sort out who wasn't a Nazi and who was lying about it. Between questionnaires, he'd been fingerprinted, completed even more paperwork for personnel files, and had his belongings searched for contraband. By the fourth day, he hoped he was close to the end of the process.

Having stood in line for hours, he finally reached the table, handing over his information. The American sitting there was young, though not much younger than Friedrich, checking boxes and making sure all the abundant and so-called essential details had been acquired. Friedrich sighed while he waited, looking past the hangar to the bright blue sky in the distance. A panic seized him, his muscles going taut as he realized he had no clue where to go from here. Devotion would have him look for his mother and brother, but practicality insisted it would be less painful to just start life over somewhere else. But without his family, he didn't know where he belonged; he didn't know where to go. *Where was he going to go?*

"Here are your discharge certificates," the young American said, showing his boredom with what had become routine, "as well as forty marks. Go to the train station, show them your certificate and they'll give you a free ride to your hometown or the city closest to it. Next!"

Aware of the heaviness of his own breathing, Friedrich picked up the slips of paper and currency off the table, stuffing them into the pocket of his tunic.

Adjusting the rucksack on his shoulder, he walked out of the hangar. As a soldier—and later, a prisoner—there'd always been someone telling him what to do. In America, though, he'd come to embrace independent thought. It was all he had now—that, along with a piddling forty marks and the worn book in his rucksack. There was no corral; there were no reins. There was no one telling him where to take the next step; there was no one to tell him if searching for his family would be a futile effort or if it was what he was supposed to do. He had to decide this for himself.

"...Naumann. Mr. Naumann!"

Friedrich hesitated outside, seeing the young American jogging up to him. "There was a notification on one of your forms. I'm sorry, but I can't let you leave yet."

He whistled, motioning over an American that was standing guard nearby. It was like déjà vu, remembering the day they had come for him at the camp; he hadn't done anything wrong this time, either.

"I am not understanding," Friedrich said, eyeing the rifle-toting guard. "The others are leaving after you discharge them."

"This one goes to Tyler," the young American said, ignoring him.

Friedrich watched him walk back to his station as the guard walked in the other direction. Friedrich followed the guard.

Had he answered a question wrong? Had his answers been consistent with that of an unsalvageable Nazi, rather than a changed man? Had he broken a rule somewhere? Why would they keep someone as inconsequential as he in custody, when they allowed so many more valuable or suspicious others to go free?

The guard was leading him away from the hangar. Around the corner was a parked jeep, and with uncertainty, Friedrich climbed in beside the guard.

Surely he would have been put in handcuffs if he was thought to be dangerous. Though it occurred to him to be offended that they were delaying his freedom. But, if he was honest with himself, he didn't know what he was going to do with it anyway.

The guard operated the vehicle with unsettling casualness, its bulky metal body jostling as it careened over small debris and pot holes in the road. He didn't even slow down when approaching pedestrians, presuming they would scatter before he reached them. Passing by a rather intact café, Friedrich spotted a couple of German girls flirting with a pair of attentive GIs outside. At one time, he would've cared—been jealous even—that these girls preferred their conquerors over their own men.

Instead, he turned his gaze ahead. Unlike most of the returning men, he'd known before even leaving America that his future wasn't here.

The guard drove toward a compound surrounded by tall fences garnished with barbed wire. The buildings it encompassed seemed to be undamaged and Friedrich listened with leery curiosity as his escort told the guard at the gate that he had 'another one for Tyler.'

The gate was opened and the guard hit the gas, swinging into a makeshift parking spot in front of the first building. Grabbing his bag, Friedrich hopped out, following the guard inside.

Men donning the standard khaki and olive drab American uniforms were everywhere. They stared at him as he walked by, making him conscious of the khaki green uniform of the enemy that he wore while strolling their halls. He was glad the guard that accompanied him seemed to know where they were going; Friedrich was certain he wouldn't be able to find his way out of the labyrinth of hallways later.

Turning down a short corridor, Friedrich stopped as the guard knocked on a door with a fog-stained window pane. He didn't even speak before opening it.

"Oh. Of course," a voice inside said. "Send him in."

The guard took a step back, holding open the door, and Friedrich assumed he was supposed to enter.

A man with dark hair in need of a good trim—or at least a comb—was sitting behind a desk, pushing at the bridge of his black-rimmed glasses. He wasn't in standard military dress. He stood as Friedrich walked in, straightening his tie, tucking in the edges of his wrinkled collared shirt.

"Mark Tyler," the man said. He came around his desk, extending his hand. "How do you do?"

Up close, the sea foam eyes behind his lenses were alert, though his lids were puffy from lack of sleep. The office had a sense of organized chaos; mountains of paper covered his desk, yet it was evident they hadn't been put there in a haphazard manner. Books slumped over on the shelves from empty spaces, the missing ones left open in stacks on the floor or what little room could be found on his desk. Friedrich's gaze was drawn to a picture of what looked like some sort of mermaid-aboriginal hybrid in a polished frame on the wall. She was naked—except for the blue paint on her face and shoulders—sitting on a rock and holding a spear while her tail fin grazed the water.

"You...*do* speak English?"

Friedrich realized they were still shaking hands. Mark Tyler was giving him a sideways look, brow raised over his glasses. Friedrich gave a slow nod, eyes straying back to the mermaid. It seemed out of place in such a setting. "I am just noticing your picture—"

"I'm assuming you're here because you've been discharged from service," Tyler said, returning to his desk. He was flipping through a binder.

Friedrich sat in one of the wobbly wooden chairs in front of him. "They discharge me, yes. But I know not why I am here."

"Name?"

"Friedrich Naumann."

Tyler never looked up. Tyler never spoke. He continued trailing a finger down each page in the binder before finally crossing something off. "I've read through your file, Mr. Naumann—"

"Friedrich."

Tyler put the cap on his pen. His expression was like that of a man who just realized he wasn't alone in the room. "Friedrich. I've looked through your file. It says you attended a program that focused on reacquainting you with Christianity."

Friedrich gave a curt nod.

"These...courses, for lack of a better word, were mandatory. Correct?"

Again, Friedrich nodded. "Eventually, I attend even if they are not mandatory."

"Why is that?"

His fingers tightened on impulse around the strap of his rucksack. "I enjoy the program. More than I think I might."

Tyler studied him. Closing the binder, he tossed it aside, dropping into his chair. "In your opinion, how successful do you think this program was?"

Pulling the cap off the pen repeatedly and putting it back on, Tyler swiveled in his chair, never blinking as he waited for Friedrich to answer. If it weren't for Tyler's attentiveness, he would've thought Tyler was bored.

"For me? Very successful."

"Why?"

Friedrich shrugged. "It matters what you are looking for. I am not the person I once am. My life is changing during my time at Camp Rockmont."

"Again, why? How?"

Friedrich stared at him. Was this a serious interest in his faith, or was this all leading to her? Why would Mark Tyler care about either?

"There are things about God and faith and life that I never know before the program," Friedrich finally said. "The things I understand changes me. I am not who I am then. Not because of anything I do, but because of the effect God is having in my life."

Because of her.

Tyler's sea foam eyes narrowed as he leaned back in his chair, crossing his arms. "Okay. Now, tell me what I need to know to believe that."

"Excuse me?"

"Tell me what I need to hear to know that you truly believe what you just told me."

Friedrich shook his head out of uncertainty. "I am not...I am not sure what you are asking."

Tyler didn't coach him any further. He merely watched Friedrich, rocking back and forth in his chair.

Friedrich swallowed. "When they take me to America, it is only a place for me to wait until the war is over. When the program starts, I think it is a strategy of the Americans to waste our time. But then..."

Her hazel eyes twinkled, nose scrunching as she laughed from across the table. She was so beautiful, even in a memory. His chest ached.

"I become curious. The more I read, the more I...interact, the more it weakens everything I think I know up to this point. I become aware of the decision I have to make. '*Niemand kann zwei Herren dienen.*'" He lifted his eyes to Tyler. "A servant cannot have two masters. I give my loyalty to a new master. I ask God to take what remains of my life and use it as He wants. I choose Him, because He offers things that exist not on the other side."

Tyler stopped moving. "Which are what?"

"Hope. Redemption. Forgiveness." *Cassie.*

Even for the length of time Tyler considered him, Friedrich never blinked away. It surprised him when Tyler's eyes crinkled. Tossing the pen next to the binder, Tyler leaned forward, clasping his hands over his desk. "I have a proposition for you, Friedrich."

Friedrich listened as Tyler spoke. He couldn't deny his interest, but he felt unqualified; perhaps there had been a mistake. Maybe there was another Friedrich Naumann out there Tyler was supposed to be asking instead. It was foreign to him, feeling and acknowledging his shortcomings when he was so used to pretending they didn't exist. If there was anything he could have kept from his old life, he wished it could have been his self-confidence, especially now.

Tyler was sitting on the edge of his desk. He had stopped talking, giving Friedrich a moment to absorb the offer.

Friedrich stared at his rucksack in thought. "I like time to search for my family first. I am not knowing if they are still alive. I need to know for certain."

Tyler was unmoved. "Very well. I'll hold a place for you in the meantime, as long as you're interested."

Friedrich nodded. Of course he was interested; he just felt incapable. Tyler noticed.

"This isn't short-term, Friedrich. I need someone who isn't just in it for the pay and benefits. I need someone with focus who will put all of his energy into this; I need someone who believes in it. If you're that person, I'm ready to take you on today; if not, you're free to go now with no hard feelings. What's it going to be?"

Friedrich stared at him before rising, holding out his hand. "Yes. I believe in it. I am doing it."

With a firm handshake that felt like a contract had just been signed, Tyler looked satisfied. Friedrich reached for his bag as Tyler started for his desk. "I'd like to keep in contact until we meet again. What's the address where you can be reached?"

Friedrich looked toward the window, slinging his rucksack over his shoulder. "I am not knowing this yet."

Tyler glanced at him. "Right. Well, you write to me." He scribbled his address on a sheet of paper, holding it out to Friedrich.

Friedrich stared at the paper, even as Tyler fell into his chair. Folding it up, he stashed it in his pocket alongside his discharge certificate and the forty marks. Tyler was already busy writing at his desk.

Friedrich took a couple steps toward the door before turning. "There is something I feel I should tell you. In the program at Camp Rockmont, the girl who is assigned to work with me..."

He went silent longer than he meant to. "She and I become...involved. I am sent to Camp Huntsville because we are discovered. I am not wanting you to find out and think —"

Tyler never looked up. "I read the reports. I already know."

Taking that as his cue to leave, Friedrich found the guard waiting outside Tyler's door. Out in the compound, the engine of the jeep roared to life.

"Where am I taking you next?" the guard asked him.

"The train station. Please."

There wasn't a cloud to be seen in the bright blue sky, and Friedrich realized he had the first hint of a smile in months. It seemed there was still Someone there, telling him what he was supposed to do next.

Acknowledgements

My husband for inspiring the heroes in my novels. My wish is that every girl and woman who reads this book comes away with the knowledge that there are good men out there; men who will love them as they are while believing in all they can become. This is the way you have always loved me.

My daughter for being the most magical, perfect little being I've ever met. Everything I do, I do in the hopes of making you proud to have me as your Mommy someday. I love you, chicken-nugget-head.

My beautiful baby sister who helped inspire this story. You were only five when I penned this novel and now you're a twelve-year-old who's old enough to read it. I hope this gives you a small glimpse of how much I adore you.

My editor, Lindsey, for your unflinching determination to help make my work the best it can be, and for always seeing the potential in me.

My friends and readers for being as enthusiastic and excited about my books as I am. It is an absolute privilege to share my work with you.

And now, for the people who may never see this book, but merit my eternal gratitude. I want to thank John and Stasi Eldredge, whose books—Captivating and Wild at Heart—helped me develop the characters and message behind Love Song. Your books changed my life.

And Taylor Swift for providing myself and the rest of the world with your music. There is no other artist who has inspired my work as much as you have.

And to the Romancer of my soul, may my purpose ever be to bring You glory.

ABOUT THE AUTHOR:

Stephanie Baumgartner lives with her loving husband and beautiful daughter in the rolling hills of Tennessee. When she is not writing about her fictional friends during World War II, she is usually reading about World War II, listening to music, or spending time with her family.

For more information and short stories starring your favorite characters, visit:
stephaniebaumgartner.com
facebook.com/smbaumgartner